Mike,

The Story of One
Peter Cleague

ROBERT R HAMLYN

*Thanks for
your support.
Have fun.
Bob Hamlyn*

Published by BookLocker.com, Inc., St. Petersburg, Florida.

Printed on acid-free paper.

The characters and events in this book are fictitious. Any similarity to real persons, living or dead, is coincidental and not intended by the author.

BookLocker.com, Inc.
2018

First Edition

"Liberty lies in the hearts of men and women. When it dies, no constitution, no law, no court can save it."
Judge Learned Hand
Central Park, New York City, May 21, 1944.

"A well regulated Militia, being necessary to the security of a free State, the right of the people to keep and bear Arms, shall not be infringed."
James Madison,
The Second Amendment to The Bill of Rights to the Constitution, Ratified 1791

"... Madison did not invent the right to keep and bear arms when he drafted the Second Amendment—the right was pre-existing at both common law and in the early state constitutions."
Thomas B. McAffee & Michael J. Quinlan, writing in the North Carolina Law Review, March 1997

"All that is necessary for evil to succeed is for good men to do nothing."
Edmund Burke, 1729 – 1797 (common attribution)

This is a novel. It is a work of fiction assembled from my imagination. The characters are composite inventions and if they bear any resemblance to any real person living or dead, it is entirely co-incidental. Peninsular Island, Washington, does not exist. Port Cullis, Washington, does not exist. The 603rd Coast Artillery Battery did not exist. There is no Alders restaurant in Seattle. As of this writing the prohibitions of Brady II and the Arsenal Codes are fictional elements of this novel. Under no circumstances should the reader assume that this novel condones doing harm to government employees or to anyone else. This novel is provided solely for your entertainment.

Have fun,
R HAMLYN

Acknowledgements

I would like to thank everyone who participated in creation of this novel:

Roger S. Hamlyn, Ken Cooper, Tom Curneen, Sonya De Witt, Hans Dunshee, Mike Ferretta, Dennis Fransson, Jon Frantzen, Matt Graham, Joan Hemple, Karen Homitz, Kregg Jorgenson, Jim Kauber, Mike Kelley, Malcolm Kenyon, Randy Kinnunen, Roselind Newland, Rick Remington, Michele Salter, and Clint Smith. Thanks, everybody.

This novel is dedicated to the memory of my parents: all of them.

Prologue

He waited in the dark. With no promise of light, he sat with his back against the plywood that formed one side of the wooden box he occupied. With his arms wrapped around his legs, and his forehead on his knees, he waited. And he waited. Jack in the box.

Two days, maybe three, he waited. The numbers on his watch were just conceptual dots in a circle. The photo-luminescence of the watch dial had given up its light-bearing quality. If he held his hand in front of his face he couldn't see it. Without reference to the horizon, or day, or night, his watch was irrelevant.

Muscle cramps came and went. Sleep came and went. Awareness came and went. He could faintly hear water lapping against the hull. The ship had made port. He would simply wait until somebody opened the box.

1

Framed by minarets and other structures that had stood for millennia in an ancient land, the sun sank below the horizon as the muezzin sang the Adhan, the supplicatory call to prayer that compelled the faithful to pay homage to their God. Gulls and other sea birds coursed through the sky scratching and fighting for what bits of food could be scavenged from the docks and waterfront streets of the old port city. The call to evening prayer was a thousand year old message—a heart-felt canticle that underscored a command to embrace the law of the prophet. With sunset, the Adhan echoed from the tower through the empty streets and deserted by-ways of the ancient port as the vast population of true believers obeyed the precepts of their faith—except for the resident infidels who blindly chose to ignore the teachings of the prophet at their own peril.

At the international sea-port that operated 24/7, the semi-trucks waited in queue to receive their designated cargo containers.

The muffled rattle and hum of a small army of diesel engines drowned out the exhortations of the muezzin. One such truck with two men pulled away from the loading zone as the silhouette of the Turkish-flagged freighter grew ever dimmer in the distance until it disappeared in the darkness.

The two men drove through the night. They transited several checkpoints without incident and, with the dawn, they sought out the appropriate warehouse as directed, left the truck, and walked away. They made their way to the center of the city where they found their pre-arranged transportation back to their homeland.

The doors of the warehouse were slid shut from the inside. Men with tools cut the wire seals on the container and drug out a rather large plywood box and some smaller ones. They immediately descended on the larger of the unmarked crates carefully ripping off the boards on the top of the box so as not to harm the semi-conscious cargo inside.

2

Peter Cleague was the "number two" man in the American Department of State's Bureau of Diplomatic Security in Beirut, Lebanon. As assistant to the State Department's Regional Security Officer it was Cleague's privilege to share much of the burden of keeping the embassy secure and the people inside it safe. What he had begun to suspect barely a month into his posting took almost a year to confirm through an acquaintance in the Shin Bet. Duplicity in the advancement of one's career, although intolerable, was one thing—treason was quite another. The CIA Station Chief to the embassy, Charles Laughton Lovegrove III, ostensibly a cultural attaché with the United States Agency for International Development, was actively soliciting buyers for information.

While on a business trip back to Washington, D.C., Cleague revealed his suspicions to a retired government official, **Judge George Hillman**, who could have had Lovegrove yanked back to the United States in a heartbeat for an investigation. Cleague's friend was a retired federal judge who had significant influence within the Department of Justice, having once been the director of the Federal Bureau of Investigation. In the capacity of one of his previous duties in the Bureau of Diplomatic Security of the State Department, Peter Cleague had occasion to work in concert with the judge's former organization. Cleague had earned a reputation of competence in counter-terrorism operations and VIP protective details. He had distinguished himself in a joint operation in which the attempt on the life of a visiting dignitary had been circumvented which brought him to the attention of the judge. Cleague was the man who identified the threat and neutralized it without the VIP ever knowing of his own brush with martyrdom in the cause of peace.

When Cleague presented his case to Hillman, he was told that his evidence consisted of only the most tangential of coincidences, would never bear the scrutiny of a Senate and/or House investigative sub-committee; certainly would not hold up in a court of law. Cleague was told to keep his mouth shut, lest he lose his own hard-earned career doing very creditable work in an organization that was regarded by many to be an endeavor of fools. Cleague had expected more. He didn't know exactly what he had expected from his old mentor, just more. Cleague believed Lovegrove's sale of names to the various splinter groups in the region would have been injurious enough to CIA's HUMINT resources that the "leak" could not have been implemented as a matter of policy. The priority of any bureaucracy, regardless of its publicly proclaimed charter, is self-sustenance—not self-destruction. The tendency was to protect itself no matter the cost. But if the hallmark of a bureaucracy is self-sustenance, wouldn't the same hold true for a bureaucrat? By the time Cleague had returned to Beirut, a number of people had been killed that Cleague knew were actively involved in providing his government with critical intelligence regarding the activity of a dozen terrorist organizations—Lovegrove had found a buyer.

Coincidentally, Cleague was getting a tremendous amount of pressure from above concerning oversight. Amid rumored but unsubstantiated speculation that Cleague was a candidate for relief-for-cause, the catch phrase that included potential career-terminating embarrassment, he found his ability to perform his work unfettered increasingly curtailed. The stated concerns included accusations of inadequate coordination on his part with the Marine guard detachment, interrogatives regarding ineffectual security precautions, and a general lack of performance. The line had been drawn. Cleague had misjudged Hillman's will to act and was now being set up to lose his career. The judge may have gone to somebody and sounded an alarm. On the other hand, maybe Lovegrove had the ear of someone well-placed who wasn't afraid of a little back-splatter.

Cleague officially petitioned the ambassador in writing, having sent reams of copies to various individuals within and without oversight of the State Department's Bureau of Diplomatic Security, demanding a hearing with his accuser substantiating the accusations. Cleague had unhesitatingly taken a giant leap over Lovegrove's line in the sand.

When the news was released that **Michael DiSilva, Colonel, USMC**, most recently serving as an observer for the UN security force in Lebanon, had been abducted, tortured and murdered, Cleague made up his mind. DiSilva had been several years senior to Cleague when the latter had been in the Marine Corps. They weren't close enough in age or year group to have been friends, but Cleague had the occasion to have worked with the man and respected him for what he was, a professional Officer of Marines. Cleague arranged a meeting with his Shin Bet acquaintance.

In spite of spending his waking hours waiting for the other shoe to drop, Cleague was still required to make his regional tour of inspection. Being an assistant to the Regional Security Officer, Lebanon, Cleague was tasked with responsibilities as directed—such as making periodic security inspections and reports of the various field offices in the region. When Cleague returned to Beirut he submitted his inspection results, filed his other reports as required, and delivered by hand to the ambassador his resignation from the Bureau of Diplomatic Security of the United States. He had requested and was granted passage by air to Dulles International Airport where he would be met by another DSO and processed out. The Al Italia Airbus made its way to Dulles via Istanbul, Athens, Rome, Lisbon and Paris. Somehow or another the manifest had been unaccountably misfiled and alleged (incorrectly as it turned out) to be ferrying one of Europe's most notorious drug traffickers, to be located in Peter Cleague's assigned seat. It wasn't all that hard to do if one could access the Al Italia database.

Cleague was reported to have been detained in Turkey for suspicion of smuggling contraband substances, held without visitor's privileges in an undisclosed Turkish facility, and left incommunicado until further notice. Coincidentally, the same notorious drug trafficker turned up face down in the briny green water of a Turkish seaport. Somewhat later, Cleague was released with perfunctory apologies to the American ambassador regarding any inconvenience unintentionally caused to the American State Department.

Meanwhile, back at Dulles International Airport, Cleague was a no-show. The assigned escort waiting to meet Cleague's flight really could not have cared less. Not having to out-process Cleague by the numbers, he took the liberty of awarding himself a three-day weekend.

3

The American security man was at the designated restaurant at the appointed time and met with his Shin Bet acquaintance that confirmed his suspicions of Lovegrove's involvement in DiSilva's murder and conveyed Shin Bet's extreme concern at the viability of the source of the leak. Officially known by the acronym SHABAK—the defender that shall not be seen. Israel's internal security service is commonly referred to in English as Shin Bet. Intelligence is a highly valued commodity. However, in this situation, the Shin Bet agent had no qualms about talking to this American—the Americans had a problem and they needed to clean up their mess.

Theoretical courses of action were discussed. Logistical options were explored purely as a matter of academic inquiry. Keeping his own counsel, the American decided on a course of action. He simply regarded it as non-attributable diplomacy. He would close with and destroy the enemy by fire and maneuver, exactly as he had been taught (more or less) at the Marine Corps Development and Education Command at Quantico, Virginia. With smiles and handshakes all around, the meeting was over. The American went back to the airport. The Israeli turned to his own affairs.

4

The man awoke from his carbon dioxide-induced slumber as he was pulled from the crate. He was pleased to breathe air that had not been recycled inside of a wooden box. Movement came slowly and painfully but he was still very glad to see his colleague who had helped arrange his impromptu journey back to Beirut, the Paris of the Middle East. He bathed and was fed and set about the logistics of his brief yet poignant visit.

He had never considered himself particularly skilled with a rifle; falling back on an old Marine Corps axiom, every Marine is trained as a rifleman first and foremost. His colleague provided him with a place to practice in the dusky light after sunset, with the rifle and ammunition appropriate to that part of the world. The distance from his position to the target would be a little more than one hundred and fifty yards. His military service had been in the time when Marines were trained in the craft of marksmanship. He had been taught to engage man-sized targets out to five hundred yards with the M-14—a rifle chambered for the 7.62x51 NATO cartridge. In his mind it was the proper battle cartridge for a proper battle rifle. Later in his career he honed his skill with a rifle designed for the smaller 5.56x45mm NATO cartridge.

It is more difficult to hit a six-foot tall target at 500 yards with a smaller diameter, lighter weight bullet than it is to hit that same target with a larger diameter, heavier weight bullet. One must learn to observe and judge wind. He had enjoyed a fair amount of federally-funded practice of an honest-to-god skill that, from time to time, he found useful.

The U.S. embassy was located on Avenue de Paris, the main road along the waterfront in Beirut. There were roadblocks east and west of the compound on the road in front of the entrance situated about 100 to 200 yards out from either end of the main gate to the grounds. The roadblocks were manned by Lebanese Army troops with USMC personnel in combat gear at the main gate. A large walk bordered the other side of the street with the breakwater on the far side. Because it was right on the water it had a slight breeze. It was dusk and the harsh light of the day had softened a little; the setting sun made long shadows on the ground.

The Marine Color Detail made its way to the flagpole inside the embassy grounds. The flag shifted lazily as it was hauled down the lanyard at a steady measured pace. Laundry drying on lines in the surrounding residential community blew inland by the ocean breeze in a gentle way.

Now—at this time and in this place—the shooter had one chance to make this shot: 153 yards, with wind from the north at three to five miles per hour for a zero wind effect, firing from a prone position, and no discernible mirage. The shooter was using an SKS—a Soviet designed self-loading carbine, with iron sights, firing a 7.62 millimeter bullet weighing 124 grains. Measured at the muzzle the bullet traveled a little faster than 2200 feet per second.

Later that week, it was reported that in war-torn Beirut an American Embassy official, Charles Laughton Lovegrove III—a cultural attaché with the USAID-- had been struck down while leaving his office, ostensibly the work of an unknown assassin according to BBC world News, while CNN announced it as a stray round from the embattled rabble beyond the fortress-like embassy. Had they known, the former Marine's instructors back at Quantico would have

cause to pronounce, as they had so many times before, Good
Initiative, Poor Judgment.

5

Eugene Smith's ancestral name had been Schmidt. His father changed the family name shortly after his arrival in the New World back in the Thirties in the hopes that he would more easily assimilate into the new culture he had just adopted. As such, Smith had no affectation one way or the other regarding the cause of Irish republicanism. Eugene Smith was the Diplomatic Security Officer for the US Department of State, assigned to the American Diplomatic Mission in Belfast, Northern Ireland. This would be his last tour as a DSO prior to his retirement. He had had enough and looked forward to other opportunities that awaited him. He had spent the morning poring over documents detailing potentially calamitous events in the world. His head throbbed, his eyes burned and he thought, *enough paperwork*; he tossed this last evaluation of the current powder keg that was the Middle East onto the pile in the middle of his desk.

As he rubbed his eyes he toyed with the idea of opening a restaurant. Smith recalled his family's occupation since the patriarch had immigrated to the United States. He remembered, not at all fondly, the sixteen-hour days, the non-stop grueling work over intense heat, and the handling of customers with kid gloves; that was the restaurant business. On second thought maybe he'd just put some money into a restaurant that was already established and be a silent partner; somebody else could do the heavy lifting. After a career of traveling the world he had already decided he would retire back home, in Seattle, Washington. He was close enough to retirement that he could entertain such idle thoughts from time to time and dismiss them at will, such as when his scheduled appointment for this morning showed up.

Sergeant Major Roger Tibbett had just been rotated back to Belfast for his third tour. Having recently returned from the Falklands, where his regiment had proved itself with the customary efficiency and effectiveness that had become the benchmark of 22 Special Air Service, Sergeant Major Tibbett was scheduled to make a security inspection of mutual points of interest with the American DSO, Eugene Smith. After concluding their threat assessment to the embassy and living quarters for American diplomatic personnel, routes of travel of officers and employees, and potential points of ambush (the likelihood of which was quite remote as US public sympathy continued to be the main source of IRA support), the work day had come to an end. The two veteran security professionals mutually dispatched themselves to a convenient pub and discussed the potential for attacks on individual employees of the American Embassy over a pint, as they were now off duty.

In one year fundamentalist zealots of one stripe or another seized forty-two embassies and diplomatic missions worldwide. Thirty-two ambassadors were taken hostage, five embassies were destroyed, and fifty-three people were killed in embassy shoot-outs—a fact not lost on either of them. Smith mused that the most likely scenario would be on an individual target; Tibbett concurred, noting the unfortunate sniper attack on one of Smith's countrymen that had taken place in Beirut just the week before...what a pity.

Eugene Smith had just returned from five days leave and had spent the better part of that morning reading reports and briefs of that very incident. Smith knew of the individual involved, Lovegrove, and had heard some of the rumors about one of his former associates in counter-terrorism operations, Peter Cleague. He knew of Lovegrove and he knew Cleague and house odds were that Lovegrove needed to be killed. Always the prudent gambler, Smith would have put his money with the house. Smith kept his reservations on Tibbett's polite lamentations to himself.

6

After his brief yet unwelcome stay in Turkey ("Apologies; most regrettable—these things happen,") Peter Cleague returned to the United States. He reported to the Deputy Assistant Secretary in Charge, Personnel, Bureau of Diplomatic Security, The United States Department of State, for voluntary discharge from active service.

His charges of treason against Lovegrove were completely ignored. Speaking ill of the dead meant little without documented evidence, while speaking ill of the living seemed to be entertained as great sport in the District of Columbia. Cleague's demands that Lovegrove immediately be removed from duty pending investigation fell on deaf ears. His wild gesticulations and accusations of Lovegrove's numerous breaches of security protocol— specifically selling the names of reliable, proven human intelligence assets in the entire region of the Middle East—barely raised an eyebrow.

Without solid documentary evidence, photographs, or other witnesses it was all unsubstantiated speculation, conveniently dismissed as bad blood between Cleague and Lovegrove. His assertions, that Lovegrove's treachery was nothing less than an act of sedition and a very real and specific threat to the security of the United States, were silently disregarded. Besides, Lovegrove was dead. Cleague had been held incommunicado in Turkey and returned quietly, PNG—persona non grata. When informed of Lovegrove's death, Cleague calmly claimed ignorance.

Cleague's request for resignation had been approved and forwarded without comment. Well, so much for a course of action. Cleague's euphemistic plan of fire and maneuver had proven to be flaccid and immobile. After having been a rising star on the fast track in the world of counter-terrorism operations, he was now summarily dismissed and nobody even noticed. Peter Cleague was now free to explore the rest of his life, unencumbered, unemployed and unprepared.

7

Prior to his posting to Beirut, much of Cleague's federal service was spent in VIP protective details and counter-terrorism operations. He had managed to make a name for himself as far as anonymous assignments go, and decided to find out what was going on in the arena of real world security. Cleague's work in government service had been very real, but as such there hadn't been a great concern about profit and loss. Now the playing field was a little different. Most of the contacts he had made while assigned to VIP protective details had proven to be good working relationships, and a lot of those folks had retired from federal service with the Bureau of Diplomatic Security and had gone on to the private sector.

If this was networking, it proved to be very tenuous at best but he managed to eke out a living from it. Occasionally augmented with providing firearms safety training as an adjunct instructor, he managed to pay the rent and most of the bills. For his undergraduate degree in college he had majored in History and minored in English. Fifteen years later he was putting those assets to work, albeit with intermittent success, with some freelance gun writing under a pseudonym. In his endeavors as a gun scribe he tried to concentrate on historically unique firearms. Researching and relating in writing the relevance of firearms classified as curios and relics to a specific historical incident genuinely appealed to him and he was good at it.

He applied for and received a Curios and Relics License through the Bureau of Public Safety (BPS)—previously known as the Bureau of Alcohol, Tobacco and Firearms. Having that license allowed him to receive firearms from a legal vendor while satisfying the paper trail required by the

BPS. It simplified the process of taking possession of a firearm by not having to go through an FFL dealer. A Curios & Relics license was easier to get than a Federal Firearms License and bore slightly less governmental scrutiny, as he was not receiving modern firearms. As with all his other professional endeavors it was feast or famine but the UPS driver could always tell whenever he had begun or had finished an article because an adult signature was required to receive firearms.

8

Cleague managed to stretch it out for a couple of years, but as with many other modes of self-employment, some days were better than others. The protective work was usually short-term and was generally found through contacting people who knew people who knew somebody else that needed a little help. Sometimes the job would be to sit in a car through the night to watch somebody's front door; other times he would actually have to escort a client from here to there. Private work thus far was not anything as elaborately planned and executed as the operations he ran in the BPS, but he didn't have the BPS' budget either.

He was fortunate enough to be able to secure for himself a little house and adjoining property that had once been a part of a de-commissioned and long-since-abandoned military facility in the northern part of Puget Sound. His neighbors were few and far between but they were good people. He loved his little house on the beach and he liked the little island community. He had indeed been fortunate.

One day, out of the blue, a former associate contacted him through one of the magazine editors that occasionally published his articles. He knew the man from the Federal Law Enforcement Training Center in Glynco, Georgia. Eugene Smith had been one of the instructors for the VIP Protective Course. Their paths had crossed a number of times between Cleague's initial training and his posting to Beirut. Each man held a good opinion of the other's professional demeanor and performance "under fire". Cleague heard that Smith had retired some years earlier to the Seattle area.

Through his network of former associates Smith heard that Peter Cleague was actually the gun-writer 'Peter Stone'. He wrote a letter to the editor of the magazine in which Smith had read one of Cleague's (Stone's) articles, who then forwarded that letter on to Cleague. It interested Cleague to the extent that he agreed to make the trip in to Seattle. Cleague met Smith for dinner in one of the less pretentious bar/restaurants that festooned the city. After the obligatory catching-up Smith said, "So what happened, Pete? The last I heard you were on the short list to stardom inside the BDS. Next thing I know you're sitting at my dinner table not knowing whether you can ask me for a job reference." Smith was direct. It made Cleague smile in spite of himself; no pretense here, nor need for it.

"I resigned, that's all." Cleague answered simply.

"Why?" Smith asked. "That's what I don't get. You were well on your way to a very good career. Why throw that away?" Smith wouldn't let it go.

"Well, I didn't throw it away. It just got to the point where I couldn't do my job anymore. I was better off outside." Cleague finished, not wanting to dwell on the very definite past.

Through the din of the muffled conversations, and the clatter of silverware on china, and the occasional celebratory clink of wine glasses, Cleague could hear the pealing notes of Miles Davis' solo trumpet pleading 'Generique' over the restaurant's music system. It was a weekday night. There was no live jazz tonight at the Alders. But it was Miles.

"Do you remember," Cleague segued as he cut through his London broil, "Colonel Michael DiSilva, USMC?"

Smith paused for a minute.

"He was with the UN observation team in Beirut, wasn't he? Got killed by some hard-liners?" Smith recalled.

"Yep, that was him." Cleague answered.

"Yeah, I knew him. We went through The Basic School together." This caught Cleague off guard a little bit.

"Really?" Cleague asked.

"Yeah, why?" Smith.

"I knew you were my senior in the Bureau of Diplomatic Security but I didn't know you were that senior."

"Yeah, very funny, so what about him?" Smith asked, somewhat pointedly.

"Well, I thought I knew who was responsible for that whole episode. I contacted the people whom I thought I should contact with that information, not being able to prove anything of course, and very mysteriously I started getting all these official inquiries and reprimands from on high." Cleague responded.

"Yeah, so where was the ambassador in the middle of all this?" Smith asked.

"He was more or less out of the loop, y'know? He was a political appointee, he was a nice guy and all that, but he was just there as a reward for faithful service. Know what I mean?" Cleague asked. Smith did know. Having completed a career in the Bureau of Diplomatic Security, Smith was quite familiar with the practice of appointing good soldiers from presidential campaigns to ambassadorships whether that good soldier was qualified for diplomatic duty or not. Smith surmised that Cleague's boss had been slightly out of his element.

"Okay, so then what?" Smith pressed.

"Well," Cleague finished his meal with strong iced tea, "every time another letter of inquiry came down to 'justify this', or 'substantiate that,' it required a formal reply. I was spending all of my time conducting formal correspondence and none of my time conducting my job. I couldn't see that it would get any better. So, I quit; Gene, it was the first time I ever quit anything in my life." It was obvious to Smith that

Cleague still regretted it. Cleague finished his tea and set his glass down on the table cloth.

Smith silently concurred with Cleague's assessment; it would not have gotten any better.

"Too bad," Smith said.

"Yeah, too bad," Cleague agreed.

"You are aware that it didn't look very good that that USAID guy got killed at that same period of time, aren't you?" Smith threw it out there. It had been churned up regularly on the rumor mill ever since it happened, in a much more simplified form, of course.

"As rumor control had it, the CIA guy got the BDS guy fired. The BDS guy got the CIA guy killed. Simple as that, it was cause and effect. Night and day, one follows the other." Smith said.

Cleague just shrugged, "It wasn't me, Gene. I was in a Turkish prison that week." Cleague stated flatly.

"Well, it was awful damn convenient, wasn't it?" Smith was really pushing this and he knew it. The Alder's music system was playing random selections from a tape— Wynton Kelley tapped and tickled his way through 'Freddie Freeloader' on piano.

"No. The one thing on this earth that a Turkish prison is not," Cleague emphatically punctuated the air with his fork, "is convenient!"

Smith grunted a laugh, conceding Cleague's point.

"So, what do you make of it, wrong place wrong time?" Smith asked.

"I don't know, and I don't care." Cleague had always privately regarded Lovegrove's assassination as an act of anonymous justice and if the truth were to be known Cleague just always assumed that the Shin Bet did it.

"As far as I'm concerned, good riddance and may he rot in hell forever." Cleague was ready for this conversation to end. "Can I get a cup of coffee?" He asked.

But Smith wouldn't let it go.

"What else were you doing in Lebanon, Pete?" Cleague didn't have to answer this and Smith knew it.

"I was doing the types of things that good DSO's (Diplomatic Security Officers) do. Diplomats generally disapprove of some security operations and it apparently became felt that some of our operations were just a little too secure for good manners." Cleague put it to rest. Having been a DSO at more than one US Embassy, Smith knew what Cleague meant and let it go, finally. He noticed Cleague's glass of tea and water glass were empty and signaled his waitress, as he changed the subject. Smith paused for the waitress to deliver his next beer and clear away the clutter.

"Thanks, Susie, I'm ready for my desert now and bring a cup of coffee for my guest please."

"Sure, Gene," and Susie retreated into the din of the restaurant tending to her other tables.

"I hear you're looking for work," Smith said.

"Maybe," Cleague answered casually.

"Well, you are or you aren't. Are you?" Smith asked.

"I can use the work but it depends on who the client is. To be very truthful with you Gene, I'm tired of getting lined up with contracts for people that supposedly have a legitimate concern for their safety only to find out that the client is some two-bit criminal who fancies himself an international drug lord and has managed to piss off a competitor. I can't tell you how many street corner drug dealers have tried to hire me to be their bodyguard," Cleague responded, still incredulous at the memory.

Eugene Smith was a big man whose weathered face belied a lifetime of serious stress, but when he smiled Cleague could see the unaffected delight of a child discovering ice cream.

"Yeah," Smith nodded while wiping his mouth with a napkin, "and the sonsabitches get insulted when you turn 'em down. But if you stop and think about it, status is just as important to them as to a lot of other businessmen." Smith spoke as he poured his beer into the pilsner glass, watching the foam approach the brim. "And if you are a bodyguard, my friend, like it or not you are a status symbol."

Cleague was surprised, almost to the point of alarm. Smith had either become very careless or was unusually comfortable in his current environment. Cleague had all but sworn off drinking altogether when he started VIP protection years ago. He simply could not believe his eyes and he let his surprise show.

"Relax Peter. I'm retired. Besides, I'm a part owner of this restaurant and I live upstairs. I am literally at home; and if a man can't relax in his own home, where the hell can he relax?" He asked.

The Alders restaurant was renowned for its steaks, chops and seafood. It was annually nominated as one of the city's ten best restaurants in both local papers. An honor that Smith usually dismissed with a somewhat tolerant scorn; he regarded both newspapers as little more than "left wing fish wrappers."

9

Smith had become a bit of an entrepreneur in his retirement. He had bought into the restaurant, which left him free to pursue other interests. He found ample occasion for work as a security consultant in a city that was continuously defining technological innovation. Shortly after his retirement from the Bureau of Diplomatic Security, Smith had also been offered the opportunity to join the board of directors of a firm of security consultants located in Palm Springs, California. All of this in turn afforded him the prospect to stay reasonably current in his former career. Mr. Smith kept a lot of irons in the fire, but he managed.

"Yeah, I heard you were doing a security consultant gig. How's that working out?" Cleague asked.

"Great. It helps pay moorage for my boat at the Des Moines Marina. On a good day, it's a fifteen minute drive from here. And the older I get, any day on the boat is a good day.

Suzy returned with coffee for Cleague and a cigar, clipper, wooden matches and a glass with three fingers of bourbon, neat, for Smith. Smith took great pleasure in lighting his cigar. Cleague was really floored. Seattle, in its bid to become the socially fashionable, cause-conscious, politically-correct capital of the "left coast" had proscribed by city ordnance smoking in public places.

"Now what's the matter?" Smith had caught Cleague's disbelief. "What are they going to do, send the BATF after me?"

Peter shrugged, "I heard they changed the name; it's the Federal Bureau of Public Safety now, something about an image problem I hear."

"Bullshit, they're still a bunch of Nazis regardless of what they're calling themselves this week, or whose cabinet post they hide 'em in." Cleague had evidently hit a nerve but enjoyed seeing this aspect of his old unflappable, imperturbable instructor.

"If they want me, they know where I live and they are welcome to it."

"Well," Cleague offered, "I doubt that the BPS has been relegated to enforcing municipal smoking codes, at least not yet."

"Whatever," Smith growled. As he sat there patiently listening to Cleague, Eugene Smith dipped the butt of his cigar into the shot glass. He saw it in an old western. Dean Martin played a bad guy. Smith did not consider himself to be a bad guy...he just thought it was one of the more socially acceptable things one could do with a cigar.

"By the way," Cleague knew this was rude but he simply couldn't help himself, "Why do you live in a city?"

Smith wasn't the least bit annoyed but rather warmed to the subject.

"I live in this city because I like this city. It's my home." Smith took a draft of the cigar, the tip of it glowed cherry red. He held it in his hand, exhaled slowly, and contemplated the ash: Orson Wells' Hamlet pondering poor Yorick's skull. He went on.

"You're more likely to be raided up on that island than I am in the middle of Seattle." There it was. He threw it out there. Smith heard things. Peter did not rise to the bait. Smith pushed on, ever-so-gently.

"You know what the tactic is as well as I do: 1) Shoot the dog. 2) Starve them out. 3) Burn their house down. 4) Shoot the survivors."

Cleague immediately thought of several examples in which most or all of the "tactics" mentioned had been applied: Ruby Ridge, Idaho; Waco, Texas; Robert Mathews on Whidbey Island, Washington; and the MOVE apartment fire in Philadelphia. The principals involved were not company in which Cleague cared to be placed but Smith's assertions were pertinent.

"There is not a mayor in this country that would be willing to risk the collateral damage caused by trying to burn out one old, feeble-minded, misanthrope." Smith said.

"There was a mayor in Philadelphia that did." Cleague suggested.

"Yeah, I'll grant you that. But this boy here is relatively new to the game and he does not have the political capital to squander on such obstinate folly." Smith said, nodding in the direction of city hall.

"No, but they can fine you." Cleague pointed out.

"True," Smith conceded, "but who's going to enforce the code? The fine men and women of the Seattle Police Department have far more important things to do than to go around to all the restaurants and bars in this city and issue tickets for smoking. Besides, if I get fined for smoking a cigar in my restaurant, I'll pay the fine. At any rate, all of this is an exercise in the abstract. I am more than content to mind my own business, enjoy the restaurant, and keep my mouth shut. I'm not a threat to nobody." Smith concluded.

Cleague smiled at the double negative.

They both stood and Smith extended his hand. "It was good to see you again, Pete. Stay in touch. Maybe I can come up to that island for some fishing." Smith said.

"Yeah, you should. I hear it's supposed to be pretty good this season." Cleague replied. "And keep me in mind if you hear of anything."

"I will. Have a safe trip back up north." They shook hands and Cleague started north on the long drive home.

10

Cleague enjoyed his time at the Alders restaurant. The conversation with Smith proved resonant. He decided it was time to get out and mingle, and consequently signed himself up for one of the refresher courses offered for his profession. The quality of content presented in the two-day seminar at the Vancouver Hilton was minimal, but he did get a chance to network with some people that seemed to be gainfully employed for the most part. Many of those present were in the position of personnel management or recruiting, the rest were, as Cleague, looking for new contacts.

Bearing that in mind, he set about putting his newly-gleaned list of names to the test. Some bore promise and some of them didn't, but there was nothing imminent on Cleague's employment horizon.

Cleague had taken to scanning the headlines on the Internet. Dial-up internet access on the island was spotty and weak, but what-the-hell, he lived on an island. He noticed a headline from Associated Press with an origin in Seattle. A gay couple had been beaten nearly to death in a public park in the vicinity of the Pike Place Market. They were on an excursion from a tour boat that had put in at one of the piers just down from the ferry landing in Seattle's waterfront.

Beyond expressing shock and grief, the proprietors of Coastal Tours, home port San Francisco, had little to say about the sad affair other than: "… this event was totally un-characteristic for a port that we have traditionally regarded as progressively friendly to same sex couples, and we are sure this aberration is a totally freak occurrence, and we have the highest confidence in the city's ability to deal with this issue in short order. Coastal Tours will definitely continue to frequent Seattle as a favored port of call."

Cleague saw dollar signs on the monitor's screen. The proprietors of Coastal Tours were manifestly waving a red flag in front of every homophobe in the Pacific Northwest. They had declared open season on their own clientele. Cleague was immediately on the phone. Sometime later, when the oatmeal was getting particularly thin, he got an invitation for an interview.

11

Coastal Tours Cruise Lines was a mom-and-pop operation, or in this case a pop-and-pop operation, compared to the larger better known cruise lines, but they served a specific clientele: gay couples that wanted the "emotional space" to enjoy a vacation without being continually beleaguered. Five miles off the West Coast from Anchorage to Baja seemed safe enough but there were times, even in this new age of enlightenment, when the ships put in at some ports in which guests were harassed, sometimes beaten, and most recently, targets of attempted murder (for example, that business in Seattle). Cleague figured "what the hell." He didn't care what consenting adults chose to do in private. Clients are clients.

Coastal Tours' homeport was San Francisco. *The Adrienne* was moored within sight of the cruise line's office. He sat in a waiting room, hands folded in his lap, staring intently at the closed door of the proprietors' office. He had been waiting over an hour.

"Can I get you a coffee?" The receptionist asked. The placard on her desk read: **Linda Muller.**

"No thanks, I'm good." Cleague smiled with a barely perceptible shake of the head, and resumed staring at the door.

"Are you from out of town?" she asked.

He amiably looked in her direction, smiled, nodded and returned his attention to the closed door. The receptionist was a little more agitated at her employers' indifference than Cleague seemed to be. He wasn't demonstrably mad, or irritated or anything. He didn't seem to have any response to obviously being ignored other than to stare a hole in the office door. She was feeling a little awkward. It just wasn't polite to invite someone for a business meeting and then ignore them.

"We've never had a security guy on the ship before," she said.

That caught Cleague's attention. He pivoted his head ninety degrees, like an owl, to look at the receptionist.

"Excuse me?" he asked.

She nodded her head in confirmation.

"Yeah, we've never had a security guy before. I hope they take your offer," she smiled.

He didn't seem to be anything other than polite. "Oh," he said. In fact, Peter was stunned to learn that the cruise line did not have a security staff, a director of security or even a night watchman for that matter. He wanted to pound his fists on his head and scream: "Dumbass, Dumbass, Dumbass!!" But he didn't. He just sat there, politely. Cleague's premise was to present his services as complementing the scope of security operations he presumed were already in place. He could have kicked himself in the ass for not having researched his prospective client more thoroughly. It was too late now. The phone on the receptionist's desk buzzed. She said, "They're ready for you now."

12

Cleague's pitch was to have been as an accompaniment to ship-sponsored tour groups in the geographical areas of the Pacific coast at which the ship made port. He had tentatively hoped for an agreement to cover the territory the ship visited between the Northern Washington border and the southern California state line or from Blaine to Baja—he thought that had a nice marketing ring to it but what did he know about marketing?

He would propose that he would join tour groups departing from the ship and escort them as a somewhat subdued, low keyed, discreet, but very serious defense against the unforeseen threat—reasoning that if they knew it was coming they wouldn't go there. If anyone would feel a need to require his services separately—apart from the cruise line, for personal protection—he would certainly make arrangements with Coastal Tours, paying a commission to the cruise line. After he had made a working cruise north-to-south, and south-to-north, he would better be able to judge the need for more security personnel to help with the protective escorts when the clients left the ship just because one guy can't cover twenty people or more, but he didn't know what the need would be until he had done it.

It was explained to Cleague by the proprietors of the cruise line that the individual members of the crew were expected to fulfill the function of ship's safety and security as a part of their general duties (in between serving meals, performing show tunes badly, and organizing shipboard shuttlecock games). The owners explained to him that they felt perhaps he could be hired in a temporary capacity to wait tables and keep an eye on things till this whole mess just blew over...by the way, could he sing or dance?

At which point he lost his patience and pointed out to his prospective employers that if they were serious about protecting the lives of their passengers they needed to refocus their worldview. Safeguarding people's lives was not a part-time, collateral duty obligation, and it couldn't be done by one guy. If he were to be able to do this at all he would need more people but he would have to assess the requirement first.

When one of the partners asked Cleague what he could do that any of their crew couldn't, Cleague responded that he had many years of experience of keeping people alive and how many of their crew members have done the same? The interview went downhill from there.

"Do you carry a gun Mr. Cleague?" asked one of the partners.

"Yes I do," he responded flatly.

"And just how do you propose getting around the federal laws that prohibit the conveyance of firearms on board commercial vessels?" the partner asked.

Cleague had not considered this tiny detail but he didn't miss a beat.

"If I'm working by myself I can meet the ship at the various ports of call. Otherwise, if we have a team on board, the team can remain with the passengers and one of the team can be designated to meet us at the specific ports with whatever hardware we may require." Not a polished answer but serviceable, he thought.

"Why on earth would you feel it necessary to carry a gun?" the other partner asked.

"Because some people need to be shot." Cleague retorted louder than he should have and he regretted it the second it came out of his mouth. The man gasped. *Note to self:* Cleague thought, *You have to learn to control your emotions.*

"Who needs to be shot, what people need to be shot, what is wrong with you?" This last remark, Cleague noted, was not altogether rhetorical. He had lost his patience but he would not lose his temper. *Your mindset is your responsibility, and you must have full motor control over what you feel and how you react at all times.* He mentally admonished himself.

He sat perched on the edge of the sofa, his elbows set on his knees, doing that church, chapel, and steeple thing with his fingers until he could speak in a conversational tone of voice. Cleague knew the interview was already over but he responded calmly.

"Look, there are vicious and predatory people in the world and you do not have to go looking for them because they will come find you. And when they do, you have to be able to do two things."

"And what would they be?" one of the partners snipped.

Peter looked the man level in the eye and told him.

"You have to be able to protect yourself, and you have to be willing to do it. You guys aren't there yet, you never will be, and you know it. You need help." With that, Peter quietly rose, ran a hand over his tie, re-buttoned his jacket and smoothed out the creases, and left their office, shutting the door behind him.

13

Linda Muller hit the button to turn off the speaker phone when the office door opened. She took one look at his face and said, "It didn't go all that well I take it." She said it completely at ease, in a conversational tone, just like he was a friend. She had a really nice smile.

"Uh, no. I guess I'm not a very effective salesman." Cleague answered, still regretting having lost his patience with a prospective client.

"Well, don't take it to heart. Those two together make up one cheap son-of-a-bitch. It's really too bad; if they don't do something soon, somebody's going to get killed, they'll get sued and lose the business, the ship, everything!"

Man, she's got beautiful eyes, he thought.

"Uh, yes, well hopefully, it won't come to that." he said. Smiling and feeling just a little awkward, he thought: *Well, what have I got to lose?* And committing himself to being the very best fool he could be, said, "Hey, listen, uh..."

"Linda!" The intercom snapped, "Have you got next month's charter schedules ready yet?"

"No Mr. Leander, not yet."

"We need those now, Linda!"

"Yes, sir, I'll have them done in just a few." She pointedly hit the intercom button with her extended middle finger and mouthed "asshole!" A slight blush came over her as she realized she had been in a conversation and Cleague was still standing there.

"I'm sorry, what were you saying?" she asked sweetly, stepping back into the role of the cheerful, if unappreciated, secretary.

Oh, why bother, Cleague thought; all he could do was take a gracious way out.

"Oh, nothing," he said. "Well, I better not keep you," nodding toward the inner office.

"It was nice to meet you, Linda. Take care."

"Yeah, you too." She smiled as she shook his hand.

Boy, what a smile, he thought. *That pink in her cheeks really sets it off too.* He stood there for a moment, awkwardly, not thinking of anything to say.

Hmph, Lost his nerve, she mused, *too bad. He's kind of cute for an old guy.*

Cleague picked up his brief case and smoothed his suit jacket again, and mumbled "Bye-bye," as he walked out of the suite when she called after him: "Mr. Cleague?"

He turned and walked back toward her desk assuming he had forgotten something—perfect end to a perfect day, leave as a total idiot. Linda said, "Hey, I'm just going out for lunch, would you like to get a bite to eat?"

Cleague's smile was immediate. He was really going to have to work on controlling his emotions a little better.

"Love to," he said; and as they made their way out of the office together he asked her,

"Don't you have to finish a schedule or something?"

"What schedule? We haven't had a charter since one of the guests almost got killed last month, it was in all the papers, maybe you saw it." Linda said facetiously, she knew he had seen it; that was why he was here.

"What a coincidence, huh? They want a phony report typed up just as I'm going out to lunch." She proceeded to confide in him, "It's a territorial imperative kind of thing with those two. Some boys may like boys, but they still piss on fire hydrants." She affirmed.

"Oh." *Earthy kind of girl*, Cleague thought. *I like that*, he confided to himself.

He was an unemployed bodyguard that used to work in the foreign legion or something, she thought. Apparently in reasonable shape for his age, he wasn't bad looking for an older guy. And she sensed he had a very unique calmness about himself. He had just lost a major contract and did not seem to be the least bit disturbed. She had seen the bid and she knew how much money he had not made just now, yet he was incredibly even tempered. She wasn't used to that level of self-control in a man. That was interesting.

She was an overeducated, underpaid, way-under-employed college graduate looking for another job, Cleague thought. Linda Muller was tall, slender, attractive and confident with dark brown hair that just touched her shoulders. Her smile was absolutely beguiling and Cleague could not help himself from staring into her eyes. Well, they hit it off.

Peter went home to the island in Washington and did a truncated magazine article on the history of the Smith & Wesson #3 Schofield revolver, and took a couple of short-term jobs on protective details. Linda stayed in San Francisco. They ran up their phone bills. She started taking work on *The Adrienne* so she could make passage north to see him once every couple of months. She also hit it off with Max, Cleague's dog, whose bearing and manner seemed to indicate that her occasional visits were for his benefit.

Cleague was able to get an adjunct instructor's job through Mr. Smith at a firearms training academy near San Francisco. Although fewer and fewer people were able to jump through all the state and federally mandated hoops to buy a firearm, there was still a demand for competent instructors. It was an established school with a credible reputation that offered programs oriented toward self-protection and officer survival. Cleague was able to develop a previously underused talent for teaching. He was averaging one class every two months. The more the students complained of the difficulty of a given exercise, the more he reiterated the real world origin of that scenario, and the harder the school staff looked at him with an offer in mind for permanent employment. Peter and Linda were seeing each other an average of once a month. Things were almost working out.

14

The November wind came off the ocean as a mild breeze. It blew through the dried sea grass, huckleberry, and weeds that covered the south end of the island. Peter Cleague jogged south along the sandy road from his house about a mile down to the bridge that joined the little peninsula-made-island community to the rest of the county. During World War II the Army Corps of Engineers dug a boat channel to enhance the logistical capacity of a military outpost located on the peninsula. It was Cleague's habit to take a casual jog every other day, swim in the summer (when it was warm enough), or ride his bicycle, or paddle his kayak around the island. He joked with his neighbors that he was in training for the Olympics: the Geriatric Division.

Today was his forty-fifth birthday. He smiled and gave a casual wave to the occupants of the sedan pulled off the road and facing north. As he passed their car and turned to call to Max, his Norwegian Elkhound, he noted the distance from the car to his house—about a hundred yards. He continued on toward the bridge and crossed over the strand just north of it. Scratching his legs on the short unyielding nettle plants as he passed, he made his way through the tough sea grass, onto the shingle beach down to the tide line where the wet pebbles were smaller. He made a point of wearing high top sneakers that covered his ankles when he ran on the cobbled surface. The higher up the intertidal zone, the bigger the stones got. Running on the beach did not seem to bother the dog; all was well other than the dark, heavy clouds from the northwest that threatened rain. Peter did not want to get caught in a downpour. The shingle strand was littered with the typical flotsam and timbers that settled on the beaches of the interior islands of Puget Sound.

Max stayed with him most of the time until he got bored and trotted off to investigate an interesting scent or examine a curious movement off Cleague's routine, and for the most part, predetermined jogging trail. Cleague ran north on the beach parallel to the hillocks, rocks and gravel backfill that formed the barrier between the rocky shoreline and the interior island. When he got about a hundred yards away from his little house on the beach, Cleague visually scanned the shore line to his left and caught a flash of reflected light low on the crest of one of the hillocks almost directly to his left. He ran on without breaking stride and remembered a T-shirt slogan with some irony: "If you try to out-run a bullet you only die tired."

As Cleague ran parallel to the barrier that obscured the view of his house from the water line, Max nonchalantly passed him in an effortless gait, stopped and stuck his nose into the rocky sand close to the water, pawed at some invisible sand vermin, and ran back passing Cleague at a furious gallop, splashing him with cold salt water.

Max seemed to enjoy being spiteful at times for no apparent reason. *It must be part of his Viking heritage,* Cleague reasoned. The dog then condescendingly joined Cleague once again as they made their way from the waterline to the end of the barrier, and again jetting away from him toward the house, out of sight. Cleague found this curious, Max usually ran off in the opposite direction from which Cleague was headed. Cleague came to the end of his two-mile run and walked toward his house when he saw who had captured Max's interest.

Her car was parked at the end of the gravel drive. She was leaning against the quarter panel of her rental car fawning over the dog. She saw Cleague and stood up tall and straight. With her sunglasses atop her head, hair tight in a ponytail, her leather jacket open despite the November chill, gray sweatshirt and comfortable faded jeans, she grinned from ear to ear as she watched him make his way toward her with carefully measured self-control.

15

"Well." Other than that he was speechless. Cleague just shook his head and swept her up in a bear-hug, lifting her off her feet, kissed her and set her down—making a show of brushing off her jacket with the palms of his hands. "Ever the clown I see," she chided. Taking her hands in his, squeezing lightly, "I've missed you too." In a mutual embrace they kissed again, slower. "Happy Birthday, Peter" her smile was softer now, eyes gleaming, she wrinkled her nose and said, "Yuck. You're all sweaty."

"Yes I am. You're chilled, been waiting long?" Cleague asked as he led her by the hand toward the bungalow. "I don't know," she shrugged, "...a few minutes I guess." The mild breeze had given way to a steady wind from the west. They could feel the onshore wind as the spotty blue sky clouded over to oyster gray and just began to drizzle. Peter told her, "I wasn't expecting you today, I'm happy you're here." He couldn't remember the last time he said he was happy. He hadn't thought about it much before he met Linda. His life before her had been a series of amassed debt and the constant struggle to pay bills. It still was, but her presence seemed to brighten his prospects.

"How about some coffee?" he asked, as they crossed the back porch into the kitchen. The dog scuttled in behind them.

"Sounds great!" Linda said, enthusiastically. He pulled a ceramic jar down from a cupboard and handed it to her.

"Good. You can make it while I take a shower." He off-handedly ordered.

"Ugh! Cleague! I don't believe you. I'm here not more than ten minutes and you're already giving orders." She grumbled: "...no wonder you live alone, nobody could put up with you more than two days at a time." She found the filters and started the coffee brewing. She could hear the shower running. She moved about the kitchen searching cabinets and shelves: "I'm not your house maid y'know!" He came in wearing a wool sweater and jeans and pulled two mugs from the cabinet she hadn't gotten to yet.

"Well, how's San Francisco?" he asked.

"The same, the city is great and I still hate my job, but I was able to work on *The Adrienne* up to Vancouver. The ship made port in Bellingham. I rented the car there. I'll catch the ship on its way down south when it makes port in Seattle. We've got four days together." She was beaming again now. Cleague loved her for that. He did not believe that she had the capacity for disingenuousness. She continued, "So who are those guys in the car down the road?"

"The BPS," he replied without further comment. Max was standing at the door, he barked once and Cleague opened the door for him.

"He's got you trained pretty well," she observed.

"Yes, Ma'am," Cleague agreed without hesitation.

"For such a gorgeous dog, how could you give him such a common name? You could have called him Rover, or Spot, and not done any worse."

"You misunderstand, Miss, his name isn't Max."

"Excuse me?" she asked. Had she been calling the dog by the wrong name all these months?

"When he was a puppy, I knew, or at least had a pretty strong suspicion, that he was going to be at the high end of the breed standard for size."

"Yeah, so?"

"Max is a term of convenience; his name is Canis Maximus, or Big Dog in the vernacular."

"You're weird, Cleague."

"Yes, Ma'am."

16

"What's the BPS?" Linda asked. The weather had turned warmer. The rain clouds had blown over, and they were sitting at his little picnic table outside enjoying the breeze on the back porch. They had just finished lunch.

"The Bureau of Public Safety," Cleague answered. "Their job is to protect you from yourself according to the dictates of Executive Order. It used to be called the Bureau of Alcohol, Tobacco and Firearms. They performed a couple of publicly televised fuck-ups..."

"Watch your language buster, there's a Lady present!" She barked without reservation. This guy could be fun but sometimes he had to be reminded of his place she thought. "Uh, yeah, sorry," Cleague accepted his admonishment and continued, "...on national TV a few years ago. They got some bad press, and through the mid to late nineties they finally became enough of a political embarrassment to the administration in office at that time that their name was changed. Actually their behavior wasn't aberrant at all, they were conducting business as usual, it just happened to be broadcast live on television," Peter said. He wasn't trying to be sarcastic. He was simply relating an historic fact, to wit: the BATF had been officially and ceremoniously disbanded. The executive branch of the federal government proposed that the BATF be retired from the Department of the Treasury, having well and faithfully discharged its assigned mission, and simultaneously campaigned for a new and progressive agency concerned with the safety and well being of the American public to be instituted under the aegis of the Department of the Interior.

"Its mission would be broader in scope than that of mere revenue collection and tax law compliance. Congress signed off on it. Nobody was relieved for cause, nobody was fired, and nobody quit. They have no constitutional authority, no rules, and no congressional oversight that holds it accountable. They simply changed the format of their letterhead and had their budget increased." He took a sip of tea and set the glass on the table.

Peter continued, "This little bit of beach-front property here belongs to the Nishtillamish Indians but the U.S. Government claims it as a National Historic Site. Now technically when I take my morning jog down the beach, I am running on property under the administrative aegis of the Department of the Interior. It is ostensibly public land. Am I trespassing? But I'm also a member of the taxpaying public. But it gets complicated because all of this land is still reservation property.

"Wait!" She interjected putting both hands in front of her as if to stop the torrent. "If you're trespassing, how can you be living on a National Historic Site?" Linda asked.

"I'm not", he said.

She shook her head, furrowed her brow, and scrunched her eyes shut, and started banging her clenched fist on the picnic table and said "NO! Stop it! You're not making any sense at all." It started with a giggle and yielded to a belly laugh. It wasn't Cleague's habit to attain levity in a normal conversation about political history but this was one of the things she did for him, it helped keep him even.

He explained, "I lease this house and the property it's built on from the Nishtillamish Tribal Council. This property sits on what used to be a military base back during World War II. It was never US Government property. It always belonged to the Nishtillamish Indians. When the war came along, they leased it to the Government for the duration of the war. After the war, the coastal artillery and the other units that were here vacated the property. It became a ghost town over night. The tribe maintains that the use of the land reverted to them on V-J day. The government contends that it is land in public trust. It belongs to the tribe and the government wants it."

He took another sip of iced tea and went on. "So far they haven't bothered me. But the BPS is no longer a tax collection administration. It's a federally-chartered police agency within the Department of the Interior. In essence, the United States of America now has a National Police Force. Incidentally, the uniformed division wears brown shirts."

17

"You know, Pete, sometimes I can't tell when you're serious and when you're just clowning around. Are you really that cynical?" Linda did indeed look concerned. Nothing in their relationship to this point had in any way prepared her for Peter's depth of feeling toward the current state of the American government. Cleague just gave a little shrug and smiled.

"Linda, I've led the life I've led. My opinions are born of my experience."

Cleague looked out at the surf and inhaled deeply. He loved the sea-air. He really felt at home in this little house on the beach and hated the thought of losing it as he imagined the fellows in the rocks and the weeds south of his house aiming a directional microphone at this private conversation on his back porch. He then turned back to Linda and answered her question. "Anyway, those guys in that car work for the Bureau of Public Safety. Their jurisdiction is the physical land mass of the United States. I don't know what they're doing here but they may be keeping an eye on me." He said and took a sip of tea.

Linda wasn't sure about his reasoning and tried to sum it up to see if she had heard it right.

"You know Pete, this all sounds a little 'iffy.' You're saying that those guys are parked in front of your house because they think you might trespass on federal property?"

"Yeah, pretty much," he agreed.

Whether she loved Cleague or not, his story seemed a little too flaky to be credible.

"So what are they going to do?" she asked.

"I don't know. They are probably waiting for me to commit a firearms violation, or cut my grass the wrong way, or they could just come in and burn my house down." He shrugged, helpless, "I really don't know." He looked down at Max, who had been basking in Linda's uninterrupted attention since the conversation began.

She leaned over and peered at him through squinted eyes, "Are you one of those, rabid, right-wing, radical, militia people?"

"Hell no, I'm a GDI and proud of it!"

"What's that?"

"A Goddamned Independent."

He got up and took her by the hand. "Come on. Let's go for a walk on the beach."

"Is it safe, honey?" she mocked.

"For now," he grunted in reply.

18

They walked the beach and watched the sunset. Again he thought of how much he loved his little spot in the world and, how fragile, how tentative was his place in it. And how much this woman was becoming a reason for this thing he was feeling. As they walked he scanned the horizon, left to right, front to rear. At dusk there were no reflected glints of light off an objective lens but he could instinctively feel his place in somebody's sight picture, superimposed by a mil-dot reticle.

She woke up the next morning to the murmured noise of the TV. He lay beside her, propped up on a pillow, channel surfing. The inane babble of the Sunday show hosts was replaced by the inane babble of the infomercial hosts. That was replaced by the singular pronouncements of the TV ministers. When the TV remained on the same channel longer than three seconds she looked up at Cleague.

"What are you watching?" she asked.

"These guys are great!" he said. This came as an unexpected revelation. She had not known Cleague to be a religious person.

"Did you get religion overnight?' she asked with mock incredulity. "I knew it was good, I didn't know it was a life-changing experience." He looked at her and said, "You are a life-changing experience," and kissed her. He lay back into the pillows.

"These guys are masters of their craft," he said. "They beckon and people come; they're just like carnival barkers in front of the tent of weird and magical things. They lay out the problems and offer the solutions to every quandary known to man. It's like a wishing well. The audience throws their money into the well and the preachers' wishes come true. I mean look at this guy, that church could be Grand Central Station. Watch this, when they do a panning shot of the speaker at the podium from the balcony, the podium is so far away you can't even see the guy standing there." They watched quietly and listened to the message. After a while Linda said, "You could do that."

"No", he said, "I could do it for a couple of minutes but these guys go on for hours and hours, they're incredible." They watched some more.

"Brothers, do you believe in the power of prayer?" the T.V. minister asked the men at the altar ostensibly there to bear witness, or receive a blessing, or be cured of leprosy or something. "Now Is The Time To Give Your Hearts TO JESUS-uh."

"That's the extra little kicker when they give the extra syllable at the end of the name." Cleague interjected. She was stunned into amazement.

"Why Peter Cleague," she declared. "I had no idea you were such a fan."

The TV man went on…"Because your soul belongs to God one way or the other. It is not yours to squander, it is yours to cherish and nurture," the preacher continued. Cleague muted the sound from the TV and in his very best Southern Baptist impersonation he exclaimed, "Sister, do you believe in the power of prayer? NOW is the time to give your heart to Jesus-uh." He slapped her on the butt and pulled her to him, "Because your ass belongs to me!"

"You blaspheme!" she proclaimed and laughed and they found each other, again.

19

Peter Cleague sat on his back porch thinking about the conversation he had with Linda. Those four days had flown by and then she had left. It was getting harder for him to say good-bye to her but he held that in check. He was doodling in a sketchpad and stretching his neck from left to right and right to left, he caught a flash of light from the weeds south of his house. *Those guys really needed to invest in a sunshade for their scope.*

Having lived the life he had lived he knew that some facts of life can be reduced to basic fundamental principles. Don't carry more than you can lift. Don't eat anything larger than your head. Your situation will determine your strategy; your strategy will determine your tactics. His situation was this: he was alone in a small wood structure in a rural environment with no close neighbors. He was being surveilled by an element of the U.S. Government, and it wasn't some guy sitting in a room somewhere looking at a computer screen—it was a guy looking at him through a spotting scope. This was not some vague intimation of malevolent intent. It was an imminent threat. They would come for him with all the speed, force, and violence of action the government could bring to bear and that would be quite a bit. If he was wrong, fine. He hoped so. But if he was right…he needed to get ready.

His strategy was to get out. He wasn't going to wage a pitched battle with the BPS by himself. His tactics would be stealth and deceit. *Not by strength but by guile, good idea.*

He looked south at the terrain covered in inosculating fronds of sea grass moving gently in the breeze. He couldn't see any telltale glints of light now but they were there. He began to wonder, *if they're there, where else would they be?* He started sketching the outline of his property as it might be seen from the air. He drew the house and the storage shed across the street in spatial relationship. He added prominent terrain features of the area surrounding his house from the bridge—south of his property—to town, amply enlarging the scale of the initial lay-out: jetties, the bridge, the road, points of constriction to foot traffic. He considered, *if I were going to conduct an all out, flat-assed, no holds barred, raid on this house*:

A) How would I do it?

B) Which direction would I come from?

C) What would I use? How many troops?

He formulated the composition and conduct of the ersatz raid on his little beach house by the acronym SMEAC.

- Situation
- Mission
- Enemy
- Administration and Logistics (beans, bullets, and band aids)
- Command and Signal

After drafting a plausible raid order he thought about how he would defend against that raid and the kinds of things he would need to do it. Doing these things made him remember his time in the service and the people he knew then. If he would admit it, sometimes he missed the people and sometimes he missed the environment. But most of the time he didn't.

When he was done with the sketch Cleague went into the house and made a long distance phone call to his old platoon sergeant back in Texas, had a brief chat—long enough to get a correct E-Mail address and hung up. He came back out onto the porch, picked up his sketchbook and walked out toward the beach. "Come on, Max!"

It was time to do some drawings.

20

Cleague's house was situated approximately one mile north of the bridge that connected Peninsular Island with the mainland. The road continued north into town and was the only thoroughfare on or off. The house was situated approximately twenty-five yards east of the road. Across the road, on the west side, was a storage building...a leftover Quonset hut from the Second World War. The east side of Cleague's property was bordered by a portion of the barrier that intermittently ran from the southern tip of the island to the north end to help deflect the effects of beach erosion. The few remaining buildings and the acreage of what was left of the 603rd Coast Artillery (Anti Aircraft) Battery from World War II had been designated a National Historic Site by Executive Order a few years before, primarily because they were still standing (and to prevent the subsequent sale to private citizens, tribal challenges not withstanding).

The island was roughly six miles long and two miles wide at its widest point, split more-or-less down the middle by an inland waterway. It had originally been a peninsular spit of land which haphazardly jutted out into Puget Sound. It had been designated a strategically significant site for the placement of an anti-aircraft battery by the Continental Defense Command during World War II and therefore redesigned by the Corps of Engineers as an island to facilitate ship traffic. The anti-aircraft guns had lined the west side of the newly-hewn island from the bridge at the south tip of the island due north to what was now a modest but essential marina. The marina had come to be Peninsular Island's economic base, catering as it did to the tourist fishing traffic from May to October. The town of Port Cullis had grown around the marina.

Cleague's house had been one of the remnants of base housing hastily erected for the support personnel considered to be "permanently assigned" to the base. After the war, with the inevitable reduction-in-force, and a sudden lack of government funding to sustain it, and no justifiable reason to continue its operation, the old post was decommissioned and the buildings were left to the elements and disrepair. The guns of the battery were dismantled—their concrete parapets razed. In the scope of the war effort in the Pacific Theatre, this tiny installation and the infrequent engagements the battery sustained with the enemy (0 engagements, but there had been a lot of false alerts for the hot gun crews) seemed almost molecular by comparison; and nothing now remained of it save a neglected patinated brass plaque near a concrete pad upon which one of the guns had been emplaced, and a lot of weeds.

A gravel service road had been laid down for access to the guns and had not been used to any extent for half a century— save the occasional kid on a four wheeler or somebody letting their dogs run the San Juan swamp rabbits, which now served as the only company for the ghosts that could never leave their appointed duty station. Weeds and sea grass covered the loamy soil and much of the gravel service road as well. East of the service road ran a ditch—the raceway—which meandered from north to south. Once a supply channel for barges delivering ordnance to the gun emplacements, after sixty years of disuse it was now little more than overgrown marsh—wide enough to allow passage to the occasional rowboat.

The fact that the whole island was tribal land and subject to the disposition of the tribe was something the Federal Government seemed to overlook to suit itself. Because the property was tribal land, the tribe—the Nishtillamish—itself a sovereign nation, could and did lease the property to whom it chose. This was how Cleague could afford a house on the beach; he leased it from the tribe who leased dozens of other properties very similar to it. This practice accounted for a not insignificant portion of the tribe's annual revenue—the tribal council did not operate a casino, the tribal council believed in real estate.

The Quonset hut across the street from Cleague's house had been one of a series of supply storage buildings, which had at one time lined the road almost all the way into town. Cleague's house and the Quonset hut and a few other houses and ancillary structures that lined the road to town were all that remained of the sprawling army facility nearly seventy years after the end of the war.

21

In the time since Cleague had visited Eugene Smith at the Alders restaurant in Seattle, Smith would occasionally take his boat from the Des Moines marina south of Seattle up north through Deception Pass to Peninsular Island. The fishing wasn't bad and it gave Smith a place to go. The city was Smith's home and he loved it as such but there were times when it made him tired. He would anchor the seventeen foot Boston Whaler right off the beach and go to Cleague's house for lunch. Smith discovered that Cleague had a dog. The dog's name was Max; he was one of those Norwegian snow dogs. Smith was ambivalent about dogs, or cats, or anything which required feeding on a regular basis. Smith lived in a big, modern city and did not have the time in his life to devote to livestock. Cleague—clearly—did not live in a city. Cleague—clearly—had nothing else in his life but the dog. To Smith's sense of things that was OK. "To each his own." Max had come to accept Smith as not being worth a lot of bother and spent energy.

Max had developed a somewhat unnerving habit, when he was ready to go out in the morning, of sitting at the head of Cleague's bed and staring at Cleague until he woke up. He would occasionally pant loudly to lend a sense of urgency to the situation. Once in a great while, he'd swat Cleague in the head with his paw. His infrequent bark was usually followed by an attack of teeth propelled by the kinetic energy generated by fifty-five pounds of Norwegian Elkhound.

Cleague, immersed in his unrelenting dream of consequences unforeseen to actions long since taken, could not quite identify the sound. In his dream a man standing in a road looked left and right but there was this sound like thunder, a truck in low gear, or a dog growling. Cleague was instantly awake and fully alert. Max only growled at something he didn't like—most usually people. Forcing himself not to move a single muscle before getting his bearings, he strained to hear some foreign sound, an uncommon pattern hidden in the ubiquitous noises of a small seventy-year-old wooden bungalow on a windy beach. Reaching under his pillow, his hand closed around the grip frame of the revolver. Cleague hurled himself to the off-side of the bed furthest from the door, using his bed as a barricade. He aimed the revolver, sighting over the top of the frame, to identify his target—Eugene Smith.

Mr. Smith leaned against the doorframe casually making his observations of the world-class bodyguard in action. Ensconced behind his mattress and box spring, pillows and blankets strewn asunder, Cleague exhaled a sigh—not quite relief, not quite anger.

"Jesus Christ, Gene that was awfully foolish."

Smith looked from the dog, its nose protruding, everything else hidden under a discarded blanket, to Cleague.

"So I see. Take your dog out for his run Peter; I'll get your stuff ready. You have a job." Max, a senior, leisure class Elkhound, did not like being awakened before he was ready. If something displeased the dog, the dog growled. Cleague was not unaccustomed to receiving oblique instructions; Smith's was nothing out-of-the-ordinary.

"Okay." Standing and stretching, "Let's go Max." Cleague made way for the bathroom door, unloaded the revolver, dumped the cartridges into his hand, and handed the gun to Smith by the top-strap (butt forward, cylinder open and emptied, muzzle down). He found his sneakers in the kitchen and didn't bother to change out of the sweat pants he had slept in before going outside into the morning rain for his daily jog. He threw on a windbreaker and did a light stretch on the porch. Two miles today would be sufficient—a mile down the road and a mile back. He would pass on the beach run this morning.

He came back to find a carry-on bag, a suit bag and his shaving kit packed.

"What's up, Gene?"

"You have an interview. They want to have a look at you."

"I don't do auditions."

"This time you do, dress nice."

Cleague took his shower and dressed as he casually made note that certain things were as he had left them before running the dog; he packed a few more odds and ends into his carry-on bag. He walked into the kitchen and took the coffee Smith handed him.

"How long?" Cleague asked.

"A couple days, maybe longer, we need to get going."

"Do I need hardware?"

"No, they'll provide it. It's supposed to be a low profile job," Smith said.

"We have to check Max into the boarding kennel," Cleague responded.

"Yep, let's go. Put him in the back of the Range Rover, we've got just enough time to do it now," Smith said, indicating the rear end of his vehicle.

22

Cleague managed to keep quiet until they were over the bridge and on the rural highway that would eventually take them to the interstate freeway. Smith drove.

"Alright, what's this about?" Peter had to admire his own restraint sometimes. He thought his emotional control was getting better.

"You really do have an interview but that's beside the point. You need to get out of that house, you've been set up," Smith said.

"Oh?" Cleague was mildly curious.

"Yeah, no shit. How many people know you got that reloading gear over there in that shed?"

"You were in the shed too?" Peter asked incredulously.

"Only long enough to see that you're in deep shit. How many people?"

"Anybody that's been on the property I suppose."

"How long have the BPS had surveillance on you?"

"I don't know, five or six months I guess."

Smith momentarily moved his gaze from the road to Peter, in utter disbelief.

"And it never occurred to you that they were going to do something?"

"Well, hell yeah it occurred to me. I just always figured I'd be home when it happened. I understand that 'an eye for an eye' is their unspoken motto." Cleague said.

"And why don't you use your alarm system? I had no trouble getting into your house this morning. Why do you have it if you're not going to use it, does it even work?" Smith asked.

"It will," Cleague answered.

"Oh." Smith was a little more than curious but knew better than to ask.

"And that fierce guard dog of yours leaves something to be desired," he added.

"Max is nothing so menial as a plebeian guard dog, he's a companion. Besides If I'm ever attacked by a moose I'll be in good stead," Cleague said.

"Peter, I think you've been living alone too long. I hope you realize that your little piece of property may no longer be there when you get back."

"The loss of personal property, among other things, has been a possibility since the day I resigned," he said.

"I hope you've made provisions for yourself, Peter. I don't get the sense that you perceive this situation with an adequate degree of gravity. They're going to come in there with bulldozers on a firearms warrant for a violation of the arsenal code. How much ammo you got in that shed anyway? Well, it doesn't matter; it won't be there when you get back," Smith concluded.

"It'll be there. They don't want the ammo and they don't want the property, they want me. It's the one place they know I'll come back to as long as they leave the house alone," Cleague said.

Smith drove through the valley farmland winding his way through the rural roads that would eventually connect them to I-5 and the way south to Sea-Tac airport.

"What are you going to do?" he asked.

"You don't need to know," Cleague said bluntly.

"What?" Smith was just as blunt.

"OK," Cleague paused and re-positioned himself in the passenger seat.

"Just for the sake of discussion, let's say that something happens up here with the BPS, or whatever, and let's say, God forbid, that maybe somebody gets hurt."

"Yeah?" Smith prodded.

"And let's say that you, because you are a known associate of mine, are required to go to court, or to testify before some congressional committee about the event. You can't testify to what you do not know. You don't need to know what I'm going to do. But think of it as perimeter security." Cleague smirked.

"Wait a minute," Smith said, "Are you telling me you intend to take on the BPS? Of all the trigger happy feds with twitchy fingers the BPS is the twitchiest. And you want to take 'em on by yourself?"

"I'm not saying any such thing," Cleague replied. "We're just having a conversation—an exercise in the abstract."

Smith didn't let it go.

"Then what are you saying? Why are they coming after you?" he asked.

"I don't know and I don't care, but I am sick and tired of being pushed to conform to the nebulous whim of some unknown, unseen, bureaucrat."

"What does that mean?" Smith asked.

"Gene, I was pushed out of my career. Back in D.C. when I left the Bureau of Diplomatic Security, I was as good as blacklisted from the private security sector— which was by that time in full-bloom. I was shut out. You tell me, Gene, who has that kind of influence? And here I am, so many years later, on the opposite side of the continent because somebody inside the beltway has the opinion that I'm not a team player? And they still want to come after me? Fuck 'em!" He quoted Smith from that night in the Alders with enthusiasm.

" 'If they want me they know where I live and they are welcome to it.' Or they can send their proxy army—I don't give a shit. And I'll tell you this: I'm not starting anything, but I will end it here." Peter finished in a pique.

Smith had known Peter Cleague over the course of many years. He had known him initially as a student, and later as a colleague, and most recently as a personal friend. Smith had never seen Cleague display this degree of fervent intent.

They spent the remainder of the drive discussing details of Cleague's next contract, and the more arcane points of the distribution system of the food service industry, for example: getting things from "A" to "B".

23

Peter Cleague spent five hours, including a lay-over in San Francisco, on two different airplanes, finally arriving at a small airstrip somewhat northeast of Palm Springs. He could not imagine the attraction the desert held for some, but people had to live somewhere. He was escorted to a hangar; empty but for the group of a dozen or so men and women waiting, making small talk. The light in an office went out and two men exited. An older man, late fifties to early sixties, with a quiet self-assured demeanor, close cropped gray hair and above average posture, dressed in standard business attire, stayed in the background and watched the proceedings with a keen interest. Cleague guessed him to be retired military. Cleague noted that the door was painted in gold letters with the legend "Hereford Associates". It made him smile.

The younger man, in his late twenties, was dressed impeccably in a fine pin striped suit by A.D. Philips, London, and Italian shoes. He greeted each "candidate" in his smoothest PR persona. "Good afternoon Ladies and Gentlemen. Thank you for taking the time and trouble to participate in our evaluation process. We would also like to thank, at this time, Mr. Tibbett of Hereford Associates for providing us with your recommendations and references," he said.

Really? Cleague had no idea who this Tibbett guy might be. Why would Mr. Tibbett have provided a reference for Cleague? Then he got it—Smith, had to be.

Cleague noticed the gold Rolex President on the young man's wrist. The most recognized watch in the world, Cleague's opinion was that the gold model was just a little ostentatious. But then again, considering the man was an employee of a Middle Eastern monarch, maybe not.

After all was said and done, Cleague and three others were invited to accompany a royal family member of the House of Saud to attend the Triple Crown. The Triple Crown consists of three races for three-year-old thoroughbred horses. Winning all three races is considered the greatest accomplishment of a thoroughbred racehorse. The three races are: the Kentucky Derby at Churchill Downs in Louisville, Kentucky; the Preakness Stakes at Pimlico Race Course in Baltimore, Maryland; and the Belmont Stakes at Belmont Park in Elmont, New York. The Triple Crown starts with the Kentucky Derby on the first Saturday of May. The Preakness follows two weeks later. The Belmont Stakes is five weeks after the Kentucky Derby in early June. The prince had a colt in the Derby.

As the crown prince chose to not stay in the United States for the entire five week span from Churchill Downs to the Belmont Stakes, Cleague and the others were only required for a total time of nine days out of five weeks. Cleague had always liked Kentucky and enjoyed his brief visit.

Maryland and New York were less interesting but the job paid well. After the Preakness, Cleague made an excursion of his own down to Mountain Home, Texas, to visit some friends.

24

It was Saturday. His house had been left undisturbed. Cleague got back just in time to get Max out of the boarding kennel. Tomorrow they would celebrate their mutual unfettered freedom with a run on the beach. Tonight he would work in the shed. After his conversation with Smith about the shipping regimen of the commercial restaurant industry, he had some things to pack.

Sunday morning was quiet, except for the sea gulls. He took advantage of the opportunity to modify his "alarm system." It would extend from the shed, to his house, to the water line. Setting things up the way he wanted them was going to take a bit of time.

Before he began his summer routine of run/swim/run he walked across the street to initiate a new ritual, something he would repeat everyday for the rest of his life on the island. Stepping inside the galvanized steel Quonset hut left over from WWII he shut the door behind him and let his eyes grow accustomed to the dimness. The ancient windows set into the curved walls of his "reloading shed" let in precious little light as it was but he left the overhead light off. The interior space was one large room; there were no interior walls. The exterior walls were lined with surplus wall lockers, the kind you might find in a high school gymnasium. All of these wall lockers represented works in progress. They all contained hand-loaded ammunition in various calibers, of various bullet weights, of various powders, and various loads, and the respective dies for those calibers.

If he had been writing a magazine article comparing and contrasting the Colt's 1873 Single Action Army revolver with the U.S. Pistol, caliber 45 ACP, Model of 1911, he would naturally need to shoot each specimen. As the two guns were thirty-eight years apart in design and manufacture they would, in turn, represent thirty-eight years difference in technology. The 45 Colt cartridge utilized black powder, while the 1911 pattern handgun was designed for the (then) new 45 ACP (Automatic Colt's Pistol) cartridge loaded with smokeless powder. While the energy per grain of different brands of black powder is essentially the same, smokeless powder can be manufactured in a nearly limitless number of variations. Given the restrictions in obtaining ammunition of any variety, Cleague simply had to make the ammunition himself to be able to write his articles. That was why he had all the reloading gear in the shed.

He had on hand at least one pound of every smokeless powder commercially manufactured since 1976. He also kept several pounds of black powder in F, FF, FFF, FFFF, and Cannon on hand. When kept in a cool dry place, powder would last for a long time. The quantities of such powders in Cleague's shed would undoubtedly be a part of any legal charge brought against him as a violation of the "Arsenal Codes."

The particular wall locker he was looking for was more or less in the center of the room. It was the one nearest the reloading benches and contained the ammunition loaded with powder with the fastest burning rates. Since burning rates for modern smokeless powders are measured in microseconds it was almost moot, but Cleague just figured that if some is good more is better. The ammunition with powders of faster burning rates tended to be the smaller caliber pistol ammunition with lighter weight bullets. His intent was to create a distraction. That fact that the whole building could very well turn into a fragmentation grenade by the time he was finished would be beside the point.

When he located the particular wall locker he was looking for he opened the door and pulled out an empty metal ammo can from the bottom shelf and placed it on one of the loading benches. He had a variety of one-eighth inch steel plates of mild steel that he often used as target stock. These had been scrap pieces that fit into the empty ammo can. He now laid the ammo can containing the eighth inch steel plates on its side on the exterior top of the locker. So far so good, he walked back to the front door.

Standing just inside the Quonset hut by the front door, Cleague pulled a bandanna from his pocket and used it as a blindfold. He made his way to where he believed the particular wall locker to be. Cleague opened the locker's door again and found an aerosol paint can on the top shelf and set it on top of the ammo can. He removed the blindfold and looked around—right locker, which was important. Satisfied with his preliminary run he put the can of spray paint back on the top shelf but left the ammo can in place. His movement in the dark to accomplish this specific task would become more efficient; his time would improve with repetition. He secured the door to the loading shed and walked back across the street to the back yard of his house and stretched before he went inside to suit up.

25

Being the middle of June it was almost warm enough for him to take a swim wearing a wet suit; his wet suit was a zippered, short sleeved, short-legged apparatus. He usually wore it when he went kayaking out on open water but it served just as well for swimming. In the interest of minimizing pain, Cleague managed to go through four pairs of running shoes a year. When the primary pair gave up their ability to support his body weight they were relegated to second string status and used for supernumerary duty—like running in salt water once, and then discarded. He wore the alternate pair this morning and carried a little rubberized satchel for some other stuff, including a curved rectangular object that weighed about two and a half pounds.

He altered his route a little. Instead of running south on the road and north on the beach, he ran north on the road for half a mile, crossed the barrier dune—noted a recently cut trail—and then headed south on the beach, making his way for the first of the three jetties that crept out into the water between his house and the bridge

The jetties were 150 yards apart. They originally served as foundations for service docks for military re-supply ships during the war. Now they simply served as mute suggestions of a nation that had once been united in a common vision. Cleague ran out onto the first jetty, dove in and swam to the next, climbing out onto the rocks and on top of the jetty. A hundred and fifty yards in 55-degree water for the first swim of the season had been a little optimistic. Shivering from the cold he wriggled out of his wet suit with some effort and donned a T-shirt and stuffed the wet suit into the satchel. In a few weeks he'd be able to swim from the jetty behind his house all the way to the boat channel but for now he simply had to pace himself. He ran back onto the cobble beach and followed the water line around to the far side of the bridge, making appropriate observations en route. The jog helped him warm up a little. By now, Max had run to hell and gone but he knew how to get home when he got hungry. Cleague followed the contour of the strand as it changed in elevation from the waterline to the road surface where the asphalt road joined the bridge. He had always hated running uphill. Running uphill on a cobbled surface was worse.

This wet and dry business was a bit more of a challenge than Cleague remembered. He also realized that at this point in his life it took longer to heal. He was no longer in his twenties, nor was he in the Marines. All this beating and banging to which he subjected his joints took a toll—he knew his knees and lower back were pretty well shot. But he had to maintain a minimum level of endurance and that meant running on a hard surface as well swim a specified distance in a specified time. He was going to have to extend his time in the water by increments, building up to the standard of a three-mile swim in open water. His first goal was to repeat this same run but swimming from the first jetty, through the boat channel to the far side of the bridge at night, unnoticed and in good time. Depending on how the assault on his house would play out, he might even have to swim from the shed down the canal, through the boat channel, and out to the Channel Marker. That would be just about two, maybe two and a half miles. That would be a true bitch and hopefully it wouldn't come to that. If any of his neighbors cared to ask he would tell them he was training for an up-coming triathlon…senior division. Growing old gracefully. Hell.

26

It was a mile or so from the bridge to his house on the hard surfaced road. The BPS sedan wasn't there, it was Sunday; *they must have run out of overtime funding,* he thought. Walking in through the brush and weeds from the road and scratching the shit out of his legs, he checked the dune a hundred yards south of his house. They hadn't been all that careful in concealing their hide. Scrub pine, weeds and dried sea grass had been cleared away in a six foot by six foot square, with a nice berm, about 18" high—forward of the position to limit visibility from the north (his house), fashioned from sand, sea grass, and brushwood. The field craft made for a nice hide but the area was littered with candy bar wrappers and Styrofoam cups. From this position they had a clear view of the South side of the house, part of the porch, and the picnic table. He was careful to display no sign as he left a small token of his esteem unobtrusively behind: the two and a half pound curved rectangular object that he had carried in his satchel. Covering his tracks, he made his way back to the road and jogged back to the house at an easy pace. Tomorrow he would observe the water route by kayak.

After a shower and a short nap he looked up and noticed it was just about sunset; he was hungry. He also realized Max had been standing at the back door giving him the evil eye. It was time to let the dog out and make supper.

27

Peter Cleague's work progressed steadily on all fronts for a few weeks until he was due to leave for San Francisco to help teach a handgun class. He worked at the Port Cullis Marina part time as seasonal maintenance. As the season's revenue was down from average he was able to take time off without much bother. He tried to fill in the gaps with teaching and writing. He was looking forward to his trip to San Francisco. Again he had been offered the job of adjunct instructor. It didn't pay much but it was an excuse to see Linda. He was surprised at himself when he realized that his pre-occupation with her was bordering on obsession.

The "alarm system" for his house was not yet in place but he knew what he wanted to do and therefore half the work was done—all that remained was to do it. He was satisfied that the miscreants would leave his house alone and if they didn't, they wouldn't find anything out of the ordinary anyway. He had asked the supervisor at the sheriff's sub-station, Andy DeKooning, to keep an eye on his place while he was gone, and the deputy happily agreed. After he dropped Max off at the boarding kennel it was time to go.

The class lasted five days: four and a half days of progressive instruction concluded with an afternoon of intensive evaluation. Each day was scheduled to be eight hours of instruction but both Cleague and the primary instructor agreed to provide the students who requested it with remedial training restricted only by the amount of ammunition each student brought to the course. Some days ran an hour or two overtime but neither instructor balked at the demand on their attention.

The primary instructor, Roger Tibbett, a Welshman retired from the British Army, was a stern taskmaster. He approached serious matters seriously and he took nothing more seriously than personal survival; neither did Cleague. For his classes, Cleague used the same pseudonym under which he wrote his magazine articles. Most literate gun enthusiasts, if pressed, could recall the by-line Peter Stone. This allowed his students some assumption of familiarity yet afforded him some degree of distance.

28

Roger Tibbett felt himself at a disadvantage. His company, Hereford Associates, had been contracted to teach this class months in advance. Hereford Associates in turn leased the firing range from the local proprietor—in this case the proprietor was a community rod & gun club. At the last minute, the designated instructor had to bow out due to unforeseen circumstances. Peter had been recommended to Tibbett by another board member of Hereford Associates as quite the capable instructor and available on very short notice. In Tibbett's view, this class would be nothing more than a refresher class, albeit an intense one, in what these agents would already have been taught, but ability with a firearm is a perishable skill. For some of these students, depending on their parent organization, qualification with the handgun determined job security.

Nonetheless, Tibbett would have liked to have talked with this Stone person at length before embarking together on the arduous task of teaching real people with real guns that fired real ammunition. Tibbett assumed the duties of the primary instructor and Stone was assigned as the adjunct instructor. The only thing Tibbett had been able to ask Stone was how he would conduct the class had he been the primary instructor. Stone, it seemed to Tibbett, without pretension, answered a direct question directly.

"If it were me, Mr. Tibbett, I would review the fundamentals of marksmanship and, using that as the foundation, build from there. Ultimately this is a handgun qualification course. A qualification is a demonstration of a specific skill set. We teach, they learn, they practice, we test. If we do our job right, everybody passes and goes home happy." Peter answered as honestly and as tactfully as he could. It was like answering the question, "what shape is a circle?"

Direct, simple, guileless, thought Tibbett. *Nothing wrong with that.* Tibbett would be evaluating Stone on the merits of his ability to teach as well as evaluating the class on their ability to learn.

Tibbett began the class with the absolutely obligatory safety lecture. Regardless how many times his students had heard it before they were going to hear it again.

1) **Every Firearm Is Always Loaded.** Do not pretend this situation is true—be deadly serious about it.
2) **Don't Let The Muzzle Sweep Anything You Do Not Intend To Harm**.
3) **KEEP YOUR FINGER OFF OF THE TRIGGER UNTIL YOUR FRONT SIGHT IS ON THE IDENTIFIED THREAT AND YOU HAVE MADE THE DECISION TO SHOOT THE THREAT.** Keep your finger off the trigger when your front sight is off the target.
4) **Be Sure Of Your Target**—Identify What It is, What It Is In Line With, And What Is Behind It. NEVER SHOOT ANYTHING THAT YOU HAVE NOT POSITIVELY IDENTIFIED.

Tibbett also made the observation, giving due homage to Clint Smith, that the first rule is the only one necessary, the rest are for the slow and dim-witted. Most of the students nodded or at least smiled at this funny little Englishman's dry sense of humor.

Tibbett spent two hours reviewing the fundamentals of marksmanship: stance and posture is fluid, grip is consistent and firm, focus on the front sight, and press the trigger.

"Why do you shoot a suspected perpetrator, a target?" Tibbett asked the class in general as he strode the aisle back and forth between the two rows of tables. No answer.

"Ladies and gentlemen, this is a class on how to keep your selves alive with a handgun. You will or will not shoot a target in accordance with your individual agencies' policies on the use of deadly force, however, the target represents a threat and you will shoot the threat to stop the threat. If it were not a threat you wouldn't shoot it would you?" Tibbett's manner was casual, contemplative—the professor verbally ruminating on the philosophy of violence.

"What is the threat? A man, or a woman, a child or an octogenarian; evil does not discriminate by gender, age, or race." He let that one sink in a bit. ... "Humans have three areas of natural armor; shoot something until something better presents itself. It is important to shoot something important. Shot placement is more important than caliber. If the fight has already deteriorated to the point at which you have to use a handgun to save yourselves, you are already in the worst possible situation you can be in, until the situation gets worse. Shoot the threat until the threat stops. Shoot until the slide of the gun locks back on an empty magazine and assess the condition of the target, if necessary, while you are deftly making a magazine change, of course."

They laughed again, shoot to slide lock and assess; what a witty guy. He wasn't kidding but they would learn that in time.

Out of the classroom now and on the range, Tibbett asked Peter to get the class started with their drills in order to give him the opportunity to evaluate the skill levels of the individual students. Stone simply nodded and took a position centered on and behind the firing line. He knew Tibbett was testing him. He also understood it and carried on with what to him was routine instruction.

"Ladies and gentleman, I want you all to move forward until you are about three feet away from your respective targets." As the class moved forward, on line, Tibbett asked Stone what he was doing. Three feet? Peter told Tibbett that everybody had the potential to be a good shot at short range. Peter would start the students close, three feet, and work them backwards increasing the distance, incrementally, until they started to miss. Then he would know their limit and that would be when he could hone his attention to the particular needs of the individual students. Tibbett concurred and left Peter alone to do his teaching.

As a pair they worked well together. Cleague was adept in firearms instruction and was able to teach either half of the lesson plan while the primary instructor gave individual attention to those students who needed it, and then the two instructors would switch off. It was a class of Federal agents assigned to carry out the writs and warrants of the Federal courts. Cleague begrudged no man the right to defend his own life. Cleague held that knowledge was a tool dependent on the individual wielding it. If pressed he would also allow that some Federal employees were as idealistic as he had once been; they weren't all necessarily evil. The final day of class was a test of comprehension and performance-on-demand for all of the students. Tibbett had designed the scenarios, the tactical solutions required to solve each problem being progressively difficult. Both he and Cleague monitored each student's resolution to each problem and each gave a critique of the student's accomplishments and failures. Tibbett was genuinely impressed with Cleague's observations and his approach to problem solving.

Tibbett had had the distinct impression all week that this adjunct instructor fellow, whatever his name was—it certainly wasn't Stone—had in him far more than he presented. He surmised this man would be an operational asset rather than a risk if he were inclined to take on certain types of work. Tibbett's organization, (of which he was executive vice-president of operations), was always on the lookout for a few more good men. This adjunct fellow had all the right skills honed to an instinctive level—the lad had been at this game for some time.

After everyone had run the scenarios, they convened in the classroom for one last group critique. One thing about it, everyone agreed they had gotten more than their tax-payer-funded money's worth. After the critique there was the brief yet obligatory certificate, handshake, and photograph. Tibbett could not help but notice that the adjunct fellow, Stone, had quietly sequestered himself in the back of the room. When bidden to stand in for a photograph by a well-meaning student, he politely declined, but cheerfully offered to take the student's photograph with Tibbett. When asked why, Peter simply told them that he did not want his spirit captured in a box. With the certificates awarded and the last of the bunch on their way home, Tibbett thought he'd give it a try.

Peter was glad to see the last of the newly indoctrinated Federal fodder leave. In mere minutes he would be on his way to Linda's! Ya-hoo!

"Well Peter, that's the last of them and I can't say it's too soon. You know, I certainly don't wish to pry, but is Peter Stone your real name?" Peter smiled and said not a word.

"Yes, well I thought as much. Listen, Peter is it?" Cleague nodded and volunteered, "Peter Cleague," as he extended his hand. He briefly explained, "Upon occasion I write magazine articles under the name 'Peter Stone' it just seemed to be a natural fit." Tibbett nodded; it made sense, in an oblique way.

"Listen Peter, I'm involved with a private company that routinely runs security operations not unlike you and I have done this past week. Sometimes we teach, and sometimes we do. Beyond the recommendation of the range administrators here I don't know what your background is but you handled yourself very well both on the range and in the classroom. What is your background?" Cleague didn't mind being asked for his bona fides; he had expected it much earlier.

"I used to be with the Bureau of Diplomatic Security for the Department of State. In fact, for a brief time I taught a class, very much like this one, at the Federal Law Enforcement Training Center in Glynco, Ga." Tibbett was more than a little bemused.

"You taught at FLETC?" he asked.

Cleague nodded, "Me and a bunch of other people, the classes were quite a bit larger. I like small classes like this a lot better," he said. Tibbett simply nodded, and agreed, "Quite!"

Tibbett decided to take the opportunity to make his assistant an offer. Something he had considered since the first day of class when Stone had started the students off at three feet from the targets. "Peter, would you be interested in getting together to discuss the possibility of potential employment with my company?" Roger asked.

"Sure." Cleague's smile was a little broader now, "What's the name of it?" he asked. It was Tibbett's turn to smile, slightly.

"Hereford Associates" Tibbett said. Hereford Associates—something about the name seemed familiar. Peter couldn't think of it just now, but no matter. In his introductory safety lecture Tibbett had explained that he had retired from the British Army. Roger Tibbett had never said anything about having served with the 22d Special Air Service Regiment, but one of the people from the range office let it "slip." Rumor mills being what they are it was all the buzz amongst the students all week long. When asked by a student what his unit was in the British army Roger simply replied that his parent unit had been The Royal Electrical and Mechanical Engineers. When asked where he was stationed, he said that much of his time he had been stationed at Credenhill, England. Apparently, none of the students realized that Credenhill was a Royal Air Force base and as such was one of several sites for the 22 SAS Mobility Troop. Cleague knew that the 22 SAS was headquartered in Hereford, England. Roger had answered the students' questions truthfully and never betrayed his oath to maintain the Official Secrets Act. Cleague enjoyed dry humor and Tibbett's seemed to be absolutely arid.

"Good. Will you be staying in the area a few days then?" Roger asked.

"Yes," Cleague replied, not uncomfortably, "I'm staying with a friend in San Francisco for a few days then I'll be going home."

"Well, perhaps you and your friend would care to have dinner with my wife and me one night this week," Roger said.

"Yes, that sounds nice, I'm sure we would," Cleague answered, very pleased with the way things were turning out.

"Fine, fine, here's the number where we're staying." Tibbett handed Cleague a card. "Give us a call in the next day or so." Tibbett offered his hand, "It was good working with you Peter, well done."

Cleague shook it, firm and dry. "Thank you." And they went their separate ways.

29

Linda very much enjoyed the evening they spent with Sergeant Major (Retired) and Mrs. Roger Tibbett. She took delight in the acerbic observations of the extremely dry-humored Mary Tibbett while the men droned on about something or other. It was, after all, a business meeting. From time to time she would catch snippets of their conversation, "...oh, you know Eugene Smith from Belfast?" and "...yes, indeed I was posted to Beirut at that period of time, but of course the British Empire would certainly not admit to it," and "...that was you?"

The Tibbetts retired from the British Army, and moved to Palm Springs. During his active duty service, Tibbett had served as an exchange officer with the United States Marine Corps at 29 Palms, California, and actually liked the area. Mary Tibbett enjoyed Roger's little training junkets to the San Francisco Bay Area as it allowed her to do some shopping without Roger getting in her way. The other kinds of training junkets he was involved in from time to time were not so much welcomed as accepted. He was still able to do work that he thought was necessary; and she was glad for it, much more so than him sitting around drinking himself into a post-retirement stupor, as so many of his mates had lived through the most harrowing missions only to die of cirrhosis of the liver, growing more bitter and resentful every day. Cleague noticed the Sergeant Major allowed himself a glass of wine with dinner. All in all Cleague thought the evening went well and ended on a good note. He might even have had the possibility of future employment on a slightly more regular basis laid at his doorstep, always a good note. He then had an entire week to spend with Linda. While she was at work, he used the time available to polish up his article and sent it off to the magazine publisher; so far, so good. In the middle of the week he called the boarding kennel to check up on Max. Max was OK.

30

It was Thursday. Peter was scheduled to fly back up north on Saturday. Linda had to work Friday and they planned to spend the evening at "home" quietly on Friday night so they chose to go out to dinner on Thursday evening. Linda made the reservations from her office. They left Linda's apartment in her little blue Toyota and arrived at the restaurant a few minutes early. They didn't notice the metallic gold Buick following them. Dinner was great and Cleague let himself indulge a little, he had a glass of wine with dinner. Linda smiled but said nothing when he ordered a split of Merlot. Desert—crème de menthe—and some coffee followed the meal. As they left the restaurant, an elderly couple was coming in and Cleague held the door open for them. Linda was a few steps in front of him as they made their way to her car. Just before she got to the parking lot, a shabbily dressed man stepped up to Linda and asked her for money. She politely declined and continued on undeterred. He stepped directly in front of her again, within arm's reach, and demanded money and that she come with him. Linda was long past being polite. Beyond the incipient drama Cleague now noticed a metallic gold colored Buick parked on the street and a dark colored van pull up behind it; he also sensed movement off to his right in peripheral vision (no such thing as coincidence). The pan-handler got quite insistent about Linda coming with him—he didn't see Cleague when he made his move on the girl, he was supposed to separate her from "the subject"—and produced a knife which he held at waist level casually describing a figure eight in the air with the blade. Peter immediately sidestepped in front of Linda, effectively pushing her out of the way.

"**Brother, Do You BELIEVE in The POWER of PRAYER?**" Cleague, stepping into character and becoming the very best Pentecostal Bible thumper he could possibly be, beseeched the panhandler, and with out-stretched arms, stepped directly in front of the blade. They told him this Cleague guy was a little "iffy" but they neglected to say how far. With his hands up-raised at shoulder level, Peter continued.

"**NOW IS THE TIME TO GIVE YOUR HEART TO JESUS-UH**..." Peter firmly clasped the man's knife hand in both of his, "...because your ass belongs to me." He turned the man's wrist in on itself while removing the knife with his left hand. He held the knife at the man's crotch, pushing up until he met a slight resistance, and told him to turn around. He grabbed hold of the man's long hair at the crown, yanked his head backward exposing his neck and held the blade adjacent to the man's carotid artery, and pinned the man's right arm behind his back.

"Linda?"

"YYYeahh?" She sounded a little nervous.

"You OK? Can you walk?"

"Yeah, yes. I'm OK. I can walk."

"OK Linda, I want you to stay directly behind me. Grab my belt. We're all going to turn around now and walk to our car. "You..." lifting slightly on the man's right arm, enough to get his attention, "Tell your team mates there I'll kill every one of you if she gets hurt; you'll be first. Cleague judged that the young man was probably a little distraught. The trio of Cleague, Linda and their new very close friend started to make their way further into the parking lot, backwards. Cleague constantly scanned from his left to his right and back again, keeping the panhandler directly between him and the rest of the task force hiding behind the silhouettes and shadows of parked cars. One of the task force shooters spoke into his throat mike.

"I've got a clear shot!" It came over clearly on the panhandler's portable, which he carried tucked into his waistband concealed with a loose flannel shirt.

Cleague told his impressed escort in a more or less conversational tone, "You know he's full of shit. The only way he can have a clear shot at me is through you." The panhandler immediately recognized the wisdom in Cleague's words and started screaming, nearly coherently, "NO, NO, NO, NO, DON'T SHOOT. DON'T SHOOT!!"

The three of them arrived at Linda's car. The command to hold fire had been given. "Linda, unlock your door and get in the car," Cleague said struggling to make his words as even and unforced as he possibly could. "Lock your door and start the engine." She complied.

"Come," Cleague indicated to the panhandler with the blade of the knife. They made their way around the back of the car, Cleague keeping the car constantly at his back—his legs in contact with the vehicle at all times. Cleague's head swiveled constantly from left to right and back again, his captive in tow. They could hear the increasing timbre of rapidly approaching sirens.

31

Police and Federal law enforcement agencies don't always coordinate their activity. They also don't coordinate communication and even if they were so inclined, there's only so much traffic a radio frequency can carry— hence they don't talk to each other very much. The metropolitan division of the San Francisco Police Department hadn't had a clue as to the impending Federal operation. As far as the BPS task force was concerned, it was only supposed to be a routine arrest of an alleged domestic scoff-law. It wasn't supposed to escalate into a firefight to be conducted in the parking lot of one of the city's most exclusive restaurants by the Federal Bureau of Public Safety. An older patron of the restaurant had called 911 to report extremely suspicious activity nearby with one man holding another at knifepoint and a bunch of other men with guns spread around the parking lot and laughing at the two men.

"Where do you suppose they got those guns?" he asked his wife when he hung up the phone. "I don't know, only police and criminals are allowed to have guns, so they've got to be one or the other," was her reply.

The agents were fanning out to 180 degrees around the car. Linda saw the move, reached over, unlocked the passenger door and pushed it open. Someone took a shot and Cleague shrunk down behind his temporary companion, increasing the pressure upward on the panhandler's carotid artery, which in turn caused him to stand more erect. As a fusillade of automatic fire came Cleague's way, he pushed the panhandler in front of him and hurled himself backwards into the passenger seat. The pan-handler was immediately struck by a hail of gunfire as, in the dimness of the parking lot, a number of undisciplined, non-discriminating shooters couldn't tell where Cleague had gone, but there was somebody moving' around on the ground so that must be him.

Linda was already out of the parking lot before the panhandler hit the ground. They could hear the waning pitch of police sirens and, in their rear view mirrors, saw the police arrive, draw down, and return fire on the cleverly black-clad malefactors who were now firing blindly out into the street— at the arriving police cars.

"What should we do now?" She wasn't all that familiar with an adrenalin rush; she often welcomed new experiences with typical grace and wit.

"Leave." Cleague choked as he caught his breath. "We should leave now." And he immediately regretted it as Linda immediately executed a heart stopping 90 degree turn at the next intersection deftly threading her way away from the restaurant, parking lot, police activity, and that part of the world in general. After Cleague was able to inhale again he took a few breaths and, in a carefully measured tone, said, "You take instruction well."

She simply smiled and nodded. "We need to get out of this car." He was thinking out loud. "OK," she said and abruptly made for the underground parking garage of the hotel to their immediate right. Navigating the compressed lanes of traffic in the sodium vapor lit parking garage with a high measure of alacrity she asked, "Now what?"

"We disappear. Find a place to park. We'll leave here on foot and take a bus back to your place. I'll come back tomorrow to get the car if I can." They took the parking garage elevator upstairs to the well-appointed lobby and left through a brass and glass revolving door, boarding the first available public transit vehicle.

32

They got back to the apartment without further distraction. But out of a need to demonstrate to himself that they were at last safe at home, Cleague cleared the apartment, room to room, before he would let Linda into her own place—which she thought was shutting the barn door after the horse had left but she kept her thoughts to herself.

"Linda, I'm sorry. I never thought they'd drag you into this but I was wrong. I always thought they'd come after me at the beach with no witnesses. It never occurred to me that they would be as conspicuous as they were tonight. I'm ashamed of myself for having put you in that situation."

"Well, I expect you are, Pete." She sat down next to him on the couch; she felt awfully tired all of a sudden. "But I never said you had to be clairvoyant to take me out to dinner. Anyway, you did, and here I am—safe in my own home." She leaned over and kissed him.

"You know what you're going to have to do next don't you?" he asked her.

"Yep, I'm going to have to go to bed. I'm really tired all of a sudden." And she yawned for emphasis.

"No," he said. "You're going to have to leave, at least for a while," he told her.

"No way. Wait a minute. I can't afford rent on this place and not live here. I do have a job you know, I just can't go off for God knows how long and expect it to be there when I get back," she said. Peter said nothing for a moment but looked at her without expression.

"Linda, how do you think they knew to find us at that particular restaurant tonight?" He asked her, quietly. He did not want an argument but he had to make his point to her now.

"Because they've been following us?" she guessed.

"Yes, and because they've got your phone tapped, and they've got your phone at work tapped, and they know where you are going and what you are doing as long as you stay here," he said. She recognized the logic of his conclusion before he even mouthed it.

"Shit. So you're telling me my life is over," she concluded resignedly.

"No. It's not over, it's just changing," he told her. He put her to bed. She crashed from the adrenalin rush.

Cleague made the call from a phone booth at a convenience store.

"Speak!" Smith barked into the phone at the third ring. He had been watching CNN in his restaurant office when the commotion in San Francisco was broadcast moments after the gunplay. "Do you remember the foreign national you were liaison with when you were DSO in Ireland a few years ago?" Cleague asked without greeting. Smith thought for a minute. *Roger Tibbett.* Eugene Smith had served a tour as Diplomatic Security Officer at the American Consular Mission in Belfast. *How in the hell did Cleague know that?*

"Yes," Smith said, curtly.

"I need you to contact him and arrange for transportation for a friend of mine. My friend needs a place to stay for a few days, and an escort to get there." The fact that Cleague wanted Smith to be the escort had been left un-said. Eugene Smith was more than a little familiar with Tibbett and Hereford Associates. Although he hadn't mentioned it to Cleague, it was how he had arranged the instructor and bodyguard gigs.

The abortion in San Francisco was an attack on Peter Cleague and that simple-minded dipshit had put Linda right in the middle of it. And now Cleague expected him to go to

San Francisco and take Linda to Roger's place in Palm Springs.

"Hey," Cleague continued without prompting, "the class went great, thanks for asking. Well, that's all for now, I'll talk to you soon." The line went dead. Smith did not like leaving his restaurant at the drop of a hat, but he had a good staff, his partners were competent managers and the restaurant would carry on. He would leave for San Francisco in the morning.

33

Peter Cleague's flight arrived at SeaTac International Airport. He took the Air Porter service van to Bellingham and made his way home by ferry. He made a cursory inspection of the exterior of the house looking for signs of entry at all doors and windows. Finding none, he let himself inside and conducted a brief check of the interior of his small house. He was very tired but decided Max should be furloughed out of the boarding kennel as soon as possible. He did all the routine checks on his truck before opening the door. He paid particular attention to the wiring around the starter, looking for signs of new wires or clean spots that did not match the level of grime consistent with the rest of the engine compartment. He looked around the brake drums and checked the brake fluid reservoir and brake cable. Satisfied, he said a Hail Mary as he turned the key in the ignition—a seldom-taught technique that always seemed to work.

Max greeted Cleague with his customary nonchalance at the boarding kennel and deigned to accompany his human back to the truck, where he refused to jump into the bed but waited to be lifted into it. Cleague recognized the signs and knew that Max was going to be difficult to live with for the next few days. Other than the sheer obstinacy that was a natural part of Max's character, the dog was nine years old and showing signs of dysplasia. Having spent two weeks on the concrete floor of a kennel hadn't done his hip joints any good. *Well, we all get old—some sooner than others.*

Peter Cleague was a reluctant convert to the cult of information worship. He was not digitally inclined and he distrusted computers. He regarded the personal computer as many had regarded television technology in the early fifties— a toaster with pictures. He only grudgingly condescended to using one of the damned things simply because that was how he learned of some of the job opportunities that he pursued in the line of executive protection. An agnostic in the church of Information Technology, he fired up his obsolete personal computer—it was already over two years old—logged onto his internet service provider and checked his E-mail. He sent his query and received his response. Linda was safe. Arrangements had been made for a moving company to clear out her apartment and relocate her property to a temporary storage facility. He owed a major debt to the Tibbetts, but he would resolve that later. That would be simple—he hadn't a clue as to how he would pay his debt to Linda. He logged off and went straight to bed.

In the dream there was this man, and there was this road and with the distant sound of rumbling thunder the dream changed. That guy was standing in the parking lot in San Francisco and then he walked behind a truck that was stuck in low gear. Cleague was immediately awake with the sound of Max growling. A creaking floorboard from his back porch— the bastards were trying to get in. Barking furiously Max launched himself from his spot on the throw rug and out of the bedroom—teeth first. Cleague grabbed the shotgun that leaned on the wall next to his bed and pied his way around the doorjamb—somewhat prudently—jacking a shot shell into the chamber of the Remington 870 and pushed the mechanical safety off from right to left with his index finger. Seeing nothing in the hallway he made his way into the kitchen in a low crouch staying below the bottom edge of the windows. He saw nothing between himself and the backdoor except Max standing on his hind legs and leaning on the back door, lips curled, paws scratching at the window molding, and barking continuously at whatever was or had been on the other side of the thin sheet of glass. "Max, Off!" He didn't want his dog to get shot.

Max stared at Cleague with utmost contempt for not letting him go out there. Peter could see no indication of a presence outside his windows. He retraced his steps down the hallway toward the bedroom, pausing to peek into the bathroom... nothing there, bedroom...nothing there. He moved into the living room from the hallway...nothing there. Cleague picked up a pair of binoculars from his desk in the living room and walked to the southwest corner of his house. He engaged the mechanical safety, from left to right, on the trigger guard of the 870 and set it against the wall on his way toward the window.

He glassed the road away from his house to the south toward the bridge. It was a little after sunrise. The road remained obscured in shadow. He hadn't heard the sound of a vehicle on his gravel driveway. It was unlikely that they'd come over the barrier dunes and climbed the fence that marked the boundary of his property. But he hadn't heard the sound of an engine either. A bicycle? Probably not, too much trouble. So they either walked up from the beach or walked in from the road. Max was barking again now, he needed to go out. Cleague glassed the road again as well as he could from north to south from the window of his bedroom and repeated the process from the west and north windows of his living room. The traffic was typical for six AM on a Sunday morning...nothing there.

What the hell were they doing at the door? Did they wire the door with a motion sensor? A microphone? A trip wire for a flash bang device? Cleague could not let his imagination run away with him; at the same time he had to be professionally paranoid regarding the incursion on his house. Or, maybe there hadn't been anybody on the porch at all.

Maybe. If they had been watching his house they would know that he almost always used the back door. So if they wanted to monitor his comings and goings that would be the logical place for a sensor, which would mean they weren't always watching the house. If they wanted to stun him they would have thrown a device through his bedroom window, followed up by an immediate raid on the house to take him into custody while he was disoriented from the concussion of the device. He saw absolutely no sign of a massed army lying in wait to take down his house. These guys weren't that stealthy. "Max, come here." Max was instantly at the front door waiting eagerly. Cleague looked at his dog and ran his hand down the length of the dog's back, patting him lightly on the right flank. He opened the door and Max was off the front porch and into the bushes and gone out of sight. The dog wasn't barking.

Cleague went to the bathroom and prepared for his run to the water. He had planned to do this at night but he had to do it now, in daylight possibly within sight of the BPS depending on their vigilance.

34

He put on the "Shorty" wet suit, and covered it with a floatation vest. Cleague chose to believe that running three quarters of a mile in this get-up would not lead to heat exhaustion before he could get in the water but it would be a bit cumbersome.

In the bag he tossed his water shoes, several spools of thin wire, diagonal side cutting pliers, a roll of reflective tape, three rolls of a vaguely beige polymer material which he had weighted at one end, three small plastic boxes, three radio receivers, three long aluminum cased cylinders about an inch and a half in diameter, and a few tent pegs. He placed his facemask on top before securing the bag. He wriggled into the pack eventually, after jumping up and down a few times to get the weight settled in the middle of his back, looped the heel straps of his fins around his left arm, and was out the front door and down the road headed north.

He ran half a mile then cut east over the dune. There were no cars on the road but he noted several boot prints in the foot path—a number of people had been coming and going in the dunes north of Cleague's house. Rehearsing?

He ran onto the beach down to the first jetty, changed his sneakers for water shoes, donned the facemask and fins and walked backwards into the water until he was hip deep. He swam out to the end of the jetty, and pulled out one of the small rolls of vaguely beige polymer weighted at one end and one of the plastic boxes that contained a CO_2 bottle attached to a trigger mechanism and made the connection. He was at the very end of the jetty; he could not be seen at this position by anybody standing on the beach, let alone from the dunes. He was able to jam one of the tent pegs into a crevice in the jetty and tied one end of a wire spool to it. He attached the other end of the wire to the appropriate flange in the plastic box containing the CO_2 bottle and marked the tent peg with reflective tape.

Cleague then set one of the aluminum tubes vertically in the rocks and ran wire from its base to the trigger mechanism connected to the CO_2 bottle. He rigged a wire from the plastic trigger box, which would activate the CO_2 bottle, to a receiver he planted in the rocks He made a surface dive about six feet, unrolled the life sized, anatomically correct, polymer inflatable doll with the weight attached to the feet, which he let drop. The depth of the water at the jetty's end was sixty-five feet. The length of the wire spools was forty-five feet. Cleague was counting on the buoyancy of the rubber doll, once inflated, to keep it at least shoulder height above the water. He ascended to the surface and swam south to the next two jetties, repeating the process. He then swam into the boat channel.

As the morning wore on he was wary of boat traffic. He stayed low in the water as much as possible as he hugged the rocks that lined the island side of the channel leading to the bridge. He simply did not want to be run over and drowned by some drunken Sunday sailor. He took his fins off, threw them up on the rocky abutment, and climbed up onto the rocks from the water to the abutment for the bridge. He extricated himself from the wet suit and changed shoes. He was now wearing the dedicated runner's uniform of shorts and sneakers; everything else that had not been planted, sunk, or run, was now in the bag. He scrambled out from underneath the one lane bridge onto the roadside, slung his pack onto his back and assumed a casual jog back to the house.

Max was waiting for him on the back porch. Peter examined the back door closely looking for wires, threads, anything that didn't belong there. He could find nothing. He then examined the kitchen and bathroom windows... nothing. He stepped off the porch and washed out all his gear with the garden hose and laid the stuff out to dry.

He sat down on the top step next to Max and absentmindedly ran his hand down the fur of the dog's back, massaging the back muscles as he went—gently rubbing the area around the dog's hips. He didn't know if it helped or hurt Max's dysplasia, but Max seemed to feel better afterwards. Peter looked at the area at the bottom of the porch around the base of the steps and at the floor of the porch about him. What were they doing on the porch? He could see nothing out of the ordinary.

In an effort to stretch the muscles at the back of his neck, which were contracted and giving him the beginnings of quite a headache, he looked straight up. He could not remember a wasp nest being there. It was located directly above the back door on the inside eave of the porch roof. He sat there a moment watching the wasp nest. No wasps. Broad daylight in the middle of the summer and no wasps in a nest that he would have sworn was not there last night. A transmitter? Transmitting what? He would probably find out soon enough.

He stood on the porch looking south toward the bridge and thought he caught a glimpse of light in the weeds between the dune and the road. It could have been the sun reflecting off the windshield of a passing car. He didn't believe the BPS were manning their posts today—too much overtime. But if they had put in a second observation point about a hundred yards south of his house and in line with where he knew the sniper hide to be, they would have one OP flanking the front end of the house and one flanking the back end of the house. The attack would probably come from the north, from town.

In a small island tourist town strangers did not attract attention as a rule. But these guys would definitely stand out in a crowd, there's just something about the bureaucratic persona. Cleague had a good friend in the County Sheriff's Office who worked at the sub-station in town; he'd have to stop by for a visit pretty soon. He stood up, stretched, picked up the satchel and went into the house and treated himself to a nap.

35

On towards sunset Cleague and Max took a casual walk south on the beach. Peter wore a shoulder pack that contained three more spools of wire, six tent pegs, and a pair of wire cutters. They walked out onto the first jetty all the way out to the end and Cleague sat down. He moved around a little bit but the "scout/snipers" in the Beach OP, if they were indeed there, wouldn't be able to make out what he was doing. After a while, he walked off the first jetty over to the second jetty and did the same thing. He repeated the process at the third jetty. After a couple of hours he and Max walked back to the house. The trip wires for the BPS sentries that would likely be stationed on the jetties were now in place, roughly boot top high.

On Sunday evening Peter sent some E-mails and made some enquiries. Linda was fine and the other responses indicated co-operation. After dark he crawled back into the "Shorty" wet suit, a shoulder holster containing a .45 caliber Glock, and the flotation vest. Dress rehearsal. He turned off the light in the living room and left the light on in the kitchen. Setting his stopwatch, Cleague crawled out the front door, down the porch steps, and along the snow fence to the road. He ran across the road to the shed. Once inside he made his way to the powder locker and set an object the size of a 16-ounce beer can on top of the ammo can on top of the locker. He would repeat this one movement again with a slightly higher sense of urgency. He slipped into the spray skirt and out the shed, dragging the kayak to the water line of the interior waterway. He was going to have to cut down on some of the stuff on his upper body or he wouldn't be able to move. With his facemask and fins bungeed to the kayak, he pushed away from the sand and paddled south through the canal to the boat channel and the peninsular bridge.

He concentrated on quietly dipping the paddles into the brackish water as he silently glided down the black canal. Coming to the boat channel he turned east and hugged the bridge abutment. He paddled on through the boat channel and broke east, assuming a strong continuous rhythm in a straight line directly to the channel marker, a navigational buoy demarcating the shipping lane through Puget Sound. He checked his watch. It took thirty minutes. It would take thirty minutes by kayak if he could catch the tide going out, as he had tonight. If he caught a slack tide it would take longer. If he had to swim it, who knew?

Cleague paddled southwest back to the boat channel and pulled the kayak up onto the rocks on the island side of the channel. He took off the spray skirt and pulled the satchel out of the cargo hatch he had packed earlier. He removed several slightly convex rectangles of a dense clay-like substance wrapped in a sealed rubberized packing paper and commenced to secure them to the main load-bearing pilings that supported the bridge. Cleague inserted the radio-activated detonators and strung the receivers sufficiently high enough above the shape charges to allow for high tide. The receivers were unobtrusive and no one would notice them above the surface of the water. He set the actual shaped charges at a level that would be below the water line at low tide.

Satisfied with the installation he dragged the kayak back into the channel and felt worn out. Cleague paddled west a short distance and then north back through the interior waterway just as quietly as he had on the way south. He softly floated past the spot where he believed the BPS observers might be but he couldn't see anything from his position in the water, just as well that they could not see him.

36

On the morning of Monday, 4 July, Peter Cleague abandoned his daily physical training routine. After showering and dressing for the weather, shorts and a sweatshirt with the arms cut off halfway to the elbow, he walked across the street to the Quonset hut and orchestrated one of his more creative efforts at defensive perimeter security. When he was satisfied, he locked up the hut and walked back across the street to the house and repeated much the same process. After he put the finishing touches on his security system in the house he took advantage of the weather for a bike ride into town. He checked his mailbox at the Port Cullis, Washington, post office, stopped at the little cafe for coffee and a bagel, and then went to visit his friend at the county sheriff's sub-station.

Andy DeKooning was roughly the same age as Peter, but Andy hadn't had the problems with Federal service as had Peter Cleague. DeKooning had been in the US Army Special Forces long enough to retire and collect a partial pension after twenty years of service.

DeKooning joined the Sheriff's Department in a county comprised of tiny islands more-or-less as something to do in his spare time. He liked the people and liked the community and the job fit in nicely with his notions of community service. He had told Cleague that during the interview process for the sheriff's deputy position, he told the interview board "I've served my country and now it's time to serve my community," it was almost a guarantee he'd get the job. They liked that line. But having done the kind of work he did for twenty years he knew how oppressive regimes worked and he knew what insurrection was. He had noticed the black sedans parked down the road from Cleague's house, as had all the other locals in town, and he monitored this situation between Cleague and The Government with interest but purely as a matter of professional curiosity. As much as he was prone to back the underdog he knew enough to bet with the house or not to play.

"Hey ya Pete, how's it going'?" Andy asked.

Cleague just shrugged, "Pretty fair. You?" he asked in turn.

"Good. Good. There are an awful lot of people around here for this early in the season." DeKooning replied.

The island community garnered the bulk of its economic base during the salmon run which didn't start until late summer or early autumn.

"Oh, is there a special charter in town or something?" Cleague asked. He thought he had been rather stoic and was getting better at controlling his responses to things.

"I suppose you could call it that. I've been seeing a lot of government cars around here. Something' going' on down at the old base?" DeKooning asked.

"Not that I know of. Just more of the same, y'know?" Cleague said as he took a seat in the chair indicated by the deputy. DeKooning handed him a cup of coffee. DeKooning was shift supervisor and was usually in the office to catch up on paperwork and play at public relations as required for a couple of hours after the shift started.

"So what's new in the field of law enforcement?" Cleague inquired.

"Funny you should ask, of all people. It seems that the Department of Justice, Treasury, and if you can believe it, the Department of the Interior, are going to conduct a nation-wide crack down on enforcement of the Arsenal Code provisions."

Andy DeKooning had never set foot inside Cleague's shed but he had long suspected what Cleague had been doing in it. Before Cleague had become otherwise engaged with travel and teaching, he and DeKooning used to shoot informal pistol matches together. But in the wake of a host of draconian gun laws most recreational shooters had given up the hobby.

"From what I can see they are really going to come down hard on ammunition manufacturers, commercial reloaders, and the now proscribed hobbyist reloaders. According to the blurb I saw, if you make ammunition and you do not have a current active contract with the Federal government, you are out of business and on your way to jail. Basically, they're looking for anybody with more than a box of .22 long rifle ammunition." DeKooning saw Cleague's knuckles turn white as his right hand involuntarily contracted around the coffee cup. DeKooning wanted to see if he could make Cleague break the cup.

"Yeah boy," Andy droned on, "Those guys in D.C. are having a hell of a time with the economy and all. It looks like the National Command Authority is looking for a new policy issue to hang its hat on. Try an' get the public scrutiny off his domestic failures you know; try to emphasize the positive." DeKooning peered at Cleague over the rim of his coffee cup. He took a perverse sense of pleasure in watching Cleague's face become noticeably darker. He idly wondered if Cleague was on high blood pressure medication yet...he just never could keep his temper.

"Yes Sir, a joint operation on a grand scale. They're calling it the 'Domestic Tranquility Initiative.'" DeKooning finished his discourse.

"Andy," Cleague began, (*He's going' for it, he took the bait* DeKooning thought to himself and smiled pleasantly.)

"Did you happen to see the thing in California on CNN the other day?" Cleague asked. "Was that part of this Domestic Tranquility thing?" Cleague asked.

"You mean in San Francisco?" DeKooning asked; it was his turn to have his blood pressure raised. Cleague nodded soberly.

"Them fucking idiots, do you know what that was all about?" DeKooning asked in righteous indignation. He had no idea Cleague had been at the heart of it nor would he have been surprised to learn so. Cleague just looked innocent and shrugged.

"That goddamned mob they call the Bureau of Public Safety went into a major fucking city without telling any of the local cops what the hell they were doing and just opened up on city traffic. Can you believe that shit?" Cleague noted with barely concealed amusement that DeKooning was starting to lose it and shook his head from side to side, commiserating with his friend's injured sense of professionalism.

"And them dumb sons o' bitches wonder why their public approval rating is so fucking low. Jesus Christ!" he exclaimed, "they are so fucking blind with their own anti-gun propaganda, not only do they believe it, they are out there trying to kill citizens over it." It was a sight to behold. DeKooning had a special place in his heart for people that reflected incompetence on the law enforcement profession. And now that the spark had been struck Cleague was present to bear witness.

"But Andy, how can you be so critical of your colleagues in Federal law enforcement, after all, they do set the standard for community policing don't they?" Cleague feigned sincerity somewhat well.

"Colleagues, my rosy red rectum!" DeKooning was in fine fettle. "They aren't law enforcement; they're just a bunch of goddamned thugs. All they got to do is take the AG's 'oath of loyalty'." Cleague was familiar with DeKooning's derogatory reference popular among cops regarding the current Attorney General who, as a Senator from the state of New York, had championed the original Brady Bill through to ratification in the Senate. Although rewarded by his constituents with a lost election, the current President of the United States appointed him as the Attorney General.

"They tattoo their armpit; hang a fucking badge on 'em, and call 'em Bureau of Public Safety. My ass! Why do you think they wear Brown shirts?" Again Cleague caught his friend's thinly veiled reference, this time to the German National Socialist Party in the thirties. It was an analogy Cleague had made a time or two. At this point in the conversation Cleague concluded that the man did seem a bit vexed.

"Well, was that thing in San Francisco part of this new initiative?" Peter was not being coy. It would lend some degree of logic, albeit distorted, to what had seemed to him to be a totally random act of stupidity.

"If it was, nobody's taking responsibility for it. They're saying it was a gang turf thing." DeKooning was starting to sound a bit depressed.

37

"Pete, do you know that they're talking about confiscating privately owned firearms in the US Congress right now?" DeKooning asked. All traces of his earlier goading now dissipated. Cleague hadn't known. He hadn't listened to the news since he got back from San Francisco. Andy went on, "There is a Federal agent down in Seattle as we speak, training cops from different agencies how to use metal detectors so they can go tear up people's yards looking for buried guns. We're scheduled to have two guys go down there in the next training quarter to get 'qualified'."

Peter's heart sunk to the pit of his gut; he could feel it hit bottom. It was one thing to believe the attack on he and Linda was a part of this Domestic Tranquility Initiative thing, but to think that he may have been the unwitting catalyst for what he was sure would be the end of the Republic made his soul ache.

"What are you guys going to do when the order comes down to go pick 'em up?" Peter asked in all seriousness.

"Pete. I'm not even sure it's going to happen. If it does I think it'll be a Federally funded mandate and then left to the states to carry it out. I think the state will use the National Guard. Depleted ranks or not, those guys will do what the governor orders them to do. Damn few governors in this country are going to reject Federal funds on principle. This one sure as hell won't." DeKooning inclined his head south toward Olympia. "You know, I don't believe it'll come down to us in the Sheriff's Office, but if it does the older guys will retire or will quit. The younger guys with new families are the ones who will do it. They're the youngest, the least experienced, the most dependent on a paycheck, and they are the ones who will get killed first." Andy finished and took a sip of coffee. Peter was disconcerted.

"Do you really believe it will come down to a shooting war?" Peter asked. The histrionics and raised octaves of a few moments ago had given way to a very quiet conversation about a deadly serious subject.

"Yeah, I do Pete." DeKooning answered and went on, "Hell, there are too many guys out there our age that have had military service and remember how to shoot and what to shoot at. Even if they haven't shot anything in a while it's a skill, like riding a bicycle. Hell, you should know that better than anybody." He was right. Cleague did know it.

"Don't you think it'll come to that?" Andy asked Cleague, somewhat dubiously.

"No I don't, Andy. The whole notion of self-preservation through the force of arms is archaic for too many people. They can't relate to it so they see no use for it. Everybody thinks the Second Amendment is about duck hunting. Sure, they'll give 'em up," Peter said. DeKooning was dumbstruck for a moment. He couldn't believe what he had just heard. He had to ask.

"What are you going to do Pete when they come to get your guns?" Andy thought he knew what the answer would be but now he wasn't at all sure.

"Well Andy," Peter paused to blow off the rising steam from his coffee. "When they come to get my guns they can have 'em. 'Cause I won't need 'em anymore." He took a sip of the hot liquid. DeKooning made a good cup of coffee.

Andy got it without any further prompting. It was Cleague's oblique reference to the "Cold, dead, fingers" cliché. DeKooning knew his friend well enough to accept that it wasn't heroic posturing. It was part of Peter's character. If Cleague said, "This far and no farther," that was exactly what he meant. After an awkward silence Andy tried to change the subject.

"Hey, I saw Hoyle the delivery guy, other day; he said you must be writing up a storm." DeKooning wasn't really fishing he just enjoyed agitating people. He considered it part of the tradecraft of the career he had left behind.

"Oh, did he?" Cleague responded mildly.

"Yeah, he said he was thinking about putting in a Labor and Industries claim for a back injury just for the amount of stuff he's been picking up at your place." DeKooning quipped.

"Well, you know, stuff piles up. He's just mad because I said I'd tell his wife about his girlfriend if he didn't stop being so damned nosey. I guess I'll have to go tell her now." Cleague said. They laughed. Each knew the other's joke before he told it.

"So when are they going to have this big crack-down, Andy?" Cleague asked. It was no longer a potential threat within the realm of possibility. It was definite and it required a plan and an execution of that plan just like any other "threat" when he was on a job.

DeKooning was no longer playing the role of the jovial devil's advocate. He pointedly looked at his watch and said, "Soon, Pete. Real soon." Cleague nodded and finished his coffee. They both stood and as they walked to the front door, Cleague said, "Oh, I almost forgot, the reason I came by, Andy, is that my dog has been getting loose."

"Again?" Andy inquired.

"Yeah. Do me a favor, will ya? Y'know, when he goes off on his little jaunts he always seems to head toward town. I think he's got a girlfriend up here. If you should happen to see him in the next few days, pick him up and take care of him for me will you?" Cleague asked. "I'll catch up to you before too long."

DeKooning nodded, understanding the unspoken plea.

"Don't worry Pete I'll take care of him till you get back."

Peter said, "That might be a while."

Andy nodded, "I know."

"Thanks." Cleague meant it. Standing at the door to the sub-station they both looked out at the intersection of the town, taking note of the number of vehicles with US government license tags on them.

"Andy," Cleague paused for a second. "Back when you took your oath to protect and defend the Constitution of the United States from all enemies foreign and domestic, did it ever occur to you that one day the enemy would be the Executive branch of the United States Government?" he asked.

"No, Pete. I can honestly say it never did. But what the fuck did I know? I spent most of my adult life fighting communists and teaching people around the world how to fight communists, and now the bastards are in the White House," he said. They shook hands. DeKooning knew full well that this would be the last time he would ever see Peter Cleague.

"Well, I got to run Andy. Keep in touch OK?" Cleague said and walked away.

DeKooning wondered just how he was supposed to do that if he didn't know where Cleague was going to be.

Before Peter went home he called Eugene Smith from a pay phone in town. It was not yet noon. The trip from the Des Moines Marina could be made in a few hours. Peter thought his tentative timeline should put him at the designated point within a reasonable margin of error. If not, he would just have to tread water.

38

When Peter got home he checked his e-mail. Linda was fine. It looked as though she was settling in nicely and although he missed her dearly, he would be with her soon. He did some last minute puttering and went over everything in his head, again. It had become a silent mantra: *clicker, gun, power, wire, shed, kayak, go.* These were the things he would take, and the things he would do before he left the house and crawled away: **clicker** (the remote radio transmitter), **gun** (he had kept the Glock 21; all his beloved antiques as Smith referred to them had been sent on by courtesy of Mr. Boyle in the big brown truck), **power** (he would shut off the circuit breaker in his house and shut off all the power coming into his house—he did not want anything interfering with the signal from the "clicker"), **wire** (he would take a small spool of heavy gauge wire—enough to span the width of the road in front of his house), **shed** (once out of the house he would crawl through the yard to the end of the snow fence ,crawl across the road , and make his way into the shed...hopefully without being seen), **kayak** (once he was finished in the shed he would slip out the back door, put the kayak into the boat channel and...), **go**.

And if he was very, very lucky he could leave without being seen. All the trip wires and decoys were what he considered to be party favors. The curved rectangular object in the sniper hide over-watching the east end of his house was a contingency; he didn't plan to use it unless things really turned to shit. His main objective was to leave the party before it started and if his guests behaved themselves and were careful, nobody would get hurt...*clicker, gun, power, wire, shed, kayak, go...* He hoped.

It remained light well past 10 PM in July if it wasn't cloudy; that was one of the things he really enjoyed about living in this part of the country because you could get a lot done on a summer day. That was a good thing. This day had been heavily overcast but, overcast or not, he still had a lot left to do. He took the screen door off the front of the house and placed it over the rail of the front porch. He oiled the hinges of the front door and worked it several times to insure it would open silently inward. He looked north and south and scanned the western horizon. No sign of them yet, but there wouldn't be if they did it right. He walked back into the house. The phone rang and Cleague answered, "Hello?" The other voice replied curtly, "It's tonight, there's a bunch of Military trucks driving off the ferry." The line went quiet. Peter hung up and thought, *Thanks, Andy.*

39

Peter casually walked across the street to the shed just as he did every day, imagining that he was probably centered in the reticle of one of the west flank OP observers/snipers. He took a scythe from the side of the shed and knocked down some of the weeds that had grown too high—he wanted a clear view of the shed from his front porch when it was time to go. He walked to a spot at which he was directly in line with the snow fence that marked the border of his front yard across the street. He bent down and planted a tent peg into the sandy loam deep enough that it held securely. Since he had noticed it the previous day, he had not been able to devise a more effective method of neutralization for that second sniper hide south of his house. This was simply going to have to work...*clicker, gun, power, wire, shed, kayak, go...clicker, gun, power, wire, shed, kayak, go*. He walked across the street to his front yard and repeated the process, knocking down some weeds with the scythe, then inserting the tent peg into the ground directly in front of and in line with the iron fence post that supported the snow fence. He straightened up and stretched, his lower back was starting to bother him. Please Lord, not now.

He walked back across the street to the shed. The way he worried and pecked around in his yard he looked like any average homeowner doing routine yard work. He walked into the shed to put the scythe and the rest of the yard tools away. Once inside he shut the door and kept his eyes closed. This would be the last time for drill. The idea was to use the decoys and flares as a distraction, and then the shed itself would be a second distraction. Although he knew what their playbook said about such operations (he had taught a portion of it at Glynco), he was hoping they would prove true to historical form and employ a very weak perimeter security. Their lives were depending on it. So was his.

He made his way to the powder locker, opened the door and withdrew the object from the top shelf, and placed it on the top of the ammo can full of mild steel plates which lay on its side on top of the locker. This was the "real thing," not the ersatz can of spray paint he had been using for practice for the past few weeks. Satisfied that it would not roll off onto the floor, creating a commotion in its wake, he opened his eyes and looked around, letting his eyes adjust to the dimness and visually ensured that everything was properly set. Once he set the item on the ammo can for real he was just going to have to be fast, that's all there was to it. If he could make it across the floor in the dark without tripping over all the det cord and comm wire, he'd be achieving something.

40

Cleague then turned to the kayak which he kept in the Quonset hut and secured his swim fins under the bungee straps of the kayak and looped the headband of his face mask around one of the cleats just ahead of the cockpit and let the glass portion hang down into the open hatch so as not to make any noise. He carried the kayak out through the back door and pre-positioned it in the water well into the invasive weeds, reeds, and bulrushes that were crowding out the raceway. Thus ensconced, the kayak wouldn't go anywhere and it wouldn't be seen by the casual observer walking around out behind his shed. The tide was on its way out, and there was little likelihood of anything moving the kayak before he got back to it.

The sun, visible as a big white circle through the thin cloud cover, was low on the horizon; it was probably 8:30, or a quarter to 9:00. It would start soon. His guts felt cold and heavy inside him; he dreaded this night. *No time for that, focus!* He admonished himself. He walked back inside the shed to the wall locker, oiled the hinges, and secured the door after replacing the item he'd left on the top of the ammo can. Cleague put the paddle for the kayak next to the back door and looked around one last time; he'd hate to be the one to diffuse all this shit if it didn't go off. He oiled the hinges of the shed door, secured it, and then walked back to the house.

Cleague had not eaten since breakfast but he still wasn't hungry. He put a potato in the microwave. He didn't feel like eating but he would need the carbohydrates for his long night ahead. His mind was preoccupied and his guts were tied up in a knot; he left half the potato. He went back to the bedroom and got the stuff together that he'd need: *clicker, gun, power, wire, shed, kayak, go...clicker, gun, power, wire, shed, kayak, go*.... He gathered together these things and laid them out on the bed: the radio transmitter was set to a specific frequency, Glock, magazines, nylon shoulder holster under the flotation vest, and the shotgun –he would do without the spray skirt. It was a lot of stuff to pack but better to have it and not need it than to need it and not have it.

He put on the shoulder holster. He picked up the Glock, removed the magazine and ensured that the magazine was fully loaded. He retracted the slide just far enough so the extractor only partially backed the cartridge out of the chamber. Visually and tactilely ensuring there was actually a round in the chamber he let the slide ride forward into battery, and seated the magazine into the magazine well. This ritual took less than three seconds and assured him that the gun was loaded, and this was the ritual he performed every time he picked up a semi-automatic handgun. He put the handgun in the shoulder holster then donned the flotation vest to ensure everything fit, and then removed them. He attached his diving tool, a fixed blade knife with a blunt screw driver like tip, serrated on one side and very, very sharp on the plain edge side, to the straps on the left breast portion of his flotation vest—in an inverted position.

He changed to a pair of swim shorts and put on his water shoes. He went back into the kitchen. He heat-sealed the radio transmitter inside a plastic bag. Max was waiting by the back door; he wanted to go out. Cleague was focused on procedure and mentally ticked off the checklist in his head: *clicker, gun, power, wire, shed, kayak, go.* Max barked once, a single syllable request, and Cleague absentmindedly opened the back door from conditioned response. He noticed the sky to the east was awful dark. Max unhurriedly wandered around the back yard making his way out onto the beach, while Cleague, preoccupied, turned back to the tasks at hand.

He walked back into the bedroom and started down the checklist again: **clicker** (he picked it up and threw it on the bed), **gun** (bed), and **power**.... He walked back into the living room and made sure that the receiver connected to the det cord had been set to the correct frequency and turned it on. He made sure all connections were properly set as well, especially the line of det cord that went out to the galvanized steel tank outside his bedroom window that contained the heating oil for his house. The oil was very similar in content and combustibility to diesel fuel; in fact, you could run your car on it if it had a diesel engine.

The interior floor of Cleague's house was very nearly a mirror image of the shop floor in the shed. C-4 lined the interior baseboards of the outside walls of both buildings. In the house, C-4 lined the baseboard from the living room into the kitchen, and started again in the bedroom, again in the bathroom, and completing the circuit in the living room. Blasting caps were set into the clay-like plastic explosive every few feet but were wired in series from the radio receiver. A pound of C-4 was adhered to the large oil tank outside. The structural support beams in the Quonset hut (the shed) had been given a few more wraps of det cord for good measure. He walked to the fuse box in the kitchen and turned all the circuit breakers off, and mentally clicked off "**Power**" in his head.

He went back into the bedroom again—it occurred to him he was literally walking in circles. He strapped the watch and compass onto his wrist, and put the spool of wire into the front pocket of the vest. He wriggled into his shorty wet suit in the dark. The dog was barking, as usual—he was an Elkhound after all—and Cleague paid it no mind. Invariably

Max would follow his nose north toward town and Andy would pick him up; it wouldn't be the first time. Cleague's plan was to use the kayak, but if he had to swim, this was the gear he would carry: water shoes, dive watch and compass, spool of wire, flashlight in the front pocket of his....

The crack of a bullet breaking the sound barrier split the night air just as the yelp of a fifty-five pound, nine-year old Norwegian Elkhound stopped Peter Cleague's heart. He felt incredibly cold and forgot to inhale for a moment. When the realization of what he had just heard seeped into his conscious brain, he resolved that tonight would be the end of this BPS problem for Peter Cleague, one way or another. All bets were off.

He honestly hadn't wanted to hurt anybody...he had resolved to just leave the BPS to their own devices at their own peril. Well, that trigger happy son-of-a-bitch in the sniper hide just changed the game plan. Moving silently in the dark, Cleague put on the shoulder holster, put on the flotation vest and shoved the remote...the clicker... into the front pocket of the vest.

He picked up the shotgun--his Remington 870, disengaged the manual safety, and released the latch forward of the trigger guard allowing him to pull the fore-end (or pump) halfway to the rear. This allowed him to stick the little finger of his right hand into the chamber, manually ensuring a cleared weapon. From the underside of the shotgun, he ran his thumb along the lifter—the metal flange that covered the loading port—until his thumb came in contact with the first shell in the magazine. He pushed on the shell with his thumb about a half an inch until it stopped. This meant the magazine tube under the barrel of the shotgun was fully loaded. After ensuring he had an empty chamber and a fully loaded magazine, he pushed the trigger blocking safety behind the trigger from the left to the right. He stood there for a moment in the dark, shotgun in his hands, and fought the urge to march out to the sniper hide and blow that son of a bitch in half.

"Focus," Smith's admonishment came back to him: *"Step one, kill the dog!"* Cleague nodded silently to himself and headed toward the front door of his little bungalow on the beach. He lay on the floor in the front room, and careful not to silhouette himself in the doorway, opened the front door— letting his eyes adjust to the darkness. As he lay there he thought: *clicker (done), gun (done), power (done), wire (done).* It was time to go.

41

It was dark to the west now. He could hear yelling, noise, high-revved trucks in low gear. Military two-and-a-half-ton trucks—Deuce-and-a-half's—were being driven into position on the beach. They came out from behind the dunes just to the north of his house. The military trucks would have had to come from the National Guard Company from the mainland. He hadn't anticipated military involvement, but no matter, it had been done before despite the Posse Comitatus Act. They always got away with it and at this point in his life he really didn't care.

Goodbye Max. He pulled out the transmitter and hit the switch for the first detonation: the claymore mine he had planted at the sniper hide 100 yards south of his house. He heard a high-pitched scream cut short, other voices farther away—yelling, and indiscriminate small arms fire toward the sound of the blast. Some of those boys were a little jumpy. Before changing his position he switched the transmitter to the next freq, stuck the transmitter into his vest pocket and slowly crawled out the front door, across the porch and down the short steps into the grass, and along the junipers that lined the snow fence to the road. His recitation of the mantra was automatic now: *clicker, gun, power, wire, shed, kayak, go...clicker, gun, power, wire, shed, kayak, go.*

He could see the intense shadows cast from the Xenon searchlights mounted on the two-and-a-half-ton trucks, their combined beams focused on the back of his house but he dared not look or he would be made blind. *Clicker-done, gun-done, power-done, wire...*

"Peter Cleague!" The amplified voice was tinny and hollow. The task force commander for Operation Clean Sweep, **BPS Special Agent Walter Speeks**, was center stage in the highest profile moment of his life. His twenty-year career had prepared him for this instant: on camera, live, and in command of "Operation Clean Sweep." He continued, "You are surrounded by Federal Agents of the Bureau of Public Safety. Come out of the house unarmed and with your hands raised above your head and you will not be harmed." The sound of the loudspeaker bounced off Cleague's house and the Quonset hut across the street, which was now only twenty yards away. Peter was at the end of the fence in his front yard.

TFC Speeks elicited Cleague's sins for the benefit of the viewing audience. "You are wanted on charges of conspiracy to kill a federal agent," the task force commander asserted. The Task Force Commander went on, "violations of the Gun Violence Prevention Act Part II."

Speeks concluded the recitation, "and intent to maim and/or kill Federal Agents in the lawful commission of their duties." Speeks wrapped it up, "You are hereby under arrest by order of the…" Cleague tuned him out and carried on with his mental "to do" list.

Peter Cleague was now at the edge of the road and could see a BPS man, apparently one of the observation posts, standing by the door of the shed. Cleague took out the spool of wire, formed a double half hitch, and looped it around the tent peg he had planted earlier in the day. He looked along the road south of his position...no-one. He did not look directly north. If he did, he'd be blinded by the glare from the lights. He shielded his eyes with his hand and looked into the periphery of the road north of the Quonset hut and visually searched the shadows for movement. He saw nothing but he did offer a Hail Mary for good measure. Gathering his legs underneath him, he leaned forward into a sprinter's crouch, grasped his shotgun, and burst across the street, keeping as low a profile as possible, letting the wire play out of his hand in loops, and landed in the ditch on the other side of the road. The lone sentry in front of Peter Cleague's shed craned his neck to watch the drama playing out in the subject's back yard.

Cleague crawled back to the tent peg directly across the street from the fence, pulled the wire taut around it, and terminated the wire here; it now spanned the surface of the road at boot top height. Cleague stayed in the shadow of the trench and crawled toward the shed. The BPS man was straining to see what was going on across the street. He was too junior to be in the assault element but had been assured that he would have the best seat in the house by the team leader; it was sure to be a doozy, that's what he said—doozy. The BPS man's sound suppressed CAR-15 was held at a half-assed port arms. Clad in black BDU's (Battle Dress Utilities), the chin strap of his helmet was unsnapped, goggles slung down around his neck, war belt festooned with first aid kit, holstered side-arm, portable radio turned to maximum volume on the tactical net (*Hey, thanks!* Cleague thought), and four pouches of spare magazines he would never need.

The man was lit up by the off-cast glow from the intense lights mounted on the trucks parked across the street. Cleague crawled on his belly toward the shed, his shotgun cradled on his forearms, and stopped at the edge of the weeds along the path from the road to the back of the shed. The weeds he had trimmed that very afternoon. As the BPS man stepped closer to the edge of the road to get a better angle on the house his radio crackled: "All stations this net, radio check, over."

The responses from the various Observation Posts, remaining sniper hides, and security check points came back in sequence, more-or-less... "Unit One, all clear"... "Unit Two, all clear"... And so on. The purpose of unit designations negated the need to broadcast their positions just in case some unauthorized personnel might be listening in. Cleague understood that but he sure would have liked to have known where all the sentries were. As most of the individual units reported all clear Cleague thought, *Good, everybody's watching the house.*

"Unit Six"... the man in front of Peter Cleague responded... "all clear, over."

The order came over the TAC net... "Forward element, standby"...(*So much for 'Step Two--starve 'em out'* Cleague thought). Cleague pulled himself up into a crouch; he was now behind and slightly to the right of the BPS man. The radio commanded: "First Squad...Go!"

Cleague firmly grasped the shotgun at the fore-end, making sure that it was locked forward, and at the small of the stock, and swiftly stepped directly behind the BPS man who was now craning his neck to see the drama unfold across the street.

"Second squad, Go!" blared from the radio at the man's hip. Cleague drove the edge of his right foot into the back side of the BPS man's right knee, bringing him down hard on his knee and knocking him forward, off balance. Cleague sharply drove the butt of the shotgun into the man's first cervical vertebra, knocking off his unfastened helmet. The man's carbine clattered to the ground.

"Third squad, stand by...Go!"

Cleague immediately executed a horizontal butt stroke with the toe of the stock into the BPS man's face. The man now lay on his back from the force of the impact.

"Forward element, standby..."

Cleague came down with the butt stock as hard as he could onto the man's trachea.

"In five...four..."

And drove it downward again onto the bridge of the man's nose—breaking it; raised the shotgun again, and again brought it down sharply onto the man's nose, driving the separated portion of the bridge of the nose into the man's brain: killing him. Cleague slung his shotgun over his shoulder, picked up the dead man's carbine, laid it across his chest, and drug him by the shoulders into the shed. He monitored the dead man's radio as he withdrew the transmitter from his vest.

"...Three...two...one...deploy CS gas!"

With the next freq pre-set he held the transmitter, with his thumb poised over the switch, as he heard the sound of glass breaking. Half the forward element had fired CS projectiles into his house through his living room and kitchen windows from single shot, 40-millimeter grenade launchers; the other half followed up quickly with smoke canisters poised. He watched as the smoke grenades were lobbed through the now broken windows by the undaunted, intrepid, warriors of the BPS. He noticed a van, with the logo of a Seattle TV station emblazoned on its side, parked on the beach side of his backyard, safely nestled behind the mighty stalwart battalions of the Common Good.

He couldn't help but wonder if the Public Safety Warriors would be exhibiting the same degree of selfless heroism if the media hadn't been there. He could imagine the highlight reels of the headline news channels for the next week. From inside the Quonset hut Cleague peered around the edge of the door frame just far enough to be able to see south on the road. As he suspected, one of the observers from the West flank OP was coming up the road at a brisk pace. Cleague set the transmitter down by his left foot and picked up the 5.56 caliber carbine from its former custodian. Cleague pressed the magazine release with his right index finger, withdrew the magazine and checked with his left index finger for the tip of the bullet in the magazine to ensure that it contained ammunition. It did. Now, was the gun loaded? He re-seated the magazine and simply racked the charging handle to the rear and let it fly forward under its own inertia stripping the top round off the top of the magazine and into the chamber. Finding his spot-weld on the stock and getting his sight picture, he tracked the black clad BPS man *(What is it with these guys and black clothing?)*, up the road. The BPS man appeared to have his radio out and talking into it but wasn't getting through...

The BPS man heard a raspy clacking sound, like the charging handle of an AR-15 over there by that storage shed and sharply turned his head to the left and hit the trip wire strung at boot top height across the span of the road and sprawled out, gun in one hand, and radio in the other, and hit the pavement chin first. His helmet rolled off and skittered to a stop a few feet away.

From inside the doorway of the Quonset hut Cleague quickly aimed and took his shot. He saw the man's head move and fall back into place on the road with the impact of the 55-grain bullet. It was a catastrophic brain shot: the placement of the bullet resulted in a one-shot kill that instantly incapacitated the target and normal body reflexes could not react.

42

The radio crackled with the Task Force Commander's voice of command: "First Squad...Go!" Cleague observed intently, setting down the carbine and picking up the transmitter again. The First Squad maneuver element charged to the windows on the north side of the house and tossed in flash bang grenades. The M84 Flash Bang Grenades produced a blinding 6 million candlepower flash and a deafening 180 decibel blast. "Second Squad, Third Squad, Up!" Cleague watched the second and third squads take positions of covering fire on the front and back doors. From across the street Cleague heard someone yell, "Hey the front door's op..."

Cleague pulled himself inside the shed, flattened his back against the corrugated metal wall and hit the switch on the transmitter. The force of the explosion blew the window casements of the house out past the porch railing. The C-4 blew outward, crumpling the vertical structure of the walls it was adhered to, buckled the roof inward from the center and hurled the front door and bits of furniture and body parts out in three hundred and sixty degrees. The BPS men standing outside the house caught it in the chest and they were separated at the torso. The charge attached to the fuel oil tank simultaneously ruptured the tank, ignited the oil, and projected the galvanized steel vessel in a parabolic arc southward, snaking a flaming stream of fuel oil behind it. What was left of the cottage was now ablaze with heating oil priming the seventy-year-old dried out wooden structure. The ensuing fire engulfed what was left of the little house, as a well-disciplined and highly trained paramilitary machine fell to chaos and confusion. Smith's words came back to Cleague once again: *"Step three: set fire to the house."*

Peter withdrew further into the darkened Quonset hut and set the transmitter to the third frequency. Having the rote motion of blindfolded repetition built into his muscle memory he found the powder locker with the ammo can of metal plates and placed himself directly in front of it. He opened the locker door, felt for the top shelf, and retrieved the metal cylinder. It was about as tall as a 16-ounce beer can but slightly smaller in diameter. It was a thermite grenade. It would take less than ten seconds for the heat of the thermite grenade to cut through the steel walls of the ammo can. The ammo can had been filled with a number of rectangular eighth inch plates of mild steel. Cleague had calculated that it would take about one minute for the thermite grenade to burn through the ammo can, metal plates, and sheet metal top of the wall locker. The thermite grenade was an incendiary device that emitted intense heat and flame that would ignite, fuse or burn through whatever it came in contact with. In this case, it would come in contact with the thin sheet metal of a surplus high school wall locker that contained about seventy five pounds of black powder of various burning rates.

Each of the three walls and the door of the wall locker had a small bit of plastic explosive stuck to it. The plastic explosive was a malleable material similar to clay connected by a length of detonating cord to each of the other three wads of plastic explosive in series. The detonating cord was a plastic sheath filled with a powdered explosive compound called PETN. It is very similar in appearance to electrical cable. Det cord does not burn—it explodes. A single length of det cord had been run out the wall locker along the nearest wall, the west side—the side furthest from the house and closest to the raceway. In turn, that length of det cord was inserted into another piece of plastic explosive which ran, in continuous sections, laterally along the base of each exterior wall. At each junction with a vertical support beam det cord had been looped round each beam several times. This would cut the supporting structure of the building and cause it to collapse in on itself.

The walls were lined with wall lockers containing thousands of rounds of re-loaded ammunition, primers, component bullets of various diameter and weight, and more powder. As a backup he had rigged another receiver and had comm wire run to every other section of C-4 inserted with an electronically detonated blasting cap. He was primarily relying on the explosive energy of the black powder to sympathetically detonate the bits of C-4 stuck to the sides and door of the one powder locker, which would blow the det cord, which would in turn detonate the C-4 lining the base of the exterior walls. The wall lockers containing the re-loading components would burst, some of the loaded ammunition would cook off from the heat, but not all of the ammunition would be exposed to heat intense enough to detonate the primers. It did not matter; the entire Quonset hut would become a fragmentation grenade. There would be nothing left but rubble and a crater.

If he had been confident of having the time to radio detonate the multiple devices in the Quonset hut, that would have been his primary plan but he had learned long ago—always have a back up, always leave yourself a way out. Manually igniting the thermite grenade was a definite and positive ignition to a sequence of events that hadn't yet started. It also gave him about a minute…more or less to get out of the building. If for some reason that failed he could still set it off via radio transmitter, barring the unforeseen. The words of the Gunny came back to him now, after many, many hours of detonating charges on various obstacles the Gunny had impressed on him one thing if nothing else,

"Always remember Lieutenant, timing is everything." *Amen to that, Gunny.*

His presses, dies, scales, and the rest of his reloading gear had been sent to the Alders Restaurant in Seattle and from there, shipped to Palm Springs as tool parts, as had most of his privately owned firearms, save the Glock and the shotgun. In Palm Springs, Mr. Tibbett agreed to take delivery of some miscellaneous boxes marked "tool parts" and put them in a storage facility.

Cleague hit the transmitter switch and stuffed it into the pocket of his vest. From the three jetties the aerial flares went up in unison to their peak of two hundred feet before they started their illuminated descent, suspended from tiny but perfectly functional parachutes. The transmitter's signal which caused the flares to launch also caused the carbon dioxide triggers to trip and inflate the anatomically correct rubber dolls in the cold semi-darkness of the water. Cleague could hear over the tactical net proclamations of: "There he is!" He could hear automatic small arms fire in the distance; the OP's on the jetties were taking the bait. He pulled the cotter pin on the thermite grenade and carefully set the thermite grenade on top of the ammo can, located on top of the powder locker. With some haste, he made for the back door of the shed. The concussion alone from the exploding powder locker would be enough to kill a man.

He decided to keep the sentry's radio and ditch the shotgun; he threw the latter back into the Quonset hut and grabbed the kayak paddle on his way out the door. He plunged knee deep into the brackish water and grabbed the kayak. He pushed the kayak out of the weeds into the raceway and climbed aboard. Gliding into the canal with a measured stroke that would place him at the channel marker in good time, he directed the kayak south toward the one-lane bridge and the boat channel as the task force Commander repeatedly called for Unit Five and Unit Six to answer up. Unit five came up on the net and reported that his partner had gone north on the road to check out something.

Unit Six would not answer. Peter monitored the TAC net as the strike force commander ordered agents from what was left of the assault element to see what the problem was with Number Six. Four men cautiously approached the Quonset hut after having reported Number Five's body in the middle of the road. They stood at the doorway of the building with the beams from their weapon-mounted flashlights trailing the coiled wires across the span of the Quonset hut floor and from one wall locker to the next. They also discovered OP#6's pallid corpse with dark blood seeping from its nostrils and ears.

From his position in the canal Cleague checked his watch and noted that just about one minute had passed since he set the thermite grenade on the...

He could feel/hear the sound of distant thunder as he instinctively ducked his head and covered his ears, and opened his mouth, as pieces of tin, wood, misshapen shrapnel, and unexpended cartridges rained down about him in the water. Smith's words again: *"Step four, kill the survivors."* Cleague maneuvered the kayak ahead for the boat channel, as all hell broke loose on the radio. The TAC net was frenetic with broken transmissions, people cutting each other out, trying to issue orders and report observations. Peter Cleague was reported in a dozen different places at the same time.

43

The west flank sniper was getting lonesome. It had been a long time since his observer/partner had gone to check out something he thought he heard or saw, and now apparently he lay dead in the middle of the goddamned road. Then the sky blew up. He was monitoring the TAC net through his earpiece but he thought he heard an echo from over to the west by the sewer ditch or canal thing or whatever it was. He was starting to get spooky. First his partner was hearing stuff, now he was hearing echoes. He was pretty sure that earpieces should not echo but who could say for sure. His agency always went with the lowest bidder on stuff.

In the interest of preserving their vision the sniper teams elected not to use any sort of enhanced night vision devices on this particular op because of the Xenon lights mounted on the Deuce-and-a-halves. Rumor had it the only reason the strike force commander wanted to use those lights was so the TV crew could get good footage. Well they sure as hell ought to get something. From his position he could see the house fairly well when it went up in flames, and shot the oil tank up in the air and landing not far away enough and setting the whole goddamned area on fire; that should look pretty spectacular on the 11:00 o'clock news. But when the second explosion went up he could only see the flames but guessed that it was probably the shed across the street. Christ, he could feel the ground shake. They said this would be a doozy; they were right but he suspected that this was probably not what they had in mind.

There it was again—the sound of the radio TAC net was coming from the water to his left. The sniper in the west OP shifted his position slightly from the prone and shone the beam of his flashlight due west. He could barely make out the far bank of the waterway and a little bit of the water. Then he thought he caught something. Indistinct, he couldn't describe it, but he thought he saw something move. He tried to inform the team commander but could not get a word in edgewise; every-body was on the radio. Piss poor radio discipline, that's what it was. He swept the area again with his hand held flashlight and this time he thought he heard a splash as well as seeing an imprecise image of something moving. He couldn't stand it; he decided to go check it out for himself.

Cleague was just shy of the first OP before he would hit the boat channel and the sentries that had to be posted on the bridge. Cleague had not paddled very far when a beam of light swept the water just in front of the kayak. *Aw, Shit!* he thought. He continued to glide forward; it wasn't as if he could put on the brakes. He put the paddle deep into the water on either side, alternating from one side to the other with the flat portion of the paddle perpendicular to the motion of the kayak to slow his forward movement. In the motion of twisting his torso he dropped the radio and it slid off the fiberglass hull with a resounding splash.

"Goddammit!" *Oops.*

Now the sniper thought he heard something distinct, a voice from right over there. He left his scoped rifle in the hide and took the MP5. He paused only slightly as he came to the edge of the weeds that shielded his hide and swept left to right, illuminating the search area with a 500 lumen weapon mounted white light, scanning the area in a good hundred-degree arc. As he scanned, he used the front sight as a pointer, an indicator of the focus of his gaze. He was in search mode: he was hunting. The BPS man silently made his way across the road toward where he heard the voice. It couldn't have been anybody from the strike force 'cause they were either dead or talking on the radio. At the ready, stock at the shoulder, he moved toward the sound in a quickstep crouch reminiscent of Groucho Marx. It was a maneuver he had practiced many times and executed it with swift and sure precision. He came to the edge of the road and scanned the area again: horizontally, vertically, and in depth. He stepped into the weeds on the far side of the road making his way toward the interior waterway.

The ground was relatively level for a few yards before it dipped down to meet the water of the canal. Visibility was terrible due to the high level of the weeds, reeds, bulrushes, and cattails. He used his weapon mounted light: on two seconds, off, move. On two seconds, off, move. The sniper, now scout, was still. He concentrated on everything he was hearing trying to pick out the one thing that didn't fit. The frogs, the crickets, the water lapping at the driftwood jammed up against the bank at different spots, the scraping sound of plastic.... He suddenly pivoted his upper torso to the left, the source of the sound, and actuated the weapon-mounted light to catch the kayak scraping up against a rock as he simultaneously pressed the trigger in sympathetic response, and stitched the length of the kayak with 9mm holes. He committed the same disciplinary malfeasance that ninety-nine people out of a hundred will make when they pick up a gun. Unless one trains oneself not to, one will invariably put one's finger on one's trigger. Given the structural mass of the fiberglass hull, the 147-grain subsonic Silvertip Hollow points went right through both gunwales. It was only then that the sniper/scout realized that the kayak was abandoned. He brought the weapon down to a low ready position and scanned to his right. He heard more than saw the movement below and to the right of him.

Cleague hated to squat. He detested that position. It made his thighs burn, his calves ached, his knees suffered a torment no mortal man had been designed to endure and the persistent pain in his lower back drove him to distraction. He squatted in the fetid, dank, muddy water waist high in the raceway with the true and specific certainty that he could only emerge smelling like crab shit. He had peeled out of the kayak and righted it just after being hit with the light a few moments before. He marked the approach of the sentry by the scout/sniper's light signature: On two seconds, off, move. On two seconds, off, move. Just like Cleague had taught at FLETC so many years before. Cleague thought the man was going to trample right over him when the sentry abruptly shifted to his left and illuminated the kayak that had been let drift in to the bank a few yards ahead and ultimately rendered utterly useless. This unexpected turn of events put Cleague beside himself with fury. How many times had he admonished his own students: **KEEP YOUR FINGER OFF THE TRIGGER, UNTIL YOUR SIGHTS ARE ON THE TARGET**. He rose and swung the paddle with all of the upper body strength he could muster into the man's knees. They both toppled into the water.

The momentum of the man's forward motion caught Cleague slightly off balance so that by the time Cleague gathered his wits he realized he was in the water, supine, and pinned. The scout/sniper was face down, in agony, and temporarily crippled. He was dead weight and Cleague was running out of breath. The man's sternum was roughly even with Cleague's chin. Virtually blind, upside down, and growing desperate he could only think of one thing to make the man move. He doubled his fists and rammed them upward into the man's crotch with as much explosive energy as he could muster.

The scout/sniper moved with expedition. Cleague erupted from the water with the velocity of a Peacekeeper Missile launched from a submarine. He sucked in air and water involuntarily as he broke the water's surface. He choked, gagged and spit up water. His adversary found his center of gravity and rose out of the water turning toward Cleague. He had dropped the MP5 in the dark and the mud the instant he had been hit in the knees. He automatically transitioned to his sidearm, a tethered Sig Sauer P226, and placed the three tritium dots of the sights in the center of the hulking black shape in front of him actuating the laser grips with his firing hand. Cleague saw the source of the laser. He grabbed the diving tool from his flotation vest and lunged forward, just barely to the man's right. Cleague swung the blade down in an arc in a backhanded slash as he swept past the man catching the tendons in the back of the man's right knee. The opponent immediately went down on his right knee losing his balance as he fell. Cleague recovered, spun and stepped up behind the man who was now on his knees in the shallow part of the water close to the bank.

Without hesitation Cleague grabbed the mane of hair with his left hand, yanking back on the head and cut deeply from just below the left jaw, across the trachea, and let the blade trail across the throat to the right severing the carotid artery on the right side of the neck. The air gurgled from the slit and the corpse emptied its bowels. Peter Cleague let the body fall into the black water of the raceway. So much for *"Clicker, gun, power, wire, shed, kayak, Go!"* He secured the diving tool in its sheath strapped to the left breast panel of his flotation vest.

44

Peter Cleague stood knee high in the water of the raceway. His kayak was shot to hell. Every Federal Agent on Peninsular Island, at this moment, was looking to kill him, and he had not a clue as to how to get out to the channel marker on time. And his eye hurt. The BPS man had landed a couple of good hits on him. *Now what?*

He had to get to the water. He had to get to the east side of the island and into Puget Sound. And now he had to swim a mile in the bargain just to get to the buoy that marked the deepest part of the channel for ship traffic in Puget Sound. All his time tests and training had been from the bridge in a kayak. Not from the middle of the raceway, swimming, in the dark. If he attempted to navigate across the road, and the weeds, and the beach strand—due east of where he was now, he would have no previous reference point for the location of the channel marker. The man that lay dead at his feet had to be one of the snipers from one of the observation posts south of his house.

OK, so he was about 100 yards south of the house and roughly in line with the middle of the three jetties on the east side of the island. If he walked east across the strand he would have to negotiate both observation posts, and even though he thought the occupants would now be dead, he couldn't be sure. He would also have to negotiate the weeds, and the scrub pine, and the area would probably be on fire by now from the fuel oil tank that had been on the south wall of his house. Besides, the BPS guys on the jetties would probably still be out there. If he did make it out to the end of the middle jetty, the mile marker in the Sound would be somewhat southeast but how far south and how far east? Perfect. Or, he could walk to the bridge, kill the sentry or sentries and then swim. Sure, just like that. They would have carbines and he wouldn't. Or he could swim from here.

He slogged through the brackish water to the ventilated shell of his kayak and pulled the swim fins from underneath the bungee cord stretched behind the cockpit, and lifted the facemask from off the cleat.

He stared at what he held in his hands for a moment before it registered. His facemask was now an empty metal rim with jagged shards of glass. Absolutely perfect, in less than two seconds his very expensive ocean going kayak and very expensive diver's facemask had been shot to hell. The shotgun was gone, the BPS radio set to the tactical net was gone, and the kayak was gone. *What was it, a mile from here to the bridge? No, no it wasn't that far. Was it?* He had also lost all sense of the amount of time that had elapsed since he had left the shed. He looked at his wrist to check his watch— no watch. He must have broken the strap in the fight. Perfect. He was on a kind of a timetable, not that it mattered now. All he could do was move on, and carry on with his life, and don't look back, and so forth, and so on. Right.

Before he took off he did think about taking the MP5 but realized that the BPS guy must have emptied the entire magazine in less than three seconds. It was empty; having it would not do him a bit of good. It was also somewhere in the brackish mud and he did not have time to look for it. He sat in the water and put on the swim fins, and then, began swimming using a sidestroke. He would alternate sides until he got to the boat channel. He would not anticipate contact with an adversary until he got to the bridge. Although telephone poles lined the highway, there were no streetlights this far south out of town along the road so there was no source of illumination until he got to the bridge. As he recalled there was a streetlight on either side of the bridge, north and south. There would be plenty of light on the boat channel on the east and west sides of the bridge.

He glided through the raceway trying to keep his fins below the surface of the water. When he got to the bridge he would have to swim under water some distance to clear the lights. The purpose of wearing a flotation vest is to keep oneself afloat. He would have to get rid of it before he got into the boat channel. Great. What about the transmitter?

The current ran north and south through the raceway, though it was negligible. The center of the raceway was the deepest part, either side tended to be shallow and stagnant. At the south end of the island, the raceway tended toward marsh. It was common for logs, lumber, and other flotsam lost from tugs going through the dredged-out boat channel to accumulate at the south end of the raceway. The Corps of Engineers still had the responsibility to clear out the accumulated debris once a year. Cleague, staying in the center of the waterway, stopped his forward motion and began to quietly tread water. He took the transmitter out of the vest pocket, and stuck it in the upper portion of the wetsuit. He shrugged out of the flotation vest and made his way over to the side of the raceway. The fact that the vest was safety equipment for kayak paddlers and was International Yellow didn't help; he smeared it with mud as well as he was able and stuffed the vest under a rotted out waterlogged timber. He left the knife mounted to the vest. It was either take the knife or the transmitter and he absolutely needed the transmitter. If somebody found the vest, they found it. He couldn't help that now. He set to into the raceway again.

After another two hundred yards he came to the junction of the raceway and the boat channel and treaded water silently. Staying in the weeds out of view from the bridge he surveyed the bridge and both sides, north and south, as far as he could see. There were two men visible walking independently across the bridge span. Occasionally they would stop in the center and make a comment. Cleague couldn't hear what they were saying. He could see a sedan parked on the near side of the bridge blocking the roadway and assumed there was another car on the south side of the bridge blocking the roadway as well. Well, that made sense. They probably had the road blocked at some point between his house and town too.

He guessed he was a hundred and fifty, maybe two hundred yards from the bridge. He wouldn't be in the illuminated area of water from the streetlights on either side of the bridge until he was about twenty or thirty yards from the bridge, maybe farther. From his position in the water it was hard to tell what the distance was. He would have to swim under water for twenty or thirty yards, surface under the bridge for air, and swim another twenty or thirty yards under water to get out from under the illuminated area of water on the far side of the bridge and into the open water of Puget Sound and then out to the mile-marker. Why hadn't he thought of this, why hadn't he measured it when he had time? Why didn't he swim this at night so he knew how to prepare for it?

The answer came back to him as quickly as it was posed in his mind, *Because you didn't want to get out this way, you dip shit.* He wanted to take the kayak because that was the fastest and the easiest way and that was what he prepared for. He failed to plan for the biggest contingency that would affect his getting away. *Well, sometimes you don't get what you want*, he thought.

For his approach to the bridge he had to be absolutely quiet. He would use a breast-stroke and keep his arms and legs below the surface of the water. He would have to keep his head above the water, but as low as possible with the water line just below his nostrils, so he could watch the sentries on the bridge.

He stuck his hands into the mud once again. He rubbed the briny muck over his face and the top of his head, up and down his arms and across the backs of his hands. It felt like he was smearing shit on himself and smelled worse but he didn't want his skin reflecting the light from the street lamps. He moved out from behind the weeds and silently swam forward toward the bridge and, hopefully, the mile marker in Puget Sound.

45

The guys on the bridge were beside themselves with a confused agitation that neither had experienced before in any kind of operation they had ever been involved in. The radio was a mess, everybody was trying to talk at the same time and cutting each other off, consequently nothing intelligible was coming over the radio net. Eventually the commander had told everybody to shut up and ordered a situation report position by position. The call signs had been assigned as follows: the first, second, and third jetties south of Cleague's house on the east side of the island were Observation Posts (OP's) one, two and three. The sniper hide south of Cleague's house closest to the beach was OP-4. The sniper hide south of Cleague's house closest to the road was OP-5. The guy in front of the shed across the street from Cleague's house was OP-6. The road blockade north of Cleague's house between the house and the town was OP-7. The blockade at the bridge was OP-8. Command was "Command" and the maneuver elements were "Squads One, Two, and Three." The Observation Post teams were designated as OP (number) Actual for the senior of the two men with the radio, and OP (number) Alpha for the junior guy or assistant. Some of the guys had AR-15 M4 carbines and some had MP-5's.

When it was their turn to respond to the sit rep on the radio they replied: "OP-8 is all secure, over." Command immediately came back and said, "OP-8, are you sure, over?" OP-8 Actual responded, "Affirmative, we see nothing out of the ordinary at this time, over."

They understood that the house had somehow caught fire and the shed had somehow caught fire as well, and apparently nobody knew where the perpetrator—the object of the whole exercise—had gone. They had been positioned at the bridge to prevent vehicular traffic from approaching the area of tonight's operation. Nobody said anything about apprehending this extremely dangerous individual apparently capable of the most heinous violence. That was precisely why they had three separate assault elements. Nobody said that manning the bridge Observation Post was going to be hard or even dangerous duty, it was supposed to be a routine traffic block for which they'd be making triple time because they were working on a holiday. It was the Fourth of July, and the intermittent splashes of color from the skies above the town down at the other end of the island bore that out.

They were having their own fireworks display on their side of the little island that apparently no one in the chain of command had planned for. And this crazy guy was seemingly running around loose. He could have been killed in the house or the shed but "Command" didn't sound like it. While his partner was on the radio to Command, the other sentry on the bridge thought he saw something in the water off to the left toward that raceway water thing. He used the binoculars they had been issued and glassed both banks of the boat channel but could see nothing. There it was again, it was a splash or something almost right underneath them, and he took his MP-5 and emptied a magazine of 9mm ammo into the water directly under his position on the bridge. His partner had no idea this was coming, as he had his back turned while he was on the radio to Command, and jumped a foot up in the air when he heard the gun go off. Apparently "Command" had heard the sound of automatic gunfire come over the radio net and was screaming for a SITREP (situation report). "OP-8, what is your status, over?"

In a calm and controlled voice, the man on the radio responded, "Uh roger, Command, standby, over." And turned to his partner and screamed, "What the fuck are you doing?"

"I saw him, goddamn it!" his partner, equally agitated, responded just as loudly.

"You saw what?" Eight-Actual demanded.

"Over there" he pointed. "I saw him," Eight-Alpha replied.

Not buying this story, Eight-Actual—in a slightly calmer voice—asked in measured tones,

"What did you see?"

"I saw a splash," said Eight-Alpha, full of righteous vindication.

Incredulous, Eight-Actual responded, "A splash? You saw a splash? It was a fish you fucking Moron!"

46

When Cleague had entered what he perceived to be the area of illumination he could not make a surface dive, as it would create a splash and too much sound, thereby giving away his position. To get depth, he stopped kicking with his legs momentarily and pulled with his arms while slowly letting out breath at a controlled rate. Once he thought he was about six or seven feet under the surface of the water he started using his legs in a frog kick. Although he had the weight of the Glock, and the extra magazine, he had to fight the buoyancy of the neoprene material of his wetsuit. Maintaining a breaststroke motion required an extra hard pull and an extra hard kick. Maybe he wasn't as deep as he thought he was and broke the surface of the water with one of his flippers, because all of a sudden there was a bunch of little zippy things coming into the water right in front of him for about two and a half seconds.

All he could do was to grab great big hands full of water and kick like hell to get deeper. The lower he got, the dimmer the ambient light from the streetlamps above the bridge became. When he started to feel pressure on his inner ears he thought he was about twenty feet deep. He needed to breathe. Now! Beginning his assent, he believed he was under the bridge and assumed a vertical posture as he began a slow flutter kick with his fins.

He slowly let out air at a controlled rate and smoothly approached the surface of the water. Using his arms in a lateral sweeping motion, back and forth and kicking very gently with his fins, he broke the surface of the water with the top of his head and gradually proceeded upward until his face protruded just above the water line. He forced himself to stay low in the water and breathed through his nose. He drew the

Glock and kept it in his right hand at arm's length just underneath the surface of the water. In this position the Glock was already indexed at whatever he was looking at. From this position he could raise the Glock an inch out of the water and fire and the gun would function and he would hit his target...hopefully.

Treading water he rotated his body 360 degrees, describing a circle in the water, searching the space under the bridge and looking for anything that would indicate the presence of the adversary. Cleague's guess had been right. He was just about directly under the middle of the bridge.

After Eight-Alpha had fired his MP-5, the bolt of the firearm remained open indicating that the magazine was empty.

"Fish, my ass." The MP-5 guy responded vehemently to his partner who was still on the radio with "Command."

"I saw him, I hit him," he said, and with that, he deftly swapped magazines without having to look, and stuffed the empty magazine into one of the numerous pockets of his tactical vest. Eight-Alpha abruptly turned and walked away from his partner toward the south end of the bridge.

"Where the hell are you going?" Eight-Actual demanded.

"I hit him. He's got to be under the bridge. I'm going to find him," Eight-Alpha said, and dropped out of sight.

"OP-8, Answer up, over." Command was getting impatient.

"Roger, Command, this is OP-8 Actual, over," the radioman responded.

Mindful that they were being monitored by the media, Command tactfully inquired,

"Interrogative, what is going on down there, over?"

"Uh roger, Command, this is OP-8 Actual, OP-8 Alpha believed he saw the suspect and discharged his weapon, over."

"He fired his gun? Over," Command demanded.

"Roger that, he discharged his weapon, he believes that he hit the suspect and has gone under the bridge to find him, over."

At this "Command" lost all sense of decorum, media presence or not, "No, absolutely goddamned not. Nobody leaves his or her post without my authorization. Is that understood OP-8, over?"

"Roger that, over."

"Get his ass back on that bridge now! Command out." Command ordered.

"Roger, Command, OP-8 out."

At this point Command assembled the assault team members that were still alive and ordered them to the bridge. A small caravan of Federal Law Enforcement appointed Chevy Blazers, with de-rigueur 'low profile' black paint, blacked out grill guard, matte black push bars, tinted windows, and all the bells and whistles, and lights, and sirens, and every other black automotive accessory known to man that screamed "FED," and made their way at maximum speed south down the little island highway to the bridge. It was a little over a mile and didn't take long.

Eight-Alpha made his way down the rocky embankment that supported the foundation of the bridge. He carefully peered into the shadow under the bridge that was seemingly made darker by the contrast of the bright light from the streetlamp just above his position. He could see nothing. He made his way cautiously closer to the water line and paused. Again, nothing…wait, was that movement by the far side of the bridge? He used the weapon mounted tactical light molded into the forearm of the MP-5 and caught a reflection of something directly under the middle of the bridge on the far side of the boat channel. The light had indeed reflected off Peter Cleague's face.

47

As Cleague completed his 360 degree search in the water an intensely bright light flashed directly into his eyes and caused him momentary blindness…

Eight-Alpha instantly brought the stock of the MP-5 up and firmly into his right shoulder taking the time to find the front sight. He pressed the trigger for a one second burst, about half the number of rounds in the magazine. Cleague, at the moment the light blinded him, slammed his eyes shut, ducked his head under the water and moved away.

Spiked on adrenalin Eight-Alpha scanned the waterline on the far side of the bridge…nothing. His shots had gone high. The bullets had impacted into the rock abutment on the north side of the boat channel. The flash of a 500-lumen light had destroyed Cleague's night vision: his own innate acclimated sensitivity between his eyes and his brain to allow him to see in the dark. Now all he could see was a big red circle in front of him. When he had gone under water to escape the light and the gunfire that followed it, he had moved to his right or to the west. He very cautiously broke the surface of the water. He could only make out the dim outline of the shadow of the bridge and the outline of the south east corner of the bridge where it joined the rock abutment from the off cast glow of the streetlight above it. But he could hear the sound of motor vehicles coming to a very abrupt halt. *Great, the cavalry is here*. Above him he could hear the clamor of many boots and many agitated voices. He went underwater again. This had to work because he would only have one chance to do it.

Peter Cleague violently expelled his air, breached the surface, sucked in as much fresh air as he could and executed the fastest surface dive he was capable of.

Eight-Alpha brought the muzzle and white light to bear on the source of a big splash and emptied the rest of the magazine, and automatically executed another magazine change. He scanned the surface of the water for a trail of air bubbles, a shadow, anything. The tactical team that was sent to the bridge by "Command" lost no time scrambling down the foundation of the bridge to the rocky abutment on the north and south side. The whole team was standing underneath the bridge scanning the water with their weapon-mounted lights. "There!" one of the guys shouted and opened up on full auto at something he thought he saw in the middle of the boat channel. Everybody else followed suit stitching the surface of the water with automatic weapons fire at nothing in particular. "Command" was screaming for a SITREP. Eight-Actual was the only BPS man left standing on the bridge. Since he wasn't down below he did not know what everybody was shooting at.

When Cleague made his surface dive he got as low as he could before he leveled out and swam east. His arm strokes were heroic in their span and his kicks were ferocious in their intensity. If he surfaced now he would be shredded with the impact of a high volume of incoming rounds at a very high rate of fire. As one of his favorite instructors had once put it, "Incoming fire always has the right of way." He let out controlled breaths of air to maintain his depth. He was tired. His arms and legs felt like lead. He desperately needed air, but he had established his mindset before he crawled off the front porch of his house. He was leaving on his terms or he would die trying. He certainly wasn't going to give those bastards the satisfaction of killing him. When he thought he had gone out about thirty yards he began his assent.

After everybody had shot out at least one magazine they scanned the boat channel, their beams of white light arcing and looping on the surface of the water. Fresh magazines and bolt stops clicked and clacked with the resonance of metal on metal in the partially enclosed space between the bottom of the bridge and the surface of the water as they swapped out magazines. Some guys went back up topside to stand on the bridge. They glassed the area thoroughly east and west, north and south.

With a controlled assent Cleague broke the surface of the water. He rotated himself with circular motions of his arms and legs until he was facing the bridge due west. He kept his head low in the water and executed a continuous backstroke until he judged he was at the edge of the clicker's range, and treading water, he pulled the radio transmitter out of the top of his wet suit. From his position in the water he could now see that aid cars and fire trucks were making their way up the Mainland Coast Highway south of the bridge. He knew them to be dedicated and professional first responders on their way to render aid and assistance where needed. He had no intention of letting these people come to harm; he pressed the button on the side of the transmitter before they could cross the bridge.

Yesterday. It was just yesterday that he had placed those shaped charges on the pilings that supported the bridge that spanned the boat channel. A shaped charge, by design, focuses all of its energy on a single line, making it very accurate and controllable. When the high explosive is detonated, it forms a jet travelling at a very high rate of speed, perforating that which it is directed against.

Cleague watched as the support pilings lurched and burst and gave way to the tremendous weight of the bridge that had been erected almost seventy years ago for military truck traffic. The bridge went down into the boat channel and with it the remnants of the assault elements of the stalwart battalions of the collective good. They were coming from both directions on the Peninsula Island Highway: fire trucks and ambulances from the south, the TV news van and a sedan from the north. And a great big hole in the middle.

48

Eugene Smith sat in his seventeen foot long Boston Whaler listening to the water softly lapping against the fiberglass hull. He knew he was going to be here for a while so he had anchored on the inland portion of the channel away from the lane designated for ferry traffic. Even so he was in a straight line with the channel marker that his friend Peter had been so adamant about. He had come prepared for a day on the Sound with rods and reels, and tackle, and bait. A cooler full of sandwiches, an ice chest full of beer, a vacuum decanter of the finest coffee made in Seattle, and a baseball game on the radio kept him company as he waited.

Cleague had not told Smith what he was going to do or how he was going to do it. He just asked Smith to be here at this channel marker a little after sunset on the Fourth of July. Smith had been there in time to see the fireworks display over the Port Cullis Marina at the north end of the little island, and even from his perch way the hell out here in the water it was pretty entertaining. Then he couldn't help but notice a different type of fireworks display further south. It wasn't quite as festive and his heart sank a little when he realized it was Peter's house. He wondered if Pete had lived through it. He wondered about the dog. Well, no matter, his friend had asked him to be here and he was. He would wait till midnight.

From the moment the aerial flares went up on the east side of the jetties, Smith had his Zeiss 10X binoculars glued to his eyes. He saw the flares, then he saw small arms fire on all three jetties aimed at the water. He could see military type trucks—old deuce-and-a-halfs, mounted with Xenon search lights. Smith believed he knew who was mounting the assault on his friend's house. It was the BPS. Obviously they had picked Cleague to make an example of, because it was certainly turning out to be quite a show.

Smith could make out the logo of a TV station on the side of a van parked behind the military trucks. He saw the house go up in flames while the slow rumble of an explosion carried across the water a few seconds later. He couldn't believe it when he watched the fuel oil tank describe an arc of fire as it traveled through the night sky with the trajectory of a rainbow. Then he could see that the grass had caught fire in the trail left by the spewed oil from the tank. Almost at the same time the roof of the house disappeared and left tongues of flame licking at the sky in its place. He could hear the muffled rumble of a second explosion travel across the water and could make out the flames of a second conflagration. That had to have been the reloading shed. *Holy Shit*! He thought. "*Glad I didn't open that door.*" Smith recalled a conversation with Cleague in which Smith gave him hell for being lax in his personal security measures and why wasn't his alarm system hooked up? Cleague had made an obscure comment that it would be. Well, apparently so.

After some time had passed and nothing else was apparent on the horizon Smith began to acknowledge the possibility that the BPS very well could have been successful. The last time they had talked, Cleague had asked Smith to take care of Linda. Smith said nothing but nodded in agreement, though he had sensed a rift between the two. This was shortly after the time she had left San Francisco on short notice and moved to Palm Springs. As far as Smith knew she was doing well. He hoped so.

When Eugene Smith saw the flashing lights of the aid cars and fire trucks approach the bridge from the south he put the binoculars back up to his eyes. He glassed the area not knowing what to look for. He scanned either side of the bridge north and south. As the red lights and sirens of the fire trucks approached from the south, the TV van followed a sedan from the north. He saw a number of people on the bridge milling about; it looked like they were shining lights in the water. He couldn't make out very much detail—it was almost a mile away.

"Jeeeesus Cha-rist!" Smith couldn't help but say it out loud. The whole fucking bridge just went into the water, troops and all. Cleague had made it. Smith had no idea how but he knew that Cleague had made it. Now all he had to do was to wait. There had to have been a reason Cleague asked him to be here at the designated channel marker at this time of night. Smith started the motor of the Whaler and made his way west to the channel marker. Smith pulled to within a few yards of the buoy and mounted the ladder to the stern of the Whaler. He used to dive but in the past couple of years he had lost interest and had given up the sport. Now he was glad he had kept some of the collateral hardware.

He thought Cleague had mentioned having a kayak but Smith had no idea what to look for. He glassed the water between the buoy and the bridge but in the ambient darkness he could see nothing. All of a sudden something hit the deck of his boat with a resounding thud and an attendant splash and Smith's heart was firmly lodged right underneath his Adams apple. It was a diver's fin.

"Hey!" a familiar voice demanded. "Can a guy get a little help around here, or is this a union outfit?" Cleague had indeed made it. He threw the second fin into the boat. Cleague was exhausted and would not have made it up the ladder without Smith's help. Smith grabbed Cleague's arm and guided him over the stern of the boat. Cleague collapsed onto a bolster molded into the gunwale and feebly smiled.

In the dim light cast from the instrument panel, Smith had a hard time believing that the person he was looking at was alive. He brought out a light with a blue filter, as long as he kept the source of light below the top edge of the gunwale of the Whaler it shouldn't be visible from the island. There was no skin left on Cleague's knees or elbows. Rivulets of blood coursed down his lower legs and arms. Cleague's cheeks were puffy and one of his eyes was swollen shut. His nose was bleeding and crooked, and possibly broken. Traces of grime streaked his head, and face, and arms, and the backs of his hands. The man looked like death warmed over.

Smith handed Cleague a towel and the clothes he had asked for: a pair of jeans and a wool sweater, wool socks, and a pair of sneakers. Cleague took the transmitter out of the plastic bag, disassembled it, and threw the whole mess overboard. He reached for his knife and then remembered that he had left it on the vest that he had stuffed under the log back in the raceway…he hoped that would not prove to be a mistake. He shrugged out of the nylon shoulder holster and noticed it felt a little light. Well, no shit, the goddamned gun was gone. He must have dropped it under the bridge. Oh well, too late to worry about it now. And he had lost his watch in the bargain. No matter.

Cleague managed to climb into the dry, clean, warm clothes un-assisted. Smith helped wrap a wool blanket around him and turned to get him some food. He poured a nice mug of hot coffee from the vacuum bottle and grabbed one of the Styrofoam trays full of gourmet sandwiches, all from the Alder's kitchen. When he turned around, Cleague had slumped over on to his side; sound asleep. Smith set the food down beside the bolster and drank the coffee. He was going to have a long trip back to the Des Moines Marina.

Peter Cleague had the sensation of falling and he caught himself with a jerk that woke him up. Unsure of his surroundings, he recognized the silhouette of Eugene Smith's back standing at the wheel of the boat. He heard the steady thrumming pulse of the motor that propelled them south through Puget Sound on a course to a marina far from Peninsular Island. The motor lulled him back to sleep and he dreamed the dreams of the dead.

*****

There was this man, and there was this road, and the man was standing in the middle of the road, and he didn't know which way to turn. Left or right? He went to ask the lost man if he needed help. The man turned around; it was Peter Cleague.

49

The pilot of the VH60 Executive Transport Helicopter, a VIP-appointed Black hawk, circled the crime scene at an altitude of 200 feet off the deck to enable her passengers to glean a sense of the destruction that had occurred the night before. She was also looking for a place to land. From his seat in the cabin of the Blackhawk, **Albert Muzecko**, the Attorney General of the United States, mutely observed the results of "Operation Clean Sweep" as he considered the losses from the previous evening. He entertained the thought that several good men in faithful service to the United States Government had lost their lives in an attempt to apprehend and bring to justice an obviously delusional renegade, a self-styled "constitutionalist," a domestic right-wing terrorist, a lone wolf extremist, a rabid white supremacist…or something along those lines. Or at least that is what the press release that had not yet been drafted would state. He scribbled the appropriate notes and handed them to an aid that would see to it that the sentiment would be in the national papers by press-time. The Attorney General in turn reflected on the fact that in spite of the relatively minor loss of life, much political capital could be generated from this little fiasco. As long as the appointed spokespeople could steer the media away from asking questions about institutional incompetence, this could be a political windfall. Never let a crisis go to waste.

The scene below them was a couple of craters full of rubble, and the vehicles of the BPS forensics technicians. Everything else was in the process of being tagged, photo-documented, plotted on a grid map, bagged, and impounded as evidence.

The pilot banked the helicopter forty-five degrees to the left and crabbed the aircraft into the northwest wind back to the spot she had picked out from her visual reconnaissance. The helicopter landed in the midst of cold, wet, huddled agents forcing them to scatter out of the impromptu LZ since no one at the site had thought to establish one. It had been raining since midnight. Sand and water spun outward and upward from under the arc of the rotor blades adding insult to injury. The blast of wet cold sand pelted people who were over-tired and already miserable, several of them tending to minor lacerations and burns, and fearful of the implications of the impending investigation. Lives had been lost with bodies unaccounted for; careers would be next.

Three men alighted from the aircraft and stepped toward the large military-issue General Purpose Tent that now served as the command center for the BPS. The tent had been erected just about a mile north of what had been the house of one Peter Cleague. The two taller men deferred to the gentleman with refined patrician features of somewhat slighter stature to lead the way out from under the tip path plane described by the main rotor.

"Where is the Agent-in-Charge?" The shorter gentleman demanded, just loud enough to be heard over the descending whine of the helicopter's jet engines and decelerating rotor blades. The larger of his two companions surveyed the people standing near the GP tent and yelled "Speeks," and beckoned Special Agent Speeks with a curt gesture. Special Agent Walter Speeks presented himself without delay. Special Agent Speeks had not slept, had failed spectacularly in his assigned mission, and carried the burden of dead agents under his command. Twelve hours previous, Speeks had been a demigod with operational control over the largest special operations team the BPS had ever fielded since the organization's inception. But now he was beyond tired, demoralized, crest fallen and in his current disheveled state, he made a crew cut look greasy.

"Special Agent Speeks, I am Albert Muzecko, Attorney General of the United States," said the shorter gentleman.

"Yes, sir." Speeks gave a respectful nod.

"Special Agent Speeks, I want to see the body of one Peter Cleague." The Attorney General urged.

"We haven't found it yet, sir," Speeks replied.

"I see." The AG paused. At this point the press corps had disembarked from their chartered bus. They had been given special dispensation to be ferried to the otherwise "closed" island by the Washington State Department of Transportation.

The AG, playing to a small audience of journalists, emanated stoic objectivity for Speeks' ostensible display of incompetence. Albert Muzecko took out his reading glasses from the inside pocket of his coat with a calculated cadence and consulted the Emergency Situation Report that had been handed to him only hours ago in Washington DC, giving the press enough time to get within earshot of the conversation. The two men that had deplaned from the helicopter with AG Muzecko quietly exchanged glances.

The AG went on, "I understand that there are a number of agents estimated…" at this point the AG made a show of putting on his reading glasses, "…to be missing in the line of duty and presumed to be dead as a result of 'Operation Clean Sweep'…conducted last night." The AG finished reading the report and peered at the hapless Speeks over the top rim of his glasses.

"Yes, sir." Speeks dutifully replied.

"Well, I want to see them. I want to see the bodies," the AG stated as he put his reading glasses back in his coat.

"Uh, we haven't found them all yet, sir," Speeks answered.

"Why not? Where are they?" the AG asked.

Henry Caleb, the Director of the Federal Bureau of Public Safety, and the larger of the AG's two companions, discretely walked over to one of the BPS men in place and instructed him to gently herd the gathering reporters to an area away from the Attorney General's performance. Rumors had been in circulation that the AG would challenge his party's apparent front-runner for the Presidential nomination. Given that front-runners seldom won, it was a very credible rumor. But whether he did or not, it would not be done at the expense of this man's dignity: his career in the BPS had already been flushed down the toilet. The Director of the Bureau of Public Safety quietly resumed his place behind the Attorney General. He believed in loyalty down—to a point.

"Well, sir, uh, we think, they, uh..." Speeks stammered.

"Well?" the AG insisted. His litigious nature was coming to the surface; he could smell blood in the water.

"Well, sir. We think they were obliterated in the explosions, sir." It was all Speeks could think of to say.

"Obliterated?" The AG was incredulous.

"Well, sir, uh, yes, sir, at this point, er, uh, in the, uh, investigation, that is our, uh, presumption. Sir." Speeks gracelessly tripped through his explanation.

"I see." the AG said blindly. "Tell me something Agent Speeks." The AG held his folded arms close to his chest. Summer or not, he wasn't used to this bizarre Washington weather.

"Yes, sir?" Speeks said.

"Had you had any field experience before last night's operation?" the AG asked.

"Yes, sir. Twenty years," Speeks replied.

"Twenty years. You are in fact one of the senior field agents in the BPS are you not?" the AG inquired.

"Yes, sir," Speeks replied.

"And of all the senior field agents in the entire Bureau of Public Safety you were the most senior Special Operations Task Force Commander, were you not?" the AG asked.

"Yes, sir," Speeks said.

The Attorney General paused. In spite of his hallmark histrionics in his previous career in the Senate, he was a man of above-average personal discipline. He had not yet raised his voice above the level necessary to be heard above the on shore wind. At this point his voice dropped in timbre, tone, and volume.

"Let me share something with you Special Agent Speeks."

Speeks had to lean forward from the waist to hear the Attorney General. It put him off balance.

"This situation truly has me baffled. How does the senior field agent in the Bureau of Public Safety fail to ascertain that his target is lined with enough explosives to kill every man in the assault element, set fire to a National Historic Site, incinerate two structures on the National Historic Registry, and completely disintegrate a bridge that connects an island to a continent? How did you manage to accomplish this amazingly spectacular feat of incompetence? Please tell me. I want to know this."

Special Agent Walter Speeks, humiliated before the Attorney General of the United States, The Director of the Federal Bureau of Public Safety, and this third man whom he did not know, assumed the resigned stoicism of a man who knows he is about to be sentenced to the guillotine.

"I do not have an answer for the Attorney General at this time, sir."

The AG's facial muscles visibly went into spasms. Short of going into an apoplectic fit he managed a decree.

"Agent Speaks, as of this moment you are summarily suspended without pay. You will appear before a board of inquiry at the very least, and I should imagine you would also be required to appear before at least one Congressional sub-committee hearing if not a criminal trial. Do not do anything foolish Mr. Speaks. That will be all."

The AG gave a dismissive nod to the BPS Director. Speaks was then escorted under guard to the helicopter.

The three men were transported by courtesy of the County Sheriff's Office to the site of the failed raid. Deputy Sheriff Andy De Kooning kept his mouth shut as he drove the VIPs out to the rubble-strewn craters. It was a very quiet ride. No one voiced the notion that had been widely believed within the Federal law enforcement community at the time of the creation of the Bureau of Public Safety within the Department of the Interior, that expanding Federal law enforcement powers to agencies like Commerce, Agriculture, and Interior was, at best, ill advised. In fact, a paper by a lower level White House lawyer back in the mid-eighties had warned that as such activities as arrest and search are the most intrusive acts a government can visit upon its citizenry, he recommended that such functions be strictly limited to Treasury and Justice. Indeed, as they arrived at the site of the previous evening's debacle, the smoldering timbers and charred verdure served as mute testimony to the wisdom of that obscure junior lawyer's observation. No one in the car felt it necessary to comment on it further.

The BPS' own forensics laboratory was arguably the finest forensics criminal investigations unit in the country, if not in the world. In addition to consistently meticulous and correct lab work, they could field a full investigative team at any crime scene within the lower forty-eight contiguous states within eight hours after notification. Such had been the case here. They had been on site since five a.m. The techs were busy plotting, mapping, marking, and photographing anything that did not seem to be a natural part of the cobbled beach strand and/or the surrounding environment. Identification would come later in the lab...hopefully. Staying outside the perimeter marked off by the ubiquitous yellow crime scene tape, the three VIPs conducted themselves on a silent tour of the site. As they surveyed the area, it occurred to at least one of the three men that this had been the scene on the previous evening of a pre-planned ambush by the BPS on a private citizen. It had turned out to be a conflagration, the likes of which had not been seen before on this tiny Peninsular Island. The third man wondered, "*Who had ambushed whom?*"

The BPS' Public Relations machine had immediately begun a campaign of somewhat haphazard spin control. The spokesperson had put the appropriate curve on the unconfirmed reports coming out of the neighboring communities—there were other islands in this part of Puget Sound—that these reports were incomplete at best, unconfirmed at present, and unverified pending the findings of an on-going investigation. But the spokesperson was confident that current circumstances indicated that what seemed to have happened was that an illegal fireworks manufacturing operation had simply gotten out of hand on the Fourth of July.

The TV news crew that had been present for the raid had immediately been sequestered, supposedly removed to a hospital for observation given their close proximity to the explosion and subsequent destruction of property and immolation of human life. Such a profoundly traumatic experience required the closest examination and attentive care. The manufactured cover story had immediately been met with skepticism and would fail in short order under the weight of direct scrutiny but for now it would simply have to do.

50

John W. Luther had been summoned at an ungodly hour that morning to meet the Attorney General of the United States and the Director of the Bureau of Public Safety at Andrews Air Force Base. It took less than an hour for Luther to drive from his home in Arlington, Virginia to Prince Georges County, Maryland. The three of them shared a ride in a Lear Jet to McChord Air Force Base, Washington. A short shuttle trip by vehicular conveyance transported them to Gray Army Airfield, Fort Lewis, Washington. En route from Andrews AFB, the AG's party had notified and tasked Command Group, I Corps, to provide transportation support.

Luther was a senior investigator for the Department of Justice and as he surveyed the scene before him some things simply did not square with the information he had been given at his initial meeting with the AG that morning. *Why was all the Military equipment here? Why was a full-scale special-operations assault team necessary for somebody who was allegedly making firecrackers in their shed?* Luther mused. *If the BPS initial press release had been correct, why had a news crew been invited to film the suspect's arrest if it was only about fireworks?* Somebody on the government's side was going to have to get their story straight and soon. This thing had the hallmarks of a potential civil liberties calamity.

Drawing on what he had already been told and on what he could see around him, John Luther was able to assess the following: apparently the press was at hand when the BPS came in to arrest this person of interest, one Peter Cleague. This meant that the press had notice of the arrest, and of the case, and what the government was going to do some time prior to the arrest. And it was leaked by the government to the press so the press could be on hand, which may have been in violation of Federal criminal laws that deal with privacy.

Well, at least he didn't have to write the damned thing. But he couldn't escape the feeling of waiting for the other shoe to drop. Although he had not yet been told, John Luther knew why he was here.

The three VIPs had borrowed a walkie-talkie from the deputy to allow them to monitor radio traffic as they toured the area. They followed the crime scene tape to its end and then continued on beyond it. The forensic techs were still trying to determine how much of the area was actual "crime scene" and they had not yet decided where to establish the outside boundaries of last night's incident. As the three men walked slowly around the debris of what had been a house back toward the road which bordered the property, Luther suddenly stuck his arm out in front of the Attorney General who had been surveying the scene, sweeping his gaze from horizon to horizon, trying to take it all in.

"Watch your step, sir." Luther advised firmly preventing the AG from making any further forward movement. "We probably shouldn't be walking this close to the debris, sir." Luther prudently suggested.

"Oh, and why is that Mr. Luther?" the AG responded. Luther simply indicated with a nod of his head at what lay in the AG's path.

"What the hell is that?" the AG responded with a curt inquiry.

"It appears to be part of an animal, sir, maybe a dog of some sort. The rest of the area seems to be covered in internal tissue, sir. Probably human," Luther surmised. Surveying the area from where they stood, given their proximity to the house debris to the road, speckles and globules of glistening pink, gray and white bits of an as yet undetermined substance or substances dotted their path. The larger identifiable pieces of anatomy: hands, lengths of bone, tangible bits of muscle, etc., had already been tagged and plotted, later to be removed.

"Hey, you three, get the hell out of there! This is a crime scene, goddamn it." The man wearing the raid jacket emblazoned with the BPS logo on its back could immediately be heard on the walkie-talkie demanding to know why that sheriff's deputy had let these three tourists into his crime scene.

"Jesus Christ!" The AG was seldom given to such public display. "What the hell happened here last night? I fail to believe that federal agents died serving an arrest warrant for a two-bit gun law violation." The AG exclaimed, clearly out of very real frustration at what he saw before him. Luther's ears pricked up at this first indicator of what this whole mess had been about, but he had yet to be briefed.

"Luther," the AG commanded in a sharp staccato, "…As of now you are in charge of this investigation. I want a complete and thorough report. Thorough. And I want it before the scale of this debacle gets leaked to the press."

Too late for that, Luther thought.

"This is all I need right now with Congress in summer recess in an election year. And with the Constitutional Convention coming up this year!" the AG proclaimed.

"Yes, sir. I understand." Luther started"…I'm going to need…"

"Fine, do it. Just get it done." The AG cut him off. "You have my authorization. You will report directly to me, understand?" the AG nearly barked.

"Yes, sir," Luther simply replied. With that the AG turned on his heel and made way for the deputy's patrol vehicle, making little muffled retching noises as he began to recognize some of the body parts he had been treading upon thus far in his sojourn through the aftermath of "Operation Clean Sweep." The Director of the BPS and John Luther shared a look as the Attorney General of the United States receded toward the deputy's Ford Expedition.

The Bureau of Public Safety was an agency within the Department of the Interior, but the Attorney General could, as the senior law enforcement officer of the US, conduct an investigation regarding any branch of the cabinet, and suspend individuals from duty pending that investigation's outcome. If circumstances warranted the Attorney General could appoint a special counsel. But first a preliminary fact-gathering process would be conducted to determine if the appointment of a special counsel was required. Although it had not been said, Luther knew that the results of his investigation would form the basis for the AG's decision of whether or not to appoint a special counsel. Careers could be toppled. Fiefdoms could be vanquished. Luther could make a lot of enemies, all depending on what he committed to the report in the course of his preliminary investigation. As far as Luther was concerned, the AG's decision was irrelevant; his job was to conduct an investigation and report his findings.

The Director of the BPS simply arched an eyebrow and gave a little shrug.

"Well, I'll leave you to your investigation, Mr. Luther. Keep in touch."

"Yes, sir." John Luther was not insensitive to the director's droll wit. Luther was simply doing his best to keep from being overwhelmed with the immensity of the task that lay before him, as he surveyed the remnants of "Operation Clean Sweep."

51

The VH-60 ascended vertically under the thrust and lift of its turbine-powered main rotor, to clear ground obstructions such as the GP tent. It then proceeded in a forward rate of climb to its service ceiling of 19,000 feet as the pilot directed her craft in a southeasterly direction toward Fort Lewis.

The Attorney General of the United States sat comfortably looking out the window and thinking of the chronometric evolutions, which were about to follow—it was just a matter of time. The Director of the Bureau of Public Safety sat in the nicely up-holstered seat to the AG's right. The unfortunate Agent Speeks was sequestered in the rear of the cabin with his very own escort, who had the previous evening been under Speeks' command.

One of the three crew members of the aircraft had asked the AG and the Director of the BPS if they cared for coffee before they departed, as he would not be able to accommodate them once they were in the air. They both accepted. The hot coffee from the vacuum bottle prepared that morning in one of the Fort Lewis Dining facilities wasn't all that bad.

Henry Caleb had not been emotionally prepared for the physical reality of what he had just seen at the site of "Operation Clean Sweep." He had been aware of the raid prior to its execution but he did not get involved in the minutiae of planning the details. He stared into the middle distance and saw the retinal image of two holes in the ground and random organic matter. Those were his guys.

"Well, Henry," Said Albert Muzecko, "All-in-all, I think, this time it is going to stick." Henry Caleb had known the Attorney General for years. In fact, he first met Muzecko when the latter was a junior Senator and Caleb was a new special agent in a now defunct organization formerly under the Department of Justice. In their long friendship they mutually recognized that they shared many things - intangible things: goals, visions, ideals, and not the least of which was a sense of mission. The only reason certain objectives had not been attained within the administration of the Federal Government was because *they* hadn't been given the opportunity to try them yet. But now, they each separately realized, their moment had come.

"What do you think happened to that guy?" Henry asked.

"What guy?" Albert responded.

"That Cleague guy, back on that island." Henry said.

Muzecko shrugged and said, "Who cares? It looked to me like he's dead. Can you think of a way somebody could have lived through that obliterated mess? You saw it. They can't even find enough pieces of enough people to figure out who's not there anymore." Muzecko said. Henry smiled wanly with some misgiving.

"Yeah, I don't know. What I saw was an ambush, and it wasn't my guys that executed it. Those guys walked into something. Goddamned shame, they were good guys," he said clearly suffering the loss of well-trained highly motivated agents at his beck and call.

"Yes they were and no one will diminish their sacrifice." Muzecko consoled his friend. "But Henry, you knew this was likely to happen. It was bound to happen sooner or later. And now this is it. It is the perfect moment—it sets the stage. This gives us the opportunity to do the things we couldn't do before. We have the momentum. When this gets out in the press we will have the public's support. And if it's handled right, there's not one pro-gun lunatic in the country that will be able to turn the tide." Muzecko's eyes gleamed with the sure and certain knowledge of the true believer. He offered sympathetic re-assurance and the simultaneous promise of attaining a long-sought goal.

"So how do you think it'll happen?" Henry said as he reclined the seat back and settled in.

"You mean the convention?" Albert asked.

"No, after that. After it's repealed." Henry said, referring to the repeal of The Second Amendment to the Bill of Rights in a shorthand manner they both understood.

"Well, I haven't seen anything in writing yet, and that is probably something you should get started on, but I'll tell you, I've got some ideas." Muzecko warmed to the topic at hand. "Y'know there was this guy, he was a retired Foreign Service guy, ambassador or something. Well, after he retired he became an editor in a newspaper out in the Midwest. Well, one day he flat out said, "This is how we should do it." And I thought he had some good ideas. He said, uh…" Muzecko tried to recall the editorial that had come across his desk one day not that long ago.

"Oh yeah, he said, uh, first, we have a ninety day grace period after the repeal of the Second Amendment. Everybody that has a gun gets a three-month amnesty to turn everything in. Then we get special squads of police that are trained for this, they would be your guys obviously, but regular cops too, and they start the confiscation process. Now this is what I liked about this guy's idea, see?" Albert interjected and went on. "We make it random. We'll never have enough guys to do this everywhere all at one time, so we make it random and systematic. Random so there's no forward notice, we cordon off certain city blocks, certain neighborhoods in the suburbs, certain sections of rural counties and we go through and sweep every business, every home and every empty building. If it's a standing edifice it gets searched; gardens, rose-beds, any area of tilled soil. We'll go through peoples' yards with metal detectors if we have to." He was starting to get enthusiastic now.

"All firearms get seized. No questions asked. No ifs, ands, or buts. We take 'em all: shotguns, handguns, rifles, and BB guns. I don't care what it is. If it can launch a projectile I want it." Muzecko went on. "For all intents and purposes, pellet guns, bb guns, paintball guns, they're all firearms. If the British and Canadians can do it, we can do it. And anybody found with a gun in their possession gets prosecuted. A thousand bucks and a year in prison for every gun found.

"Now, we can't do the whole country all at once, see? But we start in D.C., and Baltimore, and Los Angeles, and Detroit. Pretty soon, we get gun-swept, gun-free, areas across the country and before you know it, the whole country's clean. He took a sip of coffee.

"Now you know as well as I that we're not going to get them all, at first. This patch-work approach is going to leave a lot of gaps, at first. So anytime we find them, those people that have them will face immediate confiscation and prosecution. Hey, a cop on the street even suspects somebody's carrying, he will execute immediate search, seizure and apprehension whether it's a Mexican in a bandanna or a grandma in a wheelchair. It's the same penalties for everybody." Muzecko smiled.

Henry Caleb thought it sounded good, and it certainly had the AG's enthusiastic support, but he also thought it had a lot of holes in it. Caleb thought that bit about search, and seizure, and metal detectors had some constitutional issues but, he presumed, that would be taken care of at the Constitutional Convention. Once convoked the whole Constitution was up for grabs, so-to-speak. No matter. He would get some of his people to work it out and they would come up with a viable solution. The actual air travel time back to Fort Lewis was quite brief, less than an hour. It helps when you travel with people that can have air traffic re-routed because of the title they bear.

52

It stopped raining; the sky was still overcast with a luminescent gray that lent its tone to the day. John Luther surveyed the area around him. He stood on the sand on the inland side west of the dune that separated Cleague's property from the beach. He stood approximately due east of the debris that had been Peter Cleague's house. He had purposely avoided reading the periodic SITREPs (Situation Reports) and Speeks' obligatory after-action report.

What Luther knew as he stood at that particular spot was that a raid had been executed and it failed. Who, what, why, and how would be determined in the course of his investigation. Interviews, reports, and press conferences would come later. What he wanted to do right now was see the physical evidence that lay before him and construct in his own mind what happened without reading it through the misleading filters of the interpretations of other people.

Luther walked east through the break in the dune out onto the beach strand. He guessed it could be fifty or a hundred yards from the dunes to the water's edge depending on the level of the tide. Right now it was slack tide, the tide was not moving in or out, it was still—much like Luther's grasp of the situation into which the Attorney General had just dispatched him.

He walked out to the water's edge and looked south. He stood just a few yards north of one of the old jetties that had been constructed as a pier for off-loading cargo ships. In its heyday this place must have really been hopping. He climbed up onto the old pier and looked south. He could barely see two more just like it between his position and the termination of the island at the boat channel just about a mile away. In spite of the recent rain the air was extremely hazy. Luther understood that this was typical weather most of the year and wondered how in the hell people could stand it. Maybe Cleague was driven mad by sunlight deprivation. *Naah.* He continued walking along the length of the jetty nearly to its end when his shoe caught on something that caused him to trip.

He caught himself with his hands, bloodying the heels of both palms with friction burns. He recovered, nonplused, and looked to see what had caused his fall. Comm wire ran the width of the jetty at about three inches off the top of the concrete. Curious, he peered over the edge of the jetty at what he guessed was about eight feet down to the water. He saw something flaccid, vaguely beige, and vaguely familiar. It didn't float away, or drift in to shore. One end dipped down beneath the surface of the water so it had apparently been anchored—quite curious. After some minutes Luther realized what it was...a novelty doll, albeit deflated, of the sort that could be ordered through certain types of web-sites. Luther thought he was beginning to understand what had occurred the previous evening.

John Luther left his position from atop the jetty, keeping as far away from the crime scene as he could manage, and walked north along the beach past the burnt out hulk of a pickup truck. Olive drab deuce-and-a-halves with million candlepower Xenon search lights mounted to their flat beds stood in mute testimony to the spectacular failure of last night's raid. Luther continued north past the property line of Cleague's house until he could see a break in the long grass on the barrier dune. He cut through the trail and crossed the Island Highway and headed south again back toward what had been Cleague's Quonset hut. He crossed the yellow tape marking the boundary of the investigation but kept to the edge of the perimeter to survey what was actually a shallow crater in the ground. Luther showed his credentials to the BPS forensic technician making notes on a clipboard that nodded but said nothing. Luther mutely nodded in return.

What had been a small Quonset hut built of galvanized steel seventy years ago was now shrapnel strewn across brush and weeds and grass from the highway due west into the brackish water of the island's inland waterway. From appearances Luther's eye told him that an explosive of some force had erupted around the entire perimeter of the building. The resultant pile of metal reached as high as Luther's chest in some places. The foundation of the building had been blown out from under it and the building had collapsed in on itself like a house of cards. This crime scene would literally take months for the forensic technicians to excavate, let alone evaluate and analyze. They would methodically sort through it with toothbrushes and whiskbrooms removing and hauling away a layer at a time.

Luther carefully skirted the perimeter of the shed as best he could as he walked west toward the inland water way. There was an expanse of sand that led from the west side of Cleague's shed to the waterline. He noted foot prints in the sand that led from the water's edge to the west wall of where the hut had stood. To a doorway, a sliding door maybe, or an opening in the wall...maybe like a garage door? A glance at the rubble beside him indicated he would have to wait to read the forensic report. That might be a problem as his own report was to be presented to a very impatient Attorney General in short order. He walked east along the perimeter of the hut and the scrubby flora that had reclaimed most of the former Army AA battery support facility.

How come there weren't more Quonset huts? If this was base housing, how come there weren't more houses? Luther scribbled questions in a notebook and he was going to have to determine which ones would even have any bearing on his investigation before he could ask them.

Heading east toward the road he noted parallel drag marks, twelve to eighteen inches apart—just about shoulder width—in the sand from the edge of the road back toward what had been the shed. Not hard to guess what happened there. In reviewing what he had seen up to this point Luther had to admit that the BPS came up short this time. He stood at the edge of the Island Highway noting that the Quonset hut lay directly across from the driveway to Cleague's house. The Island Highway would have been blocked off north and south of the house and the place would have been flooded with light from the xenon searchlights mounted on the military trucks while the assault squads performed their execution of a raid on a barricaded position by the numbers. Yep, it would have been a doozy.

Luther felt a vague tug of remorse for the life of a young motivated BPS man who had his whole career in front of him. *Did the boy have a family? Was he married? Kids?* No matter, not Luther's concern at this point in the investigation. He made a note in his memo pad to get the cause of death from the forensic examination unit for the bodily remains he was sure they would find under the rubble of tin and plywood that had been the Quonset hut. They would do it as a matter of course, but Luther was particularly interested. *It had to have been something very close, very intimate, a neck having been broken or maybe a throat having been cut. Where would this Cleague guy learn to do something like that? In the military? Maybe. Or he could have learned it in prison,* Luther thought.

Luther walked south in the direction of the bridge along the west edge of the Island Highway eyeing something in the middle of the road just a few yards away. It lay in a crumpled heap generally in front of the site of Peter Cleague's house— maybe twenty or thirty yards from where the door of the Quonset hut might have been. Three BPS forensic technicians huddled in Cleague's front yard photographing the rubble that had been a house and plotted it on their site map. As he approached he could smell what the lump in the road was before he was able to visually identify it. He quickly walked to a position upwind and did not approach the man's body but stayed on the edge of the road west of it as he tried to visualize what had happened.

The head of the corpse pointed in a northward direction. It lay face down, its arms out-flung, its helmet lay on the far side of the street about ten feet forward of the corpse. Its feet were tangled in the tandem stranded wire: one aluminum, one copper, each sheathed in a rubber coating, spanning the highway from the edge of the fence line in Cleague's front yard, across the street to Luther's position on the west side of the road. *Goddamned comm wire; it's all over this island*, he thought. The dead man in the middle of the road had been an observer or something, probably saw or heard something peculiar at or near the Quonset hut, and went to investigate. He had tripped on the wire just as Luther had done on the jetty.

Luther visualized: *the observer tripped on the wire, hit the road surface, probably chin first, knocking him unconscious or at least dazing him. His helmet was doffed in the fall and skittered to its present resting place. He had then been shot in the head.*

This Cleague fellow was turning out to be one ruthless son of a bitch. The distance from this spot in the road to the shed would have been twenty-five, maybe thirty yards at most. The bullet had done the same thing to the man's head that had been done to the dog. Payback? This whole scenario was beginning to look like payback.

It was becoming obvious to Luther that the BPS walked into this with their eyes closed, expecting a cakewalk, and sprung a bear trap instead. It would have taken Cleague a long time to set this up. *Had he known about the raid or was he one of those paranoid survivalist types that cached their guns when they planted the vegetable garden?* Luther wondered.

If the BPS had planned the raid, Cleague would have been under continuous surveillance for days if not weeks. Luther made another note to dig up those reports pertinent to the pre-raid surveillance from BPS files. *If he had been under surveillance how could they have not known that he had set a trap? Unless they had conducted a half-assed surveillance because Cleague had never been considered to be a serious threat to begin with, but then why do the raid?* He wrote.

The answers that Luther saw did not fit with a career's experience in Federal law enforcement. The Attorney General said that Federal agents were killed in a raid over a two-bit gun law violation. *If it was indeed a "two-bit" violation, why was it considered to warrant a raid at all? And if the violation had been that serious why let an agency of the Department of the Interior execute it and not the FBI? If it was in fact a two-bit gun law violation, ostensibly a threat to public safety at most, why mount a paramilitary operation? Why not just have the County Sheriff serve a summons?* Things at this point simply did not square with the physical reality before him.

Luther pulled out his notebook again. He wrote: *"two-bit gun law violation," Quote from AG, and the day's date.* He remembered the AG also muttered something about a Constitutional Convention right before he left. Luther was cognizant of the news blurbs over the past few months that various interest groups in several states were pushing for the repeal of the Second Amendment. Almost all of the broadcast news organs had had at least one story about it each week. Luther knew there had been talk in both houses of the Congress but it came as a surprise to him that a Constitutional Convention was definite if not imminent. He didn't know if they had voted on it yet. Under his preceding notation Luther wrote: *"Constitutional Convention coming up." Any link?* The Attorney General sounded quite sure of himself when he made the comment. Well, he was the Attorney General.

A crow landed near the corpse lying in the street in front of Cleague's house. Luther cast about for something to throw at the bird but he could find nothing at hand. The bird started inquisitorially pecking, then pulling with enthusiasm. "Hey!" No response from the forensics techs. They stood off the road surface east of the Island Highway with their backs to the corpse. The carrion fowl was pulling, tearing, and picking with glee.

"Hey, goddamn it!" Luther commanded to a disinterested audience...Nothing. That bird was destroying Luther's evidence. Luther walked directly south of the corpse, more-or-less in the middle of the road, pulled his handgun and connected with his target, the crow, on the first round. That got their attention.

"What the fuck do you think you're doing?" one of them screamed with utter disbelief. Luther suffered neither fools nor prima donnas gladly. He walked to the edge of the road. Without any mental reservation or purpose of evasion, he hopped over the ditch and approached the apoplectic tech to a conversational range of about three inches, and in quiet even tones explained.

"I think I am directly representing the Attorney General of the United States in a preliminary investigation antecedent to the appointment of a Special Counsel regarding institutional incompetence of the Federal Bureau of Public Safety. What's your name?" No answer.

Luther continued, "I want you people to get that corpse covered and out of here now." Luther said it evenly, flatly, and charged with purpose. They began to comply with his instructions in petulant slow-time—the bureaucratic answer to "whose boss?"

Luther walked away from them a few feet to a point north of the corpse and surveyed the wreckage of Cleague's house. Looking at the site from the road he saw the concrete block foundation of the house directly under the still smoldering remnants of a roof in shambles...no visible walls. What remained of the walls had collapsed from the base outward, the major portion of which was under the roof in 360 degrees, smoke noticeably rose from a non-specific source.

Luther walked south on the road, his attention fully focused on the rubble to his left. Like the Quonset hut across the street, the bottom had been blown out from under it. Standing in the road south of the house he noted that the materials on the south side of the house had received the most intense heat. Something had to have been used as an accelerant but why on the south side of the house when the threat was coming from the Northeast? This didn't make sense either. *If the man in the middle of the road had been a sentry where was his post Where had the man been coming from to wind up dead in front of Cleague's house? Where could Cleague have been to be able to shoot the dead guy without having been seen by the rest of the assault element?* Luther's head hurt; he walked away.

53

John Luther stood in the middle of the Island Highway as a flatbed truck approached to pick up the corpse. The bridge was down. There were no coroner's vehicles or ambulances to carry away the dead. He took in the sight under the pearl gray light of the Washington sky: the rubble of Cleague's house, and due south, the dunes, sand, sea grass, and scrub brush. He looked down the Island highway toward the bridge. He couldn't see it but maybe it just wasn't there to be seen. He had not looked out the portholes of the helicopter as the pilot was doing her loopty-loops before they landed. If he was required to board a plane, a straight line there and a straight line back at one altitude was all he desired. From the south looking due west all he could see was the raceway with a lot of really tall weeds. You almost couldn't see the water. *That would have been a good way out.* He thought.

Looking northward past the flatbed truck, John Luther saw the deputy's vehicle parked on the far side of the now-discarded crime scene tape. The deputy had taken the Attorney General and the Director back to their waiting helicopter, which had departed some time ago, Luther now realized. Approaching the Sheriff's vehicle Luther asked in a conversational tone

"Hi, what's your name?"

The deputy regarded Luther as another interesting phenomenon currently in his domain and as such merited further observation. The deputy responded with a polite smile, "DeKooning, what's yours?"

Andy DeKooning stood leaning against the closed driver's door of his county- issued Ford Expedition, enjoying a cigarette. Luther noted the deputy's left hand was unobtrusively tucked inside of his light uniform windbreaker;

probably just another quirky habit by just another paranoid cop. "John Luther," he said extending his right hand. DeKooning shook the man's hand with the proper tone of civility. Other than that he didn't budge.

"It was nice of you to come back for me," Luther said.

DeKooning faintly smiled, nodded and said, "Nice shot."

It was apparent they weren't going anywhere without a direct order, and maybe not then either, until DeKooning's cigarette break was over. Make the most of it, Luther thought.

"You live around here?" Luther asked.

"Yeah," DeKooning nodded. "In the Port."

Luther didn't understand, "What Port?"

DeKooning realized his local slang may have been opaque to the gentleman from the 'other' Washington, and nodded with his head due north.

"In town, Port Cullis," DeKooning added. Luther nodded, getting it.

"Tell me something," Luther said, "what do people do around here?"

"You mean for a living?" DeKooning queried.

"Yeah," Luther nodded. Just a couple of your average everyday working cops having a regular conversation.

"Some of them fish. Some of them commute on the ferry every day, but not many. Some of them work in town. A lot of frustrated artists, unpublished authors, you know, a variety of shit."

Luther nodded.

"Do a lot of people live here?" Luther asked.

DeKooning shrugged, "a couple hundred maybe year round, if you count the kids; usually a couple thousand during the summer."

Luther looked around for a minute, then said with a sudden realization, "It is the middle of the summer. There are very few people around."

DeKooning took a dry pleasure in pointing out the obvious.

"Yeah, you people got the one road on this island blockaded north and south. The one bridge is down. The State Ferry Service has been suspended, except for that busload of reporters. And the Coast Guard is warning off private craft from coming into the marina. That marina is the lifeblood of this community—these people survive because of the tourists. Oh, by the way, how long do you think folks in town are going to be able to go without food and provisions?" DeKooning asked.

Luther had been unaware of the draconian measures that had been enforced by the BPS on the island's population for the conduct of the forensics investigation. However it had been completely within the scope of the charter of the BPS; a crime had been committed on Public (Federal) land (tribal claims not withstanding) involving BPS personnel. Very few "average citizens" knew what the Bureau of Public Safety was, and 99.9% of those that did, learned about it in a negative context. It made for very little difference from when it had been called the BATF under a different cabinet department.

Luther responded simply... "It shouldn't be too much longer." It was a slightly awkward moment and he let it pass.

"So what do people do for recreation?" he asked. DeKooning flicked the ash off his cigarette.

"Well, it's an island, water sports are pretty big." DeKooning answered.

Luther noted he wasn't making much headway and decided to try a different tack. Looking to the narrow channel of water that passed to the west of what had been Cleague's shed he asked, "What's that water there, is that a river?' He wasn't being stupid, he really didn't know.

"No," DeKooning answered. "It's a naturally-occurring raceway for the current that runs north to south. The Corps of Engineers dredged it out during the war. This island was originally a peninsula. The Corps dredged out the boat channel that now separates the island from the mainland. They also dredged out the raceway to facilitate supply deliveries to the warehouses that lined it. The ordnance was kept in underground bunkers on the west side. For every gun battery on the west side of the island there was at least one warehouse on either side of the raceway. This place used to be packed with warehouses up and down the road." DeKooning indicated the phantom buildings with his chin. "Most of the warehouse buildings were dummies...empty shells made from plywood. You never knew which ones had anything in them. They dug the channel out all the way to the north end of the peninsula. The only people that use it now are kids trying to catch crabs."

Luther asked, "Aren't there any fish in it?"

"Not really, some bottom feeders, eels mostly, but nothing worth eating. It's just brackish water, stagnant for the most part. It ebbs and flows with the tide but it don't really get much circulation with the Sound water, I guess. Anyway, most fish don't like it." DeKooning answered.

"Then there's not a lot of boat traffic in it?" Luther guessed.

DeKooning thought a second then shook his head. "Not really. Once in a while, somebody in a rowboat or something." Luther asked the next question and watched the reaction with as much or more interest than the verbal response it elicited.

"Did you know this Peter Cleague?"

DeKooning took the cigarette out of his mouth, looked at the end of it and pinched the tip just below the ash between his thumb and forefinger. Leaning against the car and standing on one foot, he ground the lit end of the cigarette into the sole of his boot. He pinched the cigarette between his fingers and thumb and rolled the paper cylinder back and forth, letting the remnant tobacco fall from the paper to scatter in the breeze.

DeKooning pushed himself off the side of his vehicle, straightened his back and stood squarely with his feet shoulder-width apart. He put the cigarette butt into his jacket pocket, looked Luther straight in the eye with a level gaze.

"Yeah, I knew him."

He had his left hand in his windbreaker pocket; his right hand remained at his side. "You ready?" he asked Luther.

"Yeah, sure." Luther answered with practiced nonchalance. DeKooning withdrew the car keys from his jacket pocket with his left hand, turned toward the Expedition and got in, securing his seat belt from unconscious habit.

Luther walked around the back of the vehicle to the passenger's door and got in. DeKooning started the engine, put the transmission in gear, and then sat there with his foot on the brake. He looked at Luther without expression, waiting. Luther was getting a little confused by this guy at this point.

"What?" he asked.

"Where to?" DeKooning responded.

"Oh." Luther thought a moment. "Are there other houses on the island like Cleague's?"

"Yeah, there are a few more houses between here and town."

"Can we go see one of them?"

"I suppose, are you going to want to go inside?"

"I don't think so," Luther replied.

"OK." the deputy answered.

They were under way and headed north towards town the instant Luther secured his three-point seat restraint. The deputy drove away from the crime scene tape and the flatbed as the recovery detail loaded the observer's corpse from OP-5 onto the truck in front of the shambles of Cleague's house without ceremony. DeKooning picked up the microphone to his vehicle radio and spoke, "Two Adam Four to dispatch." The Sheriff's Department's dispatcher came back, "Dispatch to two Adam four, go ahead."

"I'm taking the Federal investigator to 115 Island Highway. Would you call the occupant and tell him we're there to look at his house but that we do not need to go inside, please?" Dispatch responded, "Ten-four."

"What was that about?" Luther asked.

"People around here might be a little jumpy after last night. I don't want to get shot." DeKooning drove north past the GP tent and remaindered BPS agents milling about, to another half mile or so until they came to the next house.

As they rode north Luther asked, "Are these houses left over from the war?" DeKooning nodded.

"Yeah, after the base was decommissioned they reverted back to the tribe. Most folks that live out here lease their houses from the Nishtillamish."

DeKooning explained how the tribe and the government were in mutual and prolonged litigation over the ownership of the land. The government asserted eminent domain and the tribe invoked the treaty obligations of the United States government.

As Luther followed the story it occurred to him that this would have made Cleague's presence either somewhat desirable or extremely unenviable depending on how badly the Federal Government wanted exclusive use of the property. As DeKooning described it, the tribe had taken the US Government, Executive Branch, to court over the matter and a resolution would not be had any time soon, probably not during the lifetime of anyone that actually lived on the island. As a National Historic site it fell under the auspices of the Department of the Interior, the parent agency of the Bureau of Public Safety, as well as the Bureau of Indian Affairs. Luther scribbled the questions in his notebook –*"Did Government want Cleague off property, why?"* Luther realized that when/if this case ever came to court, the sitting administration, the de facto defendant in the law suit, would be generations removed from the administration that had actually caused the suit to be taken. "What a fucking mess," Luther said to himself in a quiet way. DeKooning grunted agreement.

54

The house was less than twenty yards off the road and Luther could see it clearly from the car. They got out but remained at the side of the road. It was a simple wood frame structure. The front of the house was white clapboard with green trim on the shutters. Luther imagined that Cleague's house had been very similar if not the same. A few steps up to a front porch, a screen door flanked by a window on both sides, and an asphalt shingle roof with a pipe—maybe a vent for a heat source. On the south side of the house Luther noticed a large oblong tank. He asked DeKooning, "...what's that tank?"

"Heating oil." DeKooning replied simply.

"Is it combustible?"

"Yeah, it's a lot like diesel."

Luther mused silently that would explain the accelerant on the south side of Cleague's house. If an explosive had been placed around the perimeter of the base of the house, as Luther believed had been done to the Quonset hut across the street from Cleague's house, the force of the explosion might have been enough to rupture the tank.

"What are those tanks made of?" Luther asked.

DeKooning fished a cigarette out of his windbreaker and lit it, then answered, "Galvanized steel." Luther did not remember seeing a fuel tank on the south side of Cleague's house.

"Do you remember seeing a fuel tank like that at Cleague's house this morning?" The deputy considered the question a moment and then answered.

"No, I don't."

Luther dug out his memo pad and wrote...*what happened to the fuel tank? Was the explosive force from inside the house enough to rupture the tank?* Luther put the notebook away and walked the span of the front of the house while the deputy enjoyed his cigarette. Standing at the northwest corner of the house Luther could just see into the backyard and tried to visualize the scene at Cleague's house the previous evening.

The Deuce-and-a-half trucks with the big search lights had been left parked in the sand bordering what would have been Cleague's backyard. Luther looked across the street to where the Quonset hut would have been. *Cleague had seen it all...from inside the Quonset hut. That's the place from where he shot the dead guy in the middle of the road in front of his house.*

They got back in the car. Luther said, "Let's go back to the house" and then asked "...how well did you know him?"

"I knew him well enough to call him a friend. When civilians were still allowed to shoot in competitions and stuff, I used to see him at some of the matches." This raised Luther's interest a peg.

"Really, was he a very good shot?"

DeKooning gave a little shrug. "He was all right. Average probably; he usually finished in the middle of the pack."

"What kind of competitions were these?" Luther asked.

"Oh, different kinds of things—bowling pin matches mostly."

Luther didn't understand "...bowling pins?"

"Yeah." The deputy explained, "You set five bowling pins one foot from the front edge of a sheet of plywood; eight feet by four feet. You stand thirty feet away. The object is to knock each bowling pin off the table in the shortest possible time. The shooter with the fastest time wins," DeKooning concluded.

Luther was not familiar with this particular use of a firearm...or a bowling pin for that matter. Since it wasn't done any more it was totally irrelevant, but arcane subjects fascinated Luther.

He asked, "What kind of gun would someone use for this type of thing?"

"Whatever you want," DeKooning said. "But the advantage went to guys shooting the larger calibers. Guys shooting .45 autos usually did best."

Luther thought he understood and then asked, "These were handguns?"

The deputy kept his head and eyes straight to the front as he responded, "Yes."

"What kind of handgun did Cleague like to shoot?" Luther was fishing now, pretty sure this conversation might give him some insight into the sick, paranoid, mindset of one Peter Cleague. DeKooning gave him a brief sidelong glance.

"Cleague was a throw-back."

"A what?" Luther asked.

It started raining again and DeKooning had to talk over the rhythmic thump and whir of the windshield wiper motor.

"He thought people got too spun up in the game aspect of it. He was never really that competitive about it, but some people would put a lot of money into getting their guns tricked out just for shooting bowling pins," DeKooning replied.

"So what did he shoot?" Luther insisted.

"Cleague shot a revolver."

"What kind of advantage did that give him?"

"It didn't. He liked to keep it light, he was just out to have a good time."

Luther could not fathom it.

"Then why do it?"

"Because he liked revolvers," DeKooning answered, matter-of-fact.

"No, I mean why shoot bowling pins at all?"

They had arrived back at the house. DeKooning stopped the vehicle and put it in park and turned off the engine.

"Because it was fun."

"Oh." That had never occurred to Luther.

Luther stood on the road in front of the debris of Peter Cleague's house. The flatbed had come and gone and the three forensic technicians had moved on to another part of the property. Luther looked back across the street at the wreckage of the Quonset hut. He turned back again to the house before moving to his right, south, in the direction of the bridge. He walked to the south border of the property marked by a lightweight wood slatted fence. He followed the fence line due east a few yards to where he guessed the fuel tank would have been. There was a badly seared portion of the shingled roof; the visible remnant of that section of the wall was almost charcoal. That section of the fence was knocked down, the individual wood slats splayed out southward and partially burned to charcoal. It stopped raining but the air was still heavy with humidity.

Luther wondered if the force of the explosion would have been enough to propel the fuel tank out into the grass for any distance. He started walking south a few yards following a trail of charred grass when he caught a glimpse of something rusty in the foliage. He walked over to it and saw that a good size hole had been ripped into one side of the fuel tank; the two ends bent toward each other almost forming a 90-degree angle. The grass around it had burned in a rough circle. He guessed the fuel tank to be about a hundred feet or so from the house. The ground had been indented form the impact from the fuel tank. Apparently it had landed with some force.

He surveyed the area from where he stood. Just a few yards to the east he saw where the grass ended and the beach began. He turned around and looked at the house again. He couldn't see DeKooning anywhere; *he must have stayed at the car* Luther thought.

If the dead BPS man in front of Cleague's house had been a sentry or an observer, where had he come from? The assault had been mounted from the north side of the house. Luther was standing on the south side of the house. So if there was an observation post, and there had to be, it was probably somewhere to the south of the house.

Luther walked southward. The weather was starting to get warmer. He took note of the shift in the terrain; with no measurable change in elevation there were an awful lot of furrows, dips and rises. The knee-high sea grass made it all look flat from a distance. The stunted shrubbery tangled underfoot. What a great place for an OP; then remembering the dog in Cleague's backyard he considered... or a sniper hide. He was starting to sweat under his suit jacket, and his dress shirt, and his tie. Walking roughly in a straight line, varying little from left to right, he noticed an area to his left, more toward the beach, where some vegetation had been buried in sand as if the sand had welled out from a crater. He approached more out of curiosity than due diligence because it just looked odd.

First he heard the flies. As he approached he instinctively slowed his pace, then the stench hit him. He reflexively vomited the contents of his stomach: coffee and no breakfast. He involuntarily gagged as he struggled to inhale air that was not tainted with the fetid odor of decaying flesh. He walked west into the slight breeze until he was able to breathe. He was shaking from the spontaneous convulsions of all his abdominal muscles in contraction and began to rub his belly to relax them. The odor had tripped his gag reflex. The body in the middle of the road with its head blown open didn't quite stink this much.

He was able to stand upright after a few minutes and looked around. He judged himself to be about a hundred yards south of the house. *How in the hell could Cleague get this far south of his house from the Quonset hut with nobody seeing him?* Luther steeled himself and walked back to the OP. The hide was more or less in line with the back wall of Cleague's house. Walking clockwise around the hide Luther noticed something gleaming, he almost stepped on it. Bending to examine it he saw that it was a fired brass cartridge case in .223. Donning a pair of latex gloves from his jacket pocket, he picked it up and examined the head stamp: Federal Cartridge. He put the cartridge case back where he found it.

Keeping his eyes trained on the hide trying to understand what he was seeing his foot caught on something and he went flying forward onto his face into the still wet sea grass—the saw tooth edges scraped his face. He had stumbled over another corpse. Luther wondered what kind of lunatic had wrought this sort of carnage as he leapt to his feet and propelled himself away from this latest remnant of pervasive death. He walked a few yards upwind and stopped. In the course of his lifetime he had seen many things but this degree of callous disregard for human life was bringing him to his limit. He turned around, facing the corpses, and committed the site to memory.

55

Luther stood west of the dug-out hide, and saw how Cleague could get to the first OP without having been seen. On the north perimeter of the hide, was a blackened area in the sand. The mine had an olive drab plastic casing and was supported by a set of inverted "V" shaped wire legs dug into the sand amongst the weeds. Luther knew that the words "Front Toward Enemy" would have been embossed on the front cover, which, now, after the fact, was no longer present.

The mine measured eight and a half inches long, by about three and a quarter inches high by about an inch and a half deep and would have weighed about a pound and a half prior to detonation. Cleague had used an explosive with a directional blast...he had used a Claymore mine.

The body of the observer lay prone, oriented due north. Most of its head was gone, its back awash in beads and puddles of gray and red and covered in flies. Luther looked up again. The body he had tripped over apparently wasn't killed in the direct blast, as the man had been able to crawl some distance south of the hide before bleeding to death. It's head lay sideways— it's face gone. The sniper's rifle trailed behind him attached by its sling to a point just above his left biceps.

The issued Remington 700 bolt action rifle with the MacMillan stock and the Leupold scope lay in the sand. The spotting scope had been propelled south, now just visible in the grass, its objective lens oriented upward toward the ubiquitous cloud cover. Still wearing the latex gloves, Luther squatted, balanced on the balls of his feet, and picked up the rifle. Keeping the muzzle oriented down at the dirt, he carefully lifted the bolt handle and gently pulled the bolt to the rear, partially extracting the cartridge case from the chamber. Satisfied, he pushed the bolt home, re-chambering the cartridge. This was where the shot had been made that took out the dog. *What the hell happened here last night?* These guys had demonstrated excellent training and had been issued excellent gear. At this point in his investigation John Luther suspected that judgment, planning and leadership was sorely lacking.

Luther walked directly west— straight to the road, he had to get away from the stink and the flies and the death. Luther was beginning to get an image of Cleague as being capable of inhuman savagery. Maybe the raid had not been such a bad idea after all. "You rotten bastard," he said out loud as he walked due west directly to the road. He would call the forensics team from the deputy's car.

After a few yards he was just able to see the crest of the shallow berm dug out from the sand—another OP/sniper hide. It was on a line with the first one. He took a moment and willed himself to turn around and look. He made sure he was upwind before he did so. He had walked west. It had in fact been a sniper hide. Sandbags had been deployed along the north perimeter of the dugout hide. It was directly in line with the west wall, or front porch, of Cleague's house. It was empty. Luther took a knee at the west edge of the hide and noted the Remington 700 barreled action on the Macmillan stock, with the Leupold M1 scope like the one he had just left. He saw the Zeiss spotting scope. He also noted the candy bar wrappers and the Styrofoam cups in casual disarray festooned about the hide. *Professional gear for professional operators, he thought.* But no operators to be seen. He looked at the house. The view of the porch was partially obscured by the juniper bushes that lined the slatted fence from the front of the house to the road.

Luther was pretty sure this would have been the assigned post for the guy he saw earlier in the middle of the road in front of Cleague's house. *But what about the other guy? SOP stipulated two man teams.* He thought.

John Luther walked west back out onto the Island Highway and then north to the deputy's car, removing his latex gloves and stuffing them back into one of his pockets.

DeKooning, leaning against his driver's door regarded Luther with an observant eye; now was not the time for cracking wise. Luther was a wreck—his suit trousers were covered with wet sand from the knees down and his face was scratched. As he approached, DeKooning saw that Luther's eyes were bloodshot: his coat, shirt and tie disheveled, his face pale and mottled with red splotches and a look of intense dread. If Luther had not just seen a ghost he had seen something very close.

"You all right?" DeKooning asked. With barely a nod Luther responded.

"Give me your radio." DeKooning recoiled from Luther's breath.

"Aw man, did you throw up?"

"Yes. Give me your radio, please." Luther was clearly not in the mood for cheerful banter. DeKooning dug in the car for a second and handed his portable hand held radio to Luther who took it without comment and walked away. DeKooning wasn't able to hear him. DeKooning had to wonder if Luther had found Cleague's body but knew better than to ask. After a few moments Luther returned and handed the portable radio to the deputy. DeKooning took the hand-held radio, opened the rear cargo door to the Expedition, threw it in the back of the truck, and shut the hatch. He'd deal with it later.

Luther wanted to see the rest of the area that comprised the crime scene. *Do it and be done with it*, he thought.

"Wasn't there a bridge damaged somewhere?" Luther asked.

"Apparently so," DeKooning responded. "It isn't there anymore." DeKooning's sense of humor was wearing thin on Luther. He felt really tired, he just wanted this to be over.

"Let's go."

They headed south. Luther wanted to know what kind of man this Peter Cleague was.

"What did he do for a living?"

DeKooning replied conversationally, "Different stuff. Sometimes he wrote magazine articles."

"What else did he do?" Luther asked.

"Sometimes he'd get a gig as a bodyguard. I guess he was pretty good but he said it was a feast or famine kind of business. Sometimes he did seasonal maintenance at the marina part-time," DeKooning replied.

"Anything else?" Luther asked. They had arrived at the bridge. DeKooning stopped the car, put it in park and turned off the engine.

"Well," DeKooning shifted in his seat slightly so he could look Luther in the eye.

"The way he explained it to me once, was that from time to time he would teach at one of the boutique gun schools. Nothing regular, you know, just when they asked for him."

Luther started to get impatient. "Well... What did he teach?"

DeKooning dropped all pretense of stoicism and clearly enjoyed the moment.

"He taught his students how to keep themselves alive with a handgun. The same exact course he used to teach at the

Federal Law Enforcement Training Center at Glynco, Georgia when he worked for the State Department."

Luther got out of the car and looked at the remains of the bridge. *Holy shit!* He thought. *Glynco! He fucking' taught officer survival tactics at Glynco!* Luther was ready to charge Speeks and everybody in his chain of command with negligent homicide for the deaths of the BPS agents. When he heard the deputy shut his door he turned to him.

"Do you know if he had any military service?"

DeKooning paused a moment as he was kind of fuzzy on this part of Cleague's history—it was before they had met.

"I think he was in the Marines."

"Perfect! Just fucking perfect!" Luther said as he stomped off alone toward the bridge that wasn't there anymore. DeKooning fished out another cigarette as he regarded the retreating figure with curiosity. "What a peculiar man," he said to no one in particular.

56

The bridge had spanned a distance of maybe fifty yards although the boat channel which it spanned was not more than thirty yards if that much. A chunk of asphalt about fifty feet wide was missing from the center of the bridge. Support structures stuck up out of the water on either side of the channel like broken fingers. Luther asked one of the forensic technicians who the senior technician in charge was. The young man indicated someone standing knee deep in the water on the far side of the channel that seemed to be talking on the radio.

"What's his name?" The younger agent replied, "Coleman," and went on about his business. Luther returned to the deputy's car and asked DeKooning for the radio back. DeKooning retrieved it from the back of the vehicle and gave it to Luther. Luther took it without comment and walked back to the bridge.

Ensuring it was on the proper frequency he got Coleman's attention and arranged to meet him. The Coast Guard had provided support in that it had ferried injured agents from the island to the waiting aid cars on the mainland side of the boat channel the night before. A small boat unit crew had remained in support of the technicians that were trying to piece together what had happened.

Luther walked to the edge of the water and climbed down through the rather large rocks that formed the embankment of the channel proper. He was assisted into the boat by the attending crew and was transported to the far side of the channel. After disembarking the Coast Guard boat, he approached Coleman and introduced himself. Coleman replied in kind and quickly briefed him on what they had found so far. A body had been found but it was still under water. The timbers that supported the bridge had been blown with shape charges from under the water line. The divers were still working on recording what they had found before they started retrieving anything from under water. Coleman stated that their priority would be getting the BPS agent, as well as any others that may be there, out as intact as possible, but the elements had already taken their toll in the twelve hours or so that he or they had been under water.

Coleman also informed him that they had located a kayak, apparently Cleague's, in the raceway about a mile north of the boat channel that had been abandoned.

"How do you know that it was Cleague's?" Luther asked.

Coleman answered, "Because it was floating keel up and had enough holes in it to make it look like a colander." Coleman also informed Luther that they had found another body at that time. Floating face down in the briny water, its throat was cut from just under the left mandible, through the esophagus, through to the right carotid artery. Luther immediately asked if an APB had been put out for Cleague.

"I don't know Mr. Luther; my concern is the forensic investigation. Now if you will pardon me, I'll get back to it." Coleman said.

Luther left the man to do his work. At least he seemed to have some sense of what it was.

He returned to the island by the Coast Guard and made his way back to DeKooning. In the course of their conversations something had tugged at the back of Luther's mind. He asked DeKooning the question trying not to make it an accusation.

"You seem to know quite a bit about Peter Cleague. What was your relationship to him?" DeKooning did not try to evade or misdirect. He simply answered the question that was asked.

"He was my friend."

Luther needed to determine whether DeKooning had helped his friend Cleague. This whole area from Cleague's house to the bridge was an ambush site and it was very extensive for one man to have executed alone. Did DeKooning help Cleague plan it? Did DeKooning help Cleague carry it out? How much information had DeKooning given Cleague about the raid on his house? How did DeKooning know in advance? Luther had to make a decision, either charge DeKooning with complicity and/or aiding and abetting a felon or not. But what Luther knew at this time did not give him sufficient cause to suspect that DeKooning had been involved. They had shot a few matches together; maybe they had an occasional cup of coffee together, so what?

"When was the last time you saw him?" Luther asked.

"Yesterday morning," the deputy replied. All kinds of red flags were going up in Luther's mind.

"What did you talk about?"

DeKooning sighed slightly and recalled. "He'd been having trouble with his dog running away. He asked me to keep an eye out for him."

"That's all?"

"Yeah." DeKooning replied matter-of-fact.

Luther then asked directly, "Did you tell him anything about last night's activity?"

DeKooning had just about enough. "Well, other than seeing about a hundred cars with US government license plates in town yesterday, I didn't know anything about 'last night's activity'."

That was it, no embellishment and no omission.

Luther still didn't have anything. They rode back the mile

and a quarter to the GP tent in silence. Something still bothered Luther about Cleague and DeKooning; he just didn't know what it was yet.

57

John Luther walked into the GP tent that served as a temporary command post for the forensic examination of the crime scene. He asked for and was immediately handed Speeks' after-action report. Heavily embellished in the writing style of Cover Your Own Ass, it basically stated that the raid did not go as planned and listed myriad excuses why. It did however mention the immediate disposition of the TV news crew, which nearly caused Luther to have a heart attack on the spot. Although the Second Amendment to the Constitution of the United States was apparently scheduled to be the subject of a Constitutional Convention pending repeal after the Congress re-convened from its summer recess, as far as Luther knew the Fourth and Fourteenth amendments were still valid. Luther was able to determine that the news crew had in fact been held at Saint Joseph's Hospital in Bellingham, incommunicado, since about eleven PM the previous evening. Luther then made a couple of phone calls and telephonically petitioned a justice of the U.S. District Court for the Western District of Washington to issue a subpoena and notice of restraint to everyone in the news crew pending formal investigation by the US Attorney General's Office. Luther anticipated it would be somewhat difficult to explain why people who were not in any way remotely injured during the previous evening's failed raid were required to stay for observation, but at least the gag order would theoretically keep them quiet.

In the meantime their equipment van, hardware, cameras, audiotape and any other "evidence" would be summarily seized pending review of the DOJ investigation. *Good luck with that*, Luther thought, t*hat stuff is probably already on the air.* He needed to see what the film crew had and advise the

Attorney General. The disposition of any material evidence the TV news crew may have had would be up to the AG.

Luther then called Headquarters, Department of Justice, Washington DC, Office of Budget and Procurement, and arranged for office space in an adjunct Federal Government Administrative building somewhere reasonably close. It happened to be Bellingham, Washington. He then called the Office of Personnel and Administration and arranged for: A) copies of his direct appointment from the US Attorney General sent to all BPS field offices and other departments from whom he would require assistance and or support, and, B) tasking of twelve available agents from whatever field offices had them to orchestrate this investigation, he simply couldn't do it by himself.

Scanning the interior of the GP tent Luther caught sight of a rather young (they all were anymore) female agent of the BPS desperately trying to give the appearance of being productive by moving piles of paper around on a field desk and back again. Her naive nature notwithstanding, he had to use the tools at hand.

"Excuse me young lady, what's your name?"

"BPS Agent Joan Glyndon, sir."

"Were you involved in the operation last night Agent Glyndon?" BPS Agent Joan Glyndon didn't have a clue as to who this guy might be but she did know he rode on helicopters with the Attorney General of the United States. Deference would be prudent at this point.

"No sir, I was sent out here this morning from Seattle."

"Good, you work for me now. My name is John Luther and I was appointed this morning by the Attorney General to conduct the investigation into last night's...event." Luther pulled the word out of the air for lack of a better term.

"I want you to contact DOD and acquire any and all records of military service for one Peter Cleague. Try Headquarters Marine Corps first."

"Yes, sir, sir how do I do that?" *Cute, interesting eyes, and dumber than a bag of hammers*, he thought.

"Are you a college graduate Agent Glyndon?" He wasn't abrasive and he wasn't sarcastic. It was a straight question.

"Yes, sir." She said.

"Did you attend the basic course at FLETC, Glynco, Georgia?" Luther asked.

"Yes sir." She said.

"Very well, carry on." He made to exit the tent and had another thought.

"Also, contact the IRS and get the tax returns for Peter Cleague from 113 Island Highway, Port Cullis, Washington, over the past ten years." He told her.

"Yes, sir." She said.

FLETC, Federal Law Enforcement Training Center. Luther thought a moment about what DeKooning had told him.

"Agent Glyndon?"

"Yes, sir?"

"Call Glynco and get the dates from when Cleague was a student and also the dates from when he taught there. Get a list of the courses he taught and copies of the syllabi if they're still available." This request took her by surprise and it caused her deferential tact to slip for just a moment.

"You mean he was one of us?" She asked, realizing her breach of protocol too late.

"No. He was never one of us. Make the calls please." He said. With that he went back outside to see if he could find

DeKooning. Luther needed to go look at the kayak that had been turned into a colander.

"Yes, sir." She said.

58

The office was located in a Federal administrative services building with an alphabet's worth of bureaucratic tenants. It was a couple of blocks over from the Whatcom County courthouse in Bellingham, Washington. It really hadn't been all that difficult to appropriate the necessary office equipment; John Luther had carte blanche guaranteed by the Attorney General himself.

Luther preferred an open bay type of arrangement where he could visually locate people without having to go through an assistant, or physically negotiate a bunch of office dividers. His desk was a very basic—haze gray type of affair that one saw in any number of government surplus outlets. The way he looked at it all he needed was a flat surface—a sheet of plywood and two saw horses would have been sufficient. He had located himself in one corner of the building by the window, although now he had the blinds drawn.

He began his case narrative from all the things he had noted and discovered on the island. In his report to the Attorney General he would list all the pertinent facts, his opinions of what the facts indicated, and draw logical conclusions. After the AG had read Luther's findings, opinions, and conclusions, he would then make a decision regarding the appointment of a special counsel.

Luther stared at the monitor taking in the final bit of information on Cleague, Peter, NMI (No Middle Initial). He wasn't sure he believed the word-picture that had been painted for him in the personnel reports.

Headquarters Marine Corps had directed BPS Agent Glyndon's request for Cleague's military records to Marine Corps Reserve's Records Division in Kansas City. As a result

Luther now scanned the Officer Qualification Record of a young lieutenant that didn't particularly seem to be destined to set the world on fire or play the role of domestic terrorist.

Cleague's active duty term was served from 1979 to 1982. Cleague's fitness reports for this period of time reflected mediocre tolerance on the part of his reporting seniors: average or above average. Observations, opinions, and conclusions: "...this Marine officer marches to the sound of a drummer I have not yet been able to locate." Question: "How would you regard this man's presence in your command during time of war?" Answer: "Be willing." Well that was hardly a sweeping testimony to this guy's military acumen was it? Luther considered this line of investigation might turn out to be a bit of a red herring. Cleague was a puzzle.

He was passed over for promotion to Captain and then he mustered out. Three months later he showed up in a Marine Reserve Company, Fourth Reconnaissance Battalion, 4th Marine Division, San Antonio TX. "Here we go." Luther muttered to his computer monitor. Cleague joined the Marine Corps Reserve Reconnaissance Battalion in July 1982 and, after passing the screening test, he was initially assigned to Company "C" as a platoon commander (tentative-conditional). Cleague was temporarily reassigned to Active Duty for Training and sent to Jump School at Ft Benning, GA, while waiting for a slot in Reconnaissance Indoctrination Platoon at either Camp LeJeune or Camp Pendleton. He was 26 years old. Luther mused all of Cleague's peers in jump school would have been nineteen or in their early twenties. That would have made it tough on him, more-so considering the fact that he was an officer. At that point in his life he must have been in pretty good shape; Luther knew from his own career in the Army that a tour with a Marine Reconnaissance Unit (if only by reputation) was no walk in the park. A Navy

SEAL had once made the comment to Luther that a "special operator" was just that. There were no "Special Units." It was the same animal be he in the Rangers, The Green Berets, the SEALS, Marine Recon, or the PJ's (Air Force). But not all organizations had the same mission statement, or the same budget, for that matter. The Marine Corps customarily got what was left over from the Navy's budget be it materiel, facilities or training—the historical fact was they always got hind tit.

After graduating Jump School, Cleague returned to the Reserve unit in Texas until a training slot came open for Navy dive school; nothing all that involved, essentially a three week course in basic Scuba qualification. Cleague returned to the reserve company for the duration of his tour and continued to wait for a slot in RIP. He was passed over for promotion to captain again—odd considering how much money had been spent on his training. Cleague stayed in the Recon Company for three years and then resigned from the Reserves in 1985. *He was tired of waiting*, Luther thought. Everything Cleague learned would have been OJT—on-the-job-training. Maybe he had a good platoon sergeant.

Curious, Luther noted, the junior enlisted men in Cleague's platoon always scored highest in the company in the annual General Subjects Test. Cleague's platoon always fielded a squad for the Annual Marine Infantry Skills competition at Quantico. Cleague's platoon consistently scored well with Inspector/Instructor evaluators during their annual two-week training assignments. It seemed to be a pretty good success ratio for somebody to be passed over for promotion twice. He left the reserves as a platoon commander in 1985 with the rank of first Lieutenant. After six years he should have been a Captain. No wonder he got out, but there was nothing specific in his OQR that Luther could find that explained why he was consistently passed over for promotion. Another puzzle, maybe he just pissed people off. *Problems with authority figures?* Luther mused.

Luther was getting tired of staring at the screen. His eyes burned. And the back of his head ached. He was blinking a lot. He got up and walked over to the coffee maker. He lifted the carafe from the burner to eye level: clear as mud. It must have been sitting on the burner for the better part of the day. He poured his cup and set the carafe back on the burner. He checked his watch. It had been three hours since he sat down at the computer. Time was getting away from him. He walked back over to the desk and looked over Cleague's evaluation reports that Agent Glyndon had obtained from the State Department.

In 1985 Peter Cleague was admitted to the Bureau of Diplomatic Security of the Department of State. He must have found his calling in life because here his star started to shine. Cleague had merited above-average reviews, observed while assigned to various protective details within Continental United States and abroad, from reporting seniors. Luther came across a certified original copy of a letter of commendation from the Director of the FBI, for individual performance in a joint operation in New York City from sometime in 1987.

"...This individual seems to excel in moments of great stress exemplifying an uncommon presence of mind and has demonstrated an outstanding capacity in CQB (Close Quarters Battle)...should have a rewarding career and a very bright future ahead of him..." signed, Judge George Hillman, Director.

59

Hmmmm. Luther remembered hearing about that one but thought it was just a rumor. So this was the guy. Luther's estimation of this character's potential was starting to shift somewhat. As well as Luther could recall the incident: an attempt on the lives of the participants of a peace negotiation from Northern Ireland, the Irish Republic and Great Britain while meeting in Manhattan had been discovered and foiled prior to the execution. Apparently it had been designed to be a very grand affair...very dramatic.

After that assignment, Cleague was assigned to the Diplomatic Security Office, U.S. Mission, Peru. In spite of the war on drugs, this assignment was apparently pretty uneventful. From there he was sent to the Federal Law Enforcement Training Center, Glynco Ga. as an instructor. He primarily taught small arms training, but was assigned as adjunct instructor for protective security procedures, officer survival, and tactics.

Luther was incredulous, how could the BPS plan a raid on this guy on a grand scale and not check out his background? This bothered Luther. He could not help but think that an oversight this blatant could not have been an oversight. *Could it have been intentional? That didn't make sense. Why kill any BPS agents in a vain attempt to make a show of arresting an ostensible malcontent?* Luther noted he was still thinking in terms of an unsubstantiated number, nobody yet knew how many agents had been lost. They knew how many people were unaccounted for, they just hadn't found all the remains yet. He was waiting for a forensics report. And where was the crime in being a malcontent anyway? Maybe Luther just didn't have enough pieces of this puzzle yet.

After his instructor gig at Glynco, Peter Cleague's next assignment was in the Middle East as an assistant to the Regional Security Officer for the American Embassy. Red flags started popping up all over Cleague's personnel file. At this point in his career Cleague's file contained official letters questioning his supervisory competence. *Not a good thing if one is the assistant to the regional supervisor of all State Department security officers in a given part of the world...like the Middle East,* Luther mused. Letters asserted inappropriate behavior in Cleague's personal relations with the indigenous population but never stipulated what those indiscretions had been or with whom. There were also letters that asserted Cleague's failures to follow established security procedures but neglected to enumerate what those failures had been. This did not square with his assignment of having taught security procedures at Glynco.

Luther looked at the date of these reports and something tugged at his memory that he simply could not retrieve right now, something about the US Embassy and the USAID officer. No matter, he'd think of it later.

Not quite expecting it, Luther then came upon Cleague's letter of resignation. Forwarded without comment from the Ambassador and approved. That was slightly out of the ordinary. Here was this rising star in the Bureau of Diplomatic Security particularly singled out by the then Director of the FBI for competence and clear mindedness under extreme stress and all of a sudden he starts getting disciplinary letters put into his file. Why?

Cleague had been pressured to quit. Why? Luther had a very hard time believing that so much acrimony could have been developed between the Ambassador and one of his security chiefs. *This had to come from somebody inside the*

*Beltway. Who, and Why? And why had he been of interest to
the Bureau of Public Safety to begin with?* Luther wondered.

Luther had to go to Washington DC to brief the Attorney
General and then get back to the Department of Justice to
interview Speeks, the raid commander, and read the
surveillance reports that had to have been filed on Cleague
during the weeks prior to the raid. And it would be nice to
spend one week at home in his own bed in Northern Virginia.
He copied Cleague's records onto a flash drive, logged off,
and secured his computer. He locked up the small safe he had
procured for office documents, and put the appropriate
handwritten notes, his case narrative, and the flash drive in
his brief case and locked his desk drawer.

"Agent Glyndon!" He didn't yell but since they were the
only two in the office she couldn't pretend as if she hadn't
heard.

"Yes sir?" she replied.

"I'm on my way to the airport. I should be back in a few
days. In the mean time, track down the names of everybody
that Cleague served with in the Marine Reserve Company in
Texas. Get their names, addresses, and phone numbers,
please."

"Yes sir," she said hurriedly scribbling down his orders.
"Continue with the tasking files and distribute them when the
other agents arrive." He went on while donning his suit
jacket. The tasking files were a list of doorbells to ring and
interviews to conduct, basically a lot of legwork that Luther
could not handle by himself. They had been broken down
geographically and evenly divided by the number of people
Luther had tasked to assist him.

"Yes sir," she replied.

"When that preliminary forensics report gets here notify me immediately, show it to no one, do not read it, and lock it up in the safe please," he went on.

"Yes sir." She was beginning to get a little peeved.

"And get the air conditioner fixed." And with that he was out the door.

She was slightly out of breath. Luther's rat-a-tat-tat list of staccato orders set her on a slow boil. She joined the Bureau to be a field agent, not a secretary and now she was working for someone whose social demeanor had been formed during the McCarthy era.

Still she didn't mind having been assigned to the office of a Special Investigator. It would be recorded in her personnel file as a joint operation with the Justice Department that could only make her look good at promotion time.

As of now she was the only person in an office with an unlimited budget and absolutely no one to be looking over her shoulder, until the other agents started showing up. Maybe at least then she could get out and do some field work. Until then she could kick back a little and take it easy. What the hell, why not go down to the snack bar for lunch? With that thought in mind she grabbed her wallet out of her shoulder bag and was out the door—the door to the office with classified material dealing directly with national security, which she left wide open.

60

When Joan Glyndon returned to her office, there was a man sitting behind Luther's desk. She had her head down looking at the National Enquirer as she walked through the door and didn't see him.

"Good afternoon," a voice said, not at all unkindly. She snapped her head up and simultaneously threw her newspaper up in the air as her hands clutched in front of her chest in a sympathetic response (fear). She had only met this man once but knew his face from his picture, which was posted in every BPS field office in the country.

"GGGGGood afternoon, sir," she managed to get out, eventually.

"Have a seat Agent Glyndon, I think we should have a little chat," the man said. She took her seat by her desk and expected a royal ass chewing for leaving the office.

"You know my name, sir?"

"Why certainly Agent Glyndon, it's part of my job. May I call you Joan?" The fact that she had left her checkbook in her shoulder bag hadn't hurt either.

She mutely nodded in the affirmative. Henry Caleb carried on amiably.

"You see Joan I try to get to all the field offices from time to time to see how things are, gauge the morale, try to get to know the troops out in the field as it were. So how's it going?"

"Uh, fine sir," she replied respectfully.

"Luther isn't being too hard on you, is he?"

"No sir, not at all."

"Good, glad to hear it. By the way, where is Mr. Luther?" he asked.

"He left for D.C. about an hour and a half ago sir," she answered.

"D.C.? What for?" he asked.

"I believe he has a meeting with the Attorney General, sir, an interim report or something." She shrugged. "That's all I know, sir."

"You know," Director Caleb opined, "It's just like him to take a relatively new agent, such as yourself for example, assign her to a major investigation with all sorts of National Security implications, and walk out on her, leaving her to fend for herself." The Director could see that the initial shock of his unannounced visit had not quite worn off yet. "Oh yeah, it's true" He carried on quite conversationally, "...that's the way those DOJ assholes are." Pausing for effect, "You mark my words," punctuating the air with his index finger. "You'll see it over and over again throughout your career. And you know what Joan? That's really what I wanted to talk to you about...your career."

Oh shit, here it comes. She thought.

"You know, it's no accident that you were assigned to this investigation," He went on very confidentially.

"Really?" She almost squeaked. She thought she was assigned to it because she was the first person Luther saw back in the field tent on that island.

"Absolutely." He assured her. "I don't know how much you've been told about this case but this is pretty big stuff. Like I said, major National Security implications. Mind you, this isn't just about some gun nut in a beach house out in Hell's half acre, making pipe bombs. NO SIRREE. This is serious stuff here," he said, tapping the desk with his fingers for effect. "That's why we wanted you on this case." He assured her with a conspiratorial wink and a nod.

Her eyebrows were arched so high they almost receded into her hairline. He was actually enjoying this; it was like talking to his grandkids.

"You know Joan, the people that pull their weight can recognize their own. We've had our eye on you since you left Glynco. Quiet, unassuming, get the job done, and move on to the next task. That's what we like about you, your attitude, and your work ethic. So damn few of your classmates share it. It's a damn shame." He shook his head in remorseful regret; she nodded hers sympathetically.

"Now I'm going to tell you something in the strictest confidence. Joan, this case is going to bear directly on the future of the BPS. I'm not kidding. That debacle out on that island may be the end of all our careers if we can't prepare for the worst. Joan, I need an inside track on this investigation that I won't be able to get from the DOJ. Inter-agency cooperation aside, and don't get me wrong cause I'm all for it. But if I'm going to be able to save the BPS Joan, I need your help. God knows I can't do it by myself. So that's it," he said with a modest shrug. "Will you help me Joan?"

"Yes, sir, absolutely." She nodded in enthusiastic agreement.

"Good, I'm depending on you," a thoughtful pause, "the country is depending on you."

She swallowed the lump in her throat. He rose from behind Luther's desk and softly walked to her side, laid an avuncular hand upon her shoulder, leaned over to her, and in a quiet voice he told her, "I won't forget this Joan, believe me. And neither will your country."

"Yes, sir," she squeaked.

"Very well, young lady." He assumed his normally erect posture. "Someone on my behalf will be in touch with you. In the meantime, you have to be the very best assistant to Mr.

Luther you can possibly be. When the time comes, you'll know what to do," he concluded.

"Yes, sir," she nodded.

And with that he was out the door and down the hallway and couldn't help from smiling. Not a bad little pep talk. He wished he had done it more often, he never realized it was this much fun.

61

Under Article V of the U.S. Constitution, when the legislatures of two-thirds of the states have passed a petitioning resolution, Congress is mandated to convene. The required number of states petitioning for the convention had been met. The scenes in several of the various state legislatures had been very similar. Toward the advent of spring most of the legislatures of the several states had wrapped up their business for the legislative sessions. Bills had been voted on and either passed out of committees and on to the next hurdle of lower and upper chamber votes or they hadn't. In addition to the several legislatures carrying out the business of their assemblies a significant majority of the states had managed to call for a petition to the U.S. Congress to convoke a constitutional convention for the purpose of repealing the Second Amendment to the Constitution of the United States.

In all, thirty-four of the states had agreed to the necessity of conducting the proceeding and had successfully called for the convention. It was sufficient to compel the Congress to convene to hear the case for and the case against the repeal of the Second Amendment to the Constitution of the United States, and then vote on its' repeal. The measure would then be sent out to the fifty states where at least three-fourths of the legislatures would have to ratify it.

The keynote speaker to the delegations of the Constitutional Convention would be the Presidential Nominee of the Democratic Party. The other party's spokesperson representing the view of the loyal opposition would be given equal time, more-or-less, but not nearly as bright a spotlight.

Resolution to Repeal the Second Amendment to the Constitution of the United States

Section 1. That, having served the purpose envisioned by the founding fathers and having outlived that purpose by the social, cultural, scientific, and economic realities of the several States that could not possibly have been foreseen by the founding fathers, and thus outlived, having come to present in itself by its very existence a very real threat to the life, liberty, and pursuit of happiness of the very citizens it had once been intended to preserve, the Second Amendment to the Constitution be repealed. And in that act it be posted to amend a new provision that: Immediately upon the ratification of this article the manufacture, sale, transportation, or transfer of any firearm, of any caliber, design, means of manufacture, or material of manufacture, and any type of ammunition appropriate to that firearm regardless of type, design, or composition, shall be prohibited from ownership or possession by any individual Citizen of the United States with the sole exception of the agencies of the States and that of the Federal Government of the United States, and that the importation thereof into, or the exportation thereof from the United States and all territories subject to the jurisdiction thereof, for the private possession, or use by any individual citizen be prohibited.

Section 2. The Congress and the several States shall have concurrent power to enforce this article by appropriate legislation.

Section 3. This article shall be inoperative unless it shall have been ratified as a repealed Amendment to the Constitution by the legislatures of three-fourths of the several States as provided within the Constitution.

62

Alexander Sherman watched the streamer crawling across the bottom of the TV picture. According to the ticker on the bottom of the screen, at the behest of the majority of the states, the United States Congress would meet in special session to convoke a Constitutional Convention, the purpose of which would be to repeal the Second Amendment. The main image of the television screen showed the Speaker of the House and The Senate Majority Leader on the steps of the Capitol announcing to the press that the recommendation to convoke a Constitutional Convention had been sent to the President of the United States, while the streamer at the bottom of the picture continuously proclaimed the vote to hold the Constitutional Convention.

Alexander Sherman was from Idaho. He was just about two-thirds of the way through his second, and he had decided, last term in the Senate. He had never considered himself naïve, but now he could concede that maybe he had been just a touch idealistic in believing that he could make a difference. Once again the Capitol was awash in scandal. Influence peddling, pay to play, quid-pro-quo, the names changed from session to session but it was always the same—everybody in government seemed to have a price. He had grown tired of the realpolitik. What had he been thinking?

The American electorate had grown weary of the serial antics coming out of the nation's capitol on a seasonal schedule. The mood of the people that put the Congress in office could be described as monumental ambivalence at best. The common wisdom held that if you scratched a politician, you'd get a liar. Politicians are liars, liars are politicians: simple as that. Why would anybody vote for a professional liar? Sherman resented deeply the notion that he should be thought a liar just because he ran for office. Then he looked at the TV screen again. He could see how the public had come to its conclusion. When Sherman took his oath of office he promised: "I, Alexander Sherman, do solemnly swear that I will support and defend the Constitution of the United States against all enemies, foreign and domestic; that I will bear true faith and allegiance to the same; that I take this obligation freely, without any mental reservation or purpose of evasion; and that I will well and faithfully discharge the duties of the office on which I am about to enter. So help me God." That was the oath he took and that was the oath in which he believed.

And there stood the congressional leadership on the steps of the capitol, gaily announcing that they were going to host a party to rip the Second Amendment out of the fabric that formed the nation. It made his chest ache. From his vantage point in his second term he could see that the scandals were merely symptomatic of something deeper: the legislative body, this branch of government called the Congress had lost its sense of direction, its moral compass had been irreparably broken and tossed away.

Sherman thought about all those people: other Senators, staff members, the endless parade of lobbyists and buttonholers, and everybody who thought they could extract a buck out of the saturated sponge that was the Federal Treasury by using him as the sieve. They were taking money in exchange for favors and were enticing him to do the same. *Fucking whores*, he thought, not that anyone in his party had a monopoly on morality. As practiced in the Capitol, morality seemed to be a moving target.

63

Prior to the election cycle (any election cycle) either party is betting that voter anger over perpetual scandals and discontent with the status quo will help them pick up seats in the up-coming election and either gain or maintain the majority in the House and/or Senate. Ideological polarization had become so acute that Congress had been incapacitated from performing its job. Every issue was framed in political terms so divisive that symbolism or the appearance of having passed substantial legislation was more important than actually passing substantial legislation.

It was in this atmosphere that the Congress would attend to the business of a constitutional convention. The purpose was to summarily suspend and repeal the Second Amendment to the Constitution of the United States. If the measure was approved and passed into law, the American People would no longer have the constitutionally protected right to keep and bear arms.

"We have lost the capacity for reason and now they want to dismantle the Constitution." Sherman said out loud to nobody there with the TV bearing mute witness. The very idea of it literally made him sick to his stomach. It was Sherman's personal belief that a God-given right was a God-given right, whether or not a bunch of politicians agreed to it. They could repeal a portion of a written document but they could not revoke the will of God. "We hold these truths to be self evident that all men are created equal, that they are endowed by their creator with certain unalienable rights…" Jefferson knew what he was doing, but Sherman doubted very much that his contemporaries in the separate legislatures across the country even had a clue.

The window of his office in the Dirksen Senate Office Building overlooked the traffic congestion that graced the nation's capital. He contemplated the scene below him. The traffic, the crime, the unresolved problems and undelivered solutions to the perennial election issues remained. *My God, what a shit-hole*, he thought. *Status quo.* He decided it must have been Newton's first law of politics: *Those with power tend to retain power; those without tend to remain without.* He never had ulcers before moving to the nation's capital either. His doctor had told him to stop internalizing. She said, "Yell at people , throw a flower pot, break a window. But get it out of your system. You either have to change your behavior or change your environment. But sooner is better than later." *Maybe she knew what she was talking about,* Sherman considered. Well that was that. He had had enough. He would go back to Ketchum and be a storefront lawyer again.

Now all he had to do was explain to his wife exactly why they were still in debt after the last campaign and why he wanted to quit, and how everything would be better when he was unemployed. *Well, no need to rush into that particular quagmire,* he thought, as he turned his attention to an e-mail addressed to members of the Senate Committee on the Interior, apprising him of an investigation ordered by the Attorney General. A subsequent e-mail from the chairman of the Senate Committee on the Interior assigned Senator Sherman to a sub-committee to conduct a hearing on a raid by an element of the Federal Bureau of Public Safety on a house and property on Peninsular Island in Washington State. Apparently the AG had initiated an investigation into the circumstances of some nut in Washington State blowing up a house on said property culminating in loss of life. "God save us from zealots and visionaries," Senator Sherman said, again, to an empty room.

*****

In Palm Springs, California, Peter Cleague sat in an apartment that contained two rooms, a bed, a chair, and a television. Cleague stared at the TV screen while the paid personages of this particular "news" network gaily made conjecture on how this stunning news would play in the Heartland and elsewhere. Cleague, only half numb, splashed more bourbon into the glass and proceeded to finish his journey to the bottom of the bottle. The main image on the television screen was the oft-repeated sound bite of the Senate Majority Leader and the Speaker of the House making a joint announcement to the press corps on the steps of the Capitol that the recommendation to convoke a Constitutional Convention had been sent to the President of the United States, while the streamer at the bottom of the picture continuously proclaimed the vote for the Constitutional Convention.

So, *they're going to repeal the Second Amendment. Well, no shit*, Cleague thought, and took another drink.

64

Luther's briefing of the Attorney General had been, at best, anticlimactic. The AG seemed to display polite interest in Luther's interim oral report but said that he looked forward to the full report in its finished form, emphasizing his concern for the necessity that Luther take the time required to produce a competent and well written report leaving no stone unturned. This puzzled Luther as he had been left with the impression, that day back at the crime scene on Peninsular Island, that the AG was quite anxious to see some result. He had made this trip as a courtesy to the AG who, in turn, treated it as a non-event.

The tale of a disaffected, lunatic-fringe, malcontent had hit the media and dissipated within hours as the hype about the Constitutional Convention was starting to warm up. The editorial pages were rife with dire predictions of fanatical right wing types, just like that lunatic on that island in Washington State, who would actually choose to die instead of surrendering their personal firearms to the government, thus fomenting a real civil war unless this reasonable and critically essential resolution were passed. It would seem that the news release of the events back on Peninsular Island had been auspiciously well-timed. The Attorney General did not need to be in that big a hurry.

In any event, amidst all the smoke and mirrors, one more story didn't seem to capture anyone's attention. There had been no mention of the status of the Federal agents who remained missing subsequent to the assault on Cleague's house. There was no mention at all of the incarceration of the TV news crew in St Joseph's Medical Center.

How'd they get that one by the watchdog media unless they could promise a bigger bone? Well, Luther mused, *at least the media bought it.* Luther was still convinced that Cleague had staged his own death so spectacularly that no trace of him could be found. That's why the house and Quonset hut had both been utterly, totally destroyed. He was convinced of it but he hadn't told anybody yet. What could have been a domestic disaster for the Administration had been eclipsed by the universal expectation of a political coup: the repeal of the Second Amendment to the Constitution of the United States. Apparently the appointment of a special counsel wasn't so urgent after-all. Lack of interest, lack of urgency, and as a result, lack of funding. The AG informed Luther that whatever resources he had managed to accrue would be all that he would get. There would be no more additional agents, and let's get this thing wrapped up, but be thorough. The AG instructed.

After his meeting with the AG Luther actually found himself with little to do as the meeting did not last as long as he had prepared for. He arranged to interview BPS Agent Speeks, the raid commander from the debacle on Peninsular Island, in a BPS conference room.

Luther, "Who issued the order for a raid?"

Speeks, "It came down the chain of command."

Luther, "From BPS Headquarters?"

Speeks, "Yes."

Luther wasn't quite sure of what he was hearing. "You got an order from the Director of the Bureau of Public Safety to go assault a house on a beach?"

Speeks, "No. Orders come from Operations."

Luther, "Did the Director know about it?"

Speeks, "I don't know who knew about it, I don't get that information. Orders come from Operations."

Luther, "What was the purpose of the raid?"

Speeks, "To take into Federal custody one Peter Cleague for felony violation of the Federal Arsenal Code."

Luther, "How long was he under surveillance?"

Speeks, "A few months."

Luther, "Did your people know that Cleague knew he was being surveilled?"

Speeks, "I guess so".

Luther was incredulous. "Excuse Me?"

Speeks, "They had it in their logs that he would wave to them every time he went jogging."

Luther was momentarily stunned. Speechless.

Luther, "Everything about the site out there indicates that Cleague knew a raid was coming. Your people knew that he knew that he was being observed. How could you have had him under surveillance for months and not have known he had laid out a trap?"

Speeks shrugged. "The guys on surveillance never made any indication of anything out of the ordinary. All their reports consistently said 'daily routine observed.'"

Luther, "Did you check out Cleague's background before planning the raid?"

Speeks, "No. The order came down: plan and execute a raid for felony violation of the Arsenal Code. That's what we did."

Luther wasn't learning anything. Speeks was not being uncooperative but he wasn't helping. Another day shot to hell.

Cleague had not blown up a day care center, or an abortion clinic, or shot up a shopping mall, or a grade school. Luther shut his eyes and remembered the scene at the island.

Military hardware was evident. The two-and-a-half-ton flat bed light trucks remained on the beach strand when Luther made his tour around the assault site. Cleague most likely would have heard them. The BPS was coming to his house—Cleague was not parking a truck bomb at a Federal building. It occurred to Luther that the whole thing Cleague had orchestrated was defensive in nature. The flares over the jetties, the plastic dolls floating in the water, even the explosions were all decoys designed to buy him time to leave. Luther still felt that he was missing something. What was it? He would have to go back to Peninsular Island.

It had been a very long day. Tomorrow he would head back to the office in Bellingham.

65

Luther was already at his desk in the office in Bellingham when Agent Glyndon came in at 8:00 on the dot. "Good morning," she said. He muttered something but she couldn't make it out. *Fine*, she thought. *You don't bother me, I won't bother you,* and that suited her just fine. She started the coffee in the drip coffee maker and went about her work at her desk.

John Luther was going over Cleague's evaluations as a student at FLETC, and subsequent evaluations as an agent in the Bureau of Diplomatic Security. Cleague showed promise. After his posting to the embassy in Lebanon everything went sour, but there was nothing in the records that explained it. *Inter-office politics?* Luther thought. *It wouldn't be the first time.*

Luther closed the file after reading of Cleague's departure from Federal service. Apparently there had been some sort of mix up with the flight in Turkey and Cleague had been delayed for a few days but he eventually got back to Washington, DC, and was mustered out of the Bureau of Diplomatic Security in short order. *Wonder what that was about? Well, no matter. It wasn't pertinent to this investigation into the business on Peninsular Island.* He concluded. Apparently he managed to get by on infrequent employment as a bodyguard, and a part-time job at the marina in Port Cullis. Luther looked over a copy of a 1040 form filed by one Peter Cleague for part-time seasonal employment as a maintenance worker. Luther found income tax as anathema as the next man but, from time to time, the IRS did serve a purpose to investigators such as himself—it provided a paper trail. And this trail led Luther right back to Peninsular Island. He called Andy DeKooning.

*****

The bridge to PI was still down. Luther took the ferry from Anacortes and met DeKooning at the Port Cullis Marina at 9:00 the next morning. They walked down the dock to one of the slips near the end and DeKooning threw his bag in the boat. DeKooning undid the stern line that secured the Boston Whaler to the dock.

"Hop in," DeKooning told Luther as he held the line taught. Once Luther was on board DeKoonig tossed the line into the boat and undid the bowline from its cleat on the dock and hopped in. He pushed the boat away from the dock and started the motor. They moved out of the marina at slightly faster than idle and south toward the race way. Once clear of other traffic DeKooning opened up the throttle a bit. It pushed Luther back on his heels. Unsinkable fiberglass hull or not, Luther did not care for the sensation of the water moving underneath him. The Sheriff's Office Patrol boat was a 15 foot "Guardian" manufactured by the Brunswick Commercial and Government Products Corporation. With a haze grey hull and white deck, Luther noted the boat could have a certain stealth quality if the environmental conditions were right, like rain or fog. The insignia of the Sheriff's Office was superimposed on a double diagonal green and gold line with "*Sheriff*" in cursive script aft of the image.

Unlike Luther's last visit to the island it was a nice summer day. DeKooning smiled and waved or tooted the boat's horn at the occasional kid in a row boat or at people pulling up and/or putting out crab pots. They waved back. DeKooning slowed down when he got near the area that had been the site of Cleague's place. He turned the motor off and let the boat drift south a little. He lit a cigarette and asked Luther, "Did you want to look around or keep going?"

"Let's keep going. Can you stop at about a hundred yards or so?" Luther asked.

"Sure," DeKooning answered, "Just say when." He re-started the motor and cruised south, slowly.

"I think this is it." All Luther could see was weeds and more weeds. Directly to the east Luther could see where the bank of the raceway dished out a little bit. When a car passed by on the island's highway he could catch a partial glimpse of the vehicle. He thought this was the area in which Cleague had assaulted one of the BPS agents manning one of the observation posts. It would have been the guy that had his throat cut. It left Luther cold. He looked around and noticed the kayak with the colanderized hull had been removed.

"Let's go." He said. DeKooning opened up the throttle slightly and nudged the Whaler south down the raceway to the ship channel.

"When are you people gonna wrap up this investigation?" DeKooning asked.

Luther wasn't aware that the BPS forensics section was still active on the island and just gave his best, "...It shouldn't be much longer." The south end of the island had been a crime scene from July fourth to Labor Day. That had to hurt. Ferry traffic had been re-established and the Coast Guard had re-opened the marina by the middle of July. But the bridge was still down.

"Is the bridge going to be re-built?" Luther asked.

"They're talking about it. The state claims that the Federal government owes them a bridge and the Feds claim that a state resident destroyed it so the state can build it. It'll probably go to court."

"Then what?" Luther asked.

"Who knows?" DeKooning said. "The Tribe is talking about turning the whole south end of the island into a golf course community. Some of 'em wanna build a hotel and a casino, make it a destination resort."

Luther looked around; even he could imagine the changes—it would bring a lot of money and a lot of people. Luther didn't know if that was good or bad. But it would sure change the character of the place. He shrugged it off. He didn't live there.

They had nearly gotten to the ship channel that separated the island from the mainland. Luther tried to lighten the conversation.

"What's your hurry? There's nothing down this end of the island but crabs, eels, and seagull shit." He tried to smile. DeKooning paid no notice. He was busy driving the boat.

"People are getting tired of lookin' over their shoulders. You guys left quite a legacy." DeKooning smiled quietly.

Luther was aware of the reputation the BPS enjoyed—a hangover from the old days. In any event DeKooning was right. Luther was running out of time. His investigation was precedent to the Attorney Generals' decision to appoint a special counsel.

Critics of the use of special counsels traditionally argue that they are an unconstitutional fourth branch to the government because they are not subject to limitations in spending or have deadlines to meet. But Luther did have a deadline. The fiscal year would end at the end of the month. He was running out of time.

Luther noticed something on the right bank of the raceway, pointed at it and said "What's that?" DeKooning looked as indicated and saw something bound up in some waterlogged timbers. He steered the boat to the bank and they stared at something yellow and muddy. DeKooning turned off the motor and played out the anchor. He grabbed the gaffe hook from the gunwale and poked at the log a bit. DeKooning looked at Luther. Luther nodded and said nothing.

DeKooning freed the thing from the rotted flotsam, hooked it, and brought it onto the deck of the Whaler. It was a lightweight flotation vest popular with boaters. It was yellow and mud colored and had a scabbard and knife attached upside down on the left shoulder strap. Luther remembered that the kayak had been found, stitched stem to stern with nine millimeter holes, in the reeds of the raceway slightly less than a mile north of their present position. Cleague wanted to use the kayak to slip out into Puget Sound, where, at night, he would be damn near invisible. The kayak was destroyed and Cleague had to swim out past the bridge. He would not have wanted a floatation vest keeping him on the surface of the water. If the one BPS agent on the bridge Observation Post hadn't been a little jumpy and shot at shadows, Cleague would have made a clean break. Luther had to smile in spite of himself.

"What do you want to do with this?" DeKooning asked.

"It's evidence," Luther responded. "You got any trash bags?"

"Yeah." DeKooning dug around under the console of the steering wheel and came up with a couple of big heavy duty plastic bags, and handed them to Luther. Luther opened one and held it by the brim at arm's length while DeKooning used the gaffe hook to put the floatation vest in the bag.

"I'll ship it to the forensics lab when I get back to the office." Luther said. DeKooning nodded. "Maybe they can match whatever residue is on the blade to the O/P Observer that got cut." And then, more to himself than to deKooning, "Well, that's it." Luther was thinking out loud.

"That's what?" DeKooning asked.

"Cleague is still alive, and he's still out there." Luther made an indiscriminate lift of his chin indicating the world at large.

"You say that like it's a bad thing." DeKooning said.

"Look at this," Luther gestured toward the phantom bridge and the ghosts of the BPS agents, "whether he was your friend or not, he killed a lot of people. What kind of man plants a claymore mine two feet away from his intended target's face? He needs to be found and he needs to be brought to trial, and he needs to answer for what he did." Luther said.

The thought occurred to DeKooning that maybe those particular people needed killing, but he kept his mouth shut. He knew Cleague would take care of himself and he wished his friend well. They made their way in the Whaler through the boat channel past the bridge abutments and east out into the Sound. DeKooning turned north and opened up the throttle a bit. Luther had to grab the console to keep from being seated on the deck involuntarily. They remained quiet till they got back to the marina.

"You going after him?' DeKooning asked.

"No. That's not my job. I have an investigation to finish. But I expect somebody will." Luther said, and made ready to take his leave.

"Well, thank you Deputy DeKooning." They shook hands.

"You're welcome."

Luther pulled himself up on the dock.

"And Luther?" DeKooning called after him.

"Yes?" Luther turned.

"Watch yourself. Just because you work with the BPS doesn't make them your friends." DeKooning said.

Luther walked back to the ferry dock and considered DeKooning's admonition. *He may have a point*, he thought.

66

Luther carried on with the investigation as best he could. With himself and Agent Glyndon there was only so much that could be done in a day. The help from other BPS offices in the region never materialized. It turned out to be a lot of paper shuffling and report writing and re-writing. On the First of October, Luther went to work at his office at the Bellingham Federal Office Building and received a call from the office of the US Attorney General in Washington, DC. John Luther's investigation had been moved from the fast track to the back burner. At the end of September money had evaporated and no further funds had been designated for his assignment as special investigator for the ensuing fiscal year. He was ordered to return back to Department of Justice, Washington, DC. Luther had been put in the position of having to petition the Attorney General to authorize the funding to finish his investigation. In a word he was told "no", not now, maybe later. He had never had to do that before and he vowed he would never be put in that position again. He returned to his normal job routine in DC and essentially cooled his heels.

Luther called Joan Glyndon the next day and released her to her BPS office in Seattle. He instructed her to take all the files that he had locked up in the safe with her and lock the door on the way out. He further instructed her to ship the files to him at the Department of Justice in Washington, D.C. He had an inkling that this wasn't over yet and he might be back. He told her to shut down the office in the Bellingham Federal Office Building. The lease on the office space had already been paid out of last year's budget. The space would sit empty until he could come out and terminate the lease when the current budget allowed.

What should have been accomplished in hours took days. Weeks turned into months. In a few months the anniversary of the Peninsular Island debacle would have come and gone and apparently no one from the Attorney General's office seemed to regard the matter with any sense of urgency. The numerous Presidential campaigns for candidates of both political parties as well as the upcoming Constitutional Convention were consuming all the attention of all the media.

No one senior to Luther seemed to be very concerned about the unfortunate incident on that obscure little island back in Washington State last summer. No one had actually said to Luther, "Sure, lives had been lost but, really, that's what they were paid for," but he sensed that seemed to be the attitude.

On Tuesday morning, the 2nd of October, BPS Agent Joan Glyndon sat in the office in Bellingham waiting for the other shoe to drop. When she had talked to Luther that morning he told her that their funding had been cut and they would be getting no other resources or staff. They would have to complete the investigation as best they could, when they could. Take the files, lock the door, and go back to Seattle. This left her a little ambivalent. She really didn't care for working for Luther but she thought the final result would be a little more grand than, "That's it, wrap it up. Out o' money." She sat back in her chair and sighed. And she had thought this assignment would be a springboard to something big.

The phone rang and she answered. The man replied, "Joan, you don't know me but I work for the man who came to see you a few weeks ago." This caught her totally off guard.

"Uh, what man?" was all she could think of to say.

"The man in the picture in your office in downtown Seattle." The voice on the phone said. He was talking about Henry Caleb, the Director of the Bureau of Public Safety.

"And who are you?" She asked.

"I'm the guy that's telling you that it's time to help," he said. "Why don't we meet, Joan, say 12:00 at Maritime Heritage Park? Do you know where that is?" he asked.

"Uh, yeah," she answered. It was just a couple blocks west of the old courthouse.

"Good, noon it is. We'll do lunch," he said. She frenetically excavated the top of her desk to find a pen and a pad of paper.

"Well, wait a minute, what's your name?" she asked.

"Call me Gabe," he said.

"Gabe? Is that it?" She asked, scribbling it down.

"It's all you need," he replied.

"Well, how will I know you?" Joan asked.

"It's OK," he said. "I'll know you." And he hung up.

*****

Maritime Heritage Park was a commons area in proximity to Squalicum Harbor, the waterfront part of Bellingham. Maritime Heritage Park bordered Whatcom Creek, which flowed into Bellingham Bay. On the north side of the creek a five-sided polygon incorporated a fish hatchery, a nice little grassy area with trees and bushes, and a pedestrian walkway that curved its way through it. On the south side of the creek the green space formed an irregular quadrangle bordered by Holly Street on the west, a hillside that abutted Prospect Street on the east and Champion Street on the south. Concrete benches terraced into the hillside formed stadium style seating that faced west. Part of the city's green space initiative for the coming decade, it had become a gathering space for homeless, itinerants, and the ill-defined. Joan Glyndon was not the least bit comfortable in this environment and wondered why she had agreed to meet a stranger here.

She was at the park on time and obviously ill at ease. She parked her car on Holly Street and walked to the creek. It gave her a vantage point toward the concrete benches where the most people seemed to be gathered. She scanned the faces of strangers for someone she did not know. The furtively cast glances over her shoulder, right and left, indicated her discomfort. She caught the sight of a young man coming from the parking lot to the south. Well built, fit, trim, nicely groomed, and wearing 5.11 trousers, polo shirt, windbreaker, and Oakley sunglasses—standard casual dress for Feds and law enforcement in general. This had to be the guy. "Gabe?" She asked. He smiled and held out his hand. "Hi, Joan. Why don't we go get some lunch?' He asked and led the way down the street. In a short distance they came to a corner café. Busy place, lunchtime crowd, hurried people scrambled in and out. Nobody looked at anybody else. They were invisible.

"So, Joan, we hear that the funding was cut for your project," Gabe said.

She munched on her sandwich, rolled her eyes, and nodded with a shrug.

"Well, our mutual friend had an idea." He paused and took a sip of soda from a can. She continued munching and raised her eyebrows.

"Our friend has a proposal for you, and Joan, if you pull this off, you will call the shots for the rest of your career," he said.

She didn't get all the munching done but swallowed the remainder in a lump.

"Now Joan, this is gonna be tough. It will be a one-woman show and you're it. You will need some help though and we can put you in touch with some people that are pretty good at this sort of thing. Now, I'm not kidding Joan this won't be easy. But do it right and the sky's the limit," he said. "Are you up for this Joan?"

She energetically nodded her head. "Uh-huh," she said.

"OK. It'll be a while. Go back to Seattle and do your regular job. We'll be in touch when it's time," he said. The director was right. This was fun. It was like talking to a little kid.

67

September stretched into October and October became November. Luther decided to take a bit of initiative. The wind came straight down the Potomac. John Luther looked to the Northwest and saw that rain was not far behind it. He guessed the wind to be about ten or twelve miles an hour, strong enough to bang the lanyards against the aluminum flagpoles. It made a shallow tinny sound like drumsticks being beat together. The flagpoles lined the walkway about every fifty yards. The lanyards beat a non-rhythmic dirge—winter was coming.

Luther had asked to meet with Judge George Hillman, and the judge had agreed to meet Luther here at Hains Point in East Potomac Park. They sat on a bench facing the convergence of the Anacostia and Potomac rivers. It was late in the autumn—cold, damp, and unpleasant. In the spring and summer Ohio drive would be packed with joggers, bicyclists, and skaters recreating under the sakura cherry trees. Now, the only thing on Ohio Drive was Judge Hillman's Lincoln Towne car and his attendant driver, Michael. Michael stood lightly leaning against the car at the junction of the front and rear passenger doors, his hands crossed lightly left over right, his suit coat unbuttoned and his attention did not waver from his principal. Michael wore wrap-around Oakleys and occasionally scanned the area—left to right, right to left, and in depth.

The judge was retired and had ample time to pursue his hobby. He enjoyed watching birds. Today he was counting seagulls.

"Did you know, Mr. Luther, that there are eight separate species of gulls that frequent these waters?" the judge asked. Luther regarded the former circuit court judge, former director of the FBI, and former mentor to one Peter Cleague who had once written a glowing letter of commendation for Cleague's service record.

"No Sir, I didn't," Luther responded.

"It is important that we learn from our environment, Mr. Luther. Eight different species of seagulls and they are all getting along in the same space. Of course it doesn't hurt that there is plenty of food. They live on garbage, you know," the judge said.

"Yes, sir." Luther knew that seagulls were scavengers.

"Eight different species of scavengers, somewhat like the bureaucracy by which you are employed, wouldn't you say?" Hillman asked.

"Couldn't say, sir; I wouldn't be employed for long." Luther smiled.

"Indeed," agreed the judge. "And why are we meeting, Mr. Luther?"

"As you know, sir, I am investigating the circumstances surrounding the loss of life of some Federal law enforcement agents up in Washington State this past summer," Luther said.

"And what do you suppose I would know about that?" the judge asked.

"What can you tell me about Peter Cleague, sir?" Luther asked.

Hillman sighed. He remembered Cleague, a rising star if there ever was one. That boy could have had a stellar career but he pissed it away. Hillman recounted the day Cleague approached him about someone in an embassy selling names. He told Cleague to let it go because he didn't have solid incriminating evidence. What a mess. It was said in certain quarters that Cleague had committed murder. It was only speculative gossip. Hillman did not believe that Cleague had committed murder, but whether he had or not, he had never been prosecuted because it could not be proved. Again, there was no evidence.

"Do you think Cleague committed murder, sir? Do you think he could have killed those Federal agents on Peninsular Island? Did he hold a grudge?" Luther asked.

Hillman shrugged. "I don't know. But of all the things Peter Cleague has ever been accused of, a lack of resourcefulness wasn't one of them. The pathetic thing was that he had committed political disembowelment with the stroke of a pen. What a waste. When he walked away from the State Department, he turned his back on government service and everything associated with it. He would not have harbored a grudge. He walked away from it. That was his solution. If you are asking me 'Could he have done it?' I will tell you Mr. Luther that he could have done anything he set his mind to do. If you are asking me 'Do I believe He did it?' No, I don't. Government service and its infernal machinations no longer concerned him. He had moved on." Hillman stood and clutched his overcoat at the neck. He was less tolerant of cold temperatures than he once had been. He used to not have arthritis either; time goes on. He was getting chilled; his bones ached.

Luther stood and asked, "If his intent was not murder, why would he have set such an elaborate series of booby traps?"

"I can't tell you that, Mr. Luther, but I will tell you that Peter Cleague was a man who did not like to be pushed and was quite content to be left alone. Ask yourself this: Would any of those unfortunate men have died if they hadn't been actively hunting for him? And, if they were hunting for him, why? Who stood to gain from it? Then you will have found your murderer. I am tired, Mr. Luther. Good day." Hillman left Luther standing at the bench and walked toward the waiting sedan. It started to rain.

68

Peter Cleague slept in his chair sitting up. He had left the TV on. He awoke to a video collage of Christmas trees from around the world to the background of classical guitar music—"The Dance of the Sugar Plum Ferries". He saw the National Christmas tree located on the Ellipse, just south of the White House. He saw a big Christmas tree with candles in a town square someplace in Europe, and snow-laden trees in a forest under the light of a full moon. Apparently, it had been a good year for coniferous trees.

Cleague got up and walked to the window; he didn't bother with a clock. It was still dark. That was all the information he needed for now. The TV was full of snow, and cedars, and pinecones, and a crackling log fire in a brick fireplace with fir garland strewn across the mantle. He looked outside and saw the dry asphalt of the parking lot, and garbage piled up by the dumpster under the acrid yellow glare of a sodium vapor lamp. It didn't feel like Christmas.

He walked into the kitchenette and dumped some ice cubes into his glass. He didn't drink when he was working protective details for the Bureau of Diplomatic Security. But any more there wasn't anybody to protect, at least not on a continuous basis and no desire to do so, least of all for himself.

He picked up the bottle and talked out loud to the label, "Merry Christmas Mr. Beam." The bottle replied with the silent swirl of liquid silk around and over the ice cubes that had made it into the glass. This was the way Cleague lived his life now. He had stopped writing. He had stopped teaching. Once in a while he would get a gig on a protective detail somewhere. He would sober up, go do the job, come home to his apartment and drink. Sober up, do a job, come home and drink. He didn't get to see Linda anymore. He missed her.

After he had joined her here, she had been with him long enough to tell him it was over. He started drinking. She would later learn that he stopped drinking only long enough to go on a job. Although she had told herself and him that she felt nothing for him now, that coming down here taught her that she had no business being with someone who hired himself out as a professional paranoid, the knowledge of the work he did still compelled her to worry.

Well, actually, it made her a nervous wreck. She had loved him and to know that he was willing to get himself killed for a stranger frightened her. Maybe that had been part of the rationale behind her decision. Who knew?

Cleague sat back down and watched the images float past on the screen. He sipped at his bourbon. By the time the ice had melted he had fallen asleep again. Talking heads being too jolly on the all news—all the time—channel woke him up. It was daylight. He got up and went to bed. This was the way Cleague lived his life.

69

The noise woke him up. It took him a while to fathom: where he was, what that noise was, and what to do next. He was in bed, sort of, half in and half out. He swung his feet over the edge of the bed and downward like a counterbalance on the other side of a fulcrum to pitch his upper body up. Whoa... the room was spinning. He hated it when that happened. Two and a half steps later he fell flat on his face. His unbuttoned and unbelted trousers had fallen down around his ankles just like homemade shackles. The bells, the bells: Clouseau as Quasimodo. Hitching his trousers up around his waist, he managed to stumble into the front room, locate the phone jack in the wall and follow the wire to the source of the noise—under a pillow and between the cushions of his chair.

"Hello." His mouth was dry. His throat was parched. His tongue felt like sandpaper. His nose was sore.

"Peter! Are you awake?" It was Roger Tibbett.

"Yeah, yes... Roger, go ahead." His head felt like it was the center ball in one of those perpetual motion machines.

"You have an interview. Be in my office in one hour; make sure you're at your best as the client will be here. And wear a suit. Do you understand? One hour, here." Short, sharp, clipped—the NCO issuing orders to a wayward private.

"Yeah, right, one hour I'll be there. Hey, Roger?" Peter's eyes were burning; he couldn't make them stay open.

"Yes?" Impatient, sand through the hourglass, time is money.

"What time is it?" He thought he owned a watch but he didn't know where it was, and even if he did he really couldn't see one in his current state; his eyes wouldn't focus on something that far away right now.

"Really, Peter it's one p.m.! Get a watch!" Exasperated, the Sergeant Major rang off. Peter considered it. *That's not the issue right now*, he thought glumly. He dropped the phone onto the receiver and regretted it immediately. Loud noises hurt. Stoically, the resolute warrior went about his business— finding clothing to wear and a bar of soap for the shower.

Roger Tibbett hung up with ambivalence about the choice he had just made. Peter, the name was Crane this time, was getting worse by the day. Since he had moved to Palm Springs Peter started drinking. The man literally could not tell if he was coming or going. As long as he was on a job he was sober as a judge and one of the very best protection specialists Tibbett had ever known. But the man's time off was his own and with it he proceeded to drink himself into oblivion. Tibbett's major concern was that it would begin to carry over, of course, and reflect poorly on the very low profile, very highly regarded firm of which Tibbett was the operations director. Tibbett thought that this particular assignment would be the thing Peter needed to get himself in order. Retired out of the military, Tibbett had seen a lot of good men kill themselves with a bottle. As he and his wife Mary both regarded Peter nearly as a surrogate son he hated to see the same fate befall him.

Peter showed up in a jacket and tie that looked as though they had been slept in. Since Peter had started drinking, he had stopped working out, and he ate poorly. And he drank incessantly when he wasn't working. He had put on weight. The fit of his clothes reflected the state of his health—a shambles. His complexion was sallow and ashen, his eyes pink with burst vessels, the skin around them puffy, and dark. His eyes even seemed to be recessed further into his skull if that were possible.

From the side of his head his temples throbbed. The back of his skull ached with a searing pain that numbed his nervous system while simultaneously increased his senses such that every perception was interpreted only as a different level, degree, or tone of agony. The pressure of the lights on his eyes made his brow pound relentlessly. He wanted to be dead now.

"Good Lord, Peter, you look like hell." Tibbett made no attempt to mask his disparagement. He anxiously and openly looked at the wall clock over the entrance to the foyer of his suite of offices in the industrial park near the Palm Springs airport. Tibbett pointedly looked at Peter's wrist. No watch. It was not a major affront, but it was a suggestion not taken which Tibbett mentally catalogued.

"When the client gets here you will be introduced as a professional acquaintance. Under no circumstances will you state or even intimate that you work for this enterprise. This particular client asked me for a referral. I mentioned your name as a competent independent contractor, and you show up here, in my place of business looking like this." Tibbett was nearly livid but never out of control. He was not given to histrionics and did not raise his voice above a conversational tone. He continued, "Your meeting here has been arranged as a matter of courtesy to both parties."

Tibbett issued Peter's orders. "When the client arrives, I will show him to the conference room and from there the ball is in your court. The assignment is extremely high risk and hopefully very low profile. Do not embarrass me Peter, I won't have it. As far as Hereford Associates is concerned this is your last chance to get yourself in order. If you don't pull yourself out of the gutter with this one, you're gone. Do you understand?" Tibbett pulled no punches—he was directly honest.

Peter mutely nodded and made his way to the conference room. *I know, I know,* he thought and prayed for a cup of black coffee but realized that his hands would shake so badly he'd never get the cup to his lips. That simply wouldn't do in front of a potential client. His eyes still burned; he took his glasses off.

70

He heard muffled noises, indistinct over the din of the central air conditioning. The door opened and Peter Crane stood. Tibbett was muttering something in a congenial polished fashion that intoned best intentions, professional good will, and absolute detachment from whatever was going to be discussed in this room in the next hour. The "client" was a small ageless person of androgynous features and indeterminate ancestry. Was he Asian? Hispanic? Slavic? Who knew?

The "client" was preceded and followed by two men who looked as though they had been recruited from Professional Wrestling. Crane conveyed his silent assessment to Tibbett with a sidelong glance.

"Mr. Lee, this is Peter Crane. Peter, this is Mr. Lee." Tibbett made the introductions with polite handshakes and dutiful nods all around.

"May I offer anyone anything to drink, coffee perhaps?" Tibbett said as he looked directly at Peter. Both Mr. Lee and Peter declined.

"Very well, I'll let you two get about your business." Tibbett said and smiling with a congenial air, dismissed himself. Mr. Lee's two escorts were dismissed as well with a subtle lift of the client's chin. Tibbett preceded them out of the room where they dutifully assumed their posts on either side of the door; Roger went back to his office.

Taking his seat with an air of accustomed authority the client spoke with a resonant base voice that came from the bottom of a 55-gallon drum.

"I am Filipino, Mr. Crane." *Well he's a perceptive little son-of-a-bitch, isn't he?* Crane mused.

"I am sixty-three years old and my family has been threatened. I am used to threats but I will not take risks with my children or grandchildren. My business interests are such that if I am harmed they will be in immediate jeopardy. Tell me Mr. Crane, why should I hire an alcoholic to protect my life?"

Crane did not care for the pejorative appellation in the least, yet conceded that at that moment it was applicable. He had really let himself go this far hadn't he?

"I can't tell you that." Crane's reply drew no discernible response from the little man seated at the head of the teak table.

"I can only tell you that you should hire me if you determine it to be in your own best interest."

"And what makes your skills superior to those of the gentlemen waiting patiently outside that door?" *Well, perceptive and observant, too.*

"I don't know that they are, sir." Peter answered.

"No, but you feel they are or you wouldn't be here. Why?" The little bastard had a talent. He was persistent to the point of being provocative. If this was the way he treated his business associates, whoever they may have been, no wonder he needed a bodyguard.

"I've worked with body blockers before. Some of them are excellent and some of them are less than adequate. A lot of them tend to rely on their size, bulk, and strength to intimidate people, much the same as a schoolyard bully. They have to be close to their adversary to intimidate them. That could mean that their level of awareness may not be as highly tuned as it should be. They may be outstanding in a physical confrontation but are they sufficiently aware to see the attack before it happens?" Peter asked.

"And you, Mr. Crane, are you telling me that you can see the future, can you read men's minds?" Lee questioned.

"No, sir." Peter laid out one of the fundamental principles of his craft—Situational Awareness. "But we have to observe our environment. If we are outside we need to know how to get inside, conversely if we are inside we need to know how to get outside—in a hurry. We need to be aware of obstacles and adversaries in our path. If it is an adversary what are his intentions? If he intends to do us harm, we need to be able to recognize that threat and react to it before he can act. It is a pinnacle skill, and not everybody has developed it."

"And in your professional estimation, are they capable of making such an assessment?" Lee asked, indicating the bodyguards outside the door with a casual inclination of his head.

"They are in your company, sir. That has to be your determination."

"And you, Mr. Crane? Are you sufficiently aware to see the attack before it happens, even in an alcohol-induced stupor?"

"Mr. Lee, I work very hard at what I do. So far, it has been my experience not to have lost a client. I firmly believe in situational avoidance and I never drink on a job. If we are in an environment in which I tell you to "turn right here" and you choose to ignore my advice and turn left, there isn't much I can do but tag along and hope for the best."

"And if I turn right, what then?" Lee asked.

"Then I'll get you out of the situation or you don't have to pay me." Crane couldn't help but smile at this last bit of insolence. He thought he had even caught a glint of humor in the older man's eye but wasn't sure.

"We are all creatures of habit, Mr. Crane. We may delude ourselves into thinking that our habits are borne of hard won experience and discipline. Nevertheless we all choose the path of least resistance just because the familiar is comforting and the unknown is a threat. How strongly do you seek the comfort and familiarity of a whiskey bottle, Mr. Crane?" *Persistent little son-of-a-bitch*, Peter thought.

"Mr. Lee, I am what you see. There is no pretense here. I've told you I've never lost a client and I will keep you alive during the duration of my appointment or I will die trying," Peter said.

"Yes," Mr. Lee interjected sharply, "and you've also told me you are a professional coward." Sharp to the point of being hostile, Mr. Lee abruptly rose to his feet.

"Situational hocus pocus, conflict avoidance. Just run away. What kind of bodyguard is that?" Lee demanded. Peter had had enough.

"Yeah, right, and it's those instincts that are going to keep your ass alive." Peter said as he resignedly stood up and put his eyeglasses back on. The interview was over, and with it, another job was gone before it was offered.

"Look. You want me or you don't, Mr. Lee." Peter's response ended with a slight shrug.

Lee was quiet for a moment and searched Crane's eyes. Crane could only wonder what Lee could possibly be looking for but did not look away. After a time Lee made his pronouncement.

"In spite of your appearance, Mr. Crane, you come well recommended. These gentlemen have escorted me since New York and as you say, they have been adequate. You will be part of a larger team." Lee pulled a business card from a pocket and scribbled something on the back of it as he continued. "Understand now that you will be a subordinate; you will meet the team leader at an appropriate time. Be at this address one week from today at noon." The client handed Crane a business card with the legend embossed in gold ink:

Lee LTD
Import Export
Manila Philippines

On the back of the card was written the name of a hotel in Mexico City. The client withdrew an envelope from his jacket and handed it to Crane. "This is an advance on your retainer. It will be enough to get you to Mexico City. You will be in my company, Mister Crane, please, do not embarrass me. Buy yourself a decent suit. You will be met at that address. You will be paid at a rate commensurate with the professional standard, the balance to be paid at the end of the contract. Good-bye, Mr. Crane." With that he turned and left.

71

Crane walked directly into Tibbett's office without knocking.

"He handed me an envelope full of cash, Roger, is this man dealing drugs?" Crane asked bluntly. Tibbett did not attempt to conceal his irritation at having been interrupted.

"You really do need to work on your discretion, Peter. No he is not dealing drugs; he is dealing in weapons, great big, expensive, weapons on the behalf of governments that shall remain anonymous. Whatever he told you is as much as you need to know. When do you leave?"

"Next week. What about hardware?" Crane walked to the credenza, poured himself a cup of coffee from Tibbett's machine and extracted the commercial size bottle of industrial strength aspirin from Tibbett's center desk drawer, barely allowing Tibbett time to get out of the way.

Controlled, showing only a slight degree of exasperation, Tibbett replied: "Well if he didn't mention it, I should think it will be provided. Why?"

Crane had to assume that Tibbett would know where the job was. Regardless, he would never break professional protocol, no matter what his mental/emotional state.

"It's in a country that does not allow non-governmental employees to carry calibers used by the military," Peter replied.

Tibbett saw the change in Peter's demeanor already. His old friend was coming back. He allowed himself the luxury of thinking that his call had been the right one to get the man back on his feet and out of the bottle as the conversation thus turned to logistics and tools.

Tibbett also permitted himself a rare smile at his younger friend's superstitions.

"Peter, when are you going to get over this juvenile, fetishistic obsession of yours with the caliber .45 ACP? In spite of your fervent and peculiar belief system, it does not ward off evil. Besides," less in jest now, "it tags you as an American."

"So does my passport, Roger." Crane took the chair opposite Tibbett's desk with easy familiarity.

"That man didn't say a thing to me about the nature of the threat, past attempts, or anything else. But I know by looking at him that he has pissed-off a lot of people in his lifetime, and if there's going to be an attempt it's going to be serious. I seriously doubt that a handgun will be useful at all but allow me this one concession to my superstition."

"Very well, I believe we may have a mutual acquaintance in the restaurant business. I also believe he may know someone in that country that may be able to help. Why don't you contact him?"

Crane nodded, he hadn't thought of that. Eugene Smith knew people all over the world. He also knew how to ship anything anywhere. Peter also wondered if Smith would know a good tailor in Mexico City. Peter finished his coffee in a couple of gulps, and stood to leave.

"You really do need to get some decent coffee in here Roger if you don't want your corporate buddies thinking you're running the show on the cheap and pocketing the expense budget." Tibbett grunted in reply, as he removed his wristwatch from his left wrist.

"Peter," Tibbett called catching him in the doorway. Tibbett tossed the watch, across the room, at Peter's head. Peter snatched the airborne missile out of its projected arc, inches away from his face. He opened his hand and saw Tibbett's watch, a Breitling, Aeromarine, GMT (Greenwich Mean Time). The back of the watch had been engraved with the military seal of Tibbett's old unit: a winged dagger superimposed with a banner emblazoned "*WHO DARES WINS*". It had been a retirement gift to Tibbett when he left the SAS, and Peter knew it to be one of Tibbett's very few and very treasured material possessions. "I'm afraid this may be a bad one, Peter. Watch yourself," Tibbett said simply. Crane knew this was a significant act on Tibbett's part. He silently nodded his gratitude and left.

Peter Crane drove a used, beat up, 1988 Toyota Tercel. It was an odd kind of aluminum/silver color. He always thought of it as the Silver Slug. He didn't particularly care for it but so far it had been satisfactory. In the six months that he had been in Palm Springs he only had to replace all four tires, the battery, the exhaust system, the starter motor, the transmission, and it really, really, wanted a new engine but he kept putting that item off.

He drove down the main drag of Palm Springs ruminating over the arrangements he would need to make in preparation for his trip. His eye was magnetically attracted to the newly acquired wristwatch on his left wrist. It was quite a gesture on Tibbett's part and quite unexpected. Buddy Guy sang Baby Don't Leave on the car's stereo. He turned this corner and turned that corner, and as he pulled the car into the parking lot of a grocery store, he seriously toyed with the idea of selling the car for parts to one of the rent-a-wreck dealers that populated the strip. But now to the business at hand—first things first—deal with the hangover.

Inside the store, he made his way to the beer aisle and pulled a six-pack of the highest alcohol content beverage he could find out of the cooler, and then deftly made his way to the aisle for tomato juice, picking up some Jell-O and saltine crackers on the way. Halfway to the checkout stand he remembered aspirin and smartly executed an about face and walked directly into her spilling his groceries as well as hers.

She started, "CL…"

He cut her off with a curt but subtle shake of his head.

"Well, Peter..." she looked at the mess on the floor "...pickling yourself again I see."

"Hello Linda. God, you're as gorgeous as ever. Haven't seen you in a while. How have you been?"

"Are you drunk?" When she met him he wouldn't touch a drop. Now he virtually swam in the stuff.

"Me? Oh, I've been fine, thanks for asking." Then, dropping the tone of feigned civility, "No I'm not. I'm coming out of one actually." He answered flatly.

"Oh." She said simply and began retrieving her items from the floor to the hand basket. He could not put his finger on it but something about the way she said "Oh", something about the way she simply and quietly turned to a menial task at hand, made her seem very familiar, very sad, and very missed.

He knelt down to help.

"Linda, I..." and she looked at him sharply, he lost his words.

"You what?" She probed, and pushed.

"I'm ...sorry." It was all he could think of to say. He felt small, alone, unprepared, and uniquely inadequate. She had broken up with him and his drunken demeanor had been posturing. Linda looked at him. He was most definitely not a "pretty-boy", as he was wont to call some practitioners of his peculiar profession, usually the ones in the company of celebrities. It had occurred to her many times in the past that if he had been cast in a Hollywood movie about bodyguards, he most definitely would not have been the lead. She recalled almost fondly that he might have been cast as a thug or a walk-on extra—someone in the periphery of the story. Indeed, she realized that was what he was now: someone cast far into the periphery of her story. She stood and left her basket and groceries on the floor. She gave him a look that cut him to the quick.

"Take care of yourself, Peter." And she was gone. Again. She was gone, out the door, and out of his life, forever.

After leaving the grocery store, he checked out the storage locker, withdrew what he would send on, and secured the rental space. He called Eugene Smith in Seattle who was adept at shipping things. Peter went to a light-freight/parcel service, and then went home. Everything would fall into place but right now he had to take care of his headache.

72

The flight to Mexico City was uneventful. He arrived a few days early, rented a car and drove to Sonora to meet the friend of a friend, and this particular friend ran a restaurant...of sorts. It was two in the afternoon and the sun was high in the sky on this day in the middle of January. The patrons of this establishment would not arrive before dusk. "La Casa Camino Real" was quite the nightspot.

He meticulously checked the contents of the package: an old Glock Model 21 in .45ACP. A long time advocate of the expression: "One is none, two is one, three is better," Peter endeavored to maintain at least two copies of each working gun in his personal battery. He had lost one Glock under the bridge back at PI. This was an older Model 21 with slightly more character but it was still chambered in .45ACP. That was the important part. Peter then paid the man the agreed fee, took his property, and drove back to the city.

The Zona Rosa in Mexico City pulsated with glitzy shops, restaurants, hotels and nightlife. Of the latter, one would find mariachis, troubadours, and some of the deadliest tequila in the world in abundance. On Eugene Smith's recommendation Peter Crane found his way to a comparatively discreet tailor shop not far from the hotel where he would meet the lead man for Mr. Lee's protective detail. On display in the tailor's shop were examples of the product that had earned their maker the just reputation of being a master of his craft, although Crane had very little appreciation for what he was looking at. He could guess that the articles of clothing on display were good but he had no idea why. A man stooped over with the history of a career of working with his hands asked him, "May I help you, Senor?" Peter simply told the man the truth. "I need a good suit." After a brief appraisal of Peter's attire the tailor responded. "Yes, of course you do. This way please," and led him to a fitting room. About thirty minutes later Crane emerged into the retail area a little ambivalent about the cost of the two suits, three shirts, two pair of trousers, and new tie he had just committed to, but no small consolation was the fact that the garments would be made to his specification—to conceal a large handgun without printing its impression on the fabric of the suits. The tailor, well acquainted with the unique requirements of Crane's profession, quietly trailed him to the shop floor, gently tapped his hand on Peter's shoulder and said, "Come back tomorrow at this time, it will be ready then."

On the day of his appointment with the protective team leader, Peter entered the hotel lobby, finding his bearings, when a younger, elegantly dressed man with a military manner—squared shoulders, a well-trimmed waist, an erect spine, an angular elbow, a click of the heels, and a pronounced contempt for everything civilian, abruptly extended his arm to plant his hand in the center of Peter's chest. Peter stopped just short of the man's reach, stepped off the centerline and simultaneously pivoted his torso, allowing the younger man to push his hand through the air right in front of him. Peter now stood to the man's rear. The younger man turned about, somewhat nonplussed.

"Crane?" the young man imperiously intoned. Peter nodded.

"Right, then. I'm John Pounds, team leader. Do what you're told when you're told to do it and we'll get along fine. Come with me." The hair on the back of Peter's neck tickled but not in a good way.

Pounds led Peter Crane to the two hotel floors that would be the site of operations for most of Mr. Lee's visit in Mexico City. After a cursory tour by Mr. Pounds, Peter was told to report to one of the conference rooms at 5 PM that day and was dismissed as the whole team had not yet arrived. Peter checked in at the desk and was assigned a room. Until then he was on his own. He knew that from 5 PM on, his time belonged to his employer and he would have little free time to himself. He decided now would be a good time to move the rental car, as he would not need it for the next three days, and to make other arrangements. It was important to be prudent. It was Peter's personal rule Number One: always leave yourself a way out.

73

At 5 pm Peter walked into the designated conference room and was met by six other team members. Pounds entered shortly thereafter and proceeded with the situation report, threat assessment, schedules, and duty assignments. The boy had done his homework, no doubt about it. The next day they would move in three separate vehicles to the airport to pick up the principal and deliver him to the hotel for the first day of meetings. Mr. Lee would be under escort of his own personal bodyguards, nephews apparently, who would be at his side until he stepped back on board the aircraft for his return trip to Manila.

Two of the three vehicles were standard Ford sedans. The third, designated the VIP Vehicle, was a Lincoln Town Car, manufactured in Wixom, Michigan and up-fitted in Ogden, Utah. Materials such as aramid fiber, ceramic blanket material, a steel box fabricated around the battery, polycarbonate/glass laminate, and armored plate, made the car resistant to small caliber projectiles for a limited period of time. However, the increased weight required the installation of up-graded springs, shocks, brakes, run flat tires, a non-standard chip to compensate the computer's interface with the fuel injectors, and other engine modifications to increase the horsepower. It was a state of-the-art up-armored limousine but it wasn't bullet proof. An armored vehicle can only buy time for the occupants. The amount of time would depend on the intensity and duration of the assault.

As any one of the three cars could become the VIP car in an emergency they were all equipped with standard Remington 870 shotguns and ample shot shells. Carbines and sub-machine guns were not permitted to non-governmental personnel. The three men who would function as drivers would have primary responsibility for the security of the vehicles.. Direct and succinct, Pounds proceeded through the entire operations order quickly and efficiently.

Peter would find out later what Pounds had omitted: Lee was acting as surrogate for a government that was covertly directing funds, armaments, and munitions in the guise of "foreign aid" to the recipient country that was documenting everything as foreign aid received. One of the links in the chain on the receiving end had been siphoning the lion's share of the "aid." When Mr. Lee found out about it, he shut down the entire operation. The "aid" had been miss-directed to the very element that had been the recipient government's target of suppression. The recipient government demanded that the op be turned back on and Lee insisted that they plug their leak first, then they'd re-negotiate.

Indeed, the American State department's travelers' alert spelled out concerns in plain language to the effect that Mexican drug cartels were engaged in an increasingly violent struggle for control of narcotics trafficking routes along the U.S. - Mexico border in an apparent response to the Government of Mexico's initiatives to crack down on narco-trafficking organizations. In order to combat violence, the government of Mexico had deployed military troops in various parts of the country. U.S. citizens were encouraged to cooperate fully with official checkpoints when traveling on Mexican highways. Some recent Mexican army and police confrontations with drug cartels had taken on the characteristics of small-unit combat, with cartels employing automatic weapons and, on occasion, grenades. Firefights had taken place in many towns and cities across Mexico but particularly in northern Mexico, including Tijuana, Chihuahua City and Ciudad Juarez. The travelers' advisory further cautioned that the situation in northern Mexico remained fluid; the location and timing of future armed engagements could not be predicted.

In such a fluid environment it was no surprise when the weak link had turned up dead in Ciudad Juarez the week before Peter's meeting with Mr. Lee. The series of meetings in the hotel were the sessions of "re-negotiation." The meetings would take place at the hotel for three days. What Peter and the others had not been told was that a fourth day of "meetings" would be required ostensibly to finalize the agreements between Lee and a governmental representative with authority and deniability. But the only people that knew that at this stage of the scenario were Pounds and the people who had persuaded him to view things from their perspective.

As a gesture of good will, the aid recipient had made the entire top two floors of the hotel available for the negotiations. The upper floor contained Mr. Lee's penthouse, the rooms assigned to his nephews, and the meeting spaces in which the negotiations would be held. The floor just below it was where the six bodyguards and the team leader would be billeted—if they got the opportunity to sleep. The hotel operations functioned normally with the exception that anyone going to the top floor would be stopped at the floor below it, searched, and escorted to the appropriate reception area in anticipation of the pre-arranged meeting with Mr. Lee. There were two elevators with a man posted at each. Two men were posted outside the door of whichever room Mr. Lee occupied, and accompanied him when moving from one meeting to the next in addition to his perpetually-present personal bodyguards. When not tasked with other requirements, the remaining three were on personal time (sleeping or eating). Pounds roamed about loose and supervised the other bodyguards.

It was grueling, mind numbing, boring work. Standing in a hotel hallway staring at a wall paper pattern for a twelve hour shift, and staying alert isn't much fun. After the first day the hotel management removed all the potted plants from the top two floors.

At the end of the third day of meetings everyone was looking forward to the next day's ride to the airport and then a flight home. The contract ended with the balance of the agreed fee and the customary gratuity when the principal boarded the airplane. Pounds assembled his team in the conference room and informed them of the next day's meeting that had suddenly and unexpectedly become overwhelmingly crucial. No one made an audible comment at the prospect of a fourth day of potted plant duty but it was apparent in the atmosphere in the room that all of the bodyguards shared the same opinion. The last, final, and crucial meeting would not be held at the hotel. It would instead be conducted at a public and neutral site where everyone was assured to be on his or her best behavior. The hair on the back of Peter's neck stood on end. At the end of the briefing he was on personal time and had an errand to run.

74

The site chosen for the final day's meeting was the National History Museum in Chapultepec Park, the foremost museum of anthropology and archaeology in the western hemisphere. Prior to leaving the hotel, weapons and appropriate certificates were issued to each of the protective team members. Anything larger than .38 caliber was considered a military type weapon and contraband for civilians, the possession of which carried a jail sentence of from five to thirty years. The men were issued .32 caliber handguns, the issuance of which had been approved by the Military Zone Headquarters for the Distrito Federal de Mexico.

Cleague had had his own ideas about personal safety equipment, something for which he had planned with the tailor when he had ordered his suits prior to the principal's meetings in the hotel. The cut of the suit allowed Peter to wear the .45 caliber Glock and the remaining three magazines—a total of 53 rounds—undetected...as long as he wasn't physically searched; the previous day's errand was to retrieve his hardware and check on the security of the rental car.

Peter was assigned point man for the box and would ride in the lead car with the driver. Lee, Pounds, and the nephews would ride in the center car, with the remainder of the protective team bringing up the rear of the three-vehicle convoy. They arrived at the museum without incident. Peter and another BG (body guard) were assigned exterior security at the entrance of the museum. The final meeting would be conducted inside. Mr. Lee and the ministry official had the entire building to themselves as the museum had been closed to the public due to an unfortunate yet unavoidable maintenance problem.

Even for January in the Equatorial Zone it was a very pleasant day and Peter had no problem with his assigned post, after having been in the hotel for the past seventy-two hours he enjoyed being outdoors. The museum had been completed in 1964 and was built to house one of the finest collections of Pre Columbian anthropological artifacts and Mesoamerican art in the western hemisphere. The museum was built on a verdant domain and overlooked a wooded expanse and several small lakes. Studded with flower gardens, separate arboreta, several other museum buildings, parking lots, and a network of single lane roads, the park spanned nearly five square miles. He quietly noted the passers-by— the young couples, the tourists, and the nurses with their infant charges in baby carriages and strollers. Balloon peddlers, knickknack vendors and maintenance men in overalls populated the area. The maintenance men seemed to be grounds keepers and apparently tended to something along the drive in the entrance/exit area of the museum proper; no matter, the cars would be beckoned by radio before the principal walked out the building. Peter noted the maintenance activity as a potential bottleneck—he'd have to keep an eye on it.

The drivers had stayed with the cars but Peter monitored them anyway. The cars were parked in the parking area to Peter's left; the groundskeepers were digging up bushes or something along the drive to Peter's right. They had a lot of bags of fertilizer stacked on the back of that truck. Peter wondered how many flowerbeds could be in the park. He caught himself letting his mind start to wander. *Time to pay attention,* he admonished himself. One young lady pushing a stroller, he noted, seemed to be making a circuit of the driveway in front of the museum entrance, the car park, and the sidewalks on either side of the drive.

All of the protective team was equipped with discreet Motorola radios with the telltale earplugs, clichéd but effective; they all heard Pounds give the drivers the order to bring the cars to the entrance. Peter continued watching the young woman and noticed that she changed her circuitous path of travel just then and headed back toward the museum's entrance. In his peripheral vision he caught one of the balloon vendors change his position from where he had been standing the past two hours and move toward the approach to the museum. The groundskeepers were busily fussing over something near the drive, their big flatbed Ford very nearly blocking the sole exit for vehicular traffic out of the museum parking lot.

To keep things simple for radio communication Pounds had split the detail into two teams: Alpha team for the actual VIP protective detail, and Bravo team for the drivers. Peter's colleague at the entrance was Alpha One, Peter was Alpha Two, Alpha Three and Alpha Four were inside with the nephews. The drivers were Bravo One, Bravo Two and Bravo Three. Lee was "PRINCIPAL" and the nephews were Nephew #1 and Nephew #2. Pounds was "Lead".

Peter heard Pounds give the order for "...Alpha One, Alpha Two, flank the door." Although not rehearsed, the procedure had been reviewed prior to leaving the hotel and it was fairly standard. Peter and colleague would flank the door, as the principal, who was flanked by his nephews, emerged from the entrance, Peter and colleague would step in front of them by not more than three paces. Alpha Three and Alpha Four would be immediately to PRINCIPAL'S rear and Pounds would trail them thus providing rear security and the ability to observe and direct the movement of the team—

essentially forming a box around the principal. The vehicles smartly pulled up to the curb in front of the entrance which was separated by the broad expanse of graduated shallow steps from the door down to ground level, a short distance of finely manicured lawn latticed the walkway in a geometric pattern, and the very wide sidewalk—possibly a span of about twenty-five yards from the front door to the curb.

As the team moved toward the cars, Peter was on the left, Alpha One on the right followed by Nephew #1, PRINCIPAL, and Nephew #2, followed by Alpha Three and Alpha Four followed by Team Leader Pounds. One of the biggest challenges for a close protection team is to beware distractions from the priority of getting the principal from 'A' to 'B'. At the same time, everybody in the "box" has to be aware of his or her environment. Peter heard a car door slam and noticed a dark colored sedan with darkened windows pass the VIP entourage waiting at the curb; he paid it little mind. In his peripheral vision Peter noticed movement to his right, looked, and noted that the balloon vendor had lost his huge bouquet of colorful, plastic, helium-filled, toys. They arced lazily upward into a clear blue sky.

Immediately scanning the area to his left he saw the lady with the stroller pull something out of the carriage. She was now nearly between them and the VIP car, twenty-five feet, if that. He instinctively stood erect and slowed his forward movement to put him closer to PRINCIPAL, simultaneously drawing the .45 caliber Glock from its inside waistband holster on his right side just behind the iliac crest of the hip and yelling "**CONTACT FRONT!**"

Peter indexed his front sight on the woman producing an Uzi carbine from the baby carriage as Alpha One was yelling about contact to the right. Peter brought the Glock into his line of sight as the woman began spraying the vicinity of the team with 9mm bullets. Peter prayed his silent mantra, *Sight picture, trigger, FRONT SIGHT, PRESS*. Peter put a bullet into the point of aim on his target—directly in line with the woman's medulla oblongata. Alpha One had engaged balloon man a little late. Nephew #1 was down, Alpha One was down and so were Balloon man, and the stroller lady. Peter continuously scanned the area 180 degrees to the team's front and found it odd that the radio was quiet. Thinking Pounds must have gone down in the attack he stole a glimpse behind him to see that Pounds wasn't there but Alpha Three and Alpha Four had PRINCIPAL nearly bent over double, furiously pushing him and Nephew #2 toward the cars.

Scanning to the front again Peter noted that the groundskeepers had blocked the only way out of the museum parking lot by pulling their five-ton flat bed across the driveway; he also noted the dark-colored sedan in the driveway just beyond the flatbed truck leaving the area. The "groundskeepers" were behind the truck and were directing automatic weapons fire onto the team. The team was well with-in the maximum effective range of the opposition's assault weapons, however—the opposition was comfortably removed from the maximum effective range of the .32 caliber mouse guns with which the team had been provided. Standing on the far side of the flat bed truck, the stacked bags of fertilizer providing ample mass for a bullet trap, the opposition directed their fields of fire into the team. Bravo One, the driver of the lead vehicle, flanked his car to the flatbed firing his shotgun from inside the car through the passenger window to provide the team with cover fire as they made their way to the VIP car—the up-armored Lincoln Town Car— the second in line.

While making their way to the VIP car Nephew #2 went down. Peter pulled open the back door while continuously returning fire as Alpha Three pushed PRINCIPAL to the floorboard between the armored front and rear seats. Alpha Four took a position beside the front axle and returned fire around the front end of the car. Ensconced behind the passenger side of the VIP car, Peter engaged the opposition as best he could, firing his Glock to slide lock. He executed a hasty reload and continued to provide covering fire for Bravo One who was trying to make his way back to the protective cover of the armored limousine. With Peter, Alpha Three, and Alpha Four continuously firing at the adversaries behind the flat-bed Ford, Bravo One sprinted toward the VIP car. He was cut down with small arms fire from what sounded to be AK-47s. The lead vehicle erupted in fire and glass. Peter could not see the source of the explosion, it wasn't bullets—it was too big and too loud. It had to be something man-portable, like a grenade launcher.

Alpha Three and Alpha Four were out of ammo. Peter inserted a fresh magazine into the Glock, racked the slide and chambered the next round. Scanning the area again Peter felt his heart drop in his chest when he caught sight through the laminated glass of the Lincoln of two men taking aim with RPGs ... a Soviet grenade launcher intended to disable light to medium fortifications and vehicles...like an armored sedan for example. Alpha Three saw the same thing and dove in on top of PRINCIPAL. Peter started yelling at the driver "...Go! Go! Go!" when the engine compartment exploded in shrapnel and sound.

The first grenade made contact through the center of the grill, through the radiator and into the engine block resulting in a radial burst of metal confetti—the shrapnel shower rained down, on, and through Alpha Four. The second grenade flew through the space previously occupied by the air filter and various electronic components until it crushed on impact with the firewall resulting in the release of high temperature, high-pressure energy in the engine compartment. The Monroe effect of explosive energy through the firewall caused the dashboard of the interior of the sedan to fragment and perforate everything between the steering wheel and the polyaramid reinforced vertical backs of the front seats. Peter's ears were ringing. He moved his jaw to get his ears to pop and make the high pitched squeal in his head go away—it didn't work.

Bravo Two, the VIP driver, was eviscerated. Alpha Four was dead. Peter and Alpha Three both worked to peel PRINCIPAL off the floorboard of the passenger compartment of the Lincoln while Bravo Three brought his car up alongside but slightly behind the limo when the remaining vehicle was hit by another RPG round. The grenade made impact with the driver's door killing Bravo Three. Another RPG round was fired at Vehicle #3 and the engine compartment was turned inside out. All three vehicles were destroyed and on fire.

Peter put his handgun back in its holster while he, PRINCIPAL, and Alpha Three took advantage of the little cover available at the rear axle of the Lincoln. Scanning the area again in 360 degrees Peter noticed the woman's Uzi on the ground only a few feet away and lunged for it. He handed the gun to Alpha Three and then made his way to the tail car, keeping a very low profile. Alpha Three provided a short burst of cover fire. Peter retrieved the shotgun and the shells before the fire consumed the interior cab. Cleague ducked back to the meager cover provided by the burning wreckage of the VIP car.

75

Rhetorically Alpha Three asked, "Now what?" Peter pointed to their left front toward the wooded stretch of park that sloped down to a lake and another parking lot.

"There, through the trees."

Alpha Three looked to the flatbed truck, then gauged the distance from their burning, useless sedan to the wooded area and responded very matter-of-factly.

"Are you nuts?"

"Yep. Certifiable. They'll be coming to finish us off soon," as he checked the chamber of the shotgun and topped off the tube magazine under the barrel. He dumped the rest of the shells from the box into his jacket pocket.

"I can give you cover while you carry him." Alpha Three said, indicating PRINCIPAL. Peter curtly shook his head no.

"We both need to flank him; we go on 'three'."

It was closer and safer moving forwards to the trees than it was backwards to the museum doors which Peter knew would be locked, bolted, barred, and welded shut by now. Smoke grenades to mask their movement would have been handy. Hell, rifles chambered in .308 would have been better, and not being in an ambush at all would have been preferable. But, as his Marine Corps training came back to him, you have to play the cards you are dealt: Adapt, Improvise, and Over-Come.

Firmly positioning themselves on either side of PRINCIPAL who seemed to be in shock: pale skin, dilated pupils, non-responsive manner, Peter started "...One, two, three!" The three of them ran out from behind the diminishing cover of the burning wreck, Alpha Three provided a short burst of fire as they literally carried Mr. Lee across the pavement through the grass and into the sparse cover of trees, then discarded the Uzi. Peter became the tail man—providing rear security for Principal and BG#3 as the men from behind the truck made out after them; the big flatbed moved into gear to take up another position to block their escape from the park. Using slugs, Peter effectively used the shotgun as a short-range rifle on the pursuers, reloading while moving backward with alacrity.

The lower parking lot adjacent to the small lake was sparsely populated with vehicles but several taxies were queued by the exit. Peter handed off the shotgun to Alpha Three. They made it to the nearest taxi and while Peter threw the operator out of the driver's seat, "Con permiso, per favor", and pushed Lee in ahead of him, Alpha Three continued to provide covering fire.

"Get in!" Peter yelled to Alpha Three as he started the taxi and put it in gear, barely allowing his last remaining team mate to board the vehicle as he launched out of the parking lot.

Nearing the exit from the park Peter saw the flatbed blocking their path and shouted "Hold on!" Alpha Three saw what was coming and prepared Lee for the collision.

Peter violently forced the battered Chevy Caprice Taxicab over the curb and took advantage of its big engine to cut through the trees and through the line of opposition groundskeepers that had formed nearly shoulder-to-shoulder pelting them with automatic small arms fire. Peter slumped down in his seat barely keeping his eyes above the level of the dashboard as the windshield burst in a spider-webbed fog effectively blinding him. He slapped Alpha Three on the shoulder and yelled "Glass!" Alpha Three knocked the fractured windshield out from the inside with the butt of the shotgun stock allowing Peter to see that he was headed toward a group of small children at a very high rate of speed.

Downshifting and jerking the wheel he diverted the big Chevy through a copse of trees narrowly escaping the kids. Racing them to the exit was the dark-colored sedan; windows down, sprouting the muzzles of pistol-gripped AK's with the stocks removed.

The perimeter fence to the park was a stout wrought iron affair that Peter was not about to try to penetrate, choosing instead to follow it to the Park Exit. He jumped the big Chevy over the curb and back onto the drive out of the Park. He arrived at an arched entry gate at the same time as the sedan. Taking automatic rifle fire again, he paralleled the other car, slowed, and nudged his bumper just ahead of their rear tire which propelled them around the front end of the taxi-cab and into the oncoming traffic of the Paseo de la Reforma, all without losing forward motion.

In the local fashion, Peter implanted the heel of his hand into the car's horn and glided the cab through the intersection, paying little heed to the decorative pink hues of the overhead traffic signal and made the first right turn possible. Checking the rearview mirror and seeing nothing but a cavalcade of metro police vehicles speeding to the Park. The clarion two-tone wail of their sirens peaked and receded as Peter pulled the taxi over and double-parked. "Let's Go!" he called at Alpha Three.

It took a second to register. Alpha Three was slumped against the door, his head at an odd angle to his shoulders, a deep crimson stain extended downward and outward on his shirt as Peter watched. Alpha Three's eyes stared vacantly, dully, blindly at a distant point that Peter was unable to see. He had taken a round at the junction of the neck and head just behind the ear when they were parallel to the sedan. Peter immediately checked Lee. PRINCIPAL still had a pulse.

Lee's jacket was covered in blood. Peter removed the man's suit coat, removed his tie, and loosened his collar. Mr. Lee was in shock but he still had a pulse and was breathing; that was enough for now. Peter emptied Lee's jacket pockets and stuffed Principal's Passport, ID, and wallet into his own pockets. Peter grabbed Mr. Lee's right arm just above the bicep. They walked away from the cab quickly, turned a corner and walked into the first large store he could find. They immediately left that store through another door that put them on the opposite side of the block from the abandoned cab. They hopped on a bus and stayed on it for a few blocks and got off, taking the first available taxi Peter spied. He and Mr. Lee got in the back seat this time and gave the driver an address: the tailor shop in La Zona Rosa.

So far, so good. When Peter had run his errand the previous night, he had arranged with the tailor to keep his car for him until he needed it. Now he needed it. Both Peter and Mr. Lee made a change of clothing. Peter took more time now to examine the physical condition of his charge. Lee was now verbally responsive although not quite talkative.

"My nephews, where are they?" He asked in a small voice.

"They didn't make it, sir. Your nephews were good men and they knew what they were doing. We have to leave now." Peter was not unsympathetic to the man's loss but he was direct. It is what it is—deal with the emotional impact later.

After making further logistical arrangements with the tailor, they drove to the airport without incident. He was able to arrange for Lee to get the next plane out to Manila, as Lee's private charter was not due until the following day. The tailor would provide appropriate shipping arrangements to return Peter's hardware to him via an address in Seattle, Washington, in care of one Eugene Smith with whom the tailor was familiar, as he cheerfully agreed to bill Mr. Lee for all services rendered.

Peter stayed with his charge. Waiting with Mr. Lee in the VIP lounge they exchanged few words. After a time, however, Mr. Lee turned to Peter.

"Your actions were commendable...all of you. I only regret that I did not perceive Mr. Pounds' character for what it is." A subject of sudden and intense interest, Peter immediately warmed to the conversation, keeping one eye on the door.

"If I may ask sir, where did you find Pounds?"

Lee responded with the name of an agency in Los Angeles. Peter knew of it and regarded it as a reputable company. All of the members of Lee's protective detail were provided through the agency in Los Angeles with the exception of Peter Crane. It seemed that Mr. Lee had agreed to meet with Peter as a personal favor to Roger Tibbett. Peter had not known that particular detail. The Public Address system in the first class lounge announced boarding for the flight to Manila in four languages.

"You will find him, Mr. Crane?" Lee asked, looking him straight in the eye.

"Yes Mr. Lee, I will find him if you wish. But recalling the words of someone far wiser than myself, we are all creatures of habit. It would seem to me that if you found him there once, you'll probably find him there again." Peter responded, holding the man's gaze. Lee considered Peter's observation and nodded in agreement.

"They'll be here shortly. You should be boarding now, Sir." Again Lee nodded.

"I will arrange for your legal representation Mr. Crane,

do not worry." Peter saw Mr. Lee off at the boarding gate. Shortly after Lee's departure the Federales showed up. Peter would be staying in Mexico a bit longer than he had planned.

76

The bar in West Hollywood was dark, stuffy, and crowded. It echoed with raucous laughter. He sat at a table keeping an eye on one particular party—the star of which was throwing money around without regard—obviously impressing the ladies on either side of him with the prospect of a profitable night's work. The man sitting by himself drank club soda with lime. He ordered food so that he be allowed to sit at the table and ate slowly, seemingly pre-occupied with his dinner. The star of the party—John Pounds—finally got up and made his way through the din and clutter and foot traffic of the popular nightspot to the rest room. The man sitting alone had counted at least three rounds of drinks in the past forty minutes. He threw sufficient currency on the table and walked away.

Pounds was alone in the public rest room standing at the urinal. He heard someone come in behind him but paid it no mind. Before he could react someone had grabbed his left arm just below the shoulder; their grip was extremely tight. In spite of the star's ineffective struggles, they had managed to keep hold of his arm and now had gotten their right hand into his hair. Lodging their foot behind his, they pulled back on the top of his head and instantly he was flat on his back on the floor. With their left knee in the center of his chest he felt the air escape him like a deflating balloon. The face...faces, looked vaguely familiar. For some reason he associated the face with that thing back in Mexico—that had been lucrative. It occurred to him that it was funny how he could remember that in such a detached fashion. If only he weren't so damned drunk, the guy had two heads! But he was awfully earnest. Pounds saw the other man produce a very thin-bladed, extremely sharp looking knife. He felt something cold draw deeply across his throat from right to left; everything started to feel kind of numb around his neck. His vision became less sharp, less distinct, clouded, blurred. Dim. Dark. Black.

The man folded the straight razor and neatly tucked it into the corpse's breast pocket and pulled it's tongue out through the slit made above the esophagus, then liberally dumped a number of inch-square cellophane packets filled with a white powder. An apparent turf skirmish, this tonier part of Los Angeles was a much-coveted area of operations for countless numbers of merchandisers all vying for the same clientele. The man unlocked the door, and casually left the bar for the long trip back home. He discarded the surgical gloves out the window on the outskirts of the city. His brother left by a different route. They knew that their uncle would be quietly pleased.

77

Peter Crane sat in a cell about forty feet by forty feet and shared it with many compadres. By his nature, Peter did not enjoy the company of other people—a lot of other people. Peter took solace in solitude. Peter was in hell. It was worse than Dante had ever imagined it.

February came and went. He once saw a movie about a Danish lady that had a farm in Africa. One day that lady went on a picnic with a man she had met. The man told the lady about the members of a certain warrior tribe that, if imprisoned, would die because they had no concept of tomorrow. Now Crane understood what that meant. Mr. Lee had given Peter his word. Peter just had to trust Mr. Lee to keep it. He did have the opportunity to talk with an *abogado* who assured him things were being taken care of. Peter had no idea what that meant. But Mr. Lee was standing by his promise of providing legal representation.

On the fifteenth of March Peter Crane was released from jail. He had lost a fair amount of weight. He hated Mexican food. On his release from jail he went back to the hotel where the meetings had been held to retrieve the personal belongings that were left in his room. After finding out that Crane had been sent to jail, the hotel management donated Cranes stuff to a local mission. Crane thought to himself that there had to be at least one very well-dressed homeless person somewhere on the streets of Mexico City. What the hell, at least he was out of jail. His plane ticket was still good and he took the next available flight to Los Estados Unidos; he could not get out of Mexico and back to California fast enough.

78

John Luther got a call from the AG's office that funding had been made available from a discretionary account and the investigation was back on. Luther immediately picked up the phone and made an appointment to interview a businessman in California.

When the commercial airliner rolled to a stop, Luther welcomed the opportunity to stand in the aisle for a few minutes before the passengers were allowed to disembark. He retrieved his carry-on bag from the overhead compartment and patiently waited his turn to march down the aisle, through the jet way, and onto the concourse of Palm Springs International, named one of the nation's top 10 "most stress free airports". John Luther was a tall man and hated to travel by airplane. His ankles, knees, and lower back ached without fail anytime he flew anywhere. He rented a car and made his way toward an industrial park.

Prior to shutting down the office in Bellingham, Agent Glyndon had been able to determine from IRS records that Peter Cleague had filed three copies of Schedule C for federal income tax for the year preceding the events on PI based on payment received from a couple of magazine publishers, several individuals (apparently his bodyguard work), and a company located in Palm Springs called Hereford Associates, as an independent contractor for services rendered. More bodyguard stuff? Who knew? Luther would have to go talk to them and ask. Glyndon had also informed him that she had been able to find an address for someone from Cleague's old reserve unit. A Gunnery Sergeant Schynd had a last known address of PO Box 1775, Mountain Home, Texas. Luther did not know if it would be worth the time it would take to go all the way to the Texas hill country to conduct an interview with an old Marine Gunnery Sergeant but he would worry about that later.

After a short drive he found the suite of low-keyed offices in a business park not far from the airport. It was June and quite warm in the high desert of California. God, he hated the desert. Virginia, his home, was hot and humid, but this was life-threateningly hot. How the hell did people manage to function here? The door whispered shut behind him as the cool air broke over his skin. *Oh, yeah,* he thought, *air-conditioning.*

A receptionist sat at a desk, greeted him amiably and asked if she could be of help. The reception area sported the obligatory couch and chairs, table and magazines, potted plant, and a terrarium with what Luther believed to be a rattlesnake. *Interesting choice,* he mused. Luther introduced himself and asked for Mr. Tibbett. The receptionist picked up the phone and informed Mr. Tibbett—she called him Roger— that Mr. Luther was here to see him. The earpiece of the phone made a muted noise, she said, "OK", and informed Luther that Roger would be right out. Indeed he was. He came down the short hallway and walked directly to Luther with an extended hand.

"Mr. Luther, I'm Roger Tibbett, what can I do for you?" Boy, people sure are friendly around here, Luther thought, as he shook Tibbett's hand: warm, dry, and firm.

Roger Tibbett told the receptionist, "We'll be in the conference room, Holly, no interruptions, please?" Holly responded, "Sure, Roger!" Luther noticed that Tibbett had just made a command in the form of asking a favor; he would have to try that.

Mr. Tibbett showed Mr. Luther into a conference room and offered refreshment.

"Would you like something to drink, coffee, water...?"

"Yes, please," Luther, responded with enthusiasm, "coffee—black." Luther did not eat or drink on airplanes because airplane rest rooms were designed for children. He had a caffeine deprivation headache.

Luther, unconsciously, maybe out of habit, took the chair at the end of the rectangular table. Tibbett, unfazed, served Luther his coffee, and took the chair to Luther's right.

"What can I do for you Mr. Luther?" Tibbett affably asked.

"As I mentioned on the phone, Mr. Tibbett, I'm with the Department of Justice and I am conducting an investigation. By the way, just out of curiosity, what is Hereford Associates?

"We are risk management consultants; we focus on security." Tibbett replied.

"Oh," Luther was not being intentionally obtuse, he just didn't know. "What is a risk management consultant?" He asked.

"Quite," Tibbett prepared to engage the question. "We cast a rather broad net. Risk management consultants will often be called upon to provide advice that may involve a variety of disciplines and skills such as threat assessment, threat analysis, consequence analysis, vulnerability assessment, and operational security including some aspects of managing a business. We are international in scope, Mr. Luther; we operate in every continent but one and in most countries of the world," Tibbett finished. Luther was stringing things together. "Hereford Associates," he paused, "does the name of your company have some reference to Hereford, England?"

Tibbett could not help but warm to the subject.

"Yes it does. Three of us on the board of directors who initially formed the company are all retired out of the British

Military. Our old unit, the one we retired from, has been based at Hereford in the west of England for many years." Tibbett replied with just a little bit of pride.

"Hereford, isn't that Headquarters of the Special Air Service?" Luther guessed.

"Yes it is." Roger replied.

"What did you do in the SAS?" Luther asked.

"Please understand that I am not being evasive, Mr. Luther, but even if I had been in the SAS, due to the Official Secrets Act, I wouldn't be able to say so. But if you were to research the subject, and I am sure you have better things to do, you will find that my parent unit was the Royal Electrical and Mechanical Engineers." Roger concluded amiably.

"What did you do?" Luther pressed with a smile.

"I spent a career in the British Military, Mr. Luther, and I did everything within the structure of our charter in so far as my orders dictated. When I retired I was in a training unit." Tibbett answered. *Well, that fits*, Luther mused.

"So, I'm guessing that your company would be pretty well regarded in the security industry." Luther ventured.

"Is that a question?" Tibbett asked. Luther indicated in the affirmative by raising his eyebrows and nodding his head as if prodding a slow child.

"Yes, we are. We are at the forefront of our industry, nationally and abroad: the pointy end of the spear as some of our people like to say." They both laughed at the pleasant witticism. Tibbett went on. "Our clients can range from high profile diplomats, businessmen, and celebrities to corporations, industries, and the legal profession. Indeed, some judges, unfortunately, find a pressing need for our services. Our standard is the epitome of the industry and is unsurpassed by any of our competitors." Tibbett concluded with an air of satisfaction.

Smug son-of-a-bitch Luther thought.

"That's very impressive, Mr. Tibbett, but what exactly does your company do? What is your product?" Luther asked.

"Our product," Tibbett replied, "is the design of the most complete security solution to fit a customer's specific requirement. We can design and, through our contractors, implement corporate and industrial security, residential security, special events, IT property concerns, data security, secure network systems, that sort of thing. We also provide services in personal and executive protection." Tibbett said.

"You provide bodyguards?" asked Luther.

"No, no, we analyze and assess a situation. We may recommend them, but we do not provide them. We do, however, provide a list of independent contractors. We also provide training to a client's previously existing security organization."

"What kind of training?" Luther asked.

"Small arms, defensive tactics, operating in small units, apprehension of suspects." Tibbett answered.

"That's quite a list of skills. Who does the training? You?" Luther asked.

At this point Tibbett had become painstakingly calm. After long experience of dealing with minor bureaucrats, he knew when he was being baited.

"Our training cadre is a mobile team of subject-matter experts. They are dedicated to providing state of the art current doctrine in various disciplines.' Tibbett said.

So much for the sales pitch, Luther thought. It was pretty well polished, he would concede that point.

"Mr. Tibbett, I am conducting an investigation into an event that led up to or caused the death of a number of Federal agents. One of the people we have an interest in talking to is one Peter Cleague."

Tibbett remained unmoved, unresponsive, a good poker player. Luther went on, "I understand that he works for you."

"No, not quite." Tibbett replied. "Peter Cleague was an independent contractor that did some training for us a while back."

"What did he teach?" Luther asked.

"Small arms skills and basic tactics." Tibbett answered.

Luther went on, "So what would qualify someone to teach on the behalf of Hereford Associates?"

"Competence, experience, and expertise in equal measure." Tibbett answered. Competence? That really did not seem to fit the picture Luther had gleaned from reading Cleague's Fitness Reports. Luther had to question this.

"And you're telling me Peter Cleague had those qualities?"

Roger Tibbett held John Luther's quizzical gaze as he replied.

"It is a point of fact Mr. Luther that your own State Department had enough confidence in Peter Cleague's abilities as to make him a security officer with supervisory responsibilities of a very major US installation in the Middle East. Now the fact that you people lost that embassy subsequent to Mr. Cleague's departure from Foreign Service should be somewhat of a testament to his abilities. It wasn't lost on his watch, now, was it?" Tibbett finished.

Luther considered this for a moment and had to admit, the man had a point. He could recall watching the TV news footage of that particular embassy being over-run by a really ugly mob. He remembered watching the film of the Marine helicopters leaving the embassy grounds and thinking how similar that scene looked to the US departure from Saigon some years previous.

79

Luther: "How long ago did Cleague work for Hereford Associates?"

Tibbett: "He and I taught a class together last year."

Luther: "Any bodyguard stuff?'

Tibbett: "No, primarily defensive handgun material."

Luther: "No, I mean did Hereford Associates employ him as a body guard?"

Tibbett: "No, Hereford doesn't employ bodyguards, however, he was offered and served a contract by our recommendation earlier this year."

Luther: "Who was the employer?"

Tibbett: "I can't say."

Luther: "When was the last time you saw him?"

Tibbett did not want to hurt his former friend. Neither would he lie. Whether he had used the nom de guerre of "Peter Stone" or "Peter Crane", it could be proved that Tibbett knew him to be Peter Cleague. Obfuscation at this juncture would be irrelevant and a waste of time. For whatever Peter had done, Peter would have to assume responsibility.

"Last month." Tibbett answered.

Luther nearly jumped out of his chair.

"You saw him last month?" Luther asked almost incredulous.

"Yes." Simply, matter of fact, Roger acquiesced.

"What did you talk about?" Luther asked, still managing, barely, to be civil.

"Mr. Cleague had been recommended to a client. He carried out his engagement with that client and we had an after-action briefing." Tibbett replied.

"And?" Luther probed.

"And the details of that conversation fall under confidentiality agreements we have with our clients. Even if I cared to, I could not divulge the content of that discussion." Tibbett replied.

Luther hated snags, especially from pompous, arrogant, self-righteous snobs.

"Do not stonewall me, Mister Tibbett. I can get a court order and shut down this business so fast it will make your head spin." Luther said, slightly less civilly.

Roger paused. He would not lose his temper in front of this underling, this marionette.

"Very well, go get your court order, Mr. Luther. Like your Department of Justice we maintain a battery of lawyers as well. I'm sure it will be in the courts for years. And I assure you, it will not shut us down." Tibbett was quiet and self-assured and pissing Luther off as the seconds ticked away and knew it.

"Incidentally, I am prohibited from divulging the contents of that conversation by law. As we also have contracts with the Federal government we must observe the provisions of the Privacy Act." Tibbett added. Touché.

Luther assessed. Time to drop back and punt.

"Do you know where he went?" Luther asked.

"No, I've no idea." Tibbett answered honestly.

"Did he have friends, family, relatives, anybody in the area?" Luther pressed.

"No. No-one that I know of." Well of course there was Linda but since she hadn't spoken to Cleague since he had arrived last summer, she didn't count did she? Tibbett kept his own council.

Luther was not one to waste time even if it was on the Federal dime and was quick to put an end to the interview. But it was not beneath John Luther to leave a parting gift.

"Mr. Tibbett, as this investigation progresses it's bound to get leaked to the press. It's just too big not to. It would be a shame if the reputation of Hereford Associates were to be connected to what so far seems to be an out-of-control psychopath."

Tibbett rose and opened the door. "Mr. Luther, Hereford Associates is committed to meeting the needs and expectations of our clients with professionalism, and discretion. I am confident our reputation will hold. Good day to you, Mr. Luther. Holly will see you out." Tibbett indicated down the hallway to the foyer and went back to his office.

Luther nodded and made his own way out to the receptionist's desk. *What was her name? Holly?*

"Excuse me, Holly?" Luther interrupted Holly as her fingernails clicked on a keyboard and she stared at a monitor. She stopped, glad for a break. "Yeah, hi," she beamed. *One thing about Hereford Associates*, Luther thought to himself, *they know how to pick 'em.*

"Holly, did you ever know someone who worked for this company named Peter Cleague?" Luther asked.

"Sure, I know Pete." Holly replied. Well that was certainly straightforward.

"Do you remember the last time you saw him?" Luther asked. Fishing, basically. She wouldn't tell him anything Tibbett hadn't told him, but you never know.

"Uhhh," she thought a bit, "last month I think."

"Do you have his home address?" Luther asked. She gave him Cleague's address in Palm Springs.

"How do you get there from here?" He asked.

She gave him directions and then added, "I think he left town," not wanting to get into a conversation about the argument Cleague had had with Roger that essentially got Cleague fired.

"He said something about wanting a change of scenery and moving on." She said helpfully.

"Did he say where?" Luther was starting to get his hopes up.

"No," she said, "Sorry.

"Yeah, me too. Do you know where he would have gone? Did he have any friends or family in the area? Or anywhere else?" Holly shook her head.

"No, He never talked about any family. He had a girl friend here in town but she broke it off a long time ago."'

"Do you know her name or where I can find her, it's really important."

"Gee, I'm sorry. No I don't, but I think she worked at a travel agency, or the visitor's bureau." She shook her head in doubt.

"Something like that."

Luther had to try one more time, "Don't remember her name, huh?"

"Lucy, uh, Lonnie, no, uh, Lisa? I'm sorry I just don't remember." Holly offered.

Well it was more than he had when he walked in here, and it would just have to be enough. Luther offered his thanks to Holly as he walked out of the pleasantly air conditioned office into the lung sucking heat of the California high desert. God he hated the desert.

He drove to the address for Cleague's apartment. The manager said Cleague had moved out. No problems, everything in order, always paid the rent on time, no complaints.

"Do you know where he went?" Luther asked.

"Nope. Not a clue." The manager answered.

Yeah, me neither, Luther thought.

Luther made up his mind. He had to go talk to Cleague's old buddy from the Reserves. He also had to find out who that girlfriend was. He drove to the airport and returned the rental car. He would make arrangements from there.

80

With no job, no prospects, and caustically-severed relationships there was little reason to stay in Palm Springs. Peter Cleague kept as low a profile as he possibly could while he made his way north on the I-5 corridor. Cleague went back to the Evergreen state to look for work, and found it, such as it was. A little sporting goods store north of Seattle needed a sales clerk and he was qualified on the basis of product knowledge alone. He gratefully took the position and made the conscious effort to keep his attitude in check—he was not a team leader trying to keep a high profile client alive, he was an errand boy supervised by grocery clerks—in a manner of speaking. He had heard this particular spot on the map described as the North Central Interior Puget Sound Region. He could not think of a more circumlocutionary manner of saying "Alger County".

Finding the job at the store when he did was a godsend but the downside to that was that he needed to find a place to live in two days. He was hired on a Friday and would start work on Monday. He found an apartment and would make do with it until he found something better.

Mr. Lee's generous remuneration for his performance in Mexico had left Peter a little bit ahead in the financial curve between survival and ruination. The payment received through Roger Tibbett's organization from Mr. Lee proved the Filipino to be a very generous man. In addition to the remaining balance of his agreed fee, and the legal fees incurred in Mexico City, Mr. Lee had included a very kind gratuity, along with a serious invitation to Cleague to work for Lee exclusively on a full-time basis. Cleague had accepted the compliment graciously and graciously declined the offer.

Roger Tibbett asked Cleague no questions regarding the gratuity because he simply did not want to know. But suspecting the gratuity to be linked to the murder in Los Angeles, which was broadcast for a standard news cycle the week that it happened, Tibbett told Peter it was time for him to leave; he no longer had a place at Hereford Associates. Peter did not protest, but simply asked, "Why?"

Tibbett responded, "I think we both know why, Peter."

Cleague understood Tibbett's unspoken accusation. Upon his return from Mexico City, Cleague had learned of the murder of Mr. Pounds. The little twerp had been found dead in a bar's men's room. "Well, good fucking riddance." Cleague said and offered no further explanation. He did not tell Tibbett to look at the dates of when the murder was reported to have occurred and the dates that he was an official guest of the Mexican Police. He thought it was so obvious any rational person would think of it. And the only reason to not consider the disparity in dates would be intentional. Cleague didn't feel the need to defend himself with an obvious fact. At that moment, the only thing Peter felt was a profound sense of betrayal. All the trust and empathy that had been established between these two men over time had dissolved in moments, with no residue of good-will remaining. He didn't understand it and he didn't question it. Of the many sins of human nature Cleague could forgive, betrayal was not among them. He accepted it and moved on. Cleague removed the Breitling wristwatch that Roger had given him prior to his trip to Mexico City and quietly laid it on Rogers's desk. Without saying a word Cleague turned away and walked out the door and never looked back.

He made his way up north and found the job at All North Sports. He then had to find a place to live in short order. He scoured papers, made phone calls, and this was the best (i.e.

only thing he could afford) place he could find with a vacancy—a low rent apartment complex in Sedro Woolley. On the phone the landlord was not quite brusque but not exactly effervescent either (couldn't fault him for that though) until he found out where Cleague would be working. In describing the property where the apartment house was located, the landlord painted a picture of bucolic salmon-bearing mountain-fed streams, wooded hiking trails, and quiet lifestyles in a pastoral setting.

The physical reality was somewhat different. Cleague followed the landlord's directions to the letter but wasn't sure he was at the right place when he arrived. The salmon stream turned out to be a dried creek bed and the wooded hiking trail was a scratched-out pathway between two rows of overgrown blackberry vines and alders that bordered the property line between the apartment buildings and the properties of the neighboring home owners association. Abandoned couches, busted TV sets, and stranded particle-board furniture had been left to rot in the terminus of the "hiking trail" by various former apartment dwellers.

As Cleague pulled into the driveway of the apartments' parking lot, he was greeted with the sight of trash strewn all over the pavement, tattooed people in muscle shirts working on Harleys while their common-law beer swilling husbands watched, and little kids running around in dirty t-shirts and no underwear. He found the building in which his apartment was located by virtue of the trash, clothing, and what may have served for furniture that had been piled up on the sidewalk outside his potential residence—the previous tenant had apparently left in a hurry. At the east end of his building Cleague could not help but notice the 1980 Chevy Chevelle parked on the sidewalk with the doors open, windows down and mariachi music spewing forth from sadly outlived speakers. This manner of entertainment ostensibly provided musical accompaniment to a huddled group of belligerent revelers as they passed around a communal bottle of a slightly green-tinted transparent fluid, but maybe it was just the color of the bottle. Empty cans of Olde English Stout adorned the pavement at their feet.

Cleague asked the landlord, who was there to meet him, about whom he hoped were not his new neighbors. "Oh don't worry about them," the man assured him, "I finally got them evicted."

"Oh?" Cleague asked politely.

"Yeah, they been selling drugs; they'll be out of here by the end of the day."

For some reason these assurances did not assuage Cleague's concerns. He was starting to notice the familiar feeling of a migraine headache. He was committed to renting this place for the minimum initial term of six months. After that maybe he'd be able to find something better, but for right now he was very much regretting his agreement to rent.

There are businesses and then there are businesses. The retail environment was like nothing he had ever known previously. Everything was an exception and there was no rule. After having been there a week or two he was stocking the ammo shelves behind the gun counter and heard a sound, a sole of a shoe scraping the concrete floor, a rustle of fabric, and turned to see the most captivating woman he had met in a long time. Nice eyes, too.

"May I help you?' He asked.

81

She looked down for a moment at the glass counter and raised her head. She smiled and with an embarrassed blush she said, "I'd like to look at a gun". Her eyes were a spectral green he couldn't quite name.

Cleague assumed his best sales persona. He was new at this and it was still a little rough. "How do you think you would use the gun?" He asked.

"Yeah, uh..." her head slightly lowered, she gave a little bit of a shrug. "I want it for personal defense."

"OK, did you have anything in particular in mind?" he asked. She looked at him quizzically with a light shake of the head, no. *Hazel? Were they hazel? No, brighter.* He went on: "Revolver? Semi-automatic?"

"I don't know?" she answered with a question. He walked around the corner to the revolver case and said, "Let's take a look at these." In the display case before her were probably four-dozen revolvers, all of different materials, calibers, and sizes. He opened up the back of the case and paused. Looking directly at her eyes, something he was learning to enjoy—*wasn't there a birthstone in that color?*

"Will it be a carry gun, or something you'll leave in the house?"

"Um, probably both." she said, breaking eye contact, casting glances about the store again. He saw something then—didn't catch it, didn't know what, and dismissed it without ever realizing it was there. She looked back at him and smiled. *Peridot! That was it! They were peridot!* He broke eye contact this time. He was starting to get lost in there. He looked for a small framed, two-inch barreled revolver and found the one he wanted.

Product description. This was the part he could do on autopilot, with his eyes closed, in his sleep, dreaming. Those eyes, wow. Nice features, light brown hair. He continued his spiel "...and the heavier the gun is, the more mass it has, the less recoil you'll feel."

"Why?" She asked? Wow! She had been paying attention.

"Because when you fire the gun, you have energy going out the barrel, and you have energy coming back at you. That is the recoil impulse or what some people call "kick." The lighter the gun, the more recoil you'll feel." He opened the cylinder again, checked to see that the chambers were indeed clear—again...it had become an automatic reflex—and, ensuring the muzzle did not sweep anything important, like a customer, he set the revolver down on the counter.

"How many bullets do they hold?" She asked.

"This one holds five rounds."

"But don't some of those others hold more?" She asked, pointing back at the semi-automatics.

"Yeah, some of them do." He agreed.

"Well, wouldn't one of those be better?" she asked.

"Not necessarily. The key thing is that the gun has to fit the geometry of your hand. If it fits, great! If it doesn't, you won't be able to shoot it well. The semi-automatics hold more ammunition but there are more parts moving in different directions at the same time. Because of that, it is possible to get a stoppage or some other sort of failure. A revolver is simpler. If you can drive a car you can probably run a semi-automatic, but you have to practice malfunction drills until you can do them without thinking about them." He paused to see if it had any effect or if he had just repeated a litany to the deaf. And then she fixed him with that gorgeous smile and those amazing green eyes again. "What do you carry?"

He smiled right back at her. "Why, ma'am I'm a pacifist." *Cute or not, it's none of your damn business lady.* He had been at it long enough to realize that she wouldn't be making any decisions today.

"You know there is a range not too far up the road that rents guns. You could go up there, try a couple and see what you like. They also offer an excellent class for women up there." He said.

"Why don't you teach me?"

Wow! He was dumb struck. Now what?

"As much as I hate to say this, the store has a policy against the sales staff teaching the customers. Since there is a facility so close by that has an excellent training program available, the management here would consider it bad manners, as the folks at the range are very good customers of this store." He said. And hoped the lump in his throat he just swallowed wasn't too obvious.

"Well, that's stupid!" She pouted. "What a silly rule" She said.

"Yeah, I couldn't agree more." He said with a shake of the head and an aw-shucks smile. *Especially since I just made it up,* he thought. This interchange had taken a turn in an unknown direction and he was not going to put himself in a compromised (and possibly liable) position until he knew her.

"Can you show me one of those?" she asked indicating the semi-automatics.

"Sure," he said. He put the revolvers away after checking the chambers again, and walked back toward the display case that held the semi-automatics.

"Which one?" he asked.

"I don't know, which one do you like?" Her tone had changed a little—not quite shrill but it had an edge to it. He pulled out a Glock, removed the magazine, locked the slide to the rear, and checked the chamber to ensure it was clear. He passed it to her across the counter, grip first, with the muzzle down.

"This is a Glock." He said and slipped back into the spiel. "It has a polymer grip frame, steel slide, steel barrel, can't break it with a hammer, keep your finger off the trigger until your sights are on the target..." he went on.

"Where do the bullets go?" she asked when he finished the sales patter. He indicated the magazine on the counter mat. She picked up the empty magazine and inserted into the magazine well. She pointed the gun at the wall in the empty space behind Cleague and released the slide stop which snapped the retracted slide forward into battery with a loud THWACK. "Oops," she sheepishly grinned. *How did she know to do that?* Cleague wondered. She held the gun as if to shoot it and pressed the trigger. Cleague noticed with interest that the muzzle didn't move. The girl had likely had training at some point.

"How many bullets does it hold?

"Ten."

"But this looks like it could hold more than just ten rounds."

He nodded and agreed: "Yeah, well, they used to. Now they can only hold ten."

"But can't you just change it? Can't you take something out or move something to make it hold more?" She insisted. Now he had a problem. It was not unknown for people working as agents for one or more Federal agencies, or newspapers, or TV news departments to go into licensed gun shops and bait sales staff into doing or saying something that could be construed as illegal at a later date in a court of law, or in a TV broadcast. Was this girl setting him up? He dropped his demeanor of helpful sales guy.

"I don't know, but I have to tell you this: If you were to alter a ten-round-capacity magazine that was manufactured after the Thirtieth of September of 1993 it would be a felony. If you have to have a high capacity magazine, legal ones are still available. You would be buying some-one's used private property and you would probably pay a premium for it." He answered flatly as he indicated for her to give the gun back to him. She set it on the counter with the muzzle pointed right at him.

"Isn't there a kind of bullet that's supposed to be really destructive?" She asked.

Oh Boy, he thought.

"You mean hollow points?" He asked; she nodded.

"All hollow points are designed to do the same thing: expand." He said. "Some were more effective than others but it all comes down to shot placement. There are no magic bullets. You have to be able to place your shot to stop a threat. But it is irrelevant now because hollow point ammunition was banned under Brady II. Handguns are poor tools for the purpose of stopping someone that's really intent on doing you harm. We carry handguns—within the constraints of the law—because they're unobtrusive and relatively more convenient to carry than a battle rifle or a shotgun. If you choose to get a handgun, get something that fits your hand and practice with it. A lot. If you're amped up on adrenaline and have to shoot somebody, you might hit them, and you might not if you have not taken the training required to hit a threat in a dire situation. If you don't hit the target, having the handgun doesn't matter—hollow-points or not." He concluded the sermon. He fished around at the end of the counter and handed her a wallet-sized card with the schedule of the local shooting range printed on it.

"Here. Give these guys a call and see when their next class is. It's really worthwhile and you'll be better able to make a decision after you take it."

"I have no problems making decisions." She snapped. *Whoa! where'd that come from?* he wondered.

"In spite of all your lecturing you still haven't told me what's required to buy a gun!" She demanded. *Maybe because you hadn't asked the question yet,* he thought.

"Sure." He said. It wasn't a smile any more, it was more of a grimace. "You have to be a state resident over twenty-one. You fill out two different forms. It takes about twenty minutes to do the paperwork and then you wait ten days." His words were not brusque or sharp but they were direct. He put away the gun as she exclaimed: "Ten days?! I need it now." She said.

"Well, I'm sorry but that's the law." He answered.

"But can't you make an exception? I'm not like everybody else. I have to get this now." Her throat was flushed. Her face was red. Her eyes were not bulged but the irises were completely visible.

"No I can't. But there is a way to circumvent the waiting period." He said. He had run out of patience. Cute or not, she was a pain-in-the-ass.

"Oh, really?" There was that smile again. She was all sweetness and light now. She could turn it on and off like a light-switch.

"Yes Ma'am. Go to the sheriff in your county and have him write a letter stating that you are known to him and that you have no felony or misdemeanor convictions that preclude you having a firearm and that there have been no restraining orders issued against you and that you have had no convictions, reports, or complaints of domestic violence made against you." He said in a flat monotone as if reciting from the Revised Code of Washington. "It would also be helpful if you have your sheriff call us to let us know that he has written the letter." He was finished now and turned to wait on other customers who had clustered at the counter.

She considered what he told her and said: "OK, thanks." She abruptly turned on her heel and marched out the door. Joan Glyndon got in her car and drove out of the parking lot.

82

Peter turned his attention to other customers. A man came up to the counter with a rifle that needed fixing. His horse threw him and he fell on it when he was out elk hunting last year and wanted it fixed before the next season opened. Cleague carried the rifle in two pieces back into the shop where the gunsmiths worked. Carl, the senior gunsmith, had a peculiar practice of playing the local talk radio station while listening to the police scanner. Ty, the younger gunsmith sat at a different bench listening to his own radio that continually hawked the values of an independent rock network. Peter wondered how a radio station could be independent if it were in a network but disregarded the urge to ask. He handed the rifle in two pieces to Carl and told him the complaint the customer had made. Carl took the rifle and gave it a visual inspection.

"Yep, it's broke." He then handed the pieces back to Cleague, who in turn laid them on Carl's bench.

"Hey, Pete, did you hear the news this morning?" Carl asked.

"No. What's up?"

"Somebody broke out of the mental hospital!" Carl said.

"No shit. I think I just waited on her." Peter said, half in jest.

*****

It was Peter's habit to take his lunch in his truck at a little park adjacent to the Little Creek fish hatchery just down the road from the store. He settled back with the radio on and commenced his tuna fish sandwich. The news at the top of the hour came on and he turned it up a little: "We lead with this

316

morning's top story...Officials of the Washington State Patrol have alerted this station that one or more inmates of the Woodrow Seeley Mental Hospital in Alger County may have escaped. Apparently one or more patients were unaccounted for at this morning's roll call conducted at 7:00 AM. These patients were assigned to the maximum-security section of the hospital where patients exhibiting violent and/or criminal behaviors are confined. No information has been released concerning their identity, their description, or what they may have been wearing. But listeners are strongly cautioned to be wary of strange or unknown persons acting oddly. This station contacted Woodrow Seelley's spokesperson who refused to confirm or deny the story but did add that... 'If such were the case, it could be possible that these people may simply be lost.' In other news...." Cleague smiled and finished his sandwich. *Was she?*

83

Luther had just made a reservation for the next flight out to San Antonio on Southwest. He had about thirty minutes to get the information he needed from the Navy/Marine Corps Reserve Center in San Antonio before his plane left.

By the time Luther arrived at the San Antonio airport, rented a car and got on the road it was about 7:30 in the evening. He drove west on I-10 for about an hour and took the exit for Kerrville. He made a left at the end of the exit ramp, through the underpass, past the McDonalds, past the gas station and turned right into the first hotel he came to. He checked in at the desk, drove around back and found his room. It was time to call it a night. He would deal with everything else tomorrow. He went to bed and sleep found him quickly.

The next morning Luther left the motel and headed west on I-10 for about twenty miles or so. He exited onto Hwy 41 and made a left off the exit ramp. He drove for another ten minutes and saw the small brick building that served as the post office for Mountain Home, Texas, to his left. He turned south onto Hwy 27, which eventually coursed east and drove another few miles.

Luther passed a sign for Sebastian Creek and eventually turned right onto a white rock road and followed it almost a quarter mile through the live oak and unchecked weeds, following the directions he had received from the Reserve Center in San Antonio.

The tree lined gravel drive opened up onto a barnyard with chickens running around loose, horses in a fenced place—a corral maybe, and dogs barking, albeit a pair of rather striking German Shepherds. As he slowly drove into the yard he saw what appeared to be a house, and what appeared to be a barn, and what appeared to be a shed, and what appeared to be a broken down Ford pick-up truck with an occupied pair of booted jeans sticking out from under it.

When Luther brought his car to a stop, the two dogs were immediately at his door, frenetically barking. Luther judged that if they were seventy pounds apiece, thirty-five pounds of that had to be teeth. The guy under the pickup truck seemed to be shouting something but Luther couldn't hear what it was.

He opened the car door and ventured to get out when he heard the guy, out from under the truck now, yelling at him to get back in his car. With two pairs of jaws emphatically slamming shut right at crotch level, Luther obeyed. Upon command the dogs went to heel to the man's left side and sat. Luther rolled down his window and asked, "Can I get out, now?" He opened his wallet, extended his arm, and displayed his Department of Justice credentials.

The man nodded and replied, "Slowly, and keep your hands out of your pockets."

Luther complied and asked, "Gunnery Sergeant Schynd?" Luther regarded the man standing before him; he was clearly of the old breed of Marines, one of The Old Corps that was seemingly rare in an age of computers and instant gratification. He was six feet tall, two feet wide and slim flanked, with a bone-deep sunburn. He had short cropped dark hair, gray at the temples; his eyes were sharp and clear and set above an aquiline nose in a tanned face that belied a tolerant scorn for the sad individual now standing in his barn yard: John Luther.

"That would be Mister Schynd to you, Sir, but I retired as a Master Sergeant. And who might you be?" Schynd replied.

"Mister Schynd, my name is John Luther; I am conducting an investigation for the Department of Justice. May I have a moment?" Luther asked.

"You may as well, you've already taken it." Schynd replied. He needed to replace a water pump and he did not like interruptions.

"Mr. Schynd, do you know a Peter Cleague?" Luther asked guilelessly.

Schynd stood erect, hands on his hips; feet shoulder width apart, and measured Luther at a glance.

"Mr. Luther, you would not have come out here if you hadn't already learned that I did know Peter Cleague. Now, you have come into my home, uninvited, and unannounced and have already taken up fifteen minutes. What is it that you want?" Schynd said.

Well, he is direct if nothing else, Luther thought. Luther made to cross his arms in front of him and shuffled his feet to get a wider stance, and the dogs were both immediately up on their feet, emitting a low guttural thunder from deep down in their chests. Luther took the opportunity to make light conversation in a tone of amiability.

"Those are two beautiful dogs, what are their names?" He asked. Schynd gestured toward the larger dog.

"His name is Magnum," and indicating the smaller of the two, "and she is Katie." The dogs' ears twitched when they heard their names. Magnum seemed genuinely affable with clear bright eyes and smiling—if dogs smile. Katie stared at Luther as though he was a piece of meat. *Well actually*, he reflected, *I guess I am.* He noticed the tips of Katie's canines protruded a bit from under her upper lip. K-9 Katie. Ears slightly back, tail straight, she didn't twitch and she didn't blink. She just stared at him. Luther felt uncomfortable and swallowed. All of a sudden he was feeling the heat of the

Texas sun. Luther couldn't help but make the observation, "Your dogs seem to be a little aggressive, don't they?'' To which Mr. Schynd replied. "No, sir. But they are protective. What's on your mind?" Schynd made a gesture with his left hand and both dogs lay down, each positioning itself between Luther and Schynd.

Luther's ball. "Mr. Schynd, I am investigating the circumstances surrounding the event that led up to or caused the deaths of a number of Federal law enforcement officers on Peninsular Island, Washington, last July." Luther stated flatly.

"I'm sorry to hear that," Schynd said and he meant it.

"One of the people we have an interest in talking to is Peter Cleague." Luther said. Schynd had not offered to get out of the sun, or a place to sit down, or any number of small gestures of hospitality that might suggest a willingness to be helpful or cooperative, Luther went on. "Mr. Schynd, how well did you know Peter Cleague?" Schynd had already demonstrated to Luther that he was not going to be co-operative. A subtle push might not hurt. "May I remind you, sir, this is an official Federal investigation and any false statement made by you could be determined to be a felony?" Schynd did not suffer fools, gladly or otherwise.

Luther was a tall man, with his erect carriage and flat gut; he sometimes intimidated people with his presence. It wasn't intentional but it was a happy accident, just another tool in the investigator's tool bag. However, in this yard, these dogs and their owner were having none of it. Schynd's body language and the dogs' demeanor informed Luther that they were not the least bit distressed.

"Mr. Luther I already told you I would answer your questions. I won't be intimidated."

Luther replied, "I'm just doing my job, Mr. Schynd." Luther said flatly.

"Yes sir, and when my dogs come up behind you and bite you in the ass, that is herding behavior. They're just doing their job too." Schynd said, equally level.

"Are you threatening a federal Investigator in the course of his duties Mr. Schynd?"

"Nope. Just stating the obvious." Mr. Schynd was obviously not impressed with Department of Justice credentials or the unspoken threat of an investigation dragging anyone whom Cleague had ever known into its destructive vortex. *Shit.* Luther thought: *I hate the hard ones.* Luther considered that it might just be time to drop back and punt. "Look Mr. Schynd, maybe we just got off on the wrong foot here." Had to be careful, if he tried to be too folksy he would definitely come off as a phony. Luther continued, "I don't know anything about the man but I'm hoping you can help me with that. I know from his military records that you and he were in the same unit for a period of time, were you friends?" Luther asked.

Schynd considered the question and responded truthfully. "No, when we were in the same platoon we weren't "friends", he was my platoon commander and I was his platoon sergeant. It was like he was my supervisor, and I was a foreman." Schynd tried to make the best analogy he could for someone who was ostensibly a civilian. Schynd could not have known that John Luther had retired from the Judge Advocate General's Corps of the United States Army before taking his position at the Department of Justice.

Luther saw an opening. "Was it a good relationship?" He asked.

Schynd looked Luther in the eyes. "Cleague was a good platoon leader and I like to think I was a good platoon sergeant. Our platoon consistently outscored the company in any evaluation or training evolution. Every year our platoon fielded a squad of Marines to the infantry games at Quantico. Those squads usually did well. We had a good working relationship." Schynd finished.

"Well," Luther started, "See, this is where you can help me out. If he was such a good officer, how come he never got promoted?" Luther was deliberately leading Schynd to draw a conclusion.

"I didn't say he was a good officer." Schynd stated flatly, and Luther thought *Gotcha!*

"I said he was a good platoon commander. If you want to know whether or not he was a good officer you would have to ask his reporting senior, the Company Commander." Schynd said. Luther saw this was a dead end; apparently it wasn't a gotcha after all. He decided to take another tack.

"Now, when Peter Cleague was on active duty prior to joining your Reserve company, wasn't he in the Combat Engineers?" Luther asked.

"Yes, I believe he was." Schynd replied. Luther noticed that the man answered questions with complete sentences. "He was at Camp LeJeune, if memory serves." Schynd continued.

"Well, the Combat Engineers is quite a bit different from a Reconnaissance Company, is it not?" Luther asked.

"Yes sir, it is." Schynd replied.

"Then how did Cleague learn to be such a good Recon Platoon Leader?" Luther asked.

"He had a good teacher." Schynd said.

"Who?" Luther.

"Me." Schynd.

Luther should have seen that one coming. He thought he could see Schynd smiling, but he wasn't sure.

"Now, Mr. Schynd, in Recon, don't you all use a lot of explosives? How did Cleague learn about that? Did you teach him?"

"No, I didn't. Cleague had some background with military explosives from the Engineers. In fact when breaching and demolition came up in the Company Training Schedule, it was usually the Lieutenant who taught the classes." Schynd answered.

"What kind of explosives did he use for those classes?" Luther asked.

"C-4 is a standard explosive for breaching and clearing," Schynd said with a slight shrug—he thought everybody knew that.

"Do you know where someone could get some C-4, like now?" Luther was clearly fishing.

"No Mr. Luther, I do not. If you have something on your mind, why don't you just ask it?" Schynd was pointedly direct.

"Mr. Schynd, I believe Peter Cleague deliberately blew up his own house and another building specifically to kill a number of Federal agents in the commission of their assigned duty. I need to know where and how he got that C-4. Did you get it for him?" Luther.

"No. I did not."

"When was the last time you saw him"?

Schynd considered it for a moment.

"About a year ago, maybe more. It was right around the time of the Triple Crown." Schynd said.

"The Triple Crown?" Repeated Luther.

"Yes, he said he had just finished a bodyguard job at the Preakness and that he wanted to stop by before he went home."

"Who was he body guarding?"

"He didn't say. He never discussed who his clients were."

"Well, what did you talk about?"

"Nothing specific and everything in general. Catching up. That sort of thing."

"How long had it been since you had seen him previous to that?"

"Oh, I don't know, a few years probably. It was when he came back from overseas." Schynd said.

"I thought you said that you and he were not friends." Luther said a little dubious at this point.

"We weren't friends when he was my boss. When I was reassigned as Company Gunnery Sergeant and moved out of the platoon to company staff, we were." Schynd answered simply.

"I was under the impression that enlisted and officers didn't mix." Luther said.

"They didn't in a parade field environment, but when you spend three quarters of your training cycle ass deep in mud together, you can't avoid it. Besides, he wasn't like most officers. Every staff sergeant and above in the company said the same thing about him. When he asked us for our opinions he listened to us. That was a very rare talent for an officer. We all regarded him pretty highly. I respected him, and yes, he was my friend." Schynd finished.

"Just how close are you two?"

"I don't know what you would call close, Mr. Luther. He introduced me to my current wife, and he is godfather to my son. What else do you want to know?' Schynd asked.

"When was the last time you saw him?' Luther.

"About a year ago, just like I said." Schynd.

"Do you know where he could have gotten that C-4?" Luther felt that it couldn't hurt to ask again.

"No sir, I don't and if you ask me again in another five minutes, I still won't know." Schynd was getting a little tired of playing host to a bureaucrat and a lawyer at that.

"Mr. Schynd, this is very important. Do you know where Peter Cleague is now?" Luther asked.

"No. I do not." It was Schynd's final word on the matter.

Shit, another dead end. Luther thought. The muttered cadence of human speech in the Texas sun had put the dogs to sleep. When the diction turned sharp, both dogs opened their eyes, looking straight at Luther. Luther reached into his inside jacket pocket to get a business card, with his address and phone number in Bellingham (he would have to change that, he reflected). The dogs were immediately up on their feet, ears forward, tails straight back, hackles up, perfectly synchronized to the tune of an open throated growl, in stereo. Luther carefully and slowly raised his other hand and explained: "Just a business card. OK?"

Schynd just nodded and slapped his left thigh with his hand giving his dogs the signal to sit at his left as they promptly did, albeit somewhat haphazardly as they still tried to maintain a position between the perceived threat—Luther, and their Alpha. Schynd verbally admonished them to "tuck it in", and they complied, aligning themselves directly to Schynd's left. Luther slowly withdrew the card from his jacket pocket and held it out for Schynd. Schynd flashed his left hand, palm open with fingers extended and joined, in front of the dogs' faces, and quietly stepped off on his right foot. The dogs remained in place. He took the card from Luther and quietly nodded. Luther was genuinely impressed at the work evident in the dogs' training. *What else could they do on command?* He mused.

Luther offered: "If you should happen to think of anything else, please call me."

Schynd nodded and said, "All right, I will." Schynd walked back toward the Ford pick-up, snapping his fingers as he passed the dogs. They raced back to the truck and immediately turned around and watched Luther back his rental car around and proceed down the drive out to the asphalt road and presumably back to town.

Peggy Schynd set the Marlin carbine back in its cradle by the barn door and stepped out into the Texas sunlight. It had been her turn to muck out the barn today and she looked like it as she walked through the open barn door to her husband standing by the truck. Shielding her eyes with her hand she asked, "Who was that?"

"Some Fed wanting to know about Pete." He said.

"Cleague? He in trouble?" She asked, clearly surprised.

"Evidently." Bob Schynd put his arm around his wife's shoulders and drew her close. She couldn't help but casually observe. "You were awful restrained and polite for talking to a Fed."

Schynd agreed, "Yeah, wasn't I though." Then he said, "Why don't you go get cleaned up and I'll make lunch. All of that restrained polite behavior has made me awful hungry."

They walked into the house together. The truck would wait and the dogs would find something else to entertain them. Some days went according to plan, and some days didn't.

*****

John Luther drove back to Kerrville. He still had an hour before check out time. From his room he called Hereford Associates back in Palm Springs. Holly the receptionist answered the phone. Luther gave his name and asked if she remembered him from his visit the previous day? She said she did and asked what she could do for him.

Did she remember by any chance the name of Cleague's girl friend?

She was pretty sure it was Linda but couldn't remember the last name.

Could she remember the name of the travel agency where Linda worked?

Holly couldn't but did recall that Linda had left that job and had taken a position with the Palm Springs Chamber of Commerce.

Luther got the number from directory assistance and called the Chamber of Commerce. When the phone was answered Luther introduced himself and asked if there was an employee there by the name of Linda.

The lady on the phone answered, "This is Linda Muller." He made an appointment.

Luther drove back to the San Antonio Airport and turned in the rental car. He presented himself at the Southwest ticket counter for a flight to Palm Springs. He had found Cleague's girlfriend.

84

Luther's flight arrived at Palm Springs airport more or less on time and he made it to the Chamber of Commerce in short order. He introduced himself to Linda Muller as an investigator for the Department of Justice and explained that he was investigating the circumstances leading up to or causing the loss of life of several Federal law enforcement officers on Peninsular Island, Washington, last summer. He then asked her if she knew Peter Cleague. She nodded her head and simply said "yes".

"When was the last time you saw him?" Luther asked.

"I think it was back in January. It was after Christmas, so it was right around the first of the year." Linda said. Luther did not believe that she was holding anything back but she impressed him as being a little soft around the edges. Maybe a little forceful prodding wouldn't hurt.

"Did you know him well?"

"Uh," She hesitated a little, "Yeah, pretty well. We dated for a while."

"How long were you dating him?" Luther asked.

"Just about a year, I think."

"Did you visit him on the island?" Luther, prodding.

"Yeah, a couple times." Linda was feeling somewhat misgiven at this point in the conversation.

"So you two were together around the time of last Fourth of July?"

"Well, not really. I moved here in June, and we kind of broke it off after that. After I moved down here I didn't see him till August and then we broke up."

Luther considered at this point that if she was telling the truth—and he had no reason to believe that she wasn't, he didn't have a damn thing. *Here goes nothing,* he thought.

"Did you know that Peter Cleague is suspected of killing a number of Federal agents back in Washington last year?"

It made her gasp. "No, I had no idea…"

He cut her off. "You admit having had a long term relationship with this man. It wouldn't take a great suspension of disbelief for any jury anywhere in this country to understand that you were directly involved in Cleague's murderous behavior." He said. She was stunned. She did not know what to say. This was the first she had heard of anything happening back on PI. But it was after she had left San Francisco and moved to Palm Springs. She said so. Luther put it into context.

"You went to see him at that island prior to the raid. He came to see you here after he killed those men. You aided and abetted a fugitive and a felon. You are complicit in his act after the fact." He was straight forward and blunt and maybe a little bit louder than necessary. It was working. She was visibly upset with tears welling up in her eyes. Now it was time to press.

"Tell me what he told you, tell me how he planned it, tell me where he is and we can make a deal."

It was insane. It was not logical. How could she be suspected of all those things when she and Cleague hadn't even lived together? It was ludicrous. She would call Roger Tibbett—he would know what to do. She wiped at her eyes with her fingertips and said in an even voice, "I can't tell you what I don't know, Mr. Luther, and you can't prove what didn't happen." She said.

"We don't have to prove anything, we just have to get a jury to believe it. It isn't that hard, Miss Muller, I do it for a living." Luther said. She did not doubt it.

Linda walked Luther to the door and said, "We're done here."

Shit and goddammit! He thought. He almost had her, and did not want to lose her now.

"Well, that's up to you, but when I walk away the deal is off the table." He said. She remained silent and unmoved. He gave her his card and asked her to call him if she changed her mind. She took it without comment.

She watched him walk away, get in his rental car and drive off in the direction of the airport. She stood there for no particular reason considering what he had just told her. She noticed another beige colored car pass by her office only a couple of minutes later. It was totally unremarkable and blended in with every other vehicle on the road. So why had she noticed it? For some reason it just made her remember the night outside the restaurant in San Francisco. When she broke up with Cleague she told herself he was paranoid. She told her friends simply that they had had issues which they could not resolve. If Cleague was ill, as she had maintained, was it contagious? Was she getting it too? She did not know where Cleague was or what he was doing, but she did know where Smith was and he would know how to get a hold of Cleague. She decided she would get out of town for a couple of days and not bother Roger Tibbett at all. The Tibbett's had been so kind, and had done so much to help her get resettled, but she didn't want to bother them again. Linda went inside to her office and made arrangements to fly up to Seattle. She did not notice the commercial van parked along the curb across the street.

85

Peter Cleague took solace in solitude. Being around other people required him to expend a tremendous amount of emotional energy and self control to conduct himself in a manner reflecting civility and common courtesy. He had come to the conclusion long ago that damned few people were worth the effort it took to deal with them. Most people made him tired. They wore him out. It was a very rare individual whose company he would look forward to, would cherish when present, and would miss when absent. He had very few friends. He missed his dog. Peter, the world class bodyguard, was now working retail sales and he could not imagine a more perfect non sequitur.

Events in the not too distant past were proof positive. Due to circumstances beyond his control, he had lost his dog, his home, his way of life, his few friends, the one woman that he considered significant, nearly everything he owned, and his identity.

Palm Springs had been a disappointment. Linda had moved there for her safety (but initially against her will). However, she found it to her liking, settled in, and flourished. She found someone else who could afford her newer, more discriminating tastes, e.g.: a Lexus instead of a Corolla, petite filet mignon instead of hamburger helper. So what else is new? This particular emotional landscape brought with it a sense of deja vu.

Peter had to be someone else at that point, someone different. It took him forty-six years to become the person he was, how was he to become someone else at this late stage in the game? But he needed work and "Peter Crane" was as good a name as any. He had started doing executive protection contracts for Roger Tibbett.

It provided precious little release but afforded him the opportunity to focus on something other than himself for a period of time. But when that job was finished he was in the same place as before. The center of his life had been a woman who, through no fault of her own, had been put at risk and had to be removed from her environment, further away from him. When she left, she found someone else to care for. When she left he lost the center. He lost the focal point of what his life had become. With no focus he had become loose, non-centered, ill-defined, with no sense of direction. He had become dangerous; he had nothing to prove, nothing to live for and nothing to lose. *Wasn't there a song that went like that*? He thought. He had started drinking.

Roger Tibbett sent him off on another trip but he was becoming messy. He allowed his mind to drift when presence of mind was absolutely essential, he was letting his emotions determine his behavior and, as a result, he was accused of having left a signature mess in a tony bar in an LA suburb when discretion was critical to desired mission outcome. That simply could not be had.

In spite of sterling performance on his "last-chance assignment to get himself in order", Tibbett maintained Cleague had given in to a temptation that he should have risen above. Rumor had it that Peter was responsible for the nasty mess on the bathroom floor in an up-scale LA nightclub, and it sent a double message throughout the executive protection community: A) you don't sell out your troops, and, B) you never, never, ever sell out your principal. Peter, of course, maintained his innocence. No matter, Roger Tibbett—the former sergeant major—terminated his employment. In the absence of everything else, Peter also had no job.

The dreams were becoming more frequent. Staring into the middle distance he could remember these things: the house exploding in a burst of wood and body parts, the blood on the stock of the shotgun, the blood on his hands—sticky, the dog being shot and collapsing under the explosive force of a 55 grain bullet traveling 2400 feet per second, the bridge over the boat channel exploding and collapsing, with the BPS agents on and beneath it. He saw the little island on fire. However he would not bear the brunt of that burden alone. The BPS would have to take responsibility for the consequences of their own actions.

Having been at the store a little more than a month, Peter took advantage of the Fourth of July holiday to go camping. It had been one year since his climactic termination of his previous identity. He needed to be away from people for a while, to decompress. In the foothills of the Cascade Mountains, he found a mountain that was administered by the Department of Natural Resources. Atherton Mountain was an active logging site but it also happened to be one of the primary recreational resources of the small county in which Peter now lived.

He wandered around the mountain for a while enjoying the quiet when he came upon a gravel pit which would block the wind. The wind now simply made a vague rushing, whistling noise as it swept through the cedar, alder, fir and hemlock which lined the hill up to its crest, like a freight train in the distance, or a host of angels used to being ignored. Admittedly a poor judge of distance, he guessed the summit of this particular hill to be another two hundred yards above the gravel pit. This would be a good place to camp; the mouth of the gravel pit allowed a terrific view of the Sound and the San Juan Islands.

The area was obviously being logged and the gravel pit had been used as a landing for the felled timbers. Just below the rim of the gravel pit on the western facing slope was a slash pile—the discarded tops and limbs from marketable timber. It had been explained to Peter by a customer: a slash pile is burned to reduce the potential hazard of a wildfire and to free up the land for new seedlings. One wouldn't typically start a fire in the hottest and driest part of the summer but would more likely wait till the rain started in the autumn. But, there is always an exception to any rule.

Peter set up camp in the landing. It had rained in the past couple days but he had a nice fire going without too much trouble, and broke out the book he was wont to read when he needed to re-center himself. The coffee in the old fashioned percolator brewed slowly directly over the open camp flame—an anachronism in the twenty-first century but so was he. With his tiny 6-volt flashlight close at hand, his .45 caliber Glock, and a book, he had settled in before going to bed. It was one of the beacons from his college days: Hemingway, Heinlein, Rand, Orwell; <u>Death in the Afternoon,</u> <u>Stranger in a Strange Land,</u> <u>Fountainhead,</u> <u>Animal Farm.</u>

The book still struck a chord within him—more nostalgia than inspiration. But he was far removed from the incredible idealism of his twenties; the words did not ring true for him anymore. They weren't less valid than they had been but he had changed. Reading the words he could almost remember what it felt like being that amazingly naive college kid who thought he was going to teach literature simply because he enjoyed it. That was many lifetimes ago and this one felt like it was just about over too.

86

He found it difficult to concentrate. His mind kept trailing off. In his memory's vision, he saw the silhouette of what had been his tiny bit of beachfront nestled in the San Juan Islands on fire. He could remember the way Smith's little Boston Whaler bobbed in the water. He remembered seeing the empty expanse across the boat channel that had been a one-lane bridge. He planted the charges. He triggered the signal that blew the bridge in place and effectively cut off Peninsular Island from the fire trucks and aid cars that were so desperately needed by the people...the rotten bastards that had come to burn him out. Kill his dog. Take his property and foist him in front of the lackey, bootlicking, complicit press that salivated at the hint of exclusive footage of a Federal raid on a militant madman. Make a national spectacle of him, a lone bitter gun hoarding, bible clinging lunatic that would not conform to the dictates of society. "Well fuck 'em. Let 'em try it again and see what happens."...He caught himself. *Ranting out loud again. I'll have to watch that. It just won't do to start a conversation with nobody there, especially if I do it in the store in front of a customer*. He thought.

Over the past year he had become aware that he was losing the ability to distinguish between when he was thinking silently to himself and when he was talking out loud. Reacting to the passing wave of vague paranoia brought on anytime he thought of the BPS, he withdrew the Glock from his waistband, checked the chamber to ensure it was loaded and checked the tension on the top round in the magazine to insure it was topped off. He set the gun in his lap, muzzle outward and away from himself.

Sitting cross-legged his legs had become numb. His hands relaxed in his lap—the Glock in his right hand covered by the book in his left: Ayn Rand's <u>Anthem</u>. He tried to read it but his mind wandered and he stopped. He thought of Linda again, what he could have done to allow a different outcome, choices other than the ones he made. *Right. And, "For of all sad words of tongue or pen, the saddest are these: "It might have been." (Where'd that come from?)* Sometimes snippets of recollected tracts would come back to him. Sometimes they wouldn't. Recalling his literature classes from college, he really hadn't cared for Whittier. And that was a very long time ago too.

He realized that he had been staring at the view of Puget Sound and the lower San Juans afforded by his hilltop perch. He could see scattered trails of backyard fireworks sporadically dot the valley floor. It was after nine in the evening and still daylight and quiet. The coffee was bitter, strong, and good. This time and place, and the opportunity to enjoy it unfettered by the presence of other people, was increasingly rare. It was one of the things that he enjoyed about living in this part of the country.

Wonder how long that'll last? He accepted the fact that he would just have to deal with other people in an everyday environment the same way everybody else did. In fact this could be good. He would blend in. He would be part of the crowd. His tone would be the middle shade of gray and he would take his place at the center of the herd. He would watch Monday Night Football, Must See TV. He would read the suggestions for Oprah's book club... Well, maybe not.

"Excuse me?" He turned sharply to the sound of the voice, previously unaware of the couple's presence. *Jesus, so help me, I'm losing it.* Peter thought. Had he been talking out loud again?

"I'm sorry, what was that?" Peter had been startled and was embarrassed by it.

"Oh. My mistake, I thought you were talking to us." A young man and woman in their late twenties or early thirties made their way around some boulders in the gravel pit and were coming toward the light of the campfire in the fading twilight.

"No, uhh, lost in thought I guess," Peter replied with an embarrassed smile, making a weakly dismissive shrug.

"Well that's sure easy enough to do up here." The young man paused, demonstratively admiring the breathtaking view.

"Beautiful up here, isn't it? My wife and I were just up for the day hiking and we've had a bit of a mishap with our car on the way out. We've run out of gas. By the way, I'm Ed, this is Terry..." Ed held out his hand in the common salutary gesture as he and Terry came around in front of him. Terry stood a few steps away and out of the light of the campfire. Peter nodded, smiling, and remained seated, not taking Ed's extended hand.

"Sorry, burned my hand making the fire." He said lamely indicating the small campfire and coffee pot. The hairs on the back of his neck were on end as he noticed "Terry" continually casting furtive glances over his shoulder and beyond him. She was a silhouette against the dimming light of dusk but she looked vaguely familiar. He had let himself lapse into condition White and was progressing through condition Yellow to Orange to Red in short order. If he were lucky it would turn out to be nothing but if not, he would survive it whatever "It" turned out to be. "Ed" seemingly took no offense at his declined gesture of polite introduction, and went glibly on with his spiel.

"Yeah, our car ran out of gas just down the road a ways. By the way, do you think you could give us a hand, maybe a ride out to the nearest gas station or something?"

Assuming his best retail sales persona, which after only three weeks really wasn't all that polished, Peter replied as he indicated his pack and sleeping bag: "Gosh, I wish I could help you out but I walked in." He heard some loose rock clatter from behind him, his back to the shale wall of the gravel pit. "Terry", glancing beyond him and shifting her eyes from one point to another, was making furtive gestures with her hands about her waistband. No wedding band, common law marriage? "Ed" introduced her as his wife. "Terry" stood behind "Ed" and just a little to "Ed's" right, her head fixed in the direction of what or whom-ever was behind Peter.

"Ed" rattled on amicably as stars became visible in the darkening sky. Peter was losing the details of their appearance but noted that they were dressed oddly for a day's hike in the Cascade foothills. Instead of shorts or light cotton clothing, Ed was wearing heavy denim jeans and a cut off denim jacket as an ersatz vest; boots instead of walking shoes. Terry was wearing a chambray shirt, jeans and boots. Bikers?

"Well, do you?" Ed said with less charm than irritation.

"I'm sorry?" He had drifted away again. "Ed" was noticeably annoyed. "Do you have anybody coming to get you? So we can get a ride out of here? Look man, what do you think I been telling this story for the past five minutes for? We're busted down over there and we need a way out!"

"Oh! No. I'm sorry, I don't." Peter said.

"Well ain't that grand." "Ed" looked around in disgust, letting his eyes sweep beyond Peter. His hands went to his waist band, on his hips—akimbo— then moving back behind his waist...his right arm extending behind his back. His voice became rather stentorian as if making a speech or giving a cue, "Well, since you ain't got nobody coming to get you I guess you ain't going nowhere are you?"

Peter could hear the faint clatter of gravel again. Someone failed to move silently. "Ed" was moving to his left, "Terry" was moving to her right. Cleague figured he had at least three targets.

87

"Ed" droned on while producing a Bali-song from his right rear pocket, making a display of flipping it from the closed position to the open position, this boy was quite good with a butterfly knife, wielding it with an artful sense of flourish, moving it in a continuous and fluid figure eight, then flipping one half of the handle to the other hand and reversing his hands one over the other, flipping the handles end over end from one hand to the next; back into a figure eight motion and finally snapping the handles closed with the blade extended. "And since you ain't got nowhere to go, you ain't gonna need your wallet, are you?"

"Look, I don't want any trouble with you, you can have my wallet but there isn't any money in it." Peter offered. "Terry" broke off her gaze from beyond the seated man and looked at "Ed".

The sun had gone down past the horizon; the meager light from Peter's campfire sputtered and jumped. "Oh, just cut the crap and get on with it." Terry said as she pulled something dark from her waistband, a handgun of some sort, and "Ed" yelled "Give us your fucking money, man!" as "Terry" pointed the gun at him. With his eyes locked on "Terry's" sternum, Peter raised the Glock from under the book to his eye level and fired once, using the minimal torque and recoil impulse to swing the muzzle of the Glock over onto "Ed" who was now rushing toward him and fired again, a double tap into center mass, letting the muzzle rise for the second shot.

Without waiting to see the results of the first three shots, Peter threw himself backward into a supine position and, finding his target and bringing his sights in line, fired into the dark mass coming at him from the rear. Kicking his legs out straight in front of him, he continuously pulled the trigger as he rolled to his left keeping the Glock's tritium sights roughly at the middle of the torso of his current target.

The third one was down. Coming to rest in a prone position Peter pushed himself up onto his knees. His legs were starting to hurt like hell. Kneeling, he had to get to his feet but they were still numb. Pulling his left knee up under him he lost his balance and went on to his right hand, dropping the Glock.

The blow to his right arm was crippling. He reactively grabbed his right arm with his left hand and lurched sideways to his right. A large shadow silhouetted against a pale twilight loomed above him. It brought back both its arms as if in a golf swing, apparently taking aim at his head and let fly with the baseball bat.

Peter hunched his shoulders, pulling his head into his chest and tried to roll off to his left as the bat caught him a glancing blow across his shoulder blades. He managed to get up on one knee before the shadow lunged at him again, bat poised over his head for a vertical strike. He let the shape come at him and ducked his head forward as he drove his left fist into the oncoming target's crotch with all the energy he could muster. The big shadow doubled over, dropped the bat, and grabbed at its lower abdomen. Peter struggled to his feet and grabbed his assailant's ears, pulling its face into his up swinging knee. Losing his grip on the target's ears he positioned both hands on the crown of the man's head and repeated the process, driving his knee into its face twice more, until he felt the facial bones give way. He let go of the assailant's head and the man pitched sideways into a mass of non-responsive clutter.

It was dark now. He couldn't see his feet beneath him. He stumbled back toward the campfire and found the flashlight he had left by the coffee cup. Sweeping the area with the beam from the little six-volt flashlight, he found the Glock, replaced the depleted magazine with a fully loaded magazine, slipping the former into his pocket.

He walked over to "Terry" and kicked away the handgun, a Sig Sauer— nice gun— standard issue to some Federal agencies. He then examined the torso—center punched right through the sternum. He didn't bother to look at her face; it didn't matter.

He walked over to "Ed" and picked up the Bali-Song, he had always hated those damned things...more for the people that carried them than for the knife itself; it was, after all, a simple tool. "Ed" had been bent over forward when he had been shot. The first round went into the solar plexus and traveled downward along the backbone apparently cutting and chopping along the way, as the seat of "Ed's" trousers seemed to be awfully wet. The second round had gone into the base of the throat, boring through windpipe, tissue, and third and fourth cervical vertebrae. In each case, the .45 caliber, 230 grain hollow points had certainly performed well.

The first Shadow Man lay on his face where he'd been dropped. Peter had lain supine on his back when he engaged Shadow Man consequently all his shots went low. At this point in the melee he had not bothered to count his rounds fired. He rolled the corpse over onto its back and noted the man had been disemboweled. Well, the Black Talons had certainly worked.

From behind him he heard a scrape, a scratch, a crawling sound, and walked toward Shadow Man #2; the broken lump was trying to crawl off. With the Glock trained on the figure's head he cautiously grabbed it by the shoulder and quickly turned it onto its back. Its face was broken and covered in blood.

It moaned. He could feel the depth of its pain and actually commiserated with it. "What do you people want with me?"

Nothing.

"Who are you?" Peter asked.

Nothing.

"Who sent you?" He insisted.

"Fuck you." The broken lump retorted.

Well that was a start albeit a little anti-social.

"Tell me who sent you and I'll get you to a hospital." Peter said.

"Eat shit and die." The lump replied and began choking.

"Look, you're dying and if you don't get to a hospital soon you won't make it. Why me?

Why come after me?" Peter asked.

"Rot in hell. The next time they find you, you won't be lucky. Three's a charm."

With this, Shadow Man #2, still on his back, began coughing, and then choking, and then gagging. He rolled over too late as he asphyxiated on his continuously seeping blood and phlegm. He lay motionless, quiet, and dead.

88

One had a gun and the other three hadn't. The scenario played itself out again in Peter's mind and he suspected that his year of running had come to an end. He walked over to the woman, as she had been the only one that had presented a gun, and went through her pockets. No ID of course. He took his flashlight and shined it on her face. It was the woman with the peridot eyes and the light switch personality from that day in the store. *"There are no magic bullets. You have to be able to place your shot to stop a threat."* He told her. *Well, there you go*, he thought. He wasn't happy about killing a woman. He wasn't sad. He had learned a long time ago that threats were threats. Men, women, kids, adults, it didn't matter. Stop the threat, move through it, and reconcile your feelings— whatever they may be, later.

He picked up the Bali-song from where "Ed" had dropped it and cut away her shirt. "Ed" had taken care to keep his tools sharp as the denim shirt came away from the corpse easily and quickly. Peter examined the woman's left arm pit and found exactly what he had feared...the six digit tattoo that indicated membership in the BPS.

He thoroughly wiped off the Bali-song and put it back in Ed's Hand. Other than picking up his own gear and dumping the contents of the coffee pot onto the fire, he made no attempt to re-orchestrate the event that had played out in the last ten minutes. Any good forensics team would see right through it, and the team that would undoubtedly be investigating this one was probably the best in the world.

The three men may have been bikers but they had been recruited to a task that was beyond their skill level. It came with almost a sense of relief, the realization that someone in the Bureau of Public Safety had not forgotten, had not believed that he had been killed in the inferno that took his house on Peninsular Island a year ago, the realization that there was someone in the BPS who would not quit until they destroyed the myth of the one that got away. He accepted the apparent fact that someone would not quit until they had put an end to the continuing, relentless paradigm of one Peter Cleague.

89

Cleague collected his things, put out the fire, minimized the evidence of his presence as best he could and made his way back to his car. His intent was not to impede the inevitable investigation that would be conducted upon the discovery of the four dead bodies, he just didn't want anybody coming looking for him, although that was probably inevitable too. He made his way up the inclined logging road and back to his little Toyota pick-up, newly acquired upon his arrival in Washington. It was ten years old and only had 132,000 original miles on it, barely broke in yet, as the eager seller had said. Cleague had unobtrusively parked away from the gravel pit. He drove slowly down the gravel-bedded roadway and turned south on to the main access road that led to the gate of the property administered by the DNR. Although Atherton Mountain was public property managed by the State of Washington, the investigation would be conducted by the County Sheriff's Office. Inevitably the BPS would muscle in as the investigation would ostensibly impinge on the "Public Management of Real Property" (one of the planks of the BPS' charter) however, since one or more of the bodies involved were BPS Agents, the BPS would most certainly position itself to conduct and control the tone, meter, pitch, and rhythm of the information that would be released to the public, if any.

No shit, the BPS, how appropriate. Cleague thought as he began to feel chill, nauseous and immediately recognized the oncoming symptoms of a migraine. Little wonder, combined with the throbbing ache of his upper right arm and upper back from the attack by Shadow Man 2, the thought of the BPS closing in on him always left him violently ill, sometimes even incapacitated by the hallmark headache.

He had to steer with his left hand. He suspected his left wrist was sprained from the intensity of the punch delivered into Shadow Man 2's pelvic girdle, but that couldn't be helped. He could move the fingers of his right hand but not without a searing scream of instantaneous pain tearing up through his right wrist, elbow, shoulder, and back, up the back of his neck to the base of his skull. The signal from the nerves in his wrist brought with it a rising convulsion from the pit of his gut, through his upper abdominal muscles, forcing his diaphragm to contract, and forcing him to pull the truck off to the side of the road as he wretched the meager contents of his nearly empty stomach. Sprain? Break? Tendon damage? Who knew? He managed to get the door open and fall out of the driver's seat almost in time as he succumbed to the rhythmic convulsions of dry heaves. He had learned long ago not to fight the involuntary impulse to vomit that often accompanied his migraines but to try to relax his abdominal muscles. He had to conclude his arm was broken and, like it or not, he needed to take himself to a hospital. The road from Atherton Mountain bordered a lake on two sides, more or less. Cleague walked to the white rail fence that skirted the perimeter of the water line and threw the Glock as far into the lake as he could manage. Then the magazine. That hurt. He got back in the truck and drove himself to the hospital.

The emergency room of the Alger Valley Community Hospital was not that busy for a holiday. On this particular Fourth of July there were only six people ahead of him. He walked through the short foyer and directly to the little receptionist's window. He waited politely for the woman to get off the phone. As he waited he wondered how many people had been trained to wait until a conversation-in-progress had ended, as it was rude to interrupt.

Giggling. The woman was sitting there giggling on the telephone while he stood there with a broken arm, sprained wrist, and migraine headache and god-knew-what-else.

Determining her conversation would have to wait, he spoke up, "...Excuse me." Nothing. "Excuse Me!" Nothing. She ignored him and kept chattering away, blissfully. He stuck his left hand through the window and slammed it down on the receiver (Damn! Ouch!). "EXCUSE ME, Lady, I Got A Broken Arm, May I See A Doctor Please?" Jumping with the initial shock of having had her space violated, she responded with icy courtesy, "...Fill out these forms, we'll be with you shortly," placing half a ream of printed forms on the counter in front of him and a pencil with a blunted point on top of them. He stood there in disbelief and half-wondered if he was going into shock.

"Uh, Ma'am." He was being as polite as he knew how. "Ma'am, my arm's broke. I can't write, ma'am." With an audible intake of air she made little effort to conceal a look of disgust.

"Well, have a seat and someone will help you."

"I can't wait". He walked away and made his way back to the truck. He managed to get himself to a 24-hour supermarket that had a pharmacy. He bought the highest strength Ibuprofen he could find and a bottle of water. He walked back out to the truck and steeled himself for the hour and a half drive to Seattle.

90

The Alders had become one of the premier restaurants in the city. The current in-vogue crowd brought with it style, glamour, panache, and notoriety. Their money was just as green as anybody else's—Smith just hated to see his restaurant become "trendy". He could only reconcile himself to the knowledge that once the fad wore out, the younger crowd of fashionably chic would move on to be some-one else's problem and, hopefully, the Alders would get its regular clientele back. The young lady at the hostess' podium acted as though she were really glad to see Cleague.

"Table for one, sir?" She asked.

His words were slurred and probably incoherent; she looked at him oddly. He repeated himself.

"Gene. I need to see Gene Smith." He spied Smith at his usual table, from where the pleasure and/or dissatisfaction of the guests could be monitored. Cleague started weaving his way through the dining room tables and didn't quite make it before he blacked out.

*****

Cleague woke up in a hospital bed. He was in Harbor View Regional Medical Center. When he collapsed in the middle of the Alders restaurant Smith called an ambulance. Unfortunately, the sight of an ambulance at the front door of the Alders, and a customer being hauled out on a gurney caught somebody's attention and there was a short article about it in the next day's newspaper. Apparently someone on the editorial staff took a dim view of his newspaper being called a Communist Fish wrapper and placed the article on the first page above the fold in the Arts and Leisure section. Payback.

"Oh no! How in the hell am I going to pay for this?" If Peter's head didn't hurt when he opened his eyes it sure as hell hurt now. He tried to look around but he couldn't move his head. He was wearing a neck brace. He thought, *there must be some way of getting the nurses' station,* and tried to move his right arm which he soon discovered was immobile. The battering he had taken the previous day left the nerves in his arm unresponsive. He tried to move his left arm but was also impeded by gauze and tape from his elbow to his wrist, with an intravenous drip inserted into his left forearm. He was totally exasperated. All he could see was perpetual debt. He didn't know what to do.

"Lord, Lord, heal me now Lord, I promise I'll be good. Please Lord, heal me now." He said out loud.

"Well, maybe not just yet, but soon my son, very soon." It was Smith. He had been sitting quietly in the corner. He casually rose, dragged the chair over to Peter's bedside and sat down. Peter stirred.

"Is there any aspirin or anything? My head hurts like hell." He asked, weakly, pitifully.

Smith indicated the IV dripping into Cleague's arm. "You already got enough drugs in you to choke a horse. What did you do?"

"I fell..." He was cut off by Smith's incredulous outburst of laughter. "Bull Shit!" Smith retorted. Cleague responded mildly, resolutely.

"I did Gene, I fell. I fell into a trap." At this simple declaration Smith lost all trace of joviality in his manner.

"How?" Smith asked.

"Well, evidently they have been tracking me and apparently they have found me." Cleague said nothing more.

"We'll talk about it later. It's really not as bad as it looks: sprained wrists, badly sprained and bruised right arm, and maybe a hairline fracture, compression fracture at the wrist and/or elbow, they're not sure---they didn't want to do x-rays yet. You also have a concussion and apparently there was some blood loss. They know blunt instrument trauma when they see it. I don't think you're going to be able to bullshit them with "...I fell," but I suspect you'll have enough time to think of something." Smith said.

Cleague was quiet for a time.

"I'm thirsty. God, it's hot in here. Can't you go find me a cute nurse to feed me a nice iced tea and fan me?"

Smith retorted quietly, "Don't you read the newspaper? The cost of health care continues to rise. Hospitals have been forced to cut costs by firing all the nurses to pay for the administrators." Cleague just shut his eyes (*God, my head hurts.*) He opened them.

"Speaking of ...pay for...how did I get admitted?"

Smith took this as an opportunity to take his leave. Since he had admitted Cleague into the hospital he had been harassing the attending physician on Cleague's status and progress. The doctor would reply by pressing him on the origin of Cleague's injuries. Since he didn't know, he could only respond with the truth. "I Don't Know, Doctor." She seemed to be awfully persistent and Smith wondered how Cleague would fare when he met her.

Rising to his feet Smith said it again.

"We'll talk later but you should probably know you are listed as an employee of the Alders Restaurant." This came as a shock to Cleague as no one had informed him of his new job.

"I am?" Cleague asked.

"Yep." Smith nodded confidentially, "Take good care of that arm...you're my new dishwasher." With that, Smith deftly took his leave.

Dr Elizabeth Wills walked in, smiled and went directly to the foot of Cleague's bed to examine his chart. Cleague noted shoulder length dark hair, high cheek bones, mildly furrowed brow, and well-etched laugh lines around the eyes and mouth. The lady enjoyed life. After a brief moment she looked up and greeted Cleague in a genuinely warm and good-natured manner.

"Good morning Mr. Cleague, I'm Dr Wills, how are you feeling?" Cleague thought a moment, taking inventory. "My head hurts. I'm stiff and everything hurts. I have a sore throat, I'm thirsty and it's pretty warm in here, other than that I'm fine." She obligingly walked to his bedside poured a "glass" of water into a ubiquitous plastic sippy cup with the hospital's logo on it. She inserted a bent straw, and held it up for him to take a drink. He did so gratefully and thanked her. "You're injuries are fairly extensive Mr. Cleague do you remember what happened?" Cleague shut his eyes for a moment... how to play this one he wondered?

During his stay in the hospital the lady doctor was overcome with questions as though Cleague were a variety of life form she hadn't studied in biology. How long had he been arrhythmic? ("Well, Doc, I never could dance," did not go over well.) Did he realize he displayed symptoms of aphasia? ("No, I've always been tongue-tied and absent minded"). When did he have his stroke? ("News to me; and stop by again doctor when you can't stay so long, I do so enjoy our little chats.") He meant it; he liked talking to her, but she was just so damned nosy she made him uncomfortable. How long had he been employed at the restaurant? What medical plan was he on? (Ha!) Who was his regular doctor? When was the last time he was tested for hypertension? The woman was absolutely relentless.

91

Cleague managed to convince his new employers at the store that he really had been injured in a camping accident over the Fourth-of-July holiday, and that he really had been unable to work, and that he really had been staying with friends down south, and that he really would come back to work as soon as he was able, and please don't give the job away to anybody else 'cause he really did need it. As their busy-season would not start until mid-August they agreed to keep the job open for him. From their perspective, if he wasn't there, they didn't have to pay him.

He walked into his apartment for the first time in over two weeks. Not having worked while he was recuperating from his injuries meant that he didn't get paid and now he wondered how he was going to make the rent. He had paid Smith back for footing the hospital bill from his tiny savings fund accrued from the job in Mexico.

Sometimes it was quiet, sometimes the police were responding to calls two and three times in the same evening. Cleague simply resolved to keep to himself and whatever anybody else did was their problem. He hated this place. "Well, seven weeks down and nineteen to go..." he thought. By the appearance of the apartment, no one had taken the initiative to see what kind of stuff he had during his absence. If they had, they would have been disappointed: the only things he owned were a radio, a portable TV, a microwave oven, a Salvation Army kitchen table and a folding chair, and a futon; they were still there.

Smith had given him hell for letting himself "go to seed", as Smith had put it, and he was right. In the former Peter Crane's quest to examine the inside of every bottle of Jim Beam sold in the greater Palm Springs area, he had managed to gain a bit of weight. For his entire life he had always tended toward fat but in the past year he had managed to become seventy-five pounds overweight. And although he had lost some of that weight in the Mexico City jail, he had let his upper body musculature atrophy to the point where a simple push-up was beyond his ability. He became winded for some minutes after having climbed a single flight of stairs; his brief stint at the Alders Restaurant bussing tables damn near killed him.

As he prepared to take a shower he noted that he looked like hell. He also noted that right now in his present state of mind he really and truly honest-to-god sincerely did not care. He started the shower. The hot water at the base of his skull felt good. State of Mind: order or chaos? So what? Who cares? And without a great deal of alarm he accepted the fact that he really did not care. As he took his shower, the strains of the Miles Davis tune came back to him. So What. But he resolved that today would be different. He had not had a drink since before the job in Mexico and he made up his mind that was the last one he would take. He acknowledged to himself that he had hit bottom and had been wallowing there for some time. After the shower he did one push-up and one sit-up. Not very far from where he worked was a trailhead and a very nice trail through the woods that was administered by the county parks system, Knave's Lake trail. He would drive there and take himself for a walk after work. Tomorrow he would do two push-ups and two sit-ups.

92

From: Bureau of Public Safety
Forensic Laboratory
To: Distribution List A
Subject: Summary of the Analysis of Forensic Evidence collected or noted at the subject Crime Scene (and environs) at 113 Island Road, Port Cullis, Washington

Peninsular Island, Washington, Approximately one mile north of the southern end of the island. The site of analysis consisted of three primary debris fields: two overlapping, with one adjacent. The debris fields were the result of three explosions in close time proximity. Other areas linked to the event directly south of Debris Fields #1, #2, and #3 were: an area adjacent to the naturally occurring inland raceway west of the north-south arterial road, and the bridge at the south of the island, which linked Peninsular Island to the mainland.

Debris field #1 was located at 113 Island Road, Port Cullis, Washington, the site occupied by a wood framed house on the east side of the north-south arterial road. The burst radius extended out from the base of the house in approximately 270 degrees along what had been the north, east, and west walls of the house.

Debris Field #2 was adjacent to DF #1 on the south side of the house and extended due south some 100 feet. It consisted of a fuel oil tank.

Debris Field #3 was due west of the house, west of the north-south arterial road. It had been a Quonset hut type of building. The burst radius of DF#3 extended out from the base of the building in 360 degrees. DF#1 And DF#3 overlapped at the north-south arterial road.

South of the house some 100 yards were two sites along an east–west line. Raid personnel confirm these two sites had been BPS observation posts. Other observation posts were located on the three jetties east and south of the house on the beach strand. Another OP/checkpoint was located on the bridge that spanned the boat channel south of the island. One other observation post was located just outside of and directly east of the building that constituted the site of DF#3. The final observation post was located on the road approximately ¼ mile north of DF#1 and DF#3 to re-direct south bound traffic.

DF#1) the house located at 113 Island Road was the target of a BPS raid. An explosion at the base of the walls caused the initial combustion in the house by a low order detonation. Distribution of debris from the buildings with the heaviest concentration of explosive residue around the perimeter of the two large debris fields indicated that explosive was placed around the perimeter of each building in a continuous line. Chromatographic analysis of chemicals isolated from the various items with the highest concentration of residue found in Debris Field #1, DF#2, and DF#3, showed that cyclotrimethylene trinitramine, here-in-after referred to as C-4, was used. The manufacturer of this particular sample of C-4 was Dupont Chemical for a military contract c.1980 to 1984. The charge was set off by a "pencil" type detonator modified to be activated by a radio signal. The radio signal sent an electric current through a wire filament that ignited a fuse head, which in turn ignited the priming charge, which in turn caused the main explosive charge to detonate.

A separate charge was placed on the fuel oil tank and was linked to the main explosive charge in the house by primer cord. When the charge on the fuel oil tank detonated, the tank vessel ruptured spewing heating oil on the south side of the house. The combustion of the fuel oil resulted in a high barrier reaction sufficient to propel the tank vessel southward of the house in a parabolic arc for approximately 100 feet. The resultant heat on the south side of the house from the combustion of the fuel oil was sufficient to pyrolyse the wood walls on the south side of the house and much of the shingled roof.

DF#3) The combustion in the storage building was initially caused by an explosion initiated by a thermite grenade which burned through a metal locker and caused to burn by deflagration a combination of smokeless and black powder which in turn sympathetically detonated charges of C-4 explosive which in turn detonated a linear charge of detonation cord composed of Pentaerythritol tetranitrate (PETN) as it was set around the base of the building and the weight bearing vertical supports of the building.

When this low-speed free air deflagration occurred within the closed structure of the seventy-year-old Quonset Hut, pressure effects produced damage due to expansion of gases, as a secondary effect. The heat released by the deflagration caused the ignition of still more gunpowder in the adjacent wall lockers resulting in the continuous release and combustion of gases and excess air to expand thermally as well. The net result was that the volume of the structure needed to either expand or fail to accommodate the continuously expanding combustion gases, or build internal pressure to contain them.

Since the base of the building had been lined with detonating cord and C-4 explosive at specific points, the base became the weakest part of the structure after detonation, causing the base to burst outward and the structure to fall in on itself.

Particulate residue of explosive powders were identified and traced back to their respective manufacturers through the identification of color-coded taggants left in the powder by the manufacturing process. These were identified as smokeless and black powder of various manufacture and various burn rates that had been commercially available prior to the enactment of the Arsenal Codes.

Remains

It is believed at this time that a total of twelve field agents of the Bureau of Public Safety died in the raid on the house located at 113 Island Road, Port Cullis, Washington.

Remains found in and adjacent to DF#1: It is difficult to know for certain all of the personnel affected by the explosion from DF#1, as the remains found in the debris field were scattered and co-mingled. The team closest to the house at the time of detonation took the brunt of the explosive charge approximately mid torso. The identities of those individuals that could be identified by DNA analysis are listed in Appendix A and forwarded to the Attorney General.

Four Field Agents were killed in the blast in DF#1.

A fifth body was found under the debris of the storage building located directly across the road from 113, Island Road, i.e. in Debris Field #3. The individual was killed from a blow to the bridge of the nose of sufficient force to drive the bone into the brain. Other injuries included a crushed larynx and trachea, and a fracture at C1 in the vertebral column. These injuries appear to have been sustained from a blow from a blunt object with a flat surface.

A sixth body was found on Island Road south of a line parallel to and coincident with the south wall of the house located at 113 Island Road. This agent died as a result of a catastrophic gunshot wound to the cranium. It is believed the individual was shot with a 5.56 caliber bullet. The projectile was not found.

A seventh body was found in the water of the north south raceway approximately 100 yards south of DF#1 And DF#3 on an east west line consistent with the location of the two BPS observation posts located south of the house at 113 Island Road. This agent died from a wound from a sharp instrument such as a fixed blade knife. The inflicted wound extended from just below the left mandibular angle, and transected the trachea through the carotid artery on the right side of the neck.

The eighth and ninth bodies were found in the area of the east OP 100 yards south of DF#1. They were both killed as a result from exposure in close proximity to the blast from a claymore mine. The serial number on the housing of the mine was traced to a DOD contract with Morton Thiokol running continuously from 1968 to 1975.

The tenth, eleventh, and twelfth bodies recovered so far were located in the boat channel. Cause of death to these three agents was drowning as they were pinned under the debris of the one lane bridge that was demolished as a result of a simultaneous blast from shape charges placed on the load bearing pilings of the bridge.

The number of recovered dead is consistent with the number of agents unaccounted for after the raid was concluded. However it is possible that other remains were lost to the tides and other natural phenomenon as it took several days to recover the three bodies from under the rubble of the bridge. The remains of one Peter Cleague were never found.

Senate Sub-Committee on Interior Affairs and Public Safety Oversight Hearing , Washington, DC

The chairman ceremoniously tapped the gavel and said "Thank you all for coming on some-what short notice. Shall we begin?" He asked and looked at Senator Sherman.

"Mr. Chairman, I'd like to call Mr. John Luther to the table," he requested. Luther made his way to the table, took his place and adjusted the table microphone. This was not his first appearance before a Senate sub-committee, but he didn't like it. It always gave him the feeling of somebody else looking over his shoulder.

"Mr. Luther, you were appointed by the Attorney General to determine the events leading to the death of several Agents of the Bureau of Public Safety on Peninsular Island, Washington, on the evening of 4 July of last year, were you not?" He asked.

"That is correct, Senator," Luther responded.

"Is your investigation complete?" Sherman asked.

"No, sir. Not yet." Luther answered.

"What have you determined thus far?" Sherman asked.

Luther gave a synopsis of the events that had occurred the night the BPS came for Peter Cleague. The sub-committee had Luther's interim report that he had made for the Attorney General in front of them. Luther's report was based on his own observations and on the forensic report from the BPS.

After the narration Sherman asked, "And what is your conclusion at this time?" Luther wasn't sure he heard that right. Without any sense of contention or acrimony and with no intent of being evasive Luther replied, "I don't believe I have all the facts yet Senator; the report is not finished."

"But you must have some opinion as to the conduct of the raid, what is it? Was it well planned? Was it mishandled? Was it executed with military precision? Was it yet another example of institutional incompetence on the part of the BPS? What do you suspect your conclusions will be?" Sherman pushed.

Luther was dumbfounded. He honestly did not know what to say.

"The facts do not support a conclusion at this time, Senator. I don't know what my conclusions will be until I've finished the investigation." Sherman had no further questions. Everybody else on the panel got a turn. Basically they asked the same thing Sherman had asked and Luther could only answer the questions asked. He wasn't clairvoyant. He was dismissed without further ado. Luther left the chamber and mused that whoever thought Congressional oversight was a tool to insure efficiency in governance had never sat through one of these hearings. *WAFWOT* (What a fucking waste of time)! He walked back to his car.

93

A few days after the initial hearing of the Interior Affairs and Public Safety Oversight sub-committee, John Luther received an invitation from Senator Sherman to join him for lunch in the Senate dining room. Luther had nothing to hide and no intention of obfuscation or evasion. He complied, if somewhat reluctantly. The Senate Dining Room was a place to be seen. As one restaurant critic had phrased it in "The Hill"; " it is one of those places where you don't notice, or really care, how good or bad the food is [because] what you eat is strictly secondary to whom you see or speak to in a restaurant literally filled with some of Washington's top power brokers." Luther would just as soon have been at work. Nevertheless, good grace and decorum would be the order of the day.

"Thank you for meeting me, Mr. Luther," Senator Sherman said as they shook hands.

"I'm willing to oblige the committee in whatever way I can, Senator, but you do realize that I have not completed my investigation yet." Luther offered.

"Yes, yes, I do." Sherman said as they made their way to a table and took their seats. "But there is something I think you can help me with that was not in the interim report and I have no other way to get a sense of than to ask you. You were out there," Sherman said as he scanned the menu.

"What would that be, sir?" Luther asked.

"You saw Cleague's place. It was a wood framed bungalow on a beach way the hell up in Puget Sound. It's windy and it's cold. There's nothing there. That island survives because of tourism. If you had been the director of the BPS, would you have selected Cleague for a raid, whether or not he was violating the Arsenal Code? If he was a danger to the public, why not have the sheriff serve a subpoena? Something about the rationale for that raid does not ring true to me," Sherman said. So it was out there. The sixty thousand dollar question, "Why?" indeed. Luther shook his head as he folded his hands on the table. "No, I don't believe I would have mounted a raid on him, Senator, but other than that I cannot give you an answer because I haven't found it yet. And, if I may, that would be a question to put to the Director of the Bureau of Public Safety." Luther said simply.

"Indeed. Anyway, tell me about this Mr.Cleague," Sherman said. Luther complied after the waiter had taken their order.

"Well, he was in the Marines, Combat Engineers, when he was on active duty. So he had some experience with military explosives. Basically he would have known how to breach and clear obstacles. After he satisfied his active duty commitment, he managed to get a billet in the Reserve Reconnaissance company down in Texas. Reserves or not, Marine Recon is a pretty selective bunch, so at least it speaks to his potential. According to his fitness reports, he was never going to set the world on fire with his military brilliance, but his platoons always performed well." Luther said. Senator Sherman had had military experience, ROTC in college and a reserve commission in the Army. But Sherman wanted to hear what Luther knew and he had the personal discipline not to interject.

"So what does that tell you?" Sherman asked as the meal was served.

Luther shrugged a little, waiting for the waiter to set his place. "It tells me that he had a capacity for leadership. I met with one of Cleague's old platoon sergeants. And believe me, this guy was Old Corps. Anyway, I got the sense from him that there was a certain amount of respect on the part of the staff NCOs toward whom he called The Lieutenant. It was the way he said it, like there wasn't any other lieutenant in the company. And, secondly, I just felt a very fierce loyalty on the part of this salty, sun-dried, retired Marine Master Sergeant toward his former Platoon Commander. And that had been many years ago. So that tells me that, One," Luther counted on his fingers, "Cleague had an ability for leadership, and Two, he commanded respect and loyalty from some very professional Marine NCOs. And that, Senator, is a very tough crowd to please. On the other hand his fitness reports were never above average, so whatever degree of working relationship he had with the staff NCOs in his company, he certainly did not have it with his superior officers. The guy is a real quandary." He summed up.

"Did you talk to the man's company commander or other reporting seniors?" Sherman asked. "No, sir. He had one reporting senior during the time he was in the recon company and that man has passed away. Headquarters Marine Corps gave us the names of two officers under whom he had served while he was on active duty. One of them was named William Jones with a home of record of Atlanta, Georgia. Senator Sherman, do you know how many William Jones there are in Atlanta, Georgia?" Luther asked. Sherman suppressed a smile and shook his head "no."

"Well, we contacted every one of them and none of them ever served as a Marine Company Commander of Combat Engineers." Luther went on.

"The second man's name was John Adams with a home of record listed in 1983 as Fairfax, Virginia. Well, currently, there is no one of that name, who served with Cleague, in Fairfax, Virginia. I haven't ruled out trying to find this man altogether, but time is short and I'm not sure what I would learn that would be of value." Luther said. Sherman nodded without comment.

Luther took a moment to put a forkful of braised beef in his mouth and reflexively wiped his mouth with his napkin. Sherman noted that Luther's table manners were fastidious and imagined that the rest of his mannerisms were as well. Everything about Luther's approach to the investigation on Peninsular Island suggested detailed thoroughness and due diligence. If the Attorney General wanted to whitewash this whole affair out in Puget Sound, which was Sherman's initial assumption, this Luther fellow was the wrong guy. Sherman would have conceded that the AG probably could not have picked a better man to investigate this mess. Now Sherman was confused.

"One thing to note, though," Luther carried on, "is that that master sergeant was moved out of the platoon to a company staff position in charge of training, among other things. He said that when the company had demolitions on their training schedule, Cleague was usually the instructor." Luther said.

"So, he knew explosives well enough to teach the application to young Marines." Sherman concluded while Luther worked on his lunch and nodded in agreement.

"Cleague gets passed over for promotion, again." Luther continued. "He gets out of the reserves and goes into the State Department Bureau of Diplomatic Security." This raised Sherman's eyebrows a little.

"Those guys are pretty good, he must have had something on the ball." Sherman said. He knew of the capacity and capabilities of the Bureau of Diplomatic Security from experience. He had had the opportunity to accompany the Secretary of State on a delegation to the Czech Republic at one point in his brief senatorial career. He remembered that the Diplomatic Security people had impressed him as being very professional and very competent. Luther was right. This Cleague guy was a puzzle.

"His star really started to shine. He was even singled out by the Director of the FBI, a Judge George Hillman at the time, for conspicuous competence and presence of mind in the conduct of a joint operation." Luther said.

"What was that?" Sherman asked.

"Back in the late Eighties there was a "summit" so to speak in New York City between the Sinn Fein and the Northern Ireland delegation. It was a pretty big deal. Anyway, Cleague found and stopped an attempt to upend the negotiations. I don't think it ever even made the press," he said.

Sherman could vaguely remember that something along those lines had happened but couldn't recall the details. So that was Cleague. Sherman shook his head. Luther went on.

"He went on to instruct at the Federal Law Enforcement Training Center, at Glynco, Georgia. From there he was posted to Peru, and then on to the Lebanon. Somewhere along the line he pissed somebody off, because he requested to resign and his boss, the Diplomatic Security Officer for Beirut, and the American Ambassador signed off on it. He ends up living out in Hell's Half Acre, Washington, on catch-as-catch-can gigs as a bodyguard." Luther finished. He leaned back in his chair as the waiter cleared their places. After the waiter had finished bussing the table and poured their coffee Sherman leaned forward with his elbows on the table and summarized.

"So, here is this man who is apparently an effective leader, inspires respect from his sub-ordinates, is individually competent under significant stress, but can't keep a job." He was starting to get a headache.

"Yep." Luther said.

"Where did he get the explosives? That was one hell of a lot of damage for one man to do." Sherman said.

Luther shrugged and said, "He kept it."

"What?" Sherman asked.

"He probably kept it." Luther repeated and started counting off on one hand again, "He taught the demolition classes in the Reserves. When he was on active duty in the Combat Engineers he would have had access to C-4. In both active and reserve service, Cleague was the guy who signed for it. He verified its use. And he ostensibly would have turned what was left over, if any, back in. If he kept a little bit here and a little bit there, who would have known? He did it over a period of years. The man was a human pack rat. Going by the list of estimated contents of that shed alone, from the forensic report, it would indicate that he kept every piece of brass he ever handled." Luther said.

"Brass?" Sherman questioned. "Yes, Sir, brass cartridge cases. After ammunition is expended you have remaining brass, which many people used to reload. Reloading was a popular hobby for many civilians until it was legislated out of existence." Luther said.

"Cleague wouldn't have been the first military guy, officer or enlisted, to have kept a little souvenir, you know?' He asked. Sherman nodded mutely.

"I can't verify this because there is no documentation to support it, but that is my gut feeling." Luther went on, "And he certainly had the expertise. He had been in the Combat Engineers—they blow up stuff. He had been in Recon—they blow up stuff. He used to teach people how to blow up stuff. By himself, it would have been difficult, but for him, it was certainly do-able." Luther concluded.

"So what happened to him Mr. Luther?" Sherman asked.

"I don't know that yet, sir." Luther said, "But, he didn't die on that island."

94

The Alders restaurant was about seventy-five feet across the front and maybe a hundred feet from front door to back door. The building faced east.

Immediately north of the restaurant was an antique bookstore which was, in turn, flanked by a dry cleaners. South of the building, on the other side of the alley was a pharmacy. West of the building on the other side of the alley that ran behind it was an industrial welding Supply Company. Four of those five buildings had residential units on their upper floors that were currently occupied. It stood to reason that some of the chemicals used in three of those businesses were probably flammable.

Fifteen feet in from the front door of *The Alders* restaurant, along the south wall, was a single flight staircase that led to the upper dining level. Directly below the dining level along the south wall was the bar. All along the north wall ran the open-pit spit on which were roasted the nationally-famous sides of beef—one of the reasons for the Alder's reputation as one of the finest dining spots in the city. Open gas grills (from which patrons were treated to somewhat dramatic displays of culinary excellence in the grilling, searing, and further preparation of their fare) also lined the same wall.

Everything operated on natural gas; the industrial gauge gas main fed in from the kitchen. Due to the intense heat coming from the north wall huge exhaust fans as well as prudently positioned air-conditioning ducts were located directly over the food preparation area. Antique yet functional ceiling fans were placed throughout the dining areas. The north edge of the upper dining deck was lined with a wrought iron open-work railing that allowed patrons to view food preparation from their lofty perch if they chose to do so.

The "plate glass" bay window that lined the front wall was hermetically sealed, double-paned, ballistic resistant Lexan. The foundation and main load-bearing support structures had been reinforced above and beyond code. When Eugene Smith chose this restaurant in which to invest his entire retirement nest egg, he took the rumor of an impending "Major West Coast Earthquake" very seriously: this building would stand.

Every aspect of the physical plant was above-code. Even the huge fans that served to waft away the exhaust over the grills and roasting pit funneled the aroma of freshly-prepared meat all over the neighborhood. With prevailing winds being what they are off Elliott Bay, unfortunately, most of the time the smell of roasting succulent beef wafted over the minimal security adult correctional facility administered by a community of Hare Krishna, located less than a block away from the Alders. As in other cities, Seattle had a contract with the local sect to administer and staff logistical-support functions of the city's adult corrections half-way house. It proved to be a reasonably-priced service provider to the city and the contract was great PR for the sect. Since the Hare Krishna rigidly observed a vegetarian diet, only strict vegetarian fare was served to the inmates. With no commitment of their own to abstain from meat, the inmates were driven to near riotous craving for animal flesh almost every time the wind was right, and the wind was right almost every day just as the cooks of the Alders were preparing for the day's biggest rush at dinnertime. Dinner was served daily from six PM to midnight with live jazz every weekend.

In the past year, the inmates had tried unsuccessfully to mount a class action suit against the sect for cruel and unusual punishment, and the sect repeatedly complained to the Mayor's office that the restaurant people were not acting in good faith with the community as this was a community-focused effort after all and the very least the commercial establishments could do would be to compromise on their food preparation schedule if not on their menu and why couldn't they just serve nice fresh vegetables anyway since it was so much healthier and karma-free to which Eugene Smith would characteristically respond: "Bullshit, I like my karma the way it is. Besides I was here first." Which he was.

The Alders' kitchen occupied most of the back quarter of the restaurant's total floor space with the southwest corner being Eugene Smith's office space. The rear of the dining area had a raised platform about a foot off the level of the ground floor. On evenings when live music was performed, this was the space where the performers set up. When live music was not offered, this area was used as additional dining space where Eugene Smith could generally be found holding court, strategically located to keep an eye on the front door and his guests while administering his tiny empire.

At 9:00 in the morning, Smith sat at his customary table. It was early, and he took advantage of the quiet to go over some paperwork before the restaurant opened for business. Some of the staff was getting ready for the day's guests: setting tables with fresh linens, utensils and glassware, correcting menus, preparing the foods that could be fixed ahead of time. Smith spent this time going over the previous day's deliveries and accounts payable. There was a noise at the door but Smith paid it no mind, someone would politely tell the potential customer to come back later. He loved the flourishing business he helped build, but the constant bickering over the past year with the Hare Krishnas and the Mayor's office and several shyster law firms who saw a quick buck in pending litigation had severely dampened Smith's enthusiasm for the business to which he had dedicated much of his life since his retirement from the State Department. He still loved his little restaurant but it wasn't fun anymore. He would sell it if he could find the right buyer, but the probability of Smith approving anyone to buy his baby was quite slim.

"Gene, there's a lady at the door asking to speak with you." The youngish waitress, who was one of the Alders' more senior staff members and worth her weight in gold as an employee, broke Smith's concentration without apology.

"Who is it, Susy?" he asked.

"She would only say her name is Linda and that she really has to talk with you." Smith peered around the girl but couldn't make out the figure standing at the front of the restaurant, obscured by the light coming through the leaded-glass of the front door. With a shrug Smith relented. *At least she doesn't appear to be wearing an orange bed sheet*, he mused.

"Show her in. Would you bring us a couple cups of coffee, as well please?" He asked.

"Sure Gene." And Susy was off to answer the door and get the coffee.

It hadn't occurred to him before but Suzy could run the restaurant. Smith shifted his gaze from the retreating waitress to the table in front of him. He piled up the invoices and packing slips into a somewhat manageable stack and put them off to the side of the table. He would have to think about selling the Alders with a bit more deliberation when time allowed. With age, apparently, he had become preoccupied and it seemed to be more and more common. He was thinking one thing and doing another when he heard a voice that instantly brought with it a sense of warmth and dread.

"Hello, Gene." Linda Muller said. Her smile was as beguiling as it had been the time Cleague had introduced Linda to him, but some of the sharper features had been mellowed a little, eroded, since the last time he had seen her. He was surprised and mutely gestured for her to join him at his table. His mind raced with worst-case scenarios that would have compelled her to leave the relatively safe haven of Palm Springs and Roger Tibbett's very protective wing as Susy brought coffee with dispatch and continued on about her work.

"How've you been, Linda?' Smith asked, as he reflexively stood to hold a chair out for her. She took it gracefully but couldn't help from laughing as she read the baffled expression on Smith's face.

"I've been fine, Gene, and you?"

Smith nodded... "Good, good." He said.

Seeing her here in his restaurant in Seattle was such a shock he was unable to articulate the questions that were bursting inside his brain all at once.

Well, one at a time in no particular order, "When did you get in town?" He asked.

"Last night; stayed down by the airport." And in the ceremonial chitchat that accompanies unexpected reunions, she mentioned a motel in the city of SeaTac.

95

"Does anybody else know you're here; have you called Peter yet?" Smith asked. Well, she knew this part was coming so best to get it over with quickly.

"I don't know how much Peter has told you, Gene, but we broke up last summer. I haven't talked to him very much in the past year. In fact, the last time I saw him, he was hungover and preparing to go get himself killed somewhere."

Cleague had never told Smith that he and Linda had broken up, but Smith had guessed as much. He had assumed that if Cleague wanted to tell him he would, and if not, it was not his concern.

"You know, Linda, it's his profession and he is pretty darned good at it."

"Yes, I know. He'd never let me forget. I swear Gene, you, Roger, Peter, you're all nuts. Did you ever think that maybe these people you three would risk getting killed to protect might have a reason for someone wanting to kill them? You were married once, how do you think your wife would have felt, or how do you think Mary felt every time Roger packed his bags and was gone in the middle of the night? Or how do you think I felt every time Cl... By the way, what's he calling himself now? And that's another thing! Every time I'd turn around he was somebody different. I swear to god, Gene, he got so damned paranoid he was delusional!"

Somewhere in there Smith thought he had detected the sound of a burning ember, but he really wasn't sure what he had just heard.

"As far as I know he's still using his own name." He would have to check with Cleague just to be sure since that was the name under which Cleague had been checked into the hospital.

"Why, did he change it?"

"Yeah, once or twice a week. He was driving Roger nuts; he couldn't keep track of him. I'll tell you, Gene, Pete was drinking like a fish till the last job. I never heard the details, but that's why Roger fired him."

Smith remained impassive but this news stunned him. He had never personally known Cleague to ever touch a drop of alcohol, but he really hadn't had the chance to catch up on old times with Cleague either.

"Well, anyway, I've come to tell him that someone has been asking a lot of questions about him. This one guy questioned me—he was really creepy. He kept dropping these hints about how dangerous Pete is, and who knows what he might do next. Gene, that man said Pete killed a bunch of Federal agents on the island up north, is that true?" She paused to take a sip of her coffee. Smith was on full alert now and feared what was coming next.

"Did he say who he was? A cop?" Smith added vaguely.

"No," she paused to remember. "He said he was with the Justice Department investigating the circumstances of the event in which so many of those guys got killed. He said the dead guys were in the…" she floundered and searched for the acronym.

"It was something Pete had told me about, ABP or BPF or something like that. It was those guys that were sitting outside his house at the island. Anyway, the guy gave me the creeps," she added matter-of-factly.

Without hesitation, but calmly, he asked "The B.P.S.?"

"Yeah, that's it, a guy by the name of Luther something, or something Luther. Do you know him?"

"No." Smith replied quietly and thought, *But, I will.*

"So, this Luther guy says I could be implicated in what Pete did on the island. Gene, I didn't know anything about it till this Mr. Luther told me and then he said I could be convicted in court for it as an accomplice after the fact, or something." She said and her trepidation showed. "Is it true?" She asked.

Smith was not a lawyer and he did his best to keep his distance from those who were, but it was so implausible he had to fall back on reason in his reassurances to her. "They can't prove something that didn't happen, Linda." He said.

"That's what I said. And then Luther says, 'We don't have to prove it; we just have to get a jury to believe it.' Can they?" She asked.

Smith, with his elbow on the table, his chin firmly planted in the palm of his hand, was totally focused on the story that had just been relayed to him. "It sounds to me like he was fishing for something, Linda, and he was trying to scare you to get you to tell him what he wanted to know." He surmised.

"Well, yeah, and it worked too. I'm scared shitless right now, Gene. What the hell am I supposed to do? I don't know a damn thing about any of this," she said.

"What else did he ask you?" Smith asked.

"He wanted to know how Cleague planned all that stuff on the island, and how did he find out about the raid, and where is he now?" She said.

Bingo, Smith thought. *They're coming after Cleague again.*

After an hour it had become awkward. Linda had looked around almost furtively, casting about for what to do next, when she finally took advantage of the opportunity presented by the increasing tempo of motion and clatter of the wait staff to take her leave.

"Well, I got to go and let you get back to work," she said as she stood. "If you see Pete, tell him about that guy."

"Well, hold on a minute, you don't have to rush out the door, you just got here." Smith really didn't want her to leave; he regarded her as a friend and enjoyed her company. "Why don't you stick around and tell him yourself?" Smith asked.

"I'm not the goddess that Peter put on a pedestal. I guess I didn't want to be around him when he figured that out," she told him flatly. But something didn't ring true, why would she have made the trip up here? Smith wondered.

"You really don't believe he would harm you do you?" Smith asked.

"I really don't know, Gene. He's different. If it is true about what happened on PI, he's done some things I never thought any sane man would do," she said.

This gave Smith pause. "How long will you be staying?" Smith asked.

"I don't know, I haven't made up my mind yet, but I'll come back to see you before I go. It was good to see you, Gene, take care." Linda said gathering her stuff about her.

"Yeah, you too." Smith agreed.

And with that Linda was out the door.

96

It was not like Smith to be reticent, shy, or rude but in the two days since Linda Muller had been to see him he increasingly spent more time in his office away from the guests. The Alders' staff was superb and could handle it but they worried about him. Suzy was particularly worried, as she was doing most of the PR with customer's complaints, real and imagined. It was a weekday and the lunchtime crowd did not give the staff a break. Smith was nowhere to be seen and Suzy was at wits end. As the lunchtime crowd thinned out, she went directly into Smith's office without knocking, sat down without invitation and said, "We need to talk."

"Not now, I'm busy." He brusquely announced from behind the newspaper. That was it. She pulled the newspaper from his hand and slapped it onto his desk.

"Damn it, Gene, that's what I'm talking about. You are going to lose your business and we are going to lose our jobs if you don't get back out there. I can't field customers forever and the staff is asking questions. It's affecting the quality of the service!" She was pissed. Plainly, clearly, pissed.

Smith was a little startled. He had not realized how much of a strain he had put her under as well as the rest of the staff. He hadn't planned to propose this yet but now was as good a time as any.

"Suzy," he started, "I think you're capable of a whole lot more than you...."

"No! Don't give me that, Gene, this is your business; you're place is out there." She cut him off.

Smith did not like being cut off. "May I finish?" He asked quietly.

"I'm sorry, Gene." She was and meant it.

He gestured to the office door, "Close the door, will you please?" he asked. She did so and took her seat.

"Suzy, I haven't mentioned this to anybody until right now, I'm going to sell my share of the restaurant. I think you would make a great manager if that's what you wanted to do, but more to the point, I think you would be a terrific owner. I think you should buy my share." He said simply.

That took the wind out of her sails. The Alders was Smith's dream. He had practically made it from the ground up and now it was nationally recognized. The thought had never occurred to her that he would one day walk away from it.

"Why?" It was all she could think of to say.

He sat squarely behind his desk, hands folded one over the other.

"Because it's time. I don't need an answer right now but I want you to think about it."

"Think about what? I don't have the capital to put into this place." Suzy said incredulously; she was also in shock. She did not know what the value of the business was but she did know she didn't have it.

"That can be dealt with in a number of ways. I haven't mentioned this to anybody yet except you. I'm not in a great hurry, but I think I'd like to do it within a year. All I'm asking is that you think about it for a while. You can do this if you want to." He was very calm. He had made up his mind.

"Gene, are you OK? Are you sick? Are you dying?" Each interrogative was more urgent than the one preceding it. She was really worried.

"I'm fine, Suzy." He said quietly with a smile. She knew he wasn't one to feign airs. "I'll be out there at my appointed station for dinner, I promise. But in the meantime, give it some thought." She left his office and walked back into the restaurant.

Smith had given it a lot of thought over the past couple days and had come to this conclusion: it was time to move on. Of the people he had considered for this proposition, he had the most faith in Suzie's ability to continue what he had started with the restaurant. He was confident he could talk his partners into the agreement and he would work out the financial arrangement in due course. All he needed was for Suzie to agree, the sooner the better, although he had not told her that.

As he sat there behind his desk musing on the fate of his restaurant, he watched the streamer on the bottom of the TV headline news channel. The sound was muted but he could read. Both houses of the United States Congress had voted to conduct a Constitutional Convention earlier in the year but now a date was likely to be set as soon as Congress returned from its summer recess. It was for real now—the country had never been this close to altering the foundation, the Bill of Rights, of the Constitution. Smith considered it would have to be very soon.

Smith's decision to sell his share of the Alders was definite. He just hadn't said it out loud to anyone until now. Linda Muller's visit had actually been the catalyst. If the BPS, or the Department of Justice, or whoever it was, had gone to Palm Springs to interview her, they were most certainly watching her. By coming to his restaurant she had very likely led them here to him whether she knew it or not. They may have seen Cleague or not, but it was certain that they were going to make another move and it was going to be a big one. The Constitutional Convention would be only days away; the papers would be full of it. A pre-emptive strike on a suspected pro-gun zealot would be just the keynote attention-getter the anti-gun faction would love. It was exactly what they had tried to do back on Peninsular Island, and look at what a success that had been—what a body count! What a PR coup! Smith would be damned if he was going to let it happen at his restaurant.

At any rate, Smith had since concluded that if he didn't own the restaurant, Cleague probably wouldn't be there and Smith's legacy, the Alders, would live on. Besides, he was tired.

97

Dr Elizabeth Wills grew up in the Napa Valley in California. She earned her undergraduate degree in chemistry from Stanford, and graduated from the University of Washington School Of Medicine. She worked in the trauma/critical care division at Harborview Medical Center— the only Level 1 (regional) Trauma Center serving Washington, Alaska, Montana, and Idaho. It was her profession and her passion to care for emergency surgical and trauma patients. She was tall, slender, and attractive. She had dark auburn hair that just broke at her shoulders and she smiled easily. She juggled a number of cases at any one time in addition to being one of the primary trauma doctors at Harborview. She always made time to see how her patients were mending as long as they were under her direct care. Once they were transferred or discharged she went on to the next set of problems, but this Cleague guy really intrigued her. It was not unusual for police to come asking about a patient who had received treatment for various injuries but Federal attention was rare. She had coolly declined to give an account of injuries sustained and treatment rendered in a very matter-of-fact, professional manner. But something was askew. She decided to make a very rare house call.

She went to the Alders Restaurant, Cleague's given address on the admission form. It was Friday, after the lunchtime rush, maybe she'd get a chance to speak with Mr. Smith, who had listed himself as Mr. Cleague's emergency contact on his admission forms if not with Mr. Cleague himself. Based on their conversations while he was a patient, she expected Mr. Cleague to be somewhat elusive. If the Federal Government was looking for him there had to be a reason for it other than being "a person of interest." Someone saying they were from the Government would not intimidate her, but unfortunately, the volunteers at the admissions desk were easily bullied. And the miserable bastards didn't even have a court order. If those Federal agents could threaten and willfully scare little, gray-haired women, she could make a "house-call."

It took twenty-five minutes to get from Harborview to Belltown. Another fifteen minutes to find a parking space and finally she had to park two blocks away from the Alders. She took a short cut and walked through the alley past the welding supply to the restaurant. There was a guy wrapped in a newspaper, talking to himself. She asked herself, *if we don't take care of our sick, how will they get well?*

She walked due east out of the alley and came out on Fourth Street, turned left and walked to the front door of the Alders. It was a little after two in the afternoon. Most of the lunchtime crowd had come and gone but a few stragglers were still in the dining room. Dr. Wills paused at the hostess' podium, taking everything in. It was her first time in the Alders. A beaming young woman approached from the bar with a menu in the crook of her arm.

"May I Help You?" She asked. Dr. Wills had not seen her approach and was a little off guard.

"Hi." She beamed right back; she hadn't any idea of what she was going to say. "My name is Dr. Elizabeth Wills, I wonder if I can speak with Mr. Eugene Smith?"

"I'll see," the young hostess nodded and gesturing toward the dining room, "would you like to have a seat?" Dr. Wills took the proffered chair, smiled her thanks and waited.

Smith, having been told some lady wanted to see him, first saw her from the back and presumed her to be Linda Muller. "Linda?" He said with the question in his voice. When she turned around he immediately recognized her as

Doctor Wills, Cleague's attending physician from the hospital, and was somewhat confused.

"Doctor Wills, what a pleasant surprise." He wasn't kidding. He was surprised as hell.

"Call me Lizzie." She said, and with that solar smile, she extended her hand.

98

Summer is traditionally observed in many parts of the United States between June and September with lots of sunshine and heat. Seattle, meanwhile, enjoyed its particular seasonal reality: highs in the mid-fifties or in the mid-nineties, cloudy and rainy, or occasionally hot and dry, with ten to fifteen knot winds out of the northwest or no wind at all. On this particular day in late August there was a small craft advisory in the Strait of Juan de Fuca due to a thunderstorm. Periods of intermittent sun breaks would turn to showers later on in the day. On Elliott Avenue, in brief glimpses of sky and water between the buildings lining the commercial boulevard, the weather made for a pretty spectacular view. The sun coming between the layers of ominously dark clouds presented a dramatic contrast between dark and light, reflected on the virtually still water of Puget Sound.

The van, of the unremarkable white panel variety, listed on the table of equipment for the Seattle office of the Bureau of Public Safety, had Washington State commercial license plates. Any civilian looking at the plates could not have known it was a government vehicle, as the plates did not carry the XMT or US designator. The van cruised south on Elliott Avenue past the used car lots, delicatessens, light industrial plants, dollar-an-hour parking lots, and the remnants of a lumberyard that burnt to the ground in 1988. As it maintained the speed of local traffic—35 miles an hour—it was flanked on either side of the avenue by commercial properties, fifty-one percent of which belonged to Lou Emerald.

It turned east on Denny, south on First, east on Virginia, north on Fourth and pulled into the Dollar an Hour lot at

Fourth and Bell, half a block down and across the street from The Alders Restaurant. The parking lot used to be a fancy movie theater called the Byzantine Cinerama that had finally fallen into hard times. It had failed as an art house theater and the gentrification of the Eighties and Nineties could not save it.

The van sought out the northwest-most parking spot. Its occupants adjusted their monitoring equipment and settled in for a protracted stay. It wasn't bad duty for the two technicians—they would even get their take-out meals from The Alders on occasion (that place had really good food). This was the day shift—the night shift left with no fanfare, no passing of the baton, and no exchange of information. This had been their routine since the Muller girl had been followed to this restaurant some days ago, and today was no different. However, the surveillance phase of this particular operation would soon be brought to a close. With their final transmission, their role in this operation would be at an end. They would be on their way home, and the next phase would be played out on National Television...Live from Seattle.

One thing about electronically eavesdropping on a restaurant is that it is terribly noisy. The clatter of silverware, the clanking of dishes, the background chatter, cooks yelling at the waitresses, waitresses yelling at the cooks, laughter from the bar and, on weekends, jazz made for a cacophonous mess.

The audio technician with the ear phones sat in the cargo area of the van fiddling with dials and knobs. He would hear a finer resolution from the restaurant than his partner who sat at a bank of small video screens, and had to rely on speakers—which weren't at all poor, they just weren't of the same binaural quality as the ear phones. They looked remarkably similar: medium height, medium build, Dockers, polo shirt, and windbreaker, dark horn-rimmed glasses and sideburns down to the jaw line. They could have been twins.

The transmitters in the restaurant sent signals down the block and across the street to a receiver in the van where they were graphically recorded and digitally filtered of collateral noise, thus enhancing the sound quality of the transmission. The BPS audio technicians had been quite generous in their dispersion of the tiny microphones and their corresponding digital transmitters. The other technician sat in the passenger seat watching intently and directing the video camera at the front door and left or right as necessary to pan the front of the building, zoom in, zoom out, hold, focus, repeat. For the first couple hours it was fun but after almost a week it was tedious.

The agent covering the backdoor had a much more difficult time of observing the restaurant in an unobtrusive manner. The alley between the back door of The Alders and the neighboring business to the west (a commercial welding supply company) was barely wide enough to allow one vehicle through. It certainly wasn't wide enough for two-lane traffic and was posted "One Way". It was also posted "No Loitering", which made it a pain in the ass to watch who went in and out of the restaurant's back door. Since the alley was posted, there was a fairly consistent police presence. The agent watching the back door was festooned in the common regalia of a skid row homeless person complete with grocery cart of personal items and naturally he drew the attention of the passing police: constant harassment.

However, persistence paid off. Nestled into the doorway of one of the neighboring buildings adjacent to the welding supply company he had been able to keep an eye on the back door for a couple of hours. He had been able to recognize the regular staff and could spot an unfamiliar face. After the lunch time rush, a woman who appeared to fit the description of the woman alleged to be the target's (one Peter Cleague) girlfriend walked right past him. She walked past and kind of smiled, kept walking through the alley out on to the street and turned left out of his line of sight.

With the unexpected radio transmission the audio tech in the van immediately turned the volume up on the appropriate freq and responded: "You were garbled, say again, over." To which the bum replied: "...a woman. "

The tech responded: "What woman, what about her." The bum was about ready to rip off the mike, walk out of the alley across the street to the parking lot and shove the goddamned thing up the technoweeny's ass. Career enhancement my ass he thought, he was getting sick of this surveillance bullshit. "What?" the tech demanded.

"Goddamn it, I said a woman just walked past. I think she's Cleague's girlfriend." The surveillance agent bit off the ends of his words in an effort of enunciation.

"Oh." was the tech's reply. The techs in the van told him to hold his position. His reply could not be heard over the rustling of clothing abrading the very sensitive microphone. The audio tech then hit the pre-dialed number on the cell phone as the video tech kept an eye on his equipment, pedestrian traffic on the sidewalk, and the front door at which stood a woman about the same height, weight, and description of Cleague's girlfriend.

But it was really hard to tell from here. The audio tech relayed the scant bit of information regarding a woman going in the front door of the Alders and was told to tell the video man to pan back on the camera to allow a wider shot of the front of the building to be transmitted. The images were being transmitted to a warehouse not very far away on one of the renovated piers on Elliott Bay. The surveillance team leader, watching the live feed in the warehouse on Elliot Bay, also directed that a second camera be turned to a tight shot on the front door. But by now the woman had already gone into the building. The team leader had to make some decisions. Was this woman Cleague's girlfriend? If she was, was Cleague in there? If he wasn't there, why would his girlfriend show up? He had to make a recommendation to his superior. He stared hard at the video monitor relayed from the van parked across the street from the Alders Restaurant but in spite of its sophistication the image was too grainy. Go or no go? Make a decision.

"What did you see?" The superior asked.

"We have a possible ID on Cleague's girlfriend." The tech in the van said.

"Did you see Cleague?" The superior asked.

"No sir." The tech replied.

"We don't care about the girlfriend. Call me when you have Cleague." The superior retorted and hung up.

99

Janmashtami, an Indian festival marking the birth of Krishna, is generally celebrated sometime between mid-August and mid- September. This festival marks the birth of the Hindu Savior, Lord Sri Krishna, one of the main spiritual founts of the Hindu religion.

Krishna is the symbol of devotional love and his birthday is observed in Hindu communities all over the world. Lovers down the ages are signified by the divine love of Radha and Krishna. Raslila, a special kind of dance drama is performed illustrating incidents from the life of Krishna, particularly his love for Radha.

Over a 48-hour period, the faithful forego sleep and sing traditional Hindu songs. Krishna was born at midnight, so it is at this time that the true festivities commence. In the temples, images of Krishna are bathed at midnight and placed in cradles, while the shankh (conch shell) is played and bells are rung. Holy mantras are also chanted to venerate Krishna. The festivity is one of the main holidays in India, and is widely celebrated, especially in the north of the country.

Unfortunately, in Seattle, Washington, on this twenty-sixth day of August, the Hare Krishna community that administered the adult detention center was not able to get a parade permit for midnight. Mid-afternoon, right around rush hour, would simply have to do. For the public celebration, they planned to observe Krishna's birthday all over the neighborhood, right past the front door of the Alders restaurant.

The lunch time crowd had thinned out quite a bit and Mr. Smith had talked Dr. Wills into ordering something to eat since she was here anyway and why not take advantage of the opportunity and they could sit and visit while she had her lunch? Smith found his words somewhere in between articulate and mute and gracelessly stumbled through them. He usually wasn't this flustered by guests, unexpected or not, but Dr Wills here at his restaurant was a total surprise. There seemed to be a lot of that lately. Taking in the relaxed atmosphere of the restaurant, she agreed, and called work to tell them she would be out for the rest of the day. Rounds had been made, and miraculously there were no meetings or appointments scheduled this late in the afternoon. Mr. Smith showed her to his table and took her order. She asked what he suggested. He told her and she took his suggestion along with the recommended wine. What the hell, she was off the clock and she settled in for a very pleasant lunch. "So how is Mr. Cleague getting along?" Dr Wills inquired. Smith nodded, testing his coffee, sipped, and said, "He's doing OK."

"You know," Dr. Wills carried on quite conversationally, "it is not unusual to have police interest in some patients, but we usually don't get very much Federal scrutiny. This very odd, very intense man was in this morning asking about your Mr. Cleague. Oh my god, this steak is out of this world!" She said, rapturously enjoying the best steak she had ever had. Meanwhile Eugene Smith's chromatic scale of awareness went from white to neon orange.

"Did you, uh," Smith cleared his throat, "did you get this fellow's name?" He asked.

"No, you know, that was kind of funny, he just flashed a badge and an ID card but I really didn't get the opportunity to read it." She said, noticing a discernible change in Smith's previously pleasant demeanor and although not unpleasant now, he did seem to be very, very, focused.

"Did he mention which agency he was from?" He asked.

"Yeah," she said. "It was, uh, B something, B, B...BBC? No," she corrected herself with a dismissive wave of the hand. "Uh, I think it was BP something, but who can keep up, there are so many of them." She took a sip of wine.

"Was it the BPS, Bureau of Public Safety?" Smith asked.

"Yeah," she said, nodding agreeably, "that was it." She said.

"This morning?" Smith asked for clarification in a pretty much normal conversational tone.

"Yeah, right around nine o'clock." She said.

"What'd he do? He wasn't disruptive or anything was he?" Smith was trying as best he could not to be too pointed in his inquiry.

"Well, they asked for Mr. Cleague's charts and I said they are confidential and they couldn't see them and then they asked for the admittance forms and, they are confidential as well.

"They?" Smith could feel his blood pressure going up.

"Oh yeah, there were two of them, but I didn't get either name." She said, digging into her curried rice, tried it blissfully, and continued.

"Unfortunately they bullied the admissions staff in spite of the hospital's policy of patient confidentiality. Often our admissions staff is assisted by the auxiliary league. They are very nice retired people who volunteer their time. But these Federal people were very persistent, and overbearing, and unfortunately our volunteers were intimidated." You could tell she was a surgeon by the way she handled a steak knife, not as a tool but as an instrument.

"They told these federal people that he had been released and the girls let them see his admission papers. They wanted to know, and they were really snippy about this, 'if it was just bumps and scrapes, why he was in the hospital?' I said we kept him there for observation because I was concerned about a concussion." She looked around briefly.

"Is he here by the way?' She asked Smith. "I would like to tell him about all this," she said.

"No, he sure isn't but I will definitely let him know." Smith said. If the BPS had seen the admission papers then they saw that the Alders had been listed as Cleague's address. What had he been thinking? He mentally chastised himself, all the while playing congenial host to a gracious doctor.

"Is Mr. Cleague in trouble?" She asked.

"Well, I don't know." Smith answered honestly. "I don't think he's done anything wrong. I have never known him to get mixed up with the law." As he said it, Smith realized that his idea of wrong and Dr. Wills' idea of wrong might not have been the same. What the hell, different people are different.

When she finished her meal she sat back with an obvious air of satisfied contentment.

"Would you like another glass of wine?" Mr. Smith asked.

"Oh, no thanks, I had plenty, but I would like a cup of coffee?" She turned it into a question. Smith smiled, and nodded, and cleared the table, and momentarily came back with two cups of coffee and a tiramisu for desert. It was, of course, excellent.

She had never been embarrassed by her curiosity. That was how she came to be here having a marvelous lunch on what was turning out to be a very fine day.

"Where is Mr. Cleague, may I ask?" She inquired with a smile.

"Yes you may," Smith replied. "He went back up north." He said simply.

"So soon?" She was somewhat surprised. "He probably isn't healed yet.' She said.

"Yeah, well, he was concerned about losing his job. He just hired on with that company and before you know it he calls in sick for a couple of weeks. He was afraid they'd give the job to somebody else." Smith said.

"And what does he do again?" she couldn't remember.

"Retail sales, sporting goods." Smith said.

"Oh." She smiled, nodding. "Right." Like, what else could you say? Retail was OK, but Cleague had just impressed her as someone who would have been involved in something else. Anything else.

100

The surveillance van parked across the street from the Alders had maintained its position. The undercover agent who had been in the alley earlier was now pushing his grocery cart up Fourth Street toward Wall, just now passing the front door of the restaurant. And there she was. Close enough that he could reach out and grab her, but he heard about the last time an agent tried to do that. She walked right past him, head down, typical, and never even saw him. Speaking into his sleeve, he immediately got on the mike to the van.

"I just saw Linda Muller." He said, clearly and distinctly and this time there was no static. The techs in the van sat up.

"Say again, over." They replied.

"I say again, I just saw Linda Muller." He turned to be sure. "She is walking into the restaurant right now." He said as he walked to the corner and turned around headed south. The van techs immediately pulled a tight shot on the door and saw the back of a woman, amazingly similar to the last one whom they had dismissed as a false alarm. One of the techs was immediately on the phone to the team leader down in the warehouse on the waterfront and told him that Linda Muller had just gone into the restaurant. The team leader asked, "Have you seen Cleague?" The techies in the van looked at each other.

"No." said the senior of the two.

"If you haven't seen him, and you do not know for a fact that he is in that building, why did you call me?" The team leader asked.

"Because we thought you'd want to know, besides, why would she come all the way up from California if her boyfriend isn't here?" The tech asked reasonably.

The team leader conceded they had a point. "All right, one of you go in there and find him, but do it discretely." The team leader told them and hung up. They hadn't eaten for hours and whoever went into the restaurant would have to order something or it would look weird. They flipped for it.

101

Eugene Smith spent most of his day in a restaurant, a very busy restaurant. The placement of the tables and the resultant traffic patterns by necessity made for a compressed space. He felt more than saw someone approach the table, and paying it no mind, he glanced at his watch. The afternoon had flown by and the after work crowd started drifting in toward the bar. He was enjoying this woman's company and now it was catching up to him. It was Friday and it was going to be hectic.

"Hi, Gene." He looked up sharply at the sound of Linda Muller's voice; she stood there grinning that Cheshire cat grin.

"Excuse me, Gene, I don't want to interrupt, but I just wanted to stop and say goodbye," Linda said, smiling by way of mute introduction to Smith's guest. Eugene Smith rose and presented Linda to Dr. Wills who introduced herself as "Lizzie". They shook hands amiably and Smith invited Linda to join them.

"Oh, no thanks, I'm on the way down to the airport and just wanted to let you know I was headed back home," she said.

"Did you ever see Pete?" he asked.

"No, I didn't. Too bad I missed him but I have to get back. Well, if you see him, tell him I said 'hi', huh?" She asked with a little shrug.

"Yeah." Smith said. "Too bad." And he couldn't remember a time he had meant it more than now.

"Hey. What's the deal with the parade?" She asked. Eugene Smith paid little attention to the activities of his Vedic neighbors and was unaware of their festivities.

"What parade?' He asked. Linda turned toward the Lexan front window of the Alders and said,

"That one."

Smith looked up, and from his position all he could see was swooping swirls of orange billowing past his window. He turned to his guest, Dr. Wills, excused himself, and walked toward the front of the building.

Shankh intonations on conch shells, the din of bells, the thumping of drums and tambourines, the tinkling of cymbals and some indecipherable chanting greeted Smith as he walked out the door of his restaurant onto the sidewalk, with Linda right beside him. Banners proclaiming: "Live and Let Live", "Flesh Burdens The Soul", "Veganism Lights The Path To Righteous Harmony", and "Meat Stains Your Karma" were displayed prominently by the marching celebrants.

"Oh, for crying out loud!" Smith exclaimed as he took in the cacophony before him. Linda leaned into to Smith's ear and said, "I saw that guy when I came in; he kind of freaked me out. He was talking to his wrist watch."

"What guy?" Smith asked. She subtly directed Smith's attention to his left. Smith looked in the direction indicated and saw a man, pushing a grocery cart, clearly talking into his sleeve. Smith immediately scanned the street, north and south, for the other end of that microphone. He couldn't see across the street for the peripatetic hubbub of the saffron garbed Hare Krishnas dancing and chanting their way down Fourth Street. He and Linda stood near the curb and waited for the grocery cart guy to pass them. They were out on a public street in the middle of a crowded sidewalk. Even if the BPS were there, what could they do? He reasoned. But then he remembered the debacle in San Francisco.

Smith watched the grocery cart guy turn west into the alley. He scanned the street again, left to right, right to left, and saw the antenna dish on the roof of the white panel van parked across the street and down the block in Emerald's parking lot. "Let's go inside." He suggested to Linda. The bastards were right across the street.

Smith dropped Linda off at his table and made his way into his office. He called Cleague at the sporting goods store up north. Smith used the landline. It was probably bugged but he couldn't help that. What else was he going to do, use a carrier pigeon?

"All North Sports, Can I help you?" A lady answered.

"Hi." Smith answered. "Peter Cleague, please." He said, and held for a moment.

"This is Peter, May I Help You?" Cleague answered.

"Yeah, you can get your ass down here right now." Smith said. Cleague recognized the voice and the tone instantly.

"What's up?" Cleague asked.

"Dr. Wills is here, your lady friend from California is here, and the nice young men in dark suits are sitting across the street." Smith explained.

This gave Cleague pause. He did not know that Linda had come up from California. And she brought the BPS with her, apparently. If the BPS were across the street from the Alders, they were probably on every street around the restaurant. This could be tricky.

"What is she doing there?" Cleague asked.

"She said she came to see an old friend but never connected." Smith said.

Ain't that the fucking truth! Cleague thought.

"Anyway, she's on her way back to the airport, she's got to catch her return flight. What do you want to do?" Smith asked.

"Well, I can't get down there for another two hours. Can you take her to the airport?" Cleague asked.

"Yeah, OK." Smith said.

"Do you want me to come down?" Cleague asked.

Smith reconsidered and said, "No! Don't take this the wrong way, but I don't want you anywhere near my restaurant." Cleague understood. *Couldn't blame him for that,* Cleague thought.

"OK," Cleague said, "Talk to you later."

"Yeah, bye." Smith responded and hung up.

Smith went back to the table and found the two women effusively comparing notes about...Gene Smith and Peter Cleague. Lizzy Wills was laughing and Linda was smiling that Evil Linda smile and they both looked at him with that universal "'So you're the one' look." All Smith could do was innocently ask: "What?"

Linda said "Never mind. So what's up?"

"Well, why don't I take you to the airport?" He said, and turning to Lizzy Wills he asked, "Do you have anything planned for tonight?"

"Well, no, I don't think so. This is rather sudden isn't it? Why?" she asked.

"How would you like to go for a boat ride?" Smith said.

"Only if you can swim," Linda said and both women burst out laughing. Smith was obviously not meant to be in on the joke and remained nonplussed.

"Well?" he nudged politely.

"OK, I guess." Lizzy said.

"Good. Why don't you meet me at the DesMoines Marina? Just park by the gate and I'll find you. Meanwhile, I'll take Linda to the airport. I'll be at the Marina in an hour." Smith said.

"OK." Lizzy said. *Every once in a while you get a day like this. You just never know.* She thought.

Smith marshaled his two lady friends out the door only to be intercepted by Suzy.

"Gene, where are you going?' She demanded.

"Something came up, I got to go." He said.

"Gene, we talked about this!" Suzy protested.

"I got to go." He said. "You'll be fine. Bye." He said, and was through the door as a man of medium height, medium build, Dockers, polo shirt, and windbreaker, dark horn-rimmed glasses and sideburns down to his jaw line, walked through the door at the same time, and collided into Smith's chest. With simultaneous apologies all around, Smith made his way out the door and the technician walked into the restaurant.

Smith reasoned that if he, Linda, and Cleague, were not at the Alder's, there wasn't any purpose for the BPS to be there either. Leaving now was the most prudent thing he could do. He hoped.

Smith suggested that Dr. Wills not walk through the alley and he and Linda accompanied her to her car a couple blocks over. All the while Smith was looking for the grocery cart guy or anybody else that looked like they could have been BPS. They all did. None of them did. *That's why it's called undercover* Smith admonished himself. After Dr. Wills was safely ensconced in the spacious interior of her luxury Honda Civic, Smith and Linda made the quick walk back to his car and motored south to SeaTac International Airport. He pulled the Range Rover into the drop off zone at the departures level and helped Linda with her bag. She took his hand with a gentle squeeze.

"I'm sorry to hear Pete got hurt." She searched for something else to say. "Watch out for him, will you?" She asked.

"Yeah, I will. Take care of yourself Linda; things could get a little weird." Smith answered. "Could get?" She retorted.

"You know what I mean." He said. She smiled, gave him a little hug, and a peck on the cheek, picked up her bag and went through the doors to the ticket desk. Smith made the drive to Des Moines Marina in fifteen minutes.

✻✻✻✻✻

The tech guy noted Smith and the two women in his company. He recognized one of them as Linda Muller. If they weren't here at the Alders, it was unlikely that Cleague would be here either. He made his way to the bar and ordered an iced tea as he asked for a menu. He was getting very depressed very quickly as he realized that he and his partner would be spending their Friday night and probably the rest of their weekend filtering every bit of audio that they had recorded today as well as the rest of the week of all the ambient restaurant noise to get a positive voice track on what had been said at Smith's table. It was likely their best if not only clue as to the location of one Peter Cleague. For now, he would order to go and head back to the van. They'd have chow, and then call up the supervisor. He may as well wait to be told he had to work tonight instead of volunteering for it.

102

The tech sat at the console and fiddled with dials. His partner was on the phone to the guy in the warehouse.

"Well?" The field agent asked?

"We just picked up a conversation on landline to a number out of the city." The tech replied.

"What was it?" The field agent asked.

"It's a place called All North Sports." The tech said. His partner stared at a monitor and scribbled down the address as soon as it came up. The tech on the phone conveyed the address to the guy in the warehouse.

"Where was the girl going?" The field agent asked.

"It was really garbled because of the ambient noise, but I think she's going to the airport." The tech said.

Peter Cleague obviously wasn't there. He was at this North Sports place. But better keep them in place for another day just to be safe. The agent pondered these things.

"One more thing." the tech said, although he really didn't want to volunteer this bit of news.

"What?" The field agent asked.

"We think the Smith guy burned us." He said. The field agent was instantly pissed.

"What? How?" he said.

"He came outside looking at the parade and saw Johnson talking into his sleeve mike. Then he looked right at the van." The tech said.

The field agent held his temper. If the Muller girl was leaving, and if Cleague was at this North Sports place, there wasn't any reason to keep surveillance on the restaurant.

"All right, wrap it up. Get out of there." He said and hung up. He gave the same direction to the tactical team sitting in the warehouse with him. They were going to make a move but it wasn't going to be here. And it wasn't going to be now. He had to go shopping at some sporting goods store up north first.

✱✱✱✱✱

Truth be told, Peter Cleague never really felt fully awake before nine P.M. He did not know why but just assumed that it was the vestigial remnant of some distant arboreal relative that once lived in jungles and climbed trees with its feet. He never really thought about it that much. Just as well. He didn't feel all that much at home in the world of the early rising, perky, perfect, over-achieving, go getters of the nine to five crowd. It was his natural inclination to get up after noon and to go to bed after dawn. He never felt he was missing much. Consequently, he was having adjustment issues with this retail sales job and wondered if he could hang on one more day without getting fired. This post-lunch stupor was cleanly snapped in two by the call from Eugene Smith.

Peter Cleague hung up the phone. He was behind the counter on the sales floor of the store and had his back to the store's interior, leaning on the display case. The BPS had followed Linda from California to Seattle, ostensibly to find him. She was leaving without having met with Cleague. He was not at the Alders although the BPS agents were. They had no reason to believe he was there, and no reason to launch an assault on a five star restaurant in the hubbub of downtown Seattle. The best thing he could do was stay put. But, if they had followed Linda to Seattle, more than likely they would find their way up north to him. They had once already and would likely do so again.

Linda was OK. Smith would get her to the airport. They were coming. Cleague needed to prepare for this.

"Hey Bozo"! Cleague was immediately brought back to the here-and-now of retail sales. "You want to help one of the paying customers?" As Cleague turned, the representative voice of his new clientele was not hard to locate on the sales floor. It belonged to the biggest mouth.

Right before Peter Cleague left the store for the day, he bought himself a Remington 870 with an 18" Cylinder bore barrel and a simple brass bead for a front sight. He also scrounged around the shop and found some Winchester Steel T shot, which he bought with some Federal reduced-load slugs and reduced-load buckshot. He did not know what he would find when he got home to his apartment.

103

Having mulled over his options John Luther sat in the American Airlines concourse at Dulles International Airport. He could stay put at his desk at the DOJ and accomplish nothing, or he could follow a hunch. Reviewing Cleague's service record from the State Department he saw a reference to a Eugene Smith who had been a reporting senior for Cleague when the latter was assigned to Glynco, Georgia. Subsequent efforts by BPS Agent Joan Glyndon revealed that the same Eugene Smith now had a part interest in a restaurant in downtown Seattle. It really couldn't hurt to fly back up to Washington State, tie up some loose ends in Bellingham, and touch base with Glyndon. He could even go talk to the Smith guy. Maybe he knew where Cleague was. What the hell, it couldn't hurt. The worst he could do was that he would accomplish nothing.

The details at the Bellingham Federal Building didn't take long. However it took all day to get to see the person that could find the proper document Luther was required to sign. *All day. All fucking day spent in a waiting room waiting for some GS-2 to find a piece of paper.* He thought; this was why he needed an assistant. *Why the hell didn't Glyndon take care of this before she left?* After his private little temper tantrum he acknowledged that Glyndon did not have the authority to cancel the lease. He did. *All fucking day shot to hell!* He officially terminated his lease on the office space, which he no longer needed. It was a two-hour drive from Seattle to Bellingham, give or take a couple minutes. It took five hours for somebody to find a piece of paper and five seconds to relinquish the office space, and two hours to drive back to Seattle. He was stiff by the time he got to the Federal

Building on Second Street. It was locked up. It was after five P.M. *Perfect.*

The next day he went into the BPS Field Office and asked to see Agent Joan Glyndon. Luther was dumbfounded by what he was told. Agent Glyndon had not come back to work after the Fourth of July holiday. No notice, no resignation, no phone call. Nobody knew where she was. Her absence had been reported to the Office for Personnel Management within the Bureau of Public Safety. After due course and having received no response from Headquarters, BPS, the Seattle field office manager called the Office for Personnel Management and asked if he was getting a replacement for Glyndon and when? He was told that the Office for Plans, Training, and Operations had assumed operational authority in the matter and as her absence was related to an ongoing operation, no replacement would be forthcoming.

Luther fought the urge to smack himself in the head. She had obviously been relaying information on Luther's investigation back to someone in BPS Ops: the same people who orchestrated the failed raid on Cleague's house on Peninsular Island. Apparently she had relayed to them the names of the people he had talked to and their locations: the gunny in Texas, and the girlfriend in Palm Springs. The BPS was using Luther to track down Cleague. Why? If the raid on Cleague's house on PI was all about good copy to generate support for the repeal of an Amendment—that had been accomplished. The Constitutional Convention was a done deal.

Presumably they would want to take Cleague into custody for the death of Federal agents during the raid on his house. The resultant airplay they would enjoy from the media would be so much more fuel on the burning desire across the country to repeal the Second Amendment. And they would get bragging rights for bringing down what would be portrayed as one of the most dangerous domestic terrorists in the history of the Republic, unless, of course, they just wanted to kill him. Luther asked the manager to see Glyndon's desk and any files she may have kept. Nope, sorry, all that stuff was shipped back to D.C. *Of course it was*, Luther thought.

He failed to remember the name of the restaurant that Smith guy had bought into. He asked the BPS lead if he could use the unoccupied desk previously assigned to Glyndon. The lead courteously gave his consent. Luther called the duty officer in Operations, Headquarters, BPS, and asked for the name of the restaurant. Nope, sorry, that information was material to an on-going investigation. Luther told the duty officer that it was his investigation. The duty officer asked him why he did not know the pertinent details to his own case. In any event, it didn't matter—can't give it out, sorry. Click.

It took Luther the rest of the day to track down the name of the restaurant. It annoyed the hell out of him that he had to re-do what had already been done but couldn't access because some territorial office pogue back in D.C. couldn't be persuaded to get up off his dead ass and look for it. What the hell, some days are better than others. He found it: it was the Alders Restaurant in Belltown. Luther got the address out of the phone book.

It was rush hour in Seattle on a Friday afternoon. He could not believe the traffic. The closer he got to Belltown the longer it took to get through the traffic lights. Finally he got close enough to the address that he just parked the car and started walking toward the restaurant. A block away he could see what the traffic problem had been. A loosely formulated gaggle of people in orange togas was walking down the middle of Fourth Street making some unintelligible noise on horns, and drums, and tambourines and one guy was tooting on a seashell. *What the hell,* he thought. *It is Seattle.* Luther was learning his environment.

The orange-clad crowd had passed. Luther was standing across the street from the Alders waiting for the traffic to clear. He saw a fairly large man, whom he did not know, and an attractive woman, whom he did not know, and Linda Muller walk out of the restaurant together. *What the hell was she doing here?*

He watched them walk to the end of the block and turn the corner. He looked south toward where he had parked his car and noticed a van in the corner of the parking lot. He would not have noticed it had it not been for the antenna farm on the roof of the van. It sported a variety of antennae one of which looked like a little satellite dish. He saw the dish, looked at the Alders restaurant and then looked back at the van. It was line of sight. Luther looked at the license plates; there was no indication that this van was government property. To Luther's mind it was conspicuous by its absence. Luther chose not to try to chase Linda Muller, who was probably half way to California by now. He would follow the van.

104

Damn few people are worth the time it takes to wait on them. Cleague's epiphany during his first week of retail sales proved itself over and over. His daily patois of: "May I help you, Is there anything I can show you, Are you being helped, Can I help you find anything, and Got one picked out yet?" wore thin in short order. Most of the time the answer was: "No, just looking." To which Cleague could do nothing but smile, nod, and let them look. Most of the mom and pop gun stores that had once populated the country had been put out of business by the increasingly restrictive decrees of the federal Firearms License Reform Act of 1993, and the only firearms retailers that could keep their doors open were the ones that diversified their product line with fishing tackle, camping gear, and camouflaged dog whistles. The majority of shoppers mostly went to the big box stores, leaving the smaller family-run businesses to struggle in the diminishing market.

Cleague did not mind letting people look. He did not mind helping people. In fact, he took a sense of personal satisfaction from the experience. But so many people seemed to expect to be entertained. There was a specific and definite difference between the two. A lot of people seemed to assume that Cleague was there for show and tell. He didn't.

Regardless, it provided something he needed desperately, a regular paycheck.

One day, a day not long after Eugene Smith's call informing him of Linda Muller's visit, three men came in the store together. Medium height, medium build, late twenties to early thirties, clean cut, they came through the front door and went in three separate directions.

Cleague was standing at the counter after a gun sale putting the finishing touches on the voluminous paperwork when he saw them come in, split up, and meander about the store in a casual fashion. When one of them approached him he looked up from his paperwork and asked if he could help. The man looked at Cleague very earnestly, shook his head in a negative response and continued to examine the contents of the glass cases. Cleague carried on with his paperwork.

As he finished and turned to stocking the shelves behind the counter, another man of the trio approached his direction. Cleague asked if there was anything he could show him. The second man looked straight at him and just said, "No thanks," and continued on, ostensibly taking stock of the display cases. Cleague went on about his business. The third man came in his separate time and passed by, paused to get a good look at Cleague and moved on. The three of them left the store together. Cleague walked over to the window and watched the three of them get in the same car and leave. He felt as if they were sizing the place up for a robbery, which was not out of the question; guns were guns, ammo was ammo, and, as such, held value to criminals as well as the law abiding. They were either sizing up the store or sizing up him and neither possibility sat well. The more he thought about it the more they looked like Feds. *Well, no shit. It was only a matter of time,* he thought.

It was September and the summer sun's languishing light arced further south on the horizon, but he still had time to take his nightly walk on Knave's Lake trail after work before it got dark. He monitored the traffic ahead of him and occasionally glanced in the rearview mirror. He was not being followed. Cleague pulled into the little parking area at the trail head, got out, locked the truck and started up the switchback path that led up the hill to Knave's Lake. He didn't hear or see the sedan that pulled into the parking area just a few minutes behind him.

The trail was a 15% climb for a hundred yards that switched back to a flat and level trail for two hundred yards, switched back to a 25% climb for about thirty yards, and terminated at the top of the ridge at the vaguely kidney shaped Knave's Lake. The trail followed a pedestrian bridge suspended over a waterfall fed by the run-off from the lake. From there you could follow the trail clockwise or due north or you could take it in the opposite direction, counterclockwise. In either case you would traverse hill and dale, ridge and gully, and be mindful the whole time that it hadn't changed very much from when the property had first been logged over a hundred years previously. It was in the foothills of the North Cascades. Western red cedar, western hemlock, douglas fir, and alder trees populated this portion of the mountain. Much of the ground cover was sword fern, marionberry, foxglove and licorice fern. The trail proper around the lake was about a mile and a half on a map and three and a half miles in linear distance up and down the topography. Cleague's best time so far was about forty-five minutes but he was trying to break thirty.

In that particular year in that particular part of the Pacific Northwest, it hadn't rained since Father's Day. Each footfall brought the resounding snap and pop of every dry twig, desiccated coniferous needle, and dehydrated blade of grass, along with the cacophony of all the detritus on the forest floor on a wooded mountain that hadn't had a fire in more than a hundred years. It occurred to Cleague that he was walking on fuel, a carpet of tinder and kindling. God forbid should a spark occur, whether from a lightning storm or a carelessly tossed cigarette butt, the conflagration would tax the county's resources beyond its means. This trail, this lake, this park, this wooded mountainside and the trophy homes that bordered it would be gone in a heartbeat. Damn.

There it was again. He consciously heard it that time. Someone was behind him. Cleague had traversed half way around the trail when he paused at a widened portion in the path that allowed him to look at a waterfall cascading down the mountainside from beneath him. It was a proper lookout with a boardwalk and a horizontal rail and a placard explaining the source of the waterfall and it afforded him the opportunity to get out of the way to let others pass by on the path. Knave's Lake Trail was on the border of two counties and got a fair amount of use: middle aged joggers in their designer sweat suits, twenty year olds on mountain bicycles, and city people with their Bernese Mountain dogs. Everybody enjoyed the trail. He frequently met other people and was happy to step aside and let them pass. But now there was no one within sight. They moved when he moved. They stopped when he stopped. He was being followed.

105

In spite of the typical East Coast heat and humidity, summer had come and gone in Washington D.C. Congress adjourned in August having accomplished nothing more than strife and acrimony in the weeks leading up to its summer recess. No bills were passed and no laws were sent to the White House for a Presidential signature. The majority party accused the minority party of procedural deadlock. The minority party accused the majority party of presiding over a do-nothing congressional term. The only thing the two parties seemed able to agree on was that a Constitutional Convention would take the national focus off their inability to govern.

It was the Tuesday after Labor Day. The House of Representatives and the Senate were re-convening. During the summer recess the pertinent conference committees of each house had stayed to establish the date and time to be set for the Constitutional Convention. The General Election was exactly two months from today. In each chamber it was announced that the Constitutional Convention to repeal the Second Amendment would be conducted starting on the first Monday of October. Just about midway to the election. The announcement was met with a standing ovation from both sides of the aisle in either house. Al Sherman sat in dismay.

As it was the single most pressing issue before either house, and as it had to happen before the November elections, the convention would be held one month from today. His colleagues around him acted like they had just landed a man on Mars. As the session adjourned various members of either party stood and broke away in little clumps. It seemed to Sherman, still sitting in his chair, that whatever intellectual and moral underpinning the Second Amendment may have had when it was first penned had long since eroded and it was all over save parliamentary procedure.

Sherman had, until this moment, always thought that the peoples' right to keep and bear arms acted as a surety that the government exists to serve the people—and not the people to serve the government. Watching members of both parties jovially ushering off to wherever, it struck Sherman that any fear of an armed electorate that may have been held by any potential tyrant could demonstrably no longer exist. Sherman concluded that his colleagues did not fear the peoples' wrath because they did not believe the people could or would make its wrath manifest in armed revolt.

They no longer believed the people, the electorate, the governed, held a common will to kill tyrants. The notion of the Second Amendment—the idea that an armed people can preserve their freedom by use of arms, obviously no longer held sway in the United States Senate or, for that matter, in the House of Representatives either. Sherman had not anticipated this tidal wave of support to repeal one of the bedrock principles of the Republic. They were in such a hurry.

But what if that was the driving force behind the vote, what if the rationale behind the vote was "strike while the iron is hot"? There hadn't been anything else in the mainstream media for months other than "the repeal of the Second Amendment." That was the way it had always been related to the audience, whether by print media or broadcast news. Not as: the Constitutional Convention to determine the case for repeal of the Second Amendment", but as: "the repeal of the Second Amendment," as if it had already been concluded. Well it had, by the media. Sherman considered Goebbels' dictum; "If repeated often enough, a lie will become the new truth."

Congress had just re-convened from its August recess, the traditional time for the Summer District Work Period. During this time Senators and Representatives went back home to their states and districts to hold town hall meetings, take questions from their constituents, and mix and mingle with the common folk. In his meetings with his constituents, Sherman was always asked if Congress was going to repeal the Second Amendment. He had no choice but to tell them the truth from his vantage point, which was: If the vote were held tomorrow, the majority of votes cast would most likely be in favor of repeal. It would then be up to the individual state legislatures to vote on and ratify the new Amendment. Then, predictably, all hell broke loose.

106

At one Sunday morning pancake breakfast Sherman attended, he tried to put the shoe on the other foot by asking his constituents: "If the vote were held tomorrow and the Amendment were repealed what would you do?" The consensus was: "We'll fight it." When he asked how they would fight it, people got pretty reticent because they hadn't thought that far ahead yet.

A quiet man who shared the table with him answered the question. Sherman had known the man all his life and had never known the man to tell a lie or bend the truth for the sake of a good story. It was Sherman's father. His answer was: "Start buying ammunition now. One box at a time. Before they can take them, they have to come get them."

It made quite a stir. The word got around and got compressed in the telling and re-telling as such things will and before Sherman could get back to Washington D.C., he saw bumper stickers on pickup trucks that read: "BUY AMMO". It was the Inland Empire's version of Molon Labe: Come and Take Them.

Sherman's father had been a history teacher at the local college and was now retired but he still knew when he had the attention of an audience, when that attention peaked, and when to let it go. As the other breakfast patrons convened among themselves about the desirability of re-loaded ammunition over that of factory-made ammunition, regulations, and restrictions and such, the teacher made the effort to teach one more lesson to his most cherished student.

"Do you remember your quotes from the founders?" Al nodded and replied.

"If I don't remember them, I know where to look them up."

His father smiled and said, "Then you will remember Mr. Adams' statement in his Defense of the American Constitutions: 'The moment the idea is admitted into society that property is not as sacred as the laws of God, and that there is not a force of law and public justice to protect it, anarchy and tyranny commence. If 'Thou shalt not covet' and 'Thou shalt not steal' were not commandments of Heaven, they must be made inviolable precepts in every society before it can be civilized or made free.'"

He sipped his coffee from a Styrofoam cup and made a face. Bitter. "Alexander," his father went on, "I am not a lawyer as you well know, but it seems to me that this could very simply be made a matter of eminent domain. The courts have recently been most favorable in their acquiescence to the governmental bodies claiming it. If the Second Amendment is repealed, and if for some reason the vote to repeal it is appealed to the courts, and ultimately to the Supreme Court, what would stop the Court from a finding that, based solely on the issue of a legitimate concern for public safety, the notion of eminent domain applies and the state may take possession of the private property under dispute?" One of the volunteers working the pancake breakfast came by with a carafe of hot coffee and offered to "hotten" up their cups. Mr. Sherman happily accepted; Al declined.

Mr. Sherman went on as he stirred in sweetener and cream. "The popular belief is that the Second Amendment is in the Bill of Rights to guard the republic from tyranny. The total usurpation of the affairs and property of the public by a central, collectivist government has been held at bay precisely because of the fear of that unruly mob, otherwise known as the American Electorate, would resort to force of arms against an overreaching and encroaching Administration. You know all the arguments—it is how you got into office. But consider this: if the Second Amendment is repealed, and contested, and found by the Supreme Court to be a matter of eminent domain, the government could assume any private property under the aegis of acting in benign good faith to protect the public interest. What would stop it? Private property, real estate, family farms, the nationalization of private enterprise, or financial institutions for that matter, could be assumed and redistributed by the central government at its will. It has happened in other countries. Just because it has not yet happened here does not mean that it can't." Mr. Sherman paused for another sip of coffee while Al considered the observation.

Mr. Sherman carried on, "Not very long ago, in the wake of a hurricane, a city mayor decreed that in the interest of public safety private citizens no longer had a right to privately owned firearms and directed the National Guard, with the governor's consent, to go door to door and pick them up. NO body stopped it. Those few that tried were flex-cuffed and sat on the curb while strangers went into their houses and ransacked their homes. This was done with the Second Amendment intact. That mayor was sued after the fact but most of those people never got their property back. If the amendment is repealed, the statists will have won the battle for history without ever having fought it." Senator Sherman's father finished his breakfast. There had been precedents for government confiscation of private property, variously justified as: drug seizures, eminent domain, right of way, public interest, and "public safety" notably among them. Most of those cases were contested and many of them were unresolved. To Sherman's mind, stealing was stealing, whether it was the government or a common thug. Sometimes you couldn't tell the difference. Senator Sherman contemplated his coffee, cold and bitter.

*****

Sitting in his seat in the Senate Chamber watching his colleagues make their way out of the assembly, the thought occurred to Sherman that the overwhelming air of willful confidence on the part of the pro-repeal faction that the Constitution would have a radical history making change in short order might not be a bad thing. Sherman knew for an absolute fact that this particular battle for history had not yet been won.

107

Peter Cleague went to work the next day. He had to work in the rifle department in the morning because they were short-handed on that side of the store. One young man asked to see one of the pre-ban AR-15 clones. Cleague pulled it down from the rack, pulled the charging handle back to open the bolt, locked the bolt in place and visually and manually checked the chamber before handing it over to the young customer. Mutely nodding, the young man hefted the weight of it in both hands with a sense of approval, and then swiftly mounted the butt stock into his shoulder, looking through the rear sight aperture to the front sight post—apparently he had done this before. Then without a word, he took it down from his shoulder, let the bolt slam forward on an empty chamber, and removed the pin that held the upper and lower receiver together, and before Cleague could say: "Hey, don't take that gun apart…" The young man had removed the charging handle from the back of the upper receiver and promptly dropped the bolt carrier and bolt, face first, on the concrete floor.

The young man bent over to pick up the bolt and jammed the muzzle of the rifle into the wooden counter that separated him from Cleague. Cleague said, "Just put it on the counter; I will get the rest of it." Which the young man proceeded to ignore and fumbled putting the charging handle back into the upper receiver, managing to put it in to its recess crooked and got it stuck. Cleague just pulled the rifle out of the young man's hands, picked the bolt carrier assembly up from the counter top and without another word walked to the back of the building to the gunsmith's area. He got the charging handle unstuck, cleaned each separate peace, examined the bolt face for damage from where it had been dropped on the floor, examined the muzzle for damage from where it had been jammed into the counter, and took the various parts and pieces over to Carl. He told Carl the story and asked him to check it over, and walked back out to the retail floor. Why men seemed to have a universal psychic need to disassemble a firearm that did not belong to them was beyond Cleague's power to fathom.

When Cleague got out to the retail area he was paged to the phone.

"This is Peter, may I help you?" He said somewhat pleasantly.

"Hey, we were looking at a Smith & Wesson the other day, it was a .44 Magnum; can you tell me how much they are?"

"Which model was it?" The price would vary according to model.

"It was the stainless one." The phone customer said.

"What barrel length was it?" Cleague asked. He was trying to limit the possibilities before he went on a wild goose chase trying to locate the gun the customer said he thought he saw.

"Eight or nine inches", the phone customer replied.

"Was it in the display case?" Cleague asked.

"Yeah. But it wasn't in your store." The phone customer replied, "It was somewhere else."

Cleague began biting the inside of his lip and mightily resisted the urge to repeatedly smack the handset of the telephone against the wood frame of the display cabinet to knock some sense into the nitwit on the other end of the phone line.

At lunch time he drove down to the fish hatchery, parked the truck, ate his cheese sandwich, and read the paper. After lunch he went back to work waiting on people, selling product, doing paperwork, and running out to the warehouse for this or that. It constituted the rest of the day. About half an hour before closing a customer walked up to the gun counter.

"May I help you?" Cleague asked.

"Yeah, I got a pistol that doesn't work, can you guys fix it?" The customer asked.

"Well, maybe, why don't you bring it in and we'll take a look at it." Cleague said. The customer said, "Well, I got it right here." And he pulled a small semiautomatic out of his coat pocket with his finger on the trigger and pointed it directly at Cleague's chest. Cleague side stepped off the center line and said, "Do not point that at me!" "Oh, it ain't loaded." The customer said, and to demonstrate that belief he straightened his arm, pointing the gun at the wall just past Cleague's head, and pulled the trigger. There aren't too many things that are louder than a handgun being discharged in a gun store. Cleague did not think. Cleague reacted.

He grabbed the man's wrist with his left hand and swept his right hand up and grabbed the gun by the lower portion of the frame twisting the gun out of the man's grasp. Cleague walked over to the metal trash can and pressed the magazine release letting the magazine drop free directly into the trash. Cleague looked at the man dead level and did not say a word. The gun was a Walther PPK. He racked the slide to the rear and let the ejected cartridge land on the floor. He then proceeded to disassemble the gun and dropped it, piece by piece, into the trash.

"Hey, asshole, you can't do that. That's my gun!" The upset customer yelled. Wordlessly, Cleague picked up the trash can and walked out of the building and into the parking lot. He emptied the wastebasket into the dumpster and walked back toward the store.

The customer came at him at a fair trot leaning forward at the waist. As he approached Cleague he reached out with both hands to grab Cleague by the collar. Cleague saw it coming. He planted 70 % of his weight on his front foot, 30 % on his rear foot, torqued his torso, and waylaid the metal trashcan into the customer's head. He threw the wastebasket out of his way and grabbed the man by the arm, twisting and pinning it behind him.

"Let go of me you faggot!" The man screamed repeatedly. Cleague used the momentum of the man's body weight to corkscrew him onto the ground with the man's right wrist twisted up between his shoulder blades and just about level with his neck. Cleague pinned it there with his left hand and with his right hand on the man's head, shoved the man's left ear into the asphalt.

Cleague bent down to the man's right ear and kept his voice low. A crowd was approaching from the store.

"Now, calm down and listen to me. It's not polite to walk into a gun store with a loaded gun and point it at the sales clerk. If you ever point a gun at me again, I will kill you. If you ever touch me again, I will hurt you. And if I ever see you in the store again I will call the Sheriff. Do you understand that?" The man grunted 'yes'.

"I am going to get up and let you go. Don't be foolish." Cleague said and got up. He walked to the trashcan and picked it up, keeping one eye on the sullen individual slowly getting up from the pavement.

The little crowd of customers that had gathered at the front door of the store had migrated across the parking lot to where the man now stood, bent over at the waist, hands on his knees, panting.

"You Okay?" and "Jesus, what was that about?" The huddled mass murmured best intentions.

Cleague walked toward the back door of the store where the offices were and saw all of the family ownership standing there, arms folded, with dour expressions. The matron scowled. Siblings and spouses frowned. The tow-headed heir-apparent looked off into the middle distance and drooled.

Cleague never broke stride.

"He came after me; it was self defense." He said. But the matron would have the last word in this contest.

"Well, don't let it happen again." She huffed with an imperious air.

"I didn't let it happen this time." He said and kept walking.

"You know what I mean!" She insistently called after him. He strongly suspected he would be fired before the day was over. With about ten minutes left to go in the workday he faced the shelves and cleaned up his work area but there wasn't much he could do about the bullet hole in the wall. He had his back to the gun counter when he heard someone approach. Cleague turned to see a tall slender man in a suit and tie.

"Excuse me", the man said.

"Yes sir?" Cleague inquired.

"I'm looking for one Peter Cleague." The gentleman said.

"I'm Cleague, what can I do for you?" Peter said. At this point in the conversation the tall man produced a credentials wallet that displayed a Federal Identification card issued by the United States Department of Justice.

"Mr. Cleague, my name is John Luther. Would you come with me please? I have some questions." He said.

Perfect. Cleague thought. *A perfect fucking end to a perfect fucking day.*

108

They stood out in the parking lot. Cleague leaned up against his truck, arms folded. Luther stood just out of arms reach in the classic interview position. The other employees waved to Cleague as they left for the day. From time to time Luther would look from left to right or right to left. This was not his home turf. He noticed the figure of a middle-aged woman filling the doorframe in the portion of the building that housed the offices. If looks could kill, they would both be on the ground drawing their last breath.

"Who's the evil princess?" he asked Cleague.

"She's one of the owners." Cleague replied.

Well, time to get on with it. Luther thought.

"Mr. Cleague, I am investigating the circumstances regarding the deaths of a number of Federal agents on the property you rented on Peninsular Island, last year. That event occurred on the Fourth of July." Luther said.

Cleague said nothing.

"Mr. Cleague, we know you were the subject of an arrest warrant, we know you were there at the time, we know you evaded and escaped lawful authority, and we suspect that you murdered quite a few people." Luther added.

Cleague said nothing.

"Mr. Cleague, it would really be in your best interest to assist this investigation rather than obstruct it. That would just be one more charge against you." Luther said.

"Am I under arrest? What am I being charged with?" Cleague asked.

"It's your choice, this can be hard or it can be easy but I was hoping you would be a little more co-operative." Luther said.

"Look, all I saw was a bunch of men, all dressed in black, wearing balaclavas, and carrying guns. I had no idea who those people were." This was the first time Cleague had said anything to anyone about that night on the P.I.

"We know for a fact from a statement from the team commander that he identified those agents present as agents from the Federal Bureau of Public Safety." Luther said.

"Yeah, well, why were military vehicles there? They had million candlepower searchlights on those trucks. If they were there to arrest me, why didn't they send the sheriff with an arrest warrant?" Cleague asked.

"Why did you blow up your house with all those agents surrounding it?" Luther asked.

"Who says I did? They filled my house full of CS gas and then threw flash bang grenades in there. That combination of chemicals is specifically combustible. Nobody would know that particular fact better than the Federal Government." Cleague said. "Some black clad paramilitary outfit shows up at my house at night with military hardware and they identify themselves as National Park Security guards and I am supposed to believe that? Would you have believed it?" He asked Luther.

"Then why didn't you just surrender? You killed twelve Federal agents Mr. Cleague. You will be arrested, prosecuted, and most likely found guilty because the evidence against you is overwhelming. You will likely get the death sentence. Otherwise you will most assuredly spend the rest of your life in prison. All that could have been avoided." Luther said.

"Let me ask you this, Mr. Luther. If you lived in Germany in the late thirties and funny dressed men with military trucks showed up at your house and told you to get in the back, would you? Those people showed up in the dark of night armed to the teeth. I didn't know who they were and I was scared shitless. I ran away."

Cleague paused for a bit. He did not know what Luther knew, but Cleague did know that the BPS ran one of the best forensic labs in the world. They would have found trace evidence of various compounds and probably would have identified the manufacturers. But everything he said thus far was plausible.

"Besides when they came after me the second time I just figured they were out to kill me." Cleague finished and watched Luther.

"What second time?" Luther asked.

"This past July Fourth. Didn't they tell you about that one? Funny, come to think of it, they didn't have a news crew with them either. Maybe they didn't want anybody to know." Cleague said.

This was news to Luther and obviously a red herring. But if there had been a second attempt to arrest Cleague, Luther had been left out of the loop.

"Where?" Luther asked. Cleague nodded in the direction behind Luther's back. "Up on the mountain." He said.

Luther turned briefly and looked, aware that Cleague may be baiting him. All he could see were the trees across the street. "What mountain?" He asked. "Atherton Mountain is a mile and half northeast of here. We are too close to the trees to see it from here." Cleague said.

Fuck, that's all I need. Another crime scene, Luther thought. And since it would bear directly on his investigation of the events on Peninsular Island the preceding year, he would have to go look at that one too. *Shitandgoddamnit*. He thought.

All of a sudden Luther felt really tired.

"Where?" He asked.

"You want me to take you up there?" Cleague asked.

"You're not taking me anywhere, Cleague." Luther said.

Cleague just shrugged and said, "Okay, you can drive."

"Why don't you just tell me what happened first?" Luther asked.

Cleague told his story. He told Luther about the girl with bright green eyes coming into the store a few days before the Fourth of July. That caught Luther's attention. Cleague described the sense that she was trying to coax him into making an illegal transfer of a firearm. On Fourth of July he went camping and was assaulted by three bikers and a girl with a gun. It was the same girl. He got hurt and sought medical help. He had not been back to the mountain and did not know what happened to the people that assaulted him.

"Well, what happened? Were they still alive when you left?" Luther was getting a little exasperated.

"I don't know." Cleague said. "Look, man. I did not know who those people were. They said they wanted my wallet and my truck and then the girl pulls a gun, and the guy pulls a knife? Fuck that. They came after me, they ended up on the ground, and I left." He said. Actually he knew damn right well whether they were alive or not but he was not going to tell this lawyer for the Department Of Justice, *Hell yeah, man, I killed them. Bigger than shit*. He thought.

"All right." Luther said. "Peter Cleague, you are under arrest for the suspicion of murder. Turn around." Luther said. Cleague did so. "Put your hands behind your back, thumbs up." He said. Cleague did so. Luther pulled a pair of nylon flex cuffs out of a pocket and cuffed Cleague. He then opened the rear right door to his rental Ford Taurus and told Cleague to get in. Luther got in the driver's seat—he knew he was going to regret this. "Show me." He said.

✶✶✶✶✶

A mile south of the All North Sporting Goods store was the Alger County Speedway. The sign proclaimed: "Hottest Dirt Track in the Pacific Northwest". A sign below that proclaimed: "Home of the Mud Cup Classic". And below that sign was parked a white Ford Crown Victoria, with very plain hubcaps and a little antenna sticking up from the rear window. The sedan was parked facing the highway and screamed UNMARKED POLICE CAR. The inhabitants noted that whenever another vehicle approached it slowed down noticeably.

Two miles north of the sporting goods store was a small rural convenience store with a gravel parking lot, and a dusty single gas pump, and a dusty public pay phone that did not work. A dark blue Ford Crown Victoria with very plain hubcaps and a small antenna sticking up from the rear window was parked on the south side of the lot near the payphone. Nobody in the store paid it any mind and nobody passing by on the road looked at it very hard because it screamed UNMARKED POLICE CAR. The Ford sedan was parked facing the highway due east and the inhabitants were quietly monitoring their comm. One of them glassed the mountain off in the distance about a mile or so away. Pretty, lots of trees.

A non-descript dirty white sedan with an amber flashing light on its roof proceeded due south on the highway. At every mailbox it would pull over and the driver would shove a piece of bogus junk mail in the mailbox, and drive on to the next mailbox. He had been at this game for the last half hour and was now approaching the set of mail boxes just north of the parking lot of the little sporting goods store located all the way out here in the country. It seemed to him to be an odd place to put a sporting goods store. The driver observed the Ford Taurus pull out of the parking lot and proceed due north. He looked and observed a driver, and a passenger in the rear seat. The driver of the dirty white sedan, turned into the parking lot of All North Sports, got on the radio and notified the two Crown Victorias parked down the road, that John Luther and Peter Cleague were northbound on the old highway.

109

Cleague gave Luther directions on how to get to the top of the hill. "Make a right here." He said. "Go three quarters of a mile and take the left. Follow this road around the lake and it will take you to the gate. It should be open." Luther drove the Taurus at the speed limit and noted the lake to their right. The perimeter of Parson's Lake was bordered by a white wooden rail fence. It looked like it belonged at a Kentucky horse farm. The road turned right bordering the north end of the lake and then doglegged left. They arrived at the gate to Atherton Mountain, an active logging site administered by the Washington Department of Natural Resources. The gate was open. They followed the gravel road up the mountain at a very cautious rate of speed. Luther's rental was not a four-wheel drive truck; he did not want to tear the chassis out from underneath it. The road was badly rutted from the tires of the logging trucks that traversed up and down the mountain every day. Luther navigated the meandering dirt road, turning where Cleague indicated, and stopped at the terminus; a flat expanse of dust, rock, and sand. They got out of the car. Cleague asked Luther to take the flex cuffs off him. Luther ignored him.

Luther looked around. It was a gravel pit. If he faced north, he saw the tree- lined mountainside slope up to his right or due east. Fir, cedar, hemlock, and alder trees lined the rise up to its crest. The wind made a whistling sound as it cut through the trees. Luther guessed the summit of the hill to be another hundred yards beyond the rock wall of the gravel pit to his right.

If he faced east, he saw the rocky escarpment from where rock had been claimed out from the mountainside and later transformed to gravel. If he faced south he saw the vertical slope of the gravel pit curve toward the west. He likened it to a rectangle with the north and west sides of the box missing. When he faced west he saw a striking view of the north end of Puget Sound. He could see the north part of Whidbey Island, Hat Island, Saddlebag Island, Lummi Island, and Anacortes. The oil refinery at March Point was lit up like it was Christmas. The purple and indigo silhouettes of the islands, abutted to the cerulean surface of Puget Sound, contrasted with the sunset of an Indian summer. He took a moment to absorb it. Luther checked his watch—it was 6:30. He looked for Peninsular Island, but that little spit of land could not be seen from this vantage point.

Cleague walked to a point two-thirds the distance between the eastern escarpment of the gravel pit and the west-facing ledge. He stood nearly at attention and faced Luther.

"This is where I had my campfire." Cleague said. With his arms tied together behind his back he could not gesture very well, so he used his chin.

"They came from behind me." He said.

"Who came from behind you?" Luther asked.

"The guy and the girl." Cleague said. "The guy kept moving back and forth the whole time he was talking." Cleague moved a few steps west. "The girl stood right about here" Cleague said. "She kept looking past me over my shoulder. There were two more guys behind me up there." Cleague gestured with his chin to the top of the eastern escarpment. "At least I think that's where they were. I never saw them until they were right in front of me." He said. "Any way, at first the guy was talking about how they ran out of gas and they needed a ride out and did I have anybody coming to pick me up. And then I kind of zoned out. The next thing I know he's yelling at me to give him my wallet and keys and where is my car...the girl said 'cut the crap" or something like that and pulled out a gun and aimed it at me." Cleague said.

"What did you do?" Luther asked.

"I shot her." Cleague said.

Something went cold inside Luther. Glyndon was a mediocre employee at best but she didn't deserve that. In fact she should not have been here at all. What the hell were they thinking sending her up against a man who had demonstrated he could best a BPS Tactical Team? It was like sending a child to catch a rattlesnake. Luther was getting a familiar hollow feeling in the pit of his gut.

"She went down, and then the guy charged at me with a butterfly knife. I shot him and he went down." Cleague said as he stepped to the approximate spot where he engaged the first shadow man from the ground. "I laid out supine and saw another guy coming at me and I shot him. Then I tried to get up and lost my balance because my legs were asleep. I put my arm out to break my fall and a third guy hit me with a baseball bat." Cleague said.

Luther found all this carnage a little hard to believe.

"Did you shoot him too?" Luther asked.

"No. I dropped the gun when I lost my balance. We beat the hell out of each other. He crawled away and I walked away but I thought the bastard broke my arm. The last time I saw him he was over there." Cleague indicated a spot back toward the road they had driven in on with his chin.

Luther looked around. There was nothing here to indicate that anything Cleague had just told him was true.

Luther noted that there were no indications of any sort of a struggle but there were a lot of tire tracks and the impressions of tread pads of heavy equipment like a bulldozer or something similar to it had repeatedly gone back and forth over the area. Luther pointed to a pile of ash about thirty feet in diameter down the slope from the western edge of the gravel pit.

"What's that?" He asked Cleague.

"I don't know, I don't remember it." Cleague said. "It wasn't here the night all this shit happened." He thought a minute. "There was a big pile of wood down there." He said.

"What?" Luther asked.

"It's called a slash pile." Cleague said.

110

"A logger explained it to me once." Cleague stepped toward the ledge and looked down at the pile of ash. "He said an average size of a commercial slash pile can be 30 feet in diameter and 15 to 20 feet high. It consists of tops, limbs, and other timber they can't sell. Slash piles are typically burnt under very controlled conditions to reduce the available fuel for a wildfire and to make room for more trees. A commercial logging operation will ignite the slash pile with a mixture of chemicals very similar to napalm: diesel, gasoline and a gel. They light it with a propane torch. One fuel lights easily, the other fuel burns hotter, and the gel doesn't let the fuel mixture burn off too fast. At its peak, it can reach 3200 degrees.

"When a pile gets hot enough it creates its own wind. Cold air is drawn in through the bottom of the pile. As the air gets sucked into the center of the pile where the fire is hottest, the fire heats the air. Hot air rises. The super-heated air is expelled out the top of the pile into a heat column that can rise 2000 feet high and can produce a roaring sound that is audible for a half mile. When the wood burns, the moisture inside the logs is being turned to steam; the steam splits the wood. It will crack, pop, snap and squeal. As the wood is burning, the up draft is so strong that much of the hot ash and embers will be carried up the heat column. A slash pile on fire, seen at night, will appear to have millions of burning embers glowing bright red and can be seen for miles. The up-draft is sufficient to pick up a 2-ounce chunk of burning wood, a coal, and propel it up the heat column where a breeze can carry it some distance. That's why it's important to control the time of year that the fire is started. October and November after the autumn rains have started is a popular time of year for slash pile fires.

"When the fire dies down there could be a foot of ash in a 30-foot circle. The layer of ash will insulate the wood at the bottom of the pile that did not get burned. A wind can come up and blow the ash away; get the coals hot, and start a wildfire. A commercial burn will bring in a track-mounted excavator—a machine with an articulated clam bucket—to stir up the ash. It looks like a backhoe on tank treads. It can dig in the ash and bring the burning logs to the surface, and, similarly, it can pick things up and drop them into the middle of a raging fire."

Luther regarded the pile of ash. He did not know how hot cremation fires got, but he would have bet that most crematoria didn't operate at 3200 degrees. He reasoned that a slash pile fire would be hot enough to reduce a cadaver to ash and bone, but would it be hot enough to make everything go away? Heavy things like gold or silver dental fillings would probably melt and seep down to the bottom of the pile. Acrylic, amalgam, and other kinds of plastic would evaporate. Porcelain fillings would likely melt, and settle to the bottom of the pile, having returned to a state of glass. At 3200 degrees the heat would be sufficient to reduce a carcass to ash. How long would it take to burn up four carcasses: three male, and one female?

Cleague went on, "The logger told me that as the ash pile gets rained on it gets compressed. Wood ash is organic and functions as a fertilizer. It becomes part of the soil, which is why the remnant burn pile makes a good nursery for seedlings."

Luther and Cleague both regarded the ash pile. It wasn't hard to imagine what might have happened to the four bodies Cleague said he left there. Once again Luther was left with no evidence of a crime having been committed.

"What did you do with the gun?" Luther asked.

"I threw it in the lake when I left." Cleague looked to the south and indicated the lake, just barely visible through the trees in the twilight, with his chin.

Luther wondered what to do next. He had half a mind to shoot Cleague now and be done with it. He heard an odd noise, a rhythmic buffeting sound like a big fan but incredibly loud. By instinct he looked up. The sound was omni directional; he could not pinpoint one source for it. He knew it was a helicopter. Cleague yelled.

"Time to go. Get these fucking things off me." He walked toward Luther. Luther was still thinking about shooting him. Maybe he wouldn't need to. He looked up over the crest of the east quarry wall and saw the shadow of the rotor blades, then the mast, and then the dark silhouette of the helicopter. The MD 500 helicopter was only eight and a half feet from the top of the rotor mast to the skids and presented a very compact silhouette. Noted for its high performance and stealthy low noise signature due to its four-bladed rotor and small size, it was a preferred aviation asset in the special operations community and was commonly referred to as the Killer Egg.

There was someone perched on the port skid of the helicopter. A sniper was tethered from a harness, with his feet on the skid and his ass on the lower edge of the cockpit doorframe. His rifle was balanced on a web strap that spanned the width of the door. The first shot was low and wild. The helicopter was close enough to the ground that the rotor wash was causing a full value wind effect for the shooter. He would compensate for it on his next shot.

Luther saw the sniper work the bolt and line up his scope on…Luther. Cleague dove into the back seat.

"Let's go, goddamnit!" Then for good measure he added, "They're not playing favorites Luther, they are going to kill us both." Luther jumped in the Taurus just as a bullet dug into the ground right where Luther's feet had been. They retreated down the road in short order with Luther securing his seatbelt on the way.

"How many roads lead off this mountain?" Luther asked.

"One." Cleague answered, "The same one that leads up the mountain." He said. "Get these fucking cuffs off me Luther, you need me." Cleague yelled over the complaining whine of a Ford Taurus being driven into the ground.

"For what?" Luther asked.

"Get these cuffs off of me and I will get you out of this." Cleague answered. Luther briefly looked over his shoulder into the back seat, "Excuse me?" He asked.

"It is what I do for a living Luther, I will get you out of this or we will both die in the effort." Cleague concluded his sales pitch. That really didn't sound like much of a bargain to Luther but what the hell. Luther fished around in his pocket, found something metallic, and tossed a pair of fingernail clippers over his shoulder into the back seat towards Cleague.

Cleague saw where it landed on the floor and screamed, "You fucking nitwit, how am I supposed to pick it up?" Luther yelled back, "Not my problem, I'm busy."

A bullet cracked through the left rear passenger window, shattering it into a bunch of little crystalline bits, and diagonally bisected the cab of the car, through the front passenger seat, and went out the lower portion of the right front door.

"They're not fucking around Luther, that shot was in line with your head. Get these cuffs off of me." Cleague insisted. Luther turned off the logging road onto a spur road that ran into the midst of a copse of trees. It provided marginal overhead concealment as they heard the Killer Egg over shoot their position.

Luther told Cleague to turn around as he withdrew a small elliptical articulated piece of plastic with metal jaws on one end called a scarab cutter, because it was vaguely shaped like a bug. He clipped the flex cuffs from Cleague's wrists. Luther was clearly out of his element and was willing to admit it.

"Now what?" He asked Cleague. They could hear the static whine of the Killer Egg's jet engine. It was hovering at the junction of the spur road and the logging road.

"You have to turn around and go back out the same way you came in." Cleague said as he rubbed his wrists. "Do it as fast as you can but don't go faster than you can control the car. He will hit us but he won't be able to place a precision shot on a moving vehicle. The roads are fairly dry and you'll probably kick up a lot of dust and it will help obscure his vision." Cleague said. *Hopefully*, he thought.

Luther turned the car around and paused.

"You want to drive?" He asked Cleague.

"You can do this, Luther."

Luther put the car in Drive and put his foot through the gas pedal kicking up a rooster tail of desiccated coniferous needles. He over-steered to make the turn back onto the logging road and the back end of the Taurus fishtailed a bit emitting billowing clouds of bone-dry powdered dirt into the air. Cleague said it loud enough to be heard over the helicopter, and the dry roadbed, and the whining Ford's motor.

"Calm down, don't go faster than you can steer." They could hear two rounds go through sheet metal behind them.

"Where's the gas tank on this car?" Luther asked.

"I think I'm sitting on it." Cleague replied.

Luther navigated the saw-toothed road with the washboard surface and came to the intersection with the main roadway that led up to the summit. Luther turned left down the hill. Cleague leaned over the seats and told Luther to slow down because there was a big turn coming up on Luther's blind side with a free drop of at least two hundred feet if he missed the road. Luther took his advice.

The helicopter buzzed them. The empennage of the tail rotor scudded across the car roof then the bird went into a steep climb and performed a pirouette and came back at them. The sniper put a hole in the engine compartment. Luther did not let up on the rental car. Something started smoking. After another very hard turn to the right they could see the gate that led back to the hard surface road.

"What the fuck!" Luther screamed as he realized what he was looking at.

"Ambush!" Cleague yelled. "Stop!" he said.

"What?" Luther yelled his question back at Cleague.

"Stop!" Cleague yelled.

111

They were about a hundred yards away from the barricading vehicles. The two Crown Victorias were lined up across the road not quite headlight to tail light but nearly so. The right hand car of the roadblock was perpendicular to Luther's approach. The left hand car was at more of an angle, with its headlights pointed outboard away from Luther. The road wasn't wide enough at that point to get both cars in there bumper to bumper. They were oriented due west or to Luther's right. They could hear the whine of the helicopter's turbine engines. The sound remained static. It stayed at a constant point behind and above them. The trees on either side of the narrow gravel road were jerking forward and backward with the rotor wash as clouds of dry dirt the consistency of talcum powder billowed up into the air. The pilot increased the helicopter's altitude until the trees stopped moving, thus creating Zero wind effect for the sniper. The dust cloud began to dissipate. The helicopter was now a stationary aerial platform. The sniper put another round through the rear window at a spot level with Cleague's head. The angle of the glass deflected the shot, but the glass shattered all over Cleague, and the back of Luther's neck. Since incoming fire has the right of way, Cleague gave his instructions to Luther quickly.

"Now, put the car in low gear, and drive forward. Do it now." Cleague yelled. Luther complied. Cleague pointed between the seats. "Line up your tires with the front and rear axles of those two cars, center yourself on the space between them." Cleague said, "Hit the right hand car on the rear axle. Hit the left hand car on the front axle and don't slow down."

Luther tentatively pressed on the accelerator. Cleague understood Luther's hesitation: deliberately causing a collision is counterintuitive, but they didn't have time for that.

"Stand on the gas pedal with both feet and push through it! Do it now!" Cleague yelled at Luther. Luther was focused on the cars in front of him while Cleague watched the needle arc toward the right on the speedometer. Within twenty-five yards of the gate they started taking automatic weapons fire. The gunners were shooting at the tires. Even if they did get past the roadblock they wouldn't travel very far on the metal rims. Cleague shifted his focus beyond the gate for a second and knew what was going to happen.

He yelled at Luther to keep his right hand down on the gear shifter to keep it from popping out of gear. They didn't want to be stuck in neutral in between the two Ford Crown Victorias taking the automatic weapons' fire. Luther froze. He could not take his hands off the steering wheel. Cleague got in Luther's ear.

"Put your hand on the fucking gear shifter and keep it there!" Cleague reached his hand into his pocket for his little serrated pocketknife. Cleague looked back at the speedometer. They were going ten miles an hour. The Taurus was a four door, family size, front wheel drive sedan and probably weighed about four thousand pounds (give or take), Cleague guessed. At ten miles an hour they were producing about 20,000 foot/pounds of energy against the dead weight of the two heavier vehicles. *It might work*, Cleague thought.

The smoke coming up from the engine compartment was making it hard to see. The sky was dark now; it was well past sunset.

"Keep the steering wheel straight Luther, do not try to turn, and brace yourself." When the Taurus collided with the two bigger Ford sedans, the right hand car gave way because the Taurus hit it in the lightest part of the body, the trunk.

With most of the weight of the vehicle in the front end, the lighter back end gave way freely. When the Taurus hit the left hand car in turn at slightly less than ten miles an hour, it gave way but not as much. The resistance of the heavier front end of the Crown Victoria caused the Taurus to turn slightly to the right. The tires had been shredded off their rims and the Taurus couldn't get traction in the loose gravel.

The Taurus' momentum was such that it continued on a line consistent with its direction of travel. Cleague told Luther to turn the wheel to the right. Luther did not respond. They had run out of road. The Taurus had broken through the roadblock but it was now moving through the white rail fence that bordered Parson's Lake. When the Taurus hit the two bigger sedans Luther's air bag deployed. The force of the Taurus hitting the two heavier cars in quick succession caused Luther's head to slam into the headrest centered on the driver's seat and the reciprocal inertial force in turn caused Luther's head to move sharply forward. When the airbag deployed it caught both of Luther's hands and smacked them into his face.

The Taurus continued to move through the white rail fence and into the lake because Luther was unconscious. Cleague reached up to the passenger door and tried to lower the electronic window. It didn't budge. He started frantically kicking at the window on the right rear passenger door and managed to kick it out just before the car slid into the lake. He wanted the water to come in on both sides—more or less evenly—to keep the car from tipping and turning upside down. The front end went down, and the interior cabin of the car started filling with water. When the water level reached the tops of the doors, the cabin started flooding and the car went down into the water. The front end hit the lake bottom first and the back end settled into the benthic muck. In the dark and cold Cleague forced his eyes open and withdrew his little pocketknife. He immediately went to work on Luther's seat belt with the serrated edge of the blade. Cleague couldn't see a damn thing. He wished he had thought to tell Luther to take his seat belt off but there hadn't been time.

The inside of the car was full of water. The water pressure inside the car equaled the water pressure outside the car; Cleague was able to get Luther's door open. He got Luther out of the car and kicked his way up to the surface with Luther in tow. Cleague side stroked to the edge of the lake avoiding the beams of light that played off the surface of the water from the flashlights of the BPS, and the spotlight from the helicopter. He kept Luther's head out of the water with his left arm and side stroked with his right arm.

He ducked into a pile of sword ferns and drug Luther up into them. He checked for a pulse and put his ear to Luther's nose to try and tell if Luther was breathing. Weak pulse, no air. Cleague cut Luther's necktie away with his pocketknife, opened his collar, and immediately started CPR. Cleague did not know what kind of injury Luther sustained in the collision but he was very careful with Luther's neck. He cleared an airway and started artificial respiration. After three breaths, he put one hand over the other centered on Luther's sternum and applied a rhythmic measured force to Luther's chest. Cleague shifted to artificial respiration again. Luther started to cough after a bit. Cleague covered Luther's mouth to muffle the sound.

From his position by the side of the lake Cleague could see, through the inosculating shadows of trees and ferns, the flashing red and blue lights of police cars from the local jurisdiction. Apparently someone in the BPS had communicated something to someone in an outside agency. The BPS needed back-up and here they were: both K-9 units from the Alger County Sheriff's Office had responded to offer assistance. He felt Luther's pockets for his wallet. He found the credentials and laid them out on Luther's chest. He bent over to Luther's ear and said, "Wiggle your fingers." Luther did so. Cleague could just barely see them move in the dark. "Can you move your feet?" Luther managed to move his feet at the ankles.

Cleague could hear the dogs barking. Time to go. Cleague took a moment and spoke quietly. "Luther, you are hurt. I don't think your neck is broken but it's hurt and I can't move you." He put Luther's hand on top of the open credentials wallet. "Keep your creds on your chest and they'll get you to a hospital. I can't stay here." And with that, Cleague silently slipped into the black water of the lake and was gone from sight.

112

John Luther came out of the dream and saw white. He tried to look at the source of light to his right but could not move his head. He was in a bed. The bed was near a window. It was daytime. He heard a mechanical beeping sound but could not locate the source for it. The bed had rails. There were tubes in his arms and his nose felt funny. He was in a hospital. He was tired and closed his eyes.

The doctor woke him up.

"Hi." She said. Some doctors seemed to have a penchant for being unnecessarily cheerful.

"What's your name?" She asked with a friendly smile.

"Lu…" His head really hurt. "Luther." He managed.

"Is that your first name?" She asked.

"No. John Luther, DOJ." He added. She elevated the head of his bifurcated bed frame, pulled a chair up close, and sat down so he could see her.

"It's nice to meet you, John, I'm Doctor Wills. You have some pretty serious injuries. Do you remember how you got hurt?" She asked. He had to think about it.

"Car accident." He said. "Hit another car, went into the lake."

"How did you get out of the car?" she asked.

"Don't know." He said. He couldn't remember that part. "How long have I been here?" he asked.

"You came in yesterday morning, just after midnight." Dr. Wills said.

"How did I get here?" he asked.

"By helicopter." She said. "They brought you down in the Air Ambulance from St Joseph's in Bellingham. You were taken to Saint Joe's by helicopter, which is kind of unusual. A little black helicopter, they said. Do you

449

remember any of that?" She asked. It only came in bits and pieces, it wasn't coherent.

"No." he said. "What's wrong with me?" He asked.

"So far, we know that you have a separated shoulder, a broken nose, and a neck injury. We want to take an MRI of your spine but we couldn't do it until you woke up. I will schedule that for you as soon as we can get you down there. You're going to be here for a while. Get some rest; we'll talk later." She smiled and stood up.

"Doctor?" he asked.

"Yes?" she answered.

"Where is here?" he asked.

"You're in Harborview." She said and left him to his morphine dream.

✳✳✳✳✳

He came in and out of consciousness. Drifting. They woke him up just as they were setting him on the metal table that would slide him into the magnetic resonance imaging chamber. They got him all tucked and stuffed into the tube and then the noise started. It sounded like jackhammers were pounding on the metal chamber all around his head, God that hurt. He heard someone talking to him over a loudspeaker but he didn't pay much attention. He just lay still until it was over. They pulled him out of the tube thirty-five minutes later and transferred him to a gurney. He fell asleep on the ride home.

"John, time to wake up." It seemed to him he heard that an awful lot. It was usually dark. Someone would check something, or move something, or pinch something, or move some covers to look at something and then would be gone as quietly as they had come. Not this time.

"John, wake up." It was that lady. He opened his eyes.

"Hi." She said with a smile.

"Dr. Wills." He said.

"We have the results from the MRI. John, you have a herniated disk between the second and third cervical vertebrae in your neck, and it looks like it is pinching some nerves. It requires surgery." She was on the level, matter of fact, that's that.

"Can't I go home for that? Talk to my own doctors?" He asked. The prospect of surgery on his spinal column seemed a little sudden—he hadn't been prepared for that.

"Where's home?" She smiled and asked.

"Virginia." He said.

"We're a long way from home aren't we?" She paused to let him answer. He blinked.

"Normally I would say 'sure'. In fact I would usually recommend it. But this is fairly severe, John. Until you have surgery, you have to keep your neck isolated. That pretty much means bed rest. I don't know how you would get home to talk to your doctor without having to move your neck." She said.

"Well, what happens if I move my neck?" He had to ask.

"Maybe nothing. Maybe you're paralyzed from your neck to your feet for the rest of your life." She said. He started drifting off.

"I'll come back later." Dr. Wills said and was gone.

Luther had no sense of the passage of time. It could have been twelve minutes or twelve hours since he drifted off to sleep. He lay there staring at the ceiling. It was still white. Not, the bright luminescence of reflected daylight from outside, but the antiseptic painted white of a hospital in the dreariest part of the world Luther had ever been. Dr. Wills came in, pulled up a chair beside the bed and sat down. *Doesn't this woman have a home to go to?* Luther wondered.

"Doctor Wills," Luther said. She wasn't smiling.

"Hello, John." She said, not unpleasantly. "I think you should have surgery to correct the disk in your neck but that is my opinion. This is your decision. If you choose to have the surgery we can have you in the operating room sometime tomorrow. If you choose to go home, you can be released with appropriate safeguards in place and take your chances. Should you choose to do that you will need to sign a number of forms releasing the hospital, and me, from any further responsibility for your care," she said.

"I understand. What safeguards?' He asked.

"Your shoulder and chest will be taped to minimize movement to your left shoulder and you will be wearing an orthotic brace around your neck." She said.

"A horse collar?" He asked.

"If you want to call it that." She said. She had heard them called all kinds of things—"horse collar" was probably the least derogatory.

"When can I be released?" He asked.

"I'd like you to stay one more night. You can leave tomorrow morning." She said.

"I'd like to do that." Luther said.

Elizabeth Wills thought it was a foolish choice but it was his decision. She nodded and left the room.

113

When Luther got back to Washington D.C. from the Pacific Northwest he went immediately to the headquarters of the Bureau of Public Safety. He wanted the identity of the people that staged the ambush at the foot of Atherton Mountain. They had damn near killed him. He promised locusts and brimstone and the fires of eternal damnation down upon them. The Director of the BPS was unmoved.

"I don't know what you're talking about, Mr. Luther. There was no such operation. Maybe you should take some time off." Henry Caleb suggested. Luther was at the edge of a great big chasm; he had never physically assaulted a superior administration official before.

"Well, where is Agent Glyndon?" Luther asked.

"Who?" Caleb inquired.

"Agent Joan Glyndon. Where is she?" Luther said.

"I don't know, does she work for us?" Caleb asked in turn.

"Yes, sir. She does." Luther replied.

"Well, then, you'd have to ask Personnel. Now John, you know I like to stay involved but I don't get that inquisitive about personnel assignments. We have over eight thousand agents in the BPS, and that's not enough. I could not possibly tell you who everyone is or where they are assigned. It's not like I have the time to be making appearances at every field office around the country, you know. Really, John, you need to take some time off, decompress. I could make a phone call over to the AG, if you like. I think he'd listen to me." The director offered. Stonewalled again, Luther walked out of the Director's office.

When Senator Sherman had had lunch with John Luther in the Senate Dining Room he asked Luther for a heads up before the final report on the events that had occurred on Peninsular Island the preceding year, was submitted. Luther had done so. Sherman arranged to meet Luther at the National Art Gallery. Sherman was a few minutes early and walked around the ground floor. He came to a bench near the David Smith piece and sat down. Sherman liked David Smith's sculptures. They reminded him of the farm equipment where he grew up.

Before very long Luther sat down beside the Senator. Luther agreed to meet Sherman as a courtesy, nothing more. Luther appeared quite heroic. His left arm was in a sling and he wore a collar about his neck. The black eyes were going away, the tissue around his eyes was a beigey-yellowish green. His nose did not whistle but it was apparent that he had to work at it to get air into his lungs. Sherman had not been prepared for this.

"What happened to you?" He asked. Luther was terse but not impolite.

"I was in an automobile accident," he said.

Luther told Sherman that the final report wasn't materially different from the interim report. It would be disseminated through the distribution list in due course. He had learned much but could not prove anything. Luther then told Sherman what he had not included in the final report.

Luther believed that elements within the Department of Justice and the Department of the Interior including the Attorney General of the United States and the Director of the Bureau of Public Safety had conspired and acted to murder an American citizen in an effort to launch the Domestic Tranquility Initiative (DTI).

Cleague was not important; he was nothing more than a bothersome stage prop. But he was the perfect precursor for the Constitutional Convention. The fact that Cleague saw an attack coming and ambushed the ambushers simply played into their hands. It was a spectacularly high profile news video that didn't last more than a day.

What better illustration than one lunatic that could single-handedly kill an untold number of Federal law enforcement agents, blow up a bridge, and practically burn down an island all by himself. The stock TV news footage that showed dozens of illicit weapons attributed to Cleague was simply that—stock TV news footage. That was the only thing Luther could prove. Nothing that was in the house or in the shed had escaped the pyre and nothing that had remained, that could be identified, bore any resemblance to any of the weapons that had been broadcast on TV.

Sherman told Luther it was simply implausible and, without proof, the accusation had no credibility. Luther knew that. He also knew it to be true, but without corroborating evidence he could not prove it.

114

Luther had finally strung it together. The whole time he had been conducting his "Independent Preliminary Investigation," someone had been following him. It was never about bringing an alleged felon to trial. It was about making a statement. They wanted Luther to find Cleague so they could kill him—tie up a potential loose end—just like Joan Glyndon. She had been venting classified information on an active investigation to parties outside the scope of the investigation. Luther believed that her superiors had sent her after Cleague knowing that she wouldn't survive it. Glyndon's death was one less potential embarrassment for the BPS. Luther now believed that elements within the Department of Justice and the Department of the Interior including the Attorney General of the United States and the Director of the Bureau of Public Safety had conspired and acted to murder an American citizen. Whether or not Cleague had committed a crime was a moot point. It was Luther's opinion that Cleague had acted in self-defense against a numerically superior force and had taken the steps necessary to protect himself from that Federally orchestrated conspiracy. Because Cleague had not been charged with anything and nothing had been proven in a court of law, Cleague was simply a target of opportunity.

Then there was that small matter of destroying a bridge and setting a National Historic site on fire, but Luther was somewhat confident that with the right lawyer, circumstances of mitigation and extenuation would be presented. But it was unlikely that Cleague would ever be prosecuted. Any examination of the facts would reveal, as they had to Luther, that Cleague was set up and ambushed to kick off The Domestic Tranquility Initiative. The future Chief Justice of the Supreme Court—Albert Muzecko—simply would not allow that little detail to come to light. That was why they wanted Cleague dead. It was all about votes.

Convening the Constitutional Convention, which was necessary to repeal the Second Amendment, was the keystone of the Domestic Tranquility Initiative. The repeal of the Second Amendment locked all the other parts of the DTI in place. Since the main focal point of the DTI was to confiscate private property without redress, specifically privately owned firearms, from the American People, the Second Amendment had to be repealed. The Constitutional Convention guaranteed a parliamentary fanfare rife with drama, ritual, and pageantry the likes of which had never been seen in the Post Modern era. This, in turn, would be politically expedient for both major political parties, as it would guarantee packed polls and insure the majority turnout of the electorate. The balance of power would remain split between the two parties, but clearly—one party would have the advantage of having championed societal reform. It would be heralded as: "A change we can live with," and a nice rainbow colored logo would go with it. And without threat of check or restraint, government would be allowed to behave in its own interest just like any other organism: i.e. to grow.

Luther knew for a fact that the loss of the Federal agents and the destruction of real property on Peninsular Island and the death of Agent Joan Glyndon were squarely and securely on the Attorney General's shoulders. All Luther had to do was prove it. And of course he could not do that, as there was no direct evidence linking the Attorney General to anything, neither as a party to conspiracy nor complicit act. These things sorted themselves out in Luther's mind as he sat in the anteroom to Albert Muzecko's office. He did not wear the collar or sling. He was OK as long as he stood erect and moved carefully. The aide told Luther to go in. He cautiously stood up and took a moment. He was crossing a line here and had no idea how to do it. When all else fails, he concluded, simple is good.

It was brief. Luther stated his conclusion to the AG, without elaboration, that elements within the Federal Government had conspired to establish Cleague as the focal point for the implementation of the Domestic Tranquility Initiative. By branding Cleague as an out-of-control rabble-rouser fomenting discord and paranoia amongst the civilian population through his garrulous rhetoric, Cleague was to have been presented as a clear and persistent threat to the internal security of the homeland. The televised assault on his property and the smoldering remnants of his house and storage building was meant to establish a clear, concise, and nearly irrefutable allegation that Cleague was up to an act of domestic terrorism on the scale of the Murrah Building.

Luther had surmised from the forensic report that the small arms ammunition present in the shed at the time of the raid was not on the scale in which it would be presented to the public through the media, but anybody will believe anything, especially if they hear it often enough. It was historical precedent from the Nazis: the bigger the lie, the more people will believe it.

Muzecko asked Luther if he had a written report to submit and Luther dutifully handed it over. Muzecko settled back into his chair, put on his reading glasses, and read the report from beginning to end, and laid it on his desk blotter. No emotion, no histrionics, no theatrics.

"Thank you Mister Luther, that will be all."

Luther was incredulous.

"That's it?" Luther asked. "Mr. Attorney General, have you nothing to say?"

"No. Not particularly." Muzecko replied, putting away his glasses.

"What about those men—those good men—who gave their lives on that island so you could achieve your agenda?" Luther asked.

The AG considered the question. He really didn't want things to go this way but the die was cast.

"Yeah, well, that was unfortunate. But as it turned out, it wasn't all bad." The AG said. Luther was dumbstruck.

"Sir?" Was all he could manage.

"Look, Luther. We got a lot of mileage out of that little fiasco. It was better than I could have hoped for to tell you the truth. I mean, who knew it would be that spectacular? I just wished that we could have had better film of the buildings and bridge and stuff. But it's OK. The Convention is going to happen, The Second Amendment is going to be repealed, and it's going to work out just fine. You'll see." Muzecko said.

"What about those men sir? There are a dozen families without husbands and fathers. You knew they were walking into a shit storm. You planned it." Luther charged.

"Watch it Luther. You're injured. You're upset, but you are very close to saying something you will regret. Nobody planned anything of the sort. If you will read your own report you will recall that I never ordered that raid. I didn't have anything to do with any of this, other than have to clean up the mess, which you have done admirably. This whole affair started in another cabinet department. If you want to hurl accusations, I suggest you start over there. But the smart thing is to go on with your life, and carry on with your career, and don't look back. And know that you have the appreciation of a grateful President for a job well done." Muzecko said.

"And what about those men, sir?" Luther pressed.

"Pawns are expendable, Mr. Luther." Muzecko said flatly. "Good day to you."

Luther stood and said "Yes, sir," and took his leave. As he let himself out into the anteroom, and then into the hallway, he had the feeling that he had missed something, something of consequence. The Attorney General had just virtually admitted to Luther that the whole thing had been planned—he had just openly alluded to a criminal conspiracy. But Luther still had no way to prove it and his allegation alone would never stand the scrutiny of a Congressional hearing.

The Attorney General scanned back through the report. Clearly he would not appoint, nor would he recommend to the President to direct the appointment of a special counsel. It would be redundant, time consuming, wasteful, counter-productive, anti-climactic, and distracting. He wanted all eyes on the big prize: the repeal of the Second Amendment. Appointing a special counsel would only detract from the effort. Peter Cleague's pyrotechnic temper tantrum had served its purpose—now it was time to move forward. Albert Muzecko mentally articulated the words that would be released to the press. Something along the lines of…"*an internal investigative report concluded there had been core deficiencies in the Bureau of Public Safety's surveillance and resultant raid on the home and private property of a citizen of Washington State last year on Peninsular Island. The report alleged that the warrant that permitted the raid had been constitutionally vague, and, unfortunately, due to the unforeseen escalation of events—a continuum of errors, the regrettable loss of life and loss of property could not have been avoided.*" Of course the Director of the Bureau of Public Safety would have to resign, but what the hell, Henry was a good soldier. Henry Caleb would just have to take one for the team. He could always be appointed to something else when the next Administration took over in January. *Like Interior.* He thought. *Yeah, Henry Caleb, Secretary of the Interior; that would be a good fit.*

The AG would also stipulate that the report would recommend the swift implementation of all measures of the Domestic Tranquility Initiative. The report would further advise that when the repeal of the Second Amendment had been achieved, such regrettable circumstances as had been seen on Peninsular Island would no longer be possible in a free and open society. The AG quietly smiled and picked up his phone.

*****

John Luther walked tall as he proceeded from the Department of Justice, across Pennsylvania Avenue, and down the street toward the parking garage in which he had left his car. He imagined that at some point he would probably be called to testify before some sub-committee or other, probably Senator Sherman's, but right now, the sky was clear, the air was relatively clean (for Washington, D.C.), and when all was said and done, life was good. It was finally over. Even for a bureaucrat, a lowly cog in the gargantuan mechanism that was the Federal Government of the United States of America, life was good. As he entered the parking structure and walked up the ramps to the level on which he had parked, he reflected that he needed to make an appointment to go see his doctor and get his neck checked out. It was uncomfortable, but he didn't think he needed surgery; even if he did, so what? He heard the squeal of tires and paid it no mind—he was in a parking garage.

As Luther ascended the ramp to the deck where he had left his car, he turned down the concrete apron toward his parking stall and was immediately struck by the full weight and energy of a commercial panel van going faster than was prudent in such a confined space. Luther was immediately thrown to the deck with a force he had not previously known in his life. His neck had been snapped. His back and pelvis were broken. He could see nothing, he could feel nothing, and his sense of hearing was fading. He was in shock and he knew he was dying. The words of the Attorney General came back to him. *Pawns are expendable, Mr. Luther.*

115

Albert Muzecko had received the summons to appear before the Senate sub-committee investigating the circumstances surrounding the loss of life and property on Peninsular Island, Washington. The event would be his opportunity to present Luther's final report with his own appropriate annotations to the sub-committee and by extension to the media news organs and almost simultaneously to every news distribution outlet in the country. He could not keep from smiling. You had to love a system like this. An idea could become fact in milliseconds just by the venue of presentation. He could hear the newscaster's voice now, "...the report recommends the swift implementation of all measures of the Domestic Tranquility Initiative. The report further advises that when the repeal of the Second Amendment has been achieved, such regrettable circumstances, as had been seen on Peninsular Island, would no longer be possible in a free and open society."

Muzecko's party had the majority of seats in the committee but he wanted everybody in his corner. Some of these people would be sitting on the Senate Judiciary Committee on his hearing for nomination as Chief Justice to the Supreme Court just after the first of the year. It was not that far away. Muzecko needed to reach out to the three members of the sub-committee from the opposition, two of whom he was sure he could persuade to act in his favor. But then there was that loose cannon – Sherman. The man's own Minority Leader couldn't control him. Muzecko reflected that with one vote, the one Senate vote opposed to the Constitutional Convention, Sherman had alienated himself from his own side of the aisle and had fewer friends on the other side. Zero friends equals zero influence. But then again he had heard Sherman make a speech or two; the guy could be pretty persuasive. He had to nip this in the bud. Muzecko picked up the phone and made a call to the Office of Senator Alexander Sherman.

✳✳✳✳✳

They met for lunch. When Sherman walked into the restaurant off the street he had to pause and let his eyes adjust to the light. Everything was mahogany and green baize, leather and brass, white linen and candles in glass boxes. The plates were china, glasses were crystal, and utensils were silver. Standing there at the behest of the Attorney General of the U.S., amid the tinkle and clink and the muted conversations of the power elite, it occurred to Al Sherman that he had been invited into one of the most exclusive restaurants in Washington D.C., and by extension, into the upper tier of the machine that made government function. Members only, all others need not apply.

After the obligatory meeting and greeting, they placed their orders with the hovering waiter. When the waiter left Sherman was unreserved.

"Why Cleague?" He asked. Clearly, Sherman did not yet know about Mr. Luther.

"Have you heard the old bromide about the sheep, the wolf, and the sheepdog?" Muzecko asked? Sherman shook his head in the negative. Muzecko paused as drinks were served.

"Well, a guy named Grossman put out this analogy and it's very useful. The sheep is your average ordinary citizen. He is content to go about his life in a productive manner. He is kind and decent and couldn't hurt anybody unless it was by accident." Muzecko took a piece of warm bread out of the linen covered basket, broke it and proceeded to spread butter on it.

"The wolf has a real and genuine capacity for harm. He likes to hurt people. He is an aggressive sociopath and has no empathy for the citizens around him. The wolf will feed on the sheep without mercy and without hesitation." He took a bite of the artisanal bread and watched some of the butter drip on his plate.

"But," he paused to take a sip of a fine cabernet and wipe his mouth with the linen napkin.

"What if you have a capacity for violence and a sense of empathy for your fellow citizens? You are a sheepdog. The sheep don't like the sheepdogs because they look a lot like the wolves and they are a constant reminder that the wolves really are out there," Muzecko said.

Sherman was wondering where Muzecko was going with this but he did not interrupt or interject. The waiter brought their food—prime rib for Muzecko and fish for Sherman.

"In this society, Senator, the Federal Government will provide the sheepdogs and Peter Cleague is not on that list. The fact that he was pointing at the government and yelling, 'WOLF', well, that just upset people and made them confused. And we really don't want to upset the sheeple," Muzecko tripped over his syllables, "I mean, people." He took a forkful of prime rib and quaffed his wine.

The AG went on. "Cleague was familiar with that analogy, he used it all the time in his classes to young impressionable Federal agents back at Glynco. We really didn't pay too much attention to him when he left government service until after he started teaching civilians and started publishing his ideas in those magazine articles. To be sure, his published works were obscure beyond the point of caring, but why take the risk? He was putting ideas out there in the public domain, and it would only take a few disenchanted misanthropists to act on them and then we'd have a real mess on our hands." Muzecko said.

Sherman had missed something. "What are you talking about? Why was he so dangerous?" He asked and sampled the brook trout.

"The man was a certifiable lunatic." Muzecko countered. "He was actually teaching civilians the same stuff he taught at Glynco. How to shoot guns, tactics, how to maneuver in teams, just crazy stuff!"

Sherman didn't get it. "Well, why not? So what if he was teaching that stuff to civilians?" He asked.

Muzecko gauged his luncheon companion. Was Sherman baiting him? No matter. "Because the people need to be protected." Muzecko answered. "Particularly from themselves. They can't be entrusted with that sort of skill set— it's just too dangerous. It would be Tombstone and the O.K. Corral every afternoon at rush hour on a national scale. What would keep these people from forming vigilante committees? Can you picture gangs of armed civilians roaming the streets? Rule by mob? No sir, it is just too dangerous. What's to keep them from coming after us who protect them and, make sure the country functions? If you take every Federal employee from here to Hawaii and give them a gun, all the Bubbas, and the Joe Six Packs in this country would still outnumber them by six hundred and fifty to one.

"What happens if somebody gets pissed off because he thinks his taxes are too high? Hell, they wouldn't just go after the IRS, they'd go after the people that voted for the taxes." Muzecko punctuated the point with his steak knife jutting it at Sherman from across the table.

"Now don't get me wrong. Most of the sheep are well-meaning, affable, and harmless, but it only takes one guy. Look at Oswald, look at Sirhan Sirhan, look at Hinckley. That close quarter armed combat stuff that Cleague taught is just too sensitive for ordinary citizens. They don't need it." He said.

"So, Cleague was this messenger of forbidden lore, and you wanted to kill the messenger." Sherman concluded.

"Well,' Muzecko shrugged, "Things were going in the direction we wanted them to go. I was in the Senate back then you know.' He said. Sherman nodded. He knew.

"People were getting used to the notion of incremental restriction. We had the Brady Bill, then we had the Crime Bill, then we had Brady II. In a few years the vast majority of the population would have been grateful to get rid of them." Muzecko said.

"Get rid of them? Get rid of their guns?'' Sherman asked for clarification.

"Yeah," Muzecko confirmed, "Who needs a gun?" Muzecko asked rhetorically. "Nobody needs a gun." He answered rhetorically. "Except us." And he took another bite of drippy beef.

"Things were going really well until we lost the majority in both houses. It took two terms before we got the majorities back." Muzecko claimed as he stabbed a forkful of mushrooms.

Sherman saw the opportunity that the AG must have seen.

"So, Cleague was teaching these classes to civilians and that made him the perfect focal point to kick off the Domestic Tranquility Initiative?" Sherman asked.

Muzecko nodded and chewed.

"Cleague was going to be your poster boy." Sherman said.

"Yeah, that was the idea. And as it turned out, it worked out OK, the way the timing fell into place and all." Muzecko said.

"And where is he now?" Sherman asked.

"I don't know." Muzecko shrugged. "Who cares? I heard he was dead. But it doesn't matter. It's a done deal. Finally, the domestic social policies of this country are on the right," he chortled, "Excuse me, correct, path. And it's morning again in America." Muzecko smiled, paraphrasing a line from the patron saint of the loyal opposition.

116

Like hell it is, Sherman thought. It started to sink in.

"So, what you are telling me is that all by himself, Peter Cleague did not pose a real threat to the government, or to the Constitution, or to the fabric of society. He taught people, and he wrote magazine articles, and that made him the right guy in the right place at the right time?" Sherman asked. Muzecko simply shrugged while soaking up the bloody juice from his plate with a piece of bread.

"Sure, I mean way the hell out there in Puget Sound? Who got hurt?" Muzecko said.

Sherman was incredulous.

"As I recall, there were a number of Federal law enforcement officers that got hurt. Your law enforcement officers." Sherman pointed out.

Muzecko retorted, "That's their job. They knew that sacrifice was part of the price for serving their country." He dabbed at his mouth with the linen napkin.

It was not the supreme hubris that affected Sherman, it was Muzecko's cold detached puppet-master's regard for those whom he saw as subordinate. Sherman knew in his heart that Albert Muzecko saw everyone as subordinate.

"Just for my own edification," Sherman asked, "do you believe it is the function of the government to protect the people?"

"Hey, look it," Muzecko pointed out. "The majority of people are sheep and need to be herded for their own protection. And what's more, they want to be in the flock whether they know it or not. Just look around. Pick any middle class neighborhood in any suburban district or bedroom community anywhere in the United States. What do you see? All the houses look the same. All the cars are in the same class. Everybody wants to be like everybody else. Nobody wants to be different, nobody wants to be an outsider and nobody wants to be socially ostracized. Everybody wants to be in the flock. Everybody wants governmental protection. Everybody expects entitlements. What would happen to the flock if the sheep dogs weren't there?" Muzecko asked.

"Well, OK," Sherman conceded, "but what does that make Cleague? He was alerting the flock to a perceived threat. Doesn't that make Cleague a sheepdog, the light in the darkness, the voice from the wilderness, the little voice inside your head?" Sherman enumerated at length. Muzecko was willing to yield the point just to shut Sherman up.

"Well, all right, yes, as long as we are speaking in metaphors, Cleague could have been all those things." Muzecko said, and Senator Sherman drew his own conclusion: *The removal of whom would have been necessary to accomplish the desired outcome i.e.: the Domestic Tranquility Initiative. And presented on National TV.*

Sherman went on. "The Attorney General is the chief law enforcement officer of the United States. In our system of government you are literally the people's champion in the rule of law." Sherman said as Muzecko nodded and took a sip of very strong coffee, the perfect end to a perfect meal.

"Yes, that is very true." Muzecko agreed as he scanned the tabletop for the cream decanter.

"But in this analogy, who is the sheepdog here?" Sherman asked. "Is it Cleague telling people to beware an encroaching government, or is it the AG and his governmental minions who know what is best for the good of the flock?" Sherman asked, gazing steadily into the eyes of the man whom he now regarded as the most dangerous person in the country.

Muzecko made no response other than a quiet malevolent stare in return. The hair on the back of Sherman's neck stood straight up.

Sherman silently considered the premise: *"The Government", principally Albert Muzecko, wants to initiate a domestic policy of pre-emption of constitutional rights, ostensibly for the greater good. It has to have the willing co-operation of its citizens to make it work. What better way than to broadcast the arrest of a certifiable lunatic prevented from doing harm — enter one Peter Cleague. The arrest never happened, but the video of a spectacular conflagration was so much more compelling. The malcontent having been revealed, unmasked, and brought out into the bright and bold light of justice served. But what if it hadn't worked?* Sherman considered. *What if Cleague had just gone meekly into the back of the truck?* He realized there had to have been other targets. *How many? Who were they?* All of a sudden Senator Sherman felt unwell.

"Mister Attorney General, why are we here?" He asked.

Muzecko raised his eyebrows. "What?" He asked in turn.

"Why are we having lunch?" Sherman asked.

Muzecko had been waiting for this. "I just wanted to share a pleasant meal in a pleasant environment as well as some concerns I have held privately about your vision of the future." Muzecko replied. Sherman would admit this restaurant was a pleasant environment but he had no idea how good the food had been. He had finished his filleted brook trout but hadn't tasted a thing since the conversation started.

"And what would those concerns be Mr. Muzecko?" Sherman asked.

"Your opposition to the Constitutional convention. Now that the convention is a fact, how are you going to vote?"

Muzecko asked. Sherman didn't hesitate—it was already a matter of public record.

"I am going to vote against it." He said.

"Yeah, see, that's what I wanted to talk to you about." Muzecko said in complete candor. "That's a mistake," the teacher tutoring one of the slower pupils.

"Oh?" Sherman asked, "And why is that?"

Gee, how to put this? Muzecko pondered.

"We know what your feelings are Senator, and we know they are heartfelt, and we know that you always, without fail, have put the wishes of your constituents foremost in every vote you have ever cast. But consider this: If you vote with the majority this time, and in time to come, life would be so much easier for you. Hell, you could even conceivably be chair of your own committee next term. Admittedly, it would be highly unusual but not impossible," Muzecko advised.

Yeah, right, when the cows come home. Sherman thought.

"Senator, you have been in this town long enough to know the influence a committee chair can wield." Muzecko went on. "In the next administration that could be very much in your favor. Look, you have to do what you think is right, I know that, and I understand it, but you should at least consider what I'm telling you. We will have the White House and we will have majorities in both houses next term. You would have grateful friends in advantageous places and your friends would not forget you.

OK. He got it. Sherman was being told, but not in so many words, that if he voted to repeal the Second Amendment, and if he would subsequently vote for Muzecko's approval to the Supreme Court, he would have a friend in the highest court in the land.

117

Sherman shifted the direction of the conversation.

"I hear you might be nominated to the Supreme Court. Is that True?" Sherman asked.

Muzecko shrugged noncommittally and beamed. The wine was good.

"If you do ascend to the bench who are your heroes? Who will you pattern yourself after?" Sherman asked,

Muzecko was mildly surprised, he never considered the question but it was a good one. He thought a moment, mulling over the history of the Court.

"I always admired Justice Brandeis. He never felt an embarrassment for wanting, or even for allowing, the government to do more for the people." Muzecko smiled pleasantly at the image of himself, the benefic justice, extolling favor upon the poor, tired, huddled masses from his position on the exalted high bench.

Sherman considered and nodded. *So the rumor was true. Muzecko had made a deal with Rebecca Ellery, the Senator from New York.* Upon emerging as her party's nominee for the office of President of the United States Senator Ellery promised sweetness and light after her election to the Presidency. If polls were to be believed she would easily carry the popular vote in November but that was just window dressing. A deal had been made with her closest rival, the only serious contender that could deprive her of the necessary delegates for the party's nomination, the current Attorney General. In return for not running in opposition to her candidacy, Albert Muzecko would, in turn, be nominated to and confirmed as the next Chief Justice of the Supreme Court. The current Chief Justice had already submitted notice of his pending retirement.

Rebecca Ellery got the nod for her party's candidacy for President and Muzecko would be sent to the Supremes. A President was President for not longer than eight years, but a Supreme Court Justice was there for life. This would allow Albert Muzecko to make his own unique imprint on history. Sherman considered that Muzecko was probably in his mid-fifties. *Hell, he could conceivably be on the bench for thirty-five or forty years.* Moreover, Sherman could understand Brandeis being someone's judicial hero.

"But even Brandeis said '...In the exercise of this high power, we must be ever on our guard, lest we erect our prejudices into legal principles,'" Sherman said, quoting the late justice. Muzecko shrugged.

"You say that like it's a bad thing, I don't believe it is. Our ideals, our guiding lights, are our principles. The Constitution is a living document. When we are on the bench we will act accordingly." Muzecko stared into his coffee cup and watched the cream bloom and billow into the hot black liquid. He wondered how he could use that last statement as a sound bite. It sounded awfully profound to him.

Sitting there in what was widely regarded as the benchmark restaurant in the Nation's Capitol, Alexander Sherman was fairly alarmed. In keeping with the spirit of polite conversation he said, "So you wouldn't necessarily be opposed to legislating from the bench? I mean, if it were possible?"

Muzecko replied, "Well, the structure of our system does not allow for that, does it?" And he let it go at that. "I don't want to rush you, Senator," Muzecko said as he looked at his watch. "I have very much enjoyed our lunch but I have to prepare for a committee hearing," Muzecko said, giving the most self-satisfied smile Sherman had ever seen on a human face. Lunch was over.

Sherman left the air-conditioned interior of the restaurant and walked out into the 90-degree heat and 95 percent humidity of Washington, D.C. It was like getting hit in the face with a wet towel.

God, I hate this town, he thought. After he walked out of the restaurant, Sherman pulled out his cell phone. He wanted to talk to John Luther. He got Luther's voicemail. He called his wife and told her he'd be late getting home. He was going back to the office to work on his speech. The Convention would start next week. For most everyone involved in the procedure it was already a foregone conclusion, but he had not yet given up. He was designated as the keynote speaker opposed to the vote to repeal the Second Amendment to the Constitution of the United States.

118

John Luther was dead. Hit and run in a parking garage. The cop that returned the message on Luther's cell phone said so. Last known contacts. Part of the investigation. Standard procedure. Sherman sat in his office in a saturnine gloom.

It was early on a Friday evening and most of the staffers had gone home and, being Friday, very few Senators were left in the building. He made his way into his private office and, as was his habit, he picked up a book of annotated quotes of one of the founding fathers. He had several such volumes. The books provided him some level of comfort: Adams, Madison, Jefferson, and Paine. They were masters of the Art of the Spoken Word: Whether one agreed with the particular point being made or not, it was executed with flourish and precision. It was locution ornately rich and structurally profound and, in time, had laid the foundation for the democratic style of government it was now Sherman's duty and pleasure to serve. As it is the function of the Senate to debate, Sherman's proclivity to seek the guidance of the masters of his craft was a fortunate calling.

In many ways, applying a quote at random to a current event or concern helped him think, it gave him focus, and he always valued it as a particularly useful exercise for the mind. And, of course, just as often the quote could be totally irrelevant. As he sat there, distractedly thumbing through the pages of John Adams' Thoughts on Government, 1776, this particular quote leapt out at him: *"Judges, therefore, should be always men of learning and experience in the laws, of exemplary morals, great patience, calmness, coolness, and attention. Their minds should not be distracted with jarring interests; they should not be dependent upon any man, or body of men."* He read it again, out loud.

He let his eyes roll over the words again. "Their minds should not be distracted with jarring interests; they should not be dependent upon any man, or body of men." Sherman thought of Albert Muzecko. As Attorney General of the United States not only did he enjoy the full faith, trust, and confidence of the President, he also determined the course of law enforcement throughout the land. If not directly under his control, he had overwhelming influence on all the organs of Federal law enforcement in the country. Sherman now knew that it had been Muzecko who had designed and orchestrated the Domestic Tranquility Initiative. Luther had told him so and he was reluctant to believe it—this afternoon's luncheon confirmed it. It had been Muzecko who had, at the very least, influenced if not planned to the last detail the execution of "Operation Clean Sweep" on Peninsular Island. He had effectively said so this afternoon. Luther was right. And now Luther was dead.

The Domestic Tranquility Initiative had almost been lifted word for word out of Article 48 of the Weimar Constitution. Article 48 permitted the suspension of civil liberties in time of national emergency without the consent of the German parliament. President Paul Hindenburg and Chancellor Adolph Hitler had invoked it in 1933 in the aftermath of the Reichstag Fire. Although the German constitution of 1919 was never officially repealed, the legal measures taken by the German government under Chancellor Hitler in February and March 1933, commonly referred to as "forcible coordination", meant that the government could legislate contrary to the constitution. The German constitution became irrelevant.

Sherman was nearly dumbstruck with shock. Why had he not seen the corollary before? We were re-enacting the laws of Nazi Germany. What was next, internment centers?

Muzecko's words from lunch came back to him, "The majority of people are sheep and need to be herded for their own protection. What would happen to the flock if the sheep dogs weren't there?" Again Sherman felt unwell. Even now he could hear Muzecko gloating, "People were getting used to the notion of incremental restriction. We had the Brady Bill, then we had the Crime Bill, then we had Brady II. In a few years the vast majority of the population would have been grateful to get rid of them." Muzecko proclaimed it like it was a banner across his chest.

Sherman sat with his elbows on the edge of his desk, his head cradled in his hands. He made the connections from one link to the next.

Brady II and the Arsenal Code laid the groundwork for and presaged the implementation of The Domestic Tranquility Initiative. Brady II and the Arsenal Code had been passed prior to Sherman's election to his Senate seat. Indeed, Sherman's campaign for the Senate had been framed as the one thing that his constituents of the great State of Idaho could do as a reaction to the East Coast lawmakers run amok in the halls of the Capitol. Something clicked. It had been passed before Sherman's time but some intangible thing pulled at his memory. Sherman looked up the original bills to see who had sponsored them in the Senate. He immediately felt sick.

119

Albert Muzecko had been a Senator at the time the Gun Violence Prevention Act had been introduced. He had also been one of its sponsors in the Senate as well as one of its foremost champions on the talk show circuit. Muzecko had also written the Gun Violence Prevention Act II (Brady II), and The National Uniform Ammunition Requirements Act (The Arsenal Code). He frequented the Sunday talk shows, the daytime shows, and any other venue that would have him. He ardently and articulately argued these courses of action to be in the best interest of the nation based on recommendations of the Office of Legal Counsel. *The OLC? Why drag those guys into it?* Sherman wondered. *Muzecko may have thought that it gave his proposals more credence, aside from the fact that it was totally insane. What the hell,* Sherman concluded. *It must have worked. The bills got passed into law.* It had all happened before Sherman's term started. He would have to find somebody that knew more about this stuff than he did.

Brady II and the Arsenal Code were the necessary precedents for the Constitutional Convention for the Repeal of the Second Amendment. Peter Cleague was incidental. He just happened to be the right guy in the right place at the right time. The repeal of the Second Amendment was a necessary precedent for the passage of the Domestic Tranquility Initiative. Its proponents had been making noises to get the Domestic Tranquility Initiative on the table and open for debate every term since Sherman had been in the Senate, but he had never realized until right now who had written it. Sherman had given it only a cursory glance and concluded it was a tower of Babel built on a foundation of feel-good gibberish that would never stand up to the scrutiny of a senate vote. At any rate, Sherman was able to determine that Albert Muzecko was the architect of this particular tower of Babel. He had planned and implemented the whole goddamned thing from start to finish. The Domestic Tranquility Initiative would be Muzecko's crowning achievement and perpetual glory. It was the instrument necessary to invoke the Federal confiscation of privately-owned firearms in the United States. Sherman knew in his heart and in his soul that there were American citizens in this country who would not stand by and let it happen. Americans like Peter Cleague for one.

Something else that Muzecko had said occurred to Sherman. Sheep and sheepdogs. Muzecko said that Cleague had used the analogy when he taught at Glynco. Muzecko knew that Cleague taught at Glynco, therefore he/they— whoever helped plan that debacle on Peninsular Island— knew what Cleague was capable of because Cleague taught some of those things to aspiring young Federal law enforcement officers. Everything else was in Cleague's military records, which would have been reviewed as a matter of course prior to Cleague's admittance to the State Department. They knew. It was all there: fire and maneuver, assault through an ambush, deception and misdirection. The BPS guys on Operation Clean Sweep were on a suicide mission, but apparently, nobody bothered to tell them.

Sherman picked up another book from the top of his pile at random. Hamilton, Madison, and Jay, <u>The Federalist.</u> He let the pages fan out from under his thumb and stopped at an arbitrary point, and read: "If the Federal government should overpass the just bounds of its authority and make a tyrannical use of its powers, the people, whose creature it is, must appeal to the standard they have formed, and take such measures to redress the injury done to the Constitution as the exigency may suggest and prudence justify." Alexander

Hamilton (Federalist No. 33, 3 January 1788). He closed the book and laid it back on the pile from which it came. Sherman had never been cynical about the government. Sherman had been called to serve and believed it to be his duty and his honor to do so. But his lunch with Muzecko today had torn away that veil of idealism. And on top of that, John Luther—and a dozen BPS agents—had been murdered. Sherman was seeing the beast from inside its belly.

He leaned back in his chair. His head hurt. He massaged the pain. Now, sitting in his office alone, he considered that if this Constitutional convention resulted in the repeal of the Second Amendment, or any other amendment of the Constitution, there would be a shooting war that could rival the ferocity, intensity, and loss of life of the Civil War. There were too many combat trained veterans in the country to let the constitution be dismantled. The Constitutional Convention was scheduled to begin next week. Sherman was designated first speaker to represent the faction opposed to the event. He picked up a yellow legal pad and a ballpoint pen and began to write. He thought best with a pen in his hand. He always had.

120

They met at the west end of the reflecting pool. Sherman kept a respectful distance as he watched Judge Hillman disembark from the back of the Lincoln Towne Car with the assistance of an aide—whom Sherman guessed to be a bodyguard. Well built, fit, trim, nicely groomed, and wearing Oakley sunglasses, in a well tailored black suit, the aide helped the judge down the steps and dutifully took a position behind him. Judge Hillman, a rolling ambulation of mass and inertia, willed himself across the concrete space like a tottering top and stopped at the reflecting pool. Sherman unobtrusively joined him and they shared a walk quietly for some minutes along the north side of the water. The judge noted the several species of pigeons, a dove, and, by golly, there was a red tailed hawk. Sherman noted that the healthy, robust, military looking fellow followed them at a discreet distance.

"What can I do for you, Senator?" The judge asked. It seemed to him that he had become awfully popular these past few weeks.

"If it has anything to do with that business with Peter Cleague, I was not there and I do not know what happened."

"No, Sir." Sherman answered. "It goes a little further back than that.

"And what would that be?" Asked the judge.

"If memory serves, Sir, weren't you in Justice when Attorney General Muzecko was in the Senate?" Sherman asked.

"Yes I was. What of it?" The judge replied.

"I was doing a bit of research on a proposed bill and I ran across a reference to Senator Muzecko's appearance on several TV talk shows at the time," Sherman stated.

"Yeah, So what?" The judge retorted. This interview by the numbers business was most tedious. It was like having your wisdom teeth extracted without the benefit of anesthesia. Sherman went on.

"In his campaign to garner public support for The Arsenal Codes and the other gun control measures he had written or had helped sponsor, he often cited that they were recommended by the Office of Legal Counsel. Why did he need to drag those guys into it?"

"I should think it would be obvious," The judge said. "By citing the OLC he was trying to borrow some credence from what he thought would have been perceived to be an impartial outside party. As the OLC is part of the Executive branch, it was not an unreasonable presumption on Mr. Muzecko's part." The judge said.

"Were they?" Sherman asked.

"Were who what?" Hillman replied.

"Were the OLC impartial?" Sherman asked.

"Oh, hell no. Mr. Sherman, do you know what the Office of Legal Counsel is or what it does?" Hillman asked the younger man.

"The Office of Legal Counsel is a collective of 22 White House-appointed academics. It is organized within the Department of Justice. It vets the policies, orders, and proclamations of the Executive branch and advises the President and the Attorney General as to what is or is not legal." Sherman recited it as if he had memorized it out of a book. He had.

"Yes. And no." Hillman said. "That bunch that was in the White House back then was a curious group. At once consumed with the appearance of accessibility and at the same time obsessed with unfettered control over anything they deemed to be within the purview of the Executive. They recoiled at the thought of Congressional oversight regarding anything they did. Are you familiar with the Unitary Executive Theory?" Hillman asked.

"Vaguely." Sherman answered.

"Right," The judge paused for a moment and took a deep breath. Then he took another breath as if he were winded. The aide picked up his pace and approached the judge with some sense of urgency. From his rearguard position he could see that the judge was having some sort of trouble. He swept the right side of his unbuttoned suit jacket away and formed a firing grip around the grip frame of the handgun at his hip as he started to scan the area for any potential threat. Sherman was not immune from suspicion, as he received the aide's especially intense scrutiny. The judge turned and waved the bodyguard away, saying, "It's alright, Michael, just a bit out of breath." Michael nodded, straightened and swept the jacket flat in front of him with the palms of his hands, and dropped back to his position behind the two bureaucrats. Hillman took an inhaler out of his jacket pocket, stuck it in his mouth and pumped it twice, taking deep sucking breaths of mist into his lungs.

He continued his narrative. "The OLC under that administration was defined by its particularly assertive claim to the exclusive dominion of the Executive branch over powers of governance. They contended under the unitary executive theory that the Executive branch of this Republic is not obliged to compromise to Congressional restraint on matters of national security or on policy decisions. UET is the view that the president holds total control over the Executive branch and that Congress can only hold the President accountable by censure or impeachment or Constitutional amendment. In this view, legislation restricting the executive branch has no power and is not binding," he said. "The fact that Muzecko sought to gain corroboration of the Office of Legal Counsel was an olive branch to the Administration. And look where he is now."

Hillman went further, "These OLC people believe that the executive branch is constitutionally mandated to protect, defend, and preserve the sovereignty and security of the United States by whatever means necessary. That mandate is not exclusive to the Republicans or to the Democrats. It is exclusive to whoever sits in the Oval Office and it is very jealously guarded.

"It is the position of the administration now in office that those powers pertain to domestic security as well as security from foreign incursion. It is also the position of this administration that these powers are solely discretionary. In other words, if the need arises, the Office of the President can assume the authority. Need a wiretap? Do it. Judicial concurrence can wait and be granted after the fact. Suspend habeas corpus for an individual suspected of domestic terrorism? Done. And what is domestic terrorism? Whatever they say it is. The OLC is literally making up the rules while it is playing the game.

"The Attorney General we have is not a part of the Office of Legal Counsel. But he is very aware of its inclinations and findings. He has never advised the President toward a course of action contradictory to the recommendations of the OLC. Because it is the cabal not of the AG's creation, but of the President, and it certainly enjoys the protection of the all-encompassing wing of the National Command Authority." Hillman stopped. They had passed through the World War II Memorial and had started west back toward the Lincoln Memorial. He turned and motioned to Michael that all was well. Sherman looked in Michael's direction and gave a weak smile and a slight nod. Michael looked at Sherman as if he were just another object in the target array. "I swear," Sherman said, "that man is a human Doberman." Hillman nodded slightly and said, "You have no idea."

"Invoking the National Command Authority implicates the President's position as Commander in Chief of the Armed Forces." Sherman said.

"Of course," Hillman agreed. "This administration sees everything through the lens of national security. Given the real threat that terrorism presents to the Republic, the claim of national security isn't much of a stretch, is it?" Hillman said.

121

"Was Peter Cleague a threat to National Security?" Sherman asked.

"Ah." The judge said. It seemed to him that they had taken the long way around the barn to get to the crux of the question.

"He was if they say he was. But I rather doubt that Cleague was anything more than a vehicle of convenience for a far more grand and expansive undertaking," Hillman said.

Sherman wanted to be sure of what was being said here.

"Do you mean the Domestic Tranquility Initiative?" He asked directly. The judge simply replied, "I see you've heard of it." The judge regarded the Senator with a new appraisal— the boy had been doing his homework and apparently had already put two and two together. Their meeting here today was only to confirm something Sherman had already suspected.

"I have noticed, Senator, that you are fond of quoting the founders in your speeches. Do you recall what Hamilton said of demagoguery?" Hillman asked? Sherman shook his head in the negative.

"No, I'm afraid I don't." He wanted to hear what Hillman would say.

"Of those men who have overturned the liberties of republics, the greatest number have begun their career by paying an obsequious court to the people, commencing demagogues and ending tyrants." Hillman recited and Sherman recognized the quote from the Federalist No. 1, Alexander Hamilton, October 1787.

"Is that what Muzecko was doing by going to all those talk shows?" Sherman asked.

"You tell me," Hillman replied. "At that time he was a Senator and needed the popular support to pass his proposed legislation. He was laying the legislative foundation for a more correct, more perfect society. His invocation of the Office of Legal Counsel enabled him to garner the support of the Executive branch. Now he enjoys the autonomy of the highest law enforcement position in the Federal government. He just happens to have been Attorney General while events have conspired to put that foundation into play. And who knows, a few months from now he may be sitting on the bench of the highest court in the land. That would be a fine position from which to safeguard his vision for a new and better society, wouldn't it?"

Hillman's question concluded their conversation. They had arrived back at the west end of the reflecting pool. Hillman signaled Michael that he was ready to leave. "Good day, Senator. And good luck to you." Hillman said, and with Michael's assistance, made his way back to his automobile.

Sherman watched the retreating figures and considered what he had been told.

He also considered that his suspicions from the previous evening were correct.

122

The President of the Senate gaveled the historic joint session to order.

The issue was resolved:

Section 1. That having served the purpose envisioned by the founding fathers and having outlived that purpose by the social, cultural, scientific, and economic realities of the several States that could not have been foreseen by the founding fathers, and thus outlived, having come to present in itself by its existence a very real threat to the life, liberty, and pursuit of happiness of the citizens it had once been intended to preserve, The second article of amendment to the Constitution of the United States shall be repealed.

And in that act it shall be posted to amend a new provision that: Immediately upon the ratification of this article the manufacture, sale, transportation, or transfer of any firearm, of any caliber, design, means of manufacture, or material of manufacture, and any type of ammunition appropriate to that firearm regardless of type, design, or composition, shall be prohibited from ownership or possession by any individual Citizen of the United States with the sole exception of the agencies of the States and that of the Federal Government of the United States, and that the importation thereof into, or the exportation thereof from the United States and all territories subject to the jurisdiction thereof, for the private possession, or use by any individual citizen be prohibited.

Section 2. The Congress and the several States shall have concurrent power to enforce this article by appropriate legislation.

Section 3. This article shall be inoperative unless it shall have been ratified as a repealed Amendment to the

Constitution by the legislatures of the several States as provided within the Constitution.

*****

The Constitutional Convention was convoked in the House chamber in the south wing of the Capitol building because it had more seats. After the procedural rhetoric had been properly invoked, the President of the Senate called on the keynote speakers to present the case for and the case against Constitutional reform. In order, he gravely intoned, "The chair recognizes the Senator from New York". One side of the aisle predictably launched to its collective feet in a maelstrom of cheering and applause.

Rebecca Ellery ardently strode to the rostrum with purpose and poise and waited until the ceremonial whooping, and hollering, applauding, and whistling died down. This was her time in the spotlight to demonstrate to the entire country on live TV that a woman could be Presidential. And she did so with the utmost grace and wit, which played really well on live national TV. As the echoes of the raucous welcome receded throughout the chamber, she only casually glanced at the TelePrompTer: she would not need to read this speech.

"Mr. President," she said, addressing the Vice President of the United States—the President of the Senate, "Madam Speaker," addressing the Speaker of the House, "and Distinguished Delegates." She paused as she surveyed the chamber before her and, the galleries above the chamber, accurately gauging how her image would appear on a TV screen.

"My esteemed colleagues, over two hundred years ago, our founding fathers set forth in writing for the entire world to see, and admire, the principles which have served to unify our great nation through strife and adversity. The Constitution of the United States ranks with the Magna Carta, and the Declaration of Independence, as one of the few seminal documents throughout history which have served to change the behavior of man and establish for time immemorial the destiny of a People, a Nation, a way of life, and subsequently a world view. The Constitution of the United States set forth a vision that was unique in its time and still rings as true today as it did when it was first drafted. It set forth in concrete terms not only that all "men" are created equal, and that they are endowed with certain unalienable rights, as had been previously resolved, but went on to discern exactly what those rights were."

After another pause, allowing the TV cameras to pan the jubilant hubbub taking place on the floor of the chamber she continued "...and if I may indulge"—at this point she did read from the TelePrompTer but you'd never know it—" 'We the People of the United States, in order to form a more perfect Union, establish Justice, ensure domestic tranquility, provide for the common defense, promote the general Welfare, and secure the Blessings of Liberty, to ourselves and our Posterity, do ordain and establish This Constitution for the United States of America.'

"This dissertation was written in the blood of our founders and has been paid for in blood many times since. It is a sacred document. And any attempt to re-define it or redirect it in our own vision as to "what" and "who" we are as a People must never be undertaken lightly."

She waited graciously for the enthusiastic hand clapping and foot stomping of her own side of the aisle, and the polite applause of the loyal opposition dimmed before she went on.

"But now, today, we stand at the crossroads of history. We must decide upon a course of action that will irrevocably alter the course and character of this great nation for all time to come. We must make a choice. We must choose to blindly conform to a notion, which was revolutionary in its time..." a pause and then dryly, and with just the barest hint of a twinkle in her eyes, "...two hundred and forty some years ago." Laughter and applause erupted from one side of the aisle and a strange silence seeped from the other. She continued on with a stern note and an iron-willed gleam in her eye, "... but which now, in this century, in this reality, is sadly out of place and out of touch."

Again interrupted by another burst of applause from her party's side of the aisle she stepped back slightly and assessed the audience before her. Stepping forward again to the podium she went on. "Or, we must choose to make a break with the past: the scarred, bloodied, and oftentimes, shameful past. There are those in this chamber who would have us all believe their own conveniently misleading mantra: '...being necessary to the security of a free state, the right of the people to keep and bear arms shall not be infringed.' My fellow Americans, I say to you that any nation whose citizens live in perpetual fear of crime and violence, any nation whose citizens are outnumbered nearly ten-to-one by privately-owned firearms, any nation whose citizens comprise an armed camp can be neither secure nor free." This last sound-bite she artfully emphasized by pounding her flat palm upon the podium, for this one twenty-second piece of footage would be repeated again and again on national TV until the vote was cast in both houses. "Rather, I say to you, that the integrity of a secure state demands a citizenry unencumbered of the evil demons of death, crime, mayhem, and destruction." Another outbreak of cheers and applause spewed from one side of the aisle to be met by stone silence from the other while the viewers at home saw select members of Congress celebrating the advent of a new age.

The senator from New York continued, "For far too long our citizens have lived in the shadows of fear and crime relying on their government to help them. But we cannot help them as long as our hands are tied by the out-dated, outmoded, vainly romantic notions of a handful of aristocratic slave owners who lived in the eighteenth century! We as a people have evolved from our barbaric past. We revere the founders, we honor them, and we cherish their memory. But that does not mean we have to re-enact their beliefs. In the United States there are, today, 90 guns for every 100 citizens, making it the most heavily armed society in the world. It is time for the insanity to end. It is time for all of us in this chamber, to stand up, summon the political courage and do what is right. We are a very different country than we were 200 years ago. It's time to do away with the notion of an individual right to keep and bear arms and the strife and carnage that this very dangerous notion propagates. It is time to move on to the bright and shining ideal of the collective right to be safe. The Second Amendment must be abolished."

Murmurs of concurrence signaled that she had her audience, at least the members of her own party, in the palm of her hand, and now for the Coup-de-grace. "I appeal to your sense of justice and destiny. I appeal to you all to cast the vote that will free this great nation from the bondage of misguided and inappropriate Eighteenth Century notions of self-determinism through the threat of force, and the manifestation of violence. We can no longer think of ourselves as a collection of individuals. Our great nation is but one member of the Global Community. It is time for us to assume our rightful place in that community of nations and follow the common-sense dictates of an international society without borders. It is time for us as a nation to step up and assume the mantle of responsibility of good citizenship in the international order. It is time for you to demonstrate your leadership, now, in determining the destiny of this great nation. You must vote for the repeal of the Second Amendment." Another burst of celebratory upheaval. Every breathing body in that chamber knew that she was getting close to the declaration and the anticipation was palpable. The tension radiated off the senior members of both parties.

In a clear, strong, and flawless voice she called out:

"MR. President, Madam Speaker, and Distinguished Colleagues: I move that a vote be held in both Houses of this Congress to repeal the Second Amendment to the Constitution of the United States of America."

The chamber erupted in such spectacle as had not been seen since VJ Day. The party of loyal opposition remained in their seats; a few applauded. When the cacophony died down a little bit, she continued. "I leave you now to the great and momentous task that lies before you and I pray that you will heed the better angels of your nature and do what you know in your hearts is right. Thank you."

Her conclusion was drowned out by the hand-clapping and foot-stomping, which was over-dubbed by the analytical pronouncements of the TV network political pundits. The junior Senator from New York acknowledged her thanks to an appreciative if not grateful chamber of both Houses of the Congress, as she made her way from the rostrum back to her side of the aisle.

The focus of attention went back to the President of the Senate before it was redirected in turn to the next of several Senators and Representatives who would begin to enunciate in explicit and mind numbing detail over the course of several days the exact changes to the Constitution these better political angels had in mind. But, before the motion was seconded, and before the vote was held, and before the ancillary recommendations for and the oppositional protestations against the measure were made, a brief word was required by decorum and orders from those few who might actually have held an opposing view.

123

Senator Alexander Sherman's response, representing the Congressional faction opposed to a change in the Constitution, and thereby opposed to the Constitutional Convention, for some unknown, unforeseen reason was not carried live over the four broadcast networks and the two or three cable news networks but instead was only carried on C-SPAN. If he was lucky, Senator Sherman may have had one-tenth the audience his predecessor at the rostrum had had, but that was somewhat doubtful.

Mr. Sherman's approach to the podium, by contrast, was not poetic motion, rather he laboriously trudged up to the rostrum with the weight of the task he was about to undertake: literally to save the Constitution of the United States of America. He still could not intellectually accept that the Executive branch actually had the support of enough members of Congress and enough Governors of enough States to get this enormous task underway. His mouth was dry and his throat ached and he hadn't even said a word yet.

There was a pitcher of water and a glass on a small shelf in the podium to which he helped himself. It was not done for dramatic effect. Setting the glass down, he surveyed the chamber of Congressmen, 535 in all with five non-voting Representatives present, some of them still glad-handing and slapping each other on the backs –celebrating what could be nothing less than the oratorical overture to another presidential administration under their party's banner. Other members sat quietly staring at him, waiting for him to say something. Sherman took it all in: chaotic cacophony and callow caution. He recalled a quote attributed to Madison and Jefferson that "...*In all very numerous assemblies, of whatever character composed, passion never fails to wrest the scepter from reason...Had every Athenian citizen been a Socrates, every Athenian Assembly would still have been a mob. And there it sits. "* Sherman privately thought.

"Mr. President," His throat tickled; he coughed. "Madam Speaker, distinguished colleagues..." he was almost inaudible. There had been a prepared speech but the emotional furor with which the previous speaker was met had left him stunned. He could appeal to their sense of reason all he wanted to, but it was clear to him that reason and logic had been checked at the door. He adjusted the microphone and simply spoke from his heart.

"My honored colleagues, ladies and gentleman, we were all very fortunate to have been able to hear, a few moments ago, the esteemed Senator from New York deliver her speech. We were privileged to have heard—what I am sure will prove to be one of the outstanding pieces of oratory ever delivered in these hallowed chambers." A clearly audible undercurrent of agreement swept the great hall from one side and died out just about in the middle.

'Ladies and gentlemen, please permit me to point out a few basic facts. Words mean things. We—you and I—occupy a very curious place here in the Nation's Capitol; we exist in a different dimension. There is the real world—the real America out there", Sherman said as he pointed directly at the C-SPAN TV camera. "And then there is Washington DC. The two may co-exist but they are not necessarily the same. Living where we do inside the Beltway, rhetoric is a valued skill. We can dance around a question with grace and flourish and never answer it. It is necessary; our linguistic gymkhana is a tool of our survival. Ladies and gentlemen, out there in the real United States of America a very important notion has been set forth and real honest-to-God people are waiting to see how we, here in this chamber, address it." The background commotion that greeted him had gradually receded as Sherman reminded the Congress that it was there to do the bidding of the People.

"To repeal the Second Amendment of the Constitution of the United States is no small task. As my esteemed colleague, the Senator from New York, stated most eloquently, we are about to decide...." He referred to a notepad. "...To make a choice that will irrevocably alter the course and character of this great nation for all time to come.' Ladies and Gentlemen, truer words were never spoken." Sherman said and took a sip of water. His throat and mouth were dry beyond his experience and it wasn't the first time he stood at this podium.

"My dearest colleagues, in a representative republic the leaders have to speak clearly, candidly, honestly, and truthfully. We cannot at this point in history, when we are about to vote to change the character of our nation, afford to hide behind innuendo and nuance. We have an overriding responsibility to those whom we have the privilege to represent to speak very, very, clearly." There were no catcalls; there was no derisive laughter from one side of the aisle. There was only silence.

Sherman went on. "This vote is not about lowering the crime rate. This vote is not about improving police response time to a crime scene. This vote is not about making people feel safe. This vote is not about delivering the people from the demons of death, crime, mayhem, and destruction. This vote is about disarming the citizens of the United States. Let us be very clear about that.

"Just ten years before James Madison wrote the Second Amendment, a smattering of militias scattered throughout a baker's dozen of colonies, clothed, fed, and armed by their own toil, defeated not only a numerically superior force but also the army of the greatest empire on the Earth at that time. They proved that resistance to a superior power, however dangerous, might sometimes be the only honorable choice. And they were able to do it because they owned, and refused to surrender, their own weapons. Madison had not lost sight of that lesson when he penned what we have heard described here as one of the greatest documents in human history.

"Madison was not talking about duck hunting. He was not talking about the shooting sports. He was talking about a people's right to overthrow an oppressive regime by force of arms and pursue its own destiny unencumbered by the shackles of tyranny."

This last comment brought the house down and while no one actually stood and rent their garments or spit on Sherman they certainly made their impressions known. The President of the Senate gaveled to no avail, the Sergeant at Arms accomplished nothing. Sherman took another long sip of water and refilled his glass from the pitcher as he let his esteemed colleagues stew over his remarks a little. When he thought the uproar had abated somewhat he began again.

"The Second Amendment has been called many things: 'The watchdog amendment to the Constitution', 'First among equals', 'The insurance policy of the American people against tyranny.' It is also one more thing and I beg you, consider this before you cast your vote: It is the linchpin of the constitutional freedoms the founding fathers secured for this great nation. Without it the first amendment will soon follow. How long will you be able to speak your mind openly in public if your government doesn't trust you with a gun? If you cannot be trusted with a mere tool, why should you be trusted with the freedom of speech, or with the freedom of thought, or with the freedom of religious worship, or with the freedom to peaceably assemble? Why should you expect to be secure in your persons, homes, papers, and effects, or to be tried by a jury of your peers?

He would make one more attempt to put this issue in perspective, if not for his colleagues in the Congress then for the American people, who would hear or read of his response to proffered tyranny.

"Our forefathers, desirous of being citizens of a free and independent nation, took up arms against tyranny and shed their blood to establish that independence. Our national character is defined by the will to actively pursue life, liberty, and happiness. And the Second Amendment to the Constitution of the United States is the tool by which we hold those values dear, and unalienable. The Second Amendment is the difference between being subjects and being citizens and once it is repealed the American People will surely be subject to every political whim and social folly coming down the pike." Sherman paused here. The rumble of discontent clearly became audible throughout the chamber.

"Ladies and Gentlemen, for those of you who intend to vote yes on this proposal, have you thought it through? Once you vote to take away the constitutionally affirmed right to bear firearms from the American people, how are you going to get them? How are you going to take away those firearms, ALL of those firearms from the American public? Sure, some of the states have been working piecemeal to restrict the quantity of privately-owned firearms for decades but there are still millions of guns out there. How are you going to do it? According to the Bureau of Public Safety records America is now estimated to have between 270 million and 310 million firearms, or, now as the esteemed Senator Ellery from New York has stated, 90 for every 100 people. Are you prepared to sign off on the National Guard in the separate states lumbering down the streets of Middle America to confiscate the private property of the very people that put you here? Or are you going to require by legislation the mandatory surrender of those same firearms. And then what are you going to do when nobody turns them in? What are you people thinking?

"You all know your constituents better than anyone else because they put you here. You know whether or not they have the mettle, collectively or individually, to use their legally-owned and constitutionally-protected firearms to thwart such a tyrannical piece of lawmaking as we discuss here today. You all know better than anyone else whether your constituents will fold under the pressure of big government and turn them in. And I am absolutely sure that you all know precisely how many combat-trained veterans reside in your districts. May I remind you that those veterans took an oath, as did we, to protect and defend the Constitution against all enemies foreign and domestic? But when they took it, they were willingly putting their lives at stake. I will wager with any one of you that 99.9 percent of those veterans were dead serious about that oath and intend to keep it whether they are still in service or not. Ladies and gentlemen, if the answers to those questions are what I think they are, you have to acknowledge that voting for the repeal of the Second Amendment is, at the very least, an enormous gamble. Now, the thing you need to ask yourselves is this: Is it the gamble that you are willing to take with the future of this country?

"Ladies and gentleman," Sherman pressed on, "Much has been made in recent times of the political rift, and the cultural divide that separates the two dominant political parties of this great nation. Now it is absolutely incumbent upon us, every one of us honored to be in this Congress, to come together. I implore you from the bottom of my heart, please, do not vote to throw away the bedrock of our freedoms and of our national character. You must vote NO on the proposal to repeal the Second Amendment to the Constitution of the United States!" He finished.

*****

The President of the Senate gaveled the session to recess. Alexander Sherman gathered his papers and took in the scene before him. The assembled Senators and Representatives milled about in a quiet fashion. Some spoke to their neighbors in muted tones as they prepared to leave the chamber, others remained seated. Sherman surveyed this and stepped away without ceremony. Maybe he actually had given them something to think about. Well, who knew? Who could tell? They would all know in a few days.

124

All delegates that cared to were allowed the opportunity to stand in front of the C-SPAN cameras and let their opinions, observations, recollections, and ruminations be known to God, the world, and everybody. It took two weeks. The following week, the U.S. Congress and the U.S. Senate adjourned to their separate chambers to conduct their concurrent vote.

Over the interceding weekends, phone lines into Washington D.C., the switchboard for the Senate, the switchboard for the House, internet service providers across the country, and the US Mail, were taxed beyond their capacity. The individual convention delegates were informed how to best represent the interests of their constituents.

Apparently, since the remarks of the pro-repeal keynote speaker was being carried by all the broadcast networks and three cable news networks (as a public service) at every news break, some egalitarian minded souls had posted Sherman's speech in opposition to the repeal of the Second Amendment, in toto, on various forms of social media. Leagues of internet bloggers, aligning themselves with the Pro2A Community—both pragmatists and the three per centers—embraced Sherman's message and had given him their full throated support—and a link. Alexander Sherman would only find out some time later that his daughter, Patsy, had been one of them. One particularly liberty-minded reference-librarian in fly-over country, where they grow lots of soy beans and corn, posited a novel idea on her blog. Her idea was for everyone to send the end-flap from a box of ammunition to their respective senator and representative along with a brief missive of why repealing the Second Amendment was a bad idea. The pithy appeal of "Buy Ammo" had grown beyond the boundaries of the Inland Empire. It had gone viral.

The vote was taken in the Senate. Thirty-seven members voted in favor of repealing the Second Amendment. Sixty-three members voted against repealing the Second Amendment. The motion did not carry in the Senate.

Of the votes cast in the lower house, fifty-three percent voted for repeal and forty-seven percent voted against repeal. The measure required a super majority of votes in both houses of the Congress to be forwarded to the desk of the President for his signature before it would be sent out to the separate states for ratification. The measure failed.

The national elections were held in November, nearly two weeks after the Constitutional Convention had been convened and adjourned.

*****

The party that had styled itself as the Can Do Party for Public Safety, in its demeanor and in its rhetoric, lost the National races. The office of the President went to the other side. But the electorate had not forgotten how their senators and representatives had voted in the Constitutional Convention. Every Congressional member who had voted for the repeal of the Second Amendment was turned out of office. The potential of the internet as a conductor of ideas and an engine of change was real.

On Wednesday morning in the first week of November, the Sherman's sat around the breakfast nook over oatmeal, bacon, eggs, and coffee, in their home in Ketchum, Idaho. Mrs. Sherman read the business page, Patsy Sherman read the sports page, and Al read the political analysis. When he read the results of the previous day's races he muttered.

"I bet Al Gore never saw that coming'."

"What was that Dear?" His wife asked.

Sherman broke out in a smile, hoisted his glass of orange juice for a toast and said:

"GOD BLESS THE UNITED STATES OF AMERICA!"

125

In accordance with the wishes expressed in the Bequests, So Appended, in his Last Will and Testament, John Luther was buried in a family plot in a municipal cemetery in Syracuse, New York. The victim of an unsolved vehicular hit-and-run accident in Washington, D.C., he was interred without service or ceremony. He had no friends and there were no living relatives. The corpse had lain in a morgue in Washington, D.C. for three months until someone made the effort to carry out Luther's last wishes. Former Attorney General Albert Muzecko had seen fit to let the incoming administration clean up his mess.

In the course of his investigation John Luther had discovered a pernicious will within the government to incessantly invoke claims of the threat to the national security to conceal its corrupt, illegal, and incompetent activities. In the course of his investigation Luther had learned that the government considers its citizens to be sheep and like a good shepherd, the government would never allow the flock to be disturbed or distressed in the face of reality. John Luther had discovered the truth, and the truth often presents a threat to power—one often fights power at great risk to oneself. Sometimes risk is rewarded and sometimes it isn't. Luther knew that until the nation stood united and questioned its government and held it to account for its inequities, power would prevail. He also knew that people were human and it is human nature to follow the path of least resistance.

*****

Lizzy Wills untied the bow line. Gene Smith untied the stern line and made ready to move the boat out of its berth at the Des Moines marina. He had sold his share of a profitable restaurant to Suzy, a very industrious young woman, and Smith knew he could not have picked a more worthy successor to his labor of love since his retirement from the State Department those long and many years ago. Now "the Alders" was in good hands, Smith was really retired, and he had the company of a fine woman to show for it. He also had a very nice boat. The *Alders II* was a sport sloop with an inboard diesel engine. He had traded up from the Boston Whaler.

They would make their way due north, through Deception Pass, north past the east side of Peninsular Island, and then due west, out through the Strait of Juan de Fuca, and south to Cabo. Woohoo!

As they passed the eastern shoreline of Peninsular Island, Smith veered out of the navigable waterway in close proximity to the little piece of beachfront that used to be the home of one Peter Cleague and one very obstinate Norwegian elkhound. Eugene Smith turned off the motor, dropped anchor and broke out their lunch, the last one he was likely to get from the Alders' kitchen. He poured two cups of steaming hot coffee from a thermos bottle and recounted what he knew of the story of One Peter Cleague to Lizzy Wills, leaving nothing out insofar as he knew it.

She listened intently while taking in the shoreline, as the description of Peter's daily routine jog down the beach, the sniper hides, and the assault on his home was made palpable by Smith's narration. Taking in the new bridge over the boat channel, she could visualize Peter's nighttime swim from the bridge to the channel marker, under darkness, under fire, and under water. She had questions.

"So who killed the guy in the bar in Los Angeles?" she asked.

"Mr. Lee's nephews." Smith answered simply.

"How do you know?" Lizzy asked.

"Mr. Lee provided the loan to Suzy that helped her buy my share of the restaurant. He told me, but not in so many words. I asked about his family and the nephews. He told me they were fine. When Cleague told me about what happened in Mexico, he believed the nephews were dead. He never learned otherwise. All he knew was that he didn't kill that guy…" Smith searched his memory, "Pounds." He went on. "If you look at the dates that Cleague was in jail and the date that Pounds was killed it could not have been Cleague." Smith said.

"How do you know Mr. Lee?" she asked.

"We both happen to be members on the same board of directors." Smith said.

This was news to Lizzy. "Board of Directors of what?" she asked with some small degree of astonishment.

"It's a security consultancy. It's called Hereford Associates." He said.

She sat there slightly slack jawed for a time and then said, "And you didn't think this was important enough to mention?"

"It just hadn't come up, and you hadn't asked." He said simply.

"Does Cleague know?" she asked.

"Does Cleague know what?" He responded with a question.

"Does he know you were one of his bosses?" she asked.

"No." He shook his head a little. "I don't think so."

She was a bit flabbergasted but she pushed on.

"What about Linda?"

"She went back to Palm Springs. You remember—you were there that day in the restaurant when she came in to say goodbye. As far as I know she's OK. She met some fellow down there and I guess they are getting along fine." He finished and took a deep sip of hot coffee. It felt good on his throat.

"And Mr. Tibbett?" Lizzy asked.

"He's still in Palm Springs running Hereford." Smith said.

"Did they ever reconcile? He and Peter?" she asked and took a sip of coffee.

"Not that I know of. Tibbett had virtually accused Cleague of murder, it was not true but Roger didn't know that. Cleague, to Roger's sense of things, had put Hereford Associates at risk—Roger believed that Cleague had killed Pounds and thereby jeopardized Hereford's reputation. As far as Roger was concerned his company's reputation and his integrity were one and the same. When Cleague walked out of Tibbett's office that was the end of it, that friendship did not exist anymore. And then, to cap it all off, when Luther came to see Tibbett and told him about what happened here, that sealed it. They may have been friends once but that has changed and I don't see it playing out otherwise."

It made Lizzy sad. Although she had not met Mr. Tibbett, she felt that she knew these guys and hated to see rifts come between people, especially when it was unnecessary.

"That's too bad. I feel awful for them," she said and sipped her coffee.

"Yes it is." Smith replied. "But what the hell, shit happens—life goes on. You deal with it." He said, looking at the wind move the tall grass that had grown back after the fire. He recalled to her, "You used to be able to see the roof of Cleague's house from here. Now, there's nothing left but a black mark in the sand where the foundation used to be. That was one hell of a fire." He said.

Lizzy was quiet a moment and considered the story she had just heard. She had one more question.

"Who shot the guy back in Lebanon? It seems that's how this whole thing got started." She said.

Eugene Smith looked straight at her, directly eye-to-eye and said, "I don't know."

She suspected otherwise, but said nothing. She recognized that Smith had earned his living, for most of his adult life, by knowing more than he would ever say. Even as a doctor she would admit that there are some things you can't say out loud. You just let others draw their own conclusions. Was that a lie? If so, how do you build a relationship on a lie? Smith was a good man. He was kind. He was funny. He freely gave her his time and his attention without being prompted. And she would take life as it came, one day at a time.

Lunch was over. Smith stowed the trash and pulled up the anchor. Shortly they would be on their way to the Pacific Ocean and south to Cabo San Lucas for a week's vacation. Then, it would be back to the hospital for Lizzie and Smith would think of something else to do.

He waited a moment before he started the inboard diesel and listened to the sound of the water lapping against the hull. Just like that night in that box in the black hold of a Turkish flagged freighter so many years ago. Smith hadn't thought of that night in years. That miserable son-of-a-bitch, Lovegrove could rot in hell. Too bad Cleague had to spend time in a Turkish jail. *Well, we all got to play our part, sometimes we know it and sometimes we don't.* He thought. *Just move on through and carry on with your life, and don't look back. No regrets. No remorse.* No regrets, no remorse.

510

In Ketchum, Idaho, Al Sherman held the car door for his wife who had agreed to be with him at the press conference. He took in the elegant black dress, the single strand of pearls and the nice cloth coat. "Very Republican, dear," he said with a smile as she got into the car. With his teenage and college-bound daughter warmly ensconced in the back seat, it was not a long drive. He had arranged for the press conference to be held at the same spot where, nearly twelve years ago, he had announced his candidacy for the Senate.

There was a minor representation of the local news services and the microphones were already set up. It was cold now and threatened rain, typical for January. He did not want to keep his wife and daughter and the few other supporters out in the weather any longer than necessary.

"Good Morning." He smiled at the cameras and gave a cursory glance at the notes in his hand. "Nearly twelve years ago, I announced my intention to run for the United States Senate. We had neither campaign funds nor a staff. We were challenged in a primary, and trailed the incumbent in the general election by more than 38 points in the polls. Over the next nine months we focused relentlessly on the need to reorient our national security policy and to restore fairness and accountability in our government. I will always be grateful for the spirit and energy of the many loyal and committed volunteers that helped us overcome the challenges and obstacles of our campaigns for the Senate.

"It has been a great and continuing privilege to serve in the United States Senate. I am very proud of my talented and dedicated staff, which has worked tirelessly to resolve the issues on which I based my candidacy, and to protect the interests of all Idahoans in this national forum. However, after much thought and consideration I have decided to return to the private sector, where I have spent most of my professional life. I am announcing today that I will not be seeking re-election to the United States Senate.

"This last term and the events that led up to the constitutional convention have taught me that in spite of all best intentions, one man can only do what one man can do. In representing the will of his constituents he must apply all his zeal and industry and after he has done it, it is time to move on. In the course of carrying out my best efforts for the proper representation of the fine people of Idaho, I have met, and with your help, have overcome many obstacles.

"George Mason once said 'Nothing so strongly impels a man to regard the interest of his constituents, as the certainty of returning to the general mass of the people, from whence he was taken, where he must participate in their burdens.'" It was there in Sherman's notes: George Mason at the Virginia ratifying convention, 17 June, 1788; he didn't feel the need to pad the attribution.

He continued, "It was never my intent to add to the rift and cleavage of the political culture that currently defines our nation, but rather to represent this state according to the desires of my constituents, and above all, to remain true to my own principles—many times in spite of the obiter dicta of the party leadership. Maybe my efforts were sufficient and maybe they weren't. But, in my considered opinion, I can swear to you without hesitation, I did the best I was able to do. I thank you for your continued support throughout my tenure in office, and to whomever you elect to this Senate seat, Godspeed."

There were no questions; he was already yesterday's news. The media circus would now seek out the people that actually wanted his Senate seat. He put the notes back in his coat pocket and stepped away from the microphones.

Al Sherman took his wife and daughter by the hands and leisurely strolled back to the car. In time he would worry about locating a law practice that would take him on, or perhaps he would consider starting his own. Maybe he could teach a class at the local college. In his oration to his fellow senators during the constitutional convention held to abolish the Second Amendment, he had gleefully burnt his bridges behind him, blowtorch in hand. In the end, the proposed amendment to repeal the Second Amendment to the Constitution just didn't have enough votes to make it to the President's desk. It never went to the states, but Sherman liked to think it would have met a similar fate if it had. There was something about one's home phone ringing at three o'clock in the morning and one being told that if one voted a certain way, not only would one be unemployed but also one would not be welcome back home. It seemed to get a lot of peoples' attention. Sherman had to quietly smile to himself. *God bless the grass roots effort.* With the concomitant defeat of the proponents of the abolition of the Second Amendment in the ensuing national elections, Sherman took pride in the fact that at least those miserable bastards were no longer in office either. But they would be back eventually and they would try it again. They would be back, but he was done with tilting at windmills, and today he was going to enjoy the pleasure of his family's company. As the Sherman's' car pulled out from the curb and quietly glided away none of the assembled reporters noticed the bumper sticker sporting the slogan: **BUY AMMO.**

✳✳✳✳✳

The sky in the north Central Puget Sound was clear, and cold, and blue. It was an un-commonly dry day for January in Washington state. The cold air made Peter Cleague's chest hurt as he jogged along the trail meandering in and out of the wood line that graced the periphery of the small regional airport administered by the Port of Alger County. It was a nice trail and he was moving along at a reasonable pace. Cleague still missed his dog more than a year after having lost him. It struck him that he grieved more for the dog he had lost than he had for most people he had known. He wasn't sure that that was exactly healthy, but he reflected that loss of a companion was measured in the degree to which you had opened up your heart to them. Every so often he thought of Linda, wondered how she was doing, and wished her well. It was a tough year. It taught him that shit happens, life goes forward, you learn to deal with it, and you move on. On this particular day in this particular part of the world, the sky was clear, the path was serpentine, and the future made no promises. Maybe he would get a puppy.

Epilogue

The former director of the FBI, George Hillman, sat on his favorite bench by the Mall and fed the pigeons. He ruminated on all that had passed. There were no heroes in this story, just different people doing different things, valiant things, to achieve an end. Ordinary people doing extraordinary things, wasn't that the definition of a hero? No matter. Luther was dead and his death brought with it no revelatory truth, no glimpse of a higher purpose. In the great machinery of government, the individual was irrelevant. Government employees were like so many cogs, pinions, and gears. Even the notion of "Citizen" was not what it had once been. In the unwinding of the great American experiment, the notion of "citizen" as active participant in the representative government of which he was constituent had been replaced by the notion of the component consumer.

If the function of a government is to govern, one would assume the function of leadership is to lead, but the paradigm had shifted. In this reality of constitutional conventions to spike and influence voter turn-out, and poll-based executive decision making, it seemed to Hillman that the function of leadership had become to accrue and retain as much power unto itself as possible, governance and leadership be damned. The priority was not to support and defend the Constitution, uphold the law, or protect the American people from all enemies, foreign and domestic. The priority was the pursuit of exclusive, unitary, executive power to act as the single branch of government without restraint or limitation for the nation. It was, Hillman reflected, the definition of tyranny.

So what was the point of all the work and sacrifice of people like Luther? Was their idealism misplaced at the altar of an absentee deity? But, Hillman reasoned, if it had not been for people like Luther, and Sherman, and even Cleague, the battle would have been lost long ago and there would be no remaining hope for an enlightened future, no matter how dim. It was a peculiar story.

It was the story of one Peter Cleague and the government had come up short this time. What about next time? What if there were ten Peter Cleagues? Or a hundred? Or a thousand? Cleague was an unremarkable man with a certain life experience and a specific skill set. He was a U.S. veteran with skill at arms borne of experience. The episode on Peninsular Island was a footnote in the record of unrecorded abuses, committed by a centrist government that had already been forgotten. The attempt to usurp one more right from the people, repealing the Second Amendment, had failed…barely. What about next time? At some point the republic would have to recognize that history is rife with governments expanding their powers at the expense of individual freedoms. It would be up to the people to redefine the government they would have.

He looked at the people around him: office workers on their lunch breaks, tourists from the hinterland come to the nation's Capitol, school children on a field day. Would these fine people have the courage, the temerity to tear down an abusive government and replace it with one that adhered to the Constitution instead of a government that refuted it? The judge did not know.

Judge Hillman got up from his favorite bench, threw the empty, crumpled bag in a trashcan, and walked toward the waiting Lincoln Towne Car. Michael would drive him home.

THE END

CPSIA information can be obtained
at www.ICGtesting.com
Printed in the USA
FSHW02n2202270418
47404FS